Beneath the Veil

By Sarah Michelle Lynch

Matthew,
You can officially say you were one of my earliest readers!
Sarah Michelle x

ISBN-10: 148007246X
ISBN-13: 978-1480072466

For Andrew

CONTENTS

ACKNOWLEDGEMENTS

The friends and family who have supported me – your encouragement knows no bounds. However, as ever, it is my husband who has been with me every step of the way on this long and sometimes arduous journey. Andrew, it just wouldn't be the same without your ideas, inspiration and that bended ear of yours which is so long-suffering but welcoming nonetheless.

PROLOGUE

January 5, 2063
A streetlight struggled as the blackout approached. The acrid aromas of a nearby soup vendor lingered in the air as dozens of exhausted office workers queued up for the tasteless liquid on their way back home to their cold, unwelcoming dwellings.

A lone woman, six feet tall with an imposing mane of red hair, stood on a desolate backstreet behind the decaying remains of Radio City Music Hall, an art deco masterpiece that was used as a makeshift hospital during the Ravage and never recovered. She was dressed all in black, with her battered leather journalist's bag over her shoulder. Her head bent down, she tried to look as inconspicuous as possible as she leant against the brick building, off which loosely hung the famous sign that once lit up the place. Seraph Maddon never managed to remain unnoticed; she always attracted attention, and most of the time it was unwanted, distracting even.

The intimidating skyscrapers, heavy traffic and throngs of pedestrians that swirled around her nearby somehow failed to consume entirely this towering, militant vision of womanhood; passers-by would simply never understand why she exuded a demeanour of hatred against the world and everything in it. Her thick fiery locks fell to her waist despite being perpetually pulled back, while her rounded cheekbones, purposeful features and long neck suggested a Celtic heritage. Penetrating and constantly surveying her surroundings, the windows to her soul emitted bright blue light to pierce the darkness, between thick brown lashes.

It was labouring toward evening, and the dark skies overhead reflected her irritable mood. She was waiting for an informant, and she wasn't happy about their tardiness. It had been a tough day and she just wanted to get back to her apartment and collapse. As she glanced sideways down the alley, she saw silent, dejected husks with their heads lowered and their shoulders hunched, creeping to their destinations anxiously after slaving away in cramped conditions all day long.

She avoided staring and bowed her head again. Soon she saw a pair of large, impeccably shiny black leather shoes appear in front of her. She looked up at the figure stood before her, and said in a raspy drawl, 'You're late.' He was an inch taller than her at most, dressed in a long black overcoat, with a suit underneath. He was around forty years old, with slightly greying brown hair, a mildly handsome face and a bookish look about him.

He spoke very good English, but a soupcon of a Swiss accent was still detectable. 'You're lucky I'm here at all.'

Seraph pulled the man down the alley to get out of sight, gesturing for him to shelter with her in an old side entrance of the music hall. Apparently another tropical storm was on the way, but the smog overhead always made it difficult to separate rain clouds from lingering pollution.

'So, why the need to see me face to face?' she asked.

'I can't keep giving you information like this. My employers know something. They are suspicious and keep dragging me in for one-on-one meetings and leaving memos reminding me about the clause in my contract where I agreed not to discuss my work with anyone outside of the organisation.'

'Let's just stand by and do nothing then, shall we?'

'Why are we bothering? Nobody is ever going to get to the bottom of this. We'll be dead before we do.'

Her impatience was quickening.

'Then we'll be dead, at least we'll have died trying.'

His defiance was palpable.

'Listen, I've met someone, so I can't keep doing this. I've got someone to care about now.'

Seraph recoiled at this sudden, inconvenient annoyance and recognised the reason behind the outfit. He must have been heading off for a date – probably the opening of the latest Ravage-inspired opera at the near-extinct Carnegie Hall.

'I thought romance was dead,' she mocked.

'It's not like that. It's real.'

'Yeah right. It'll never last, once she finds out who you work for.'

He got angry, and grabbed Seraph's elbow. 'Look, she already knows so shut the hell up. Just because you're so damned heartless doesn't mean everyone else is.'

She sniffed in disdain, and appeared nonchalant, but deep down she knew he was right. She was tired of his dallying, however. She had just spent another miserable Christmas alone, and being forced to spend time with her thoughts only made her feel more weighed down with hopelessness and despair at never being able to get to the truth.

Checking nobody was looking in their direction, she moved toward Ulrich and grabbed him roughly by his coat collars. A tendon strengthened in her neck as she shoved him back and held him against the brick wall, while his eyes looked as if they were about to pop out of his head. He was shocked by her swift attack and struggled to breathe. Her large eyes seemed to have turned completely black, but her facial expression was one of static iciness. 'God dammit, don't test me Ulrich, I haven't got time for you delaying on me, alright? Just tell me what you know.'

He tried to nod but she maintained her grip until she felt certain he had succumbed. He fell on the step at the bottom of the music hall's side door, catching his breath as he tried to recover. She waited impatiently, tapping her feet, with her arms crossed.

He looked up at her with exasperation. He gasped as he said, 'Head virologist Suranna Eames, she's dead.'

Seraph's eyes brightened and she knelt down to his level. 'When?'

'Two months ago. Laboratory explosion. They'll probably kill me for telling you.'

'Ulrich, if you tell me everything, I promise you'll never have to see me again.' She gave him a look that warned she wouldn't accept non-compliance.

He remained silent, but just as she was about to recommence her attack, he said, 'Seraph, you really are a tough bitch you know?'

'Don't test me, Ulrich. I've just spent another day at the morgue, picking between the bodies of suicidal factory workers to discover whether any of them bore any decent evidence of maltreatment.'

He hung his head in his hands. 'I can't do this Seraph. I'm not built like you are.'

'I need whatever you've got. Just tell me everything before I demonstrate what I'm really capable of.'

'Okay, look, some colleagues of mine in her department said she started turning up at work withdrawn and dishevelled. Something was clearly troubling her, and then she was dead. Ryken Hardy got fired just after taking over her job as head researcher.'

'Her ex? Why was he fired?'

'Dunno, something about lacklustre results in their department.'

Seraph threw her head back in disbelief. 'As if someone like him could possibly be termed lacklustre! He's bedded nearly every one of your colleagues, hasn't he?'

'He's a good guy, trust me. There must be more to it than we know, but I can't tell you any more than that.'

She contemplated these revelations, eyeing him to gauge whether he was holding something back. 'Where's Hardy now?'

'I wish I knew, he's here and there, but nobody can ever seem to get hold of him.'

'Are you sure there is nothing else? Nothing you might have overlooked?'

He looked shifty, and she reiterated, 'Just tell me.'

'They're watching you. They have been for ages. And yet, they don't ever seem to get you.'

She was unsurprised by his revelation. 'They're always watching, we all know that, but I don't do what I do without protection. For years I've had a sympathetic supporter feeding me dirt on all the scum of this city, and I've tucked some of the choicest bits away in an encrypted file hovering in cyberspace. If anything happens to me it will be released within twenty-four hours of me failing to upload my message service.'

'They won't stop, though, you know that. Your impunity won't last forever.'

'They can't touch me because my protection is unbreakable, trust me. I had my underground hacker friend the rascal shore up its impenetrability. He's smarter than the whole of Officium put together. He knows all their tricks, but even he's been unable to get any data proving their culpability in 2023.'

'Maybe you ought to just admit defeat. You know, sometimes when I sit scanning the obituaries, I often half expect to see your name amongst them.'

'Nothing else matters to me apart from getting to the bottom of this. All I want is the truth about 2023, because I doubt I'll ever discover why they murdered my family. I'll keep going until I get the information I need, whether they threaten to kill me or not.' Her face was emotionless and expressionless, and he looked saddened by her remarks.

'Ulrich, don't look at me with those pity eyes. I know what I am.'

'No, you're better than this. I remember the person you used to be before all this and she was pretty great. Deep down, you know there is more to life. I just hope you realise that before they catch up with you.' He stood up and got ready to leave, offering her a hand to shake. She took it begrudgingly, and he spoke one last word of advice, 'If you can get Hardy to talk, you might finally get to the bottom of the conspiracy. But he's a pretty tough one to crack. He's built like a marine, and perhaps smarter and more complex than anyone else I've ever known. He's the best of us, and yet, for him to have been sacked… something big must have gone down.'

Seraph smiled limply at Ulrich. 'Sorry for grabbing you before. And thanks, I hope it works out for you and your lady friend.'

He moved away from her, and offered, 'Goodbye Seraph. I really hope you find what you're looking for.'

PART I
Mors Tua, Vita Mea

CHAPTER 1

April 3, 2063
The dazzling sun of an early spring morning was battling to slice through the thick, orange-brown clouds of smog hovering above New York City. The Big Apple was just breaking into life, with yellow hover-cabs whooshing down streets, ambulance sirens howling in the distance and dew rising from the sidewalks along with steam from the grates. People were starting to pour out from subway stations, and cyclists with their masks on zoomed from one lane to another to avoid potholes along the crumbling cycle routes. What was left of Central Park, from 85th Street downwards, was the only green space remaining in the entire metropolis, since the bulldozers moved in to maximise the land for real estate. Rammed full of office workers purchasing various breakfast items from automated food dispensaries before racing off to work, the blighted park fought bravely to provide some recreation for all the inhabitants of the heaving grey city.

As Seraph stared down at the scene from her apartment window, almost burning her mouth as she drank her coffee down rapidly, she felt empty and numb. Her morning ritual allowed her no retrospect that day. She had only one thing on her mind. Her last living relative was dead, and she had been arrogant enough to ignore the warnings.

Earlier, she had been woken by the subdued fanfare of a call coming through on her Unicus. *Damn, I really could have done with more sleep this morning.* She had got in at 3am after spending the night staking out a whorehouse where a depraved senator was spending his Friday nights. She had expected it to be her Australian boss, Francesca.

Sprawled across her king-size bed in her Dakota penthouse apartment, she had shaken off the white duvet and rolled over to open the communications device on the nightstand, infuriated by the low din that was now reverberating around her head. She answered in a croaky voice, 'Hello?'

On the screen, she saw a woman's face crackle into focus and heard some muffled noises before an unfamiliar voice asked, 'Oh, hello, am I speaking to Seraph Maddon? This is the last number Eve had for you.'

The woman was middle-aged but her tied-back, light-brown hair was without grey. She had a thin mouth and large hazel eyes set wide apart between a small dainty nose. Her features were so close to the screen Seraph could barely make them out. She had quite a strong English accent, but a French twang crept in now and again as her speech rose and fell. It took Seraph a few moments to process what she had just heard, before replying, 'This is she, yes.'

'Oh thank goodness. I'm Camille, from the bridal shop. I have some sad news I'm afraid. Eve passed away early this morning in her sleep. The doctor says her heart finally gave out. I'm so sorry to be the bearer of bad tidings.'

Seraph took even longer to register that information. She sat up sharply, and the voice on the other end of the line asked, 'Are you still there? I understand this might have come as a bit of a shock.'

Seraph brought the Unicus in front of her so the woman could see her face again. 'Sorry, yeah, I'm still here. I just feel terrible I wasn't there. I mean, I knew she was… but I just didn't take it seriously I guess.'

'Yes, she seemed like the sort of person who would live forever.' Camille paused before continuing, 'Well, the funeral will take place within the next couple of days. I thought I'd better get in touch in case you wanted to attend.'

Seraph's mind went into overdrive, selfishly thinking about how she could get out of work. Even missing just one day, a weekend day even, would set her back weeks. 'Thanks for letting me know. I appreciate you calling Camille, but I have so many commitments here. I'll have to see if…'

'Of course, but I know Eve would have wanted you here.'

'Well, I'll see what I can do. I can't promise but…'

'Okay, well we'll hopefully see you here Seraph. We'd all love to meet you. I'd better get going now anyway, things to do. Call me anytime. Au revoir.'

Her father's aunt wasn't married, but had dedicated her life to the cause of marriage, an institution that had severely decreased in popularity as people had become more withdrawn and anti-social. Making couture wedding dresses at her bridal house in York, England – a walled city founded by the Romans two millennia ago – Eve's low-key, almost cottage industry, had brought thousands of people through her doors, over a fifty-year career that saw her build up an international clientele. Eve's niche business had remained, despite the fact that most garments were mass-produced in factories. Made-to-measure goods were in decline and usually cost a fortune, but for some reason, Eve had become a mainstay in an extremely limited market.

Seraph had first met Eve around thirty years ago and had remained in contact ever since. She had been in awe of her aunt's unique dress sense, wit and infectious personality. Theirs was an unexpected bond, given they were distantly related, but it was one that had survived the test of time. For the journalist, Eve was the only person Seraph ever felt she could be herself with. They were both tenacious, sharp-tongued Capricorns, who shared the same fiery hair. They were kindred spirits of sorts, and though Seraph never really understood Eve's chosen profession, she was in awe of her refusal to bend to the will of the new world. The last thing she had heard about Eve was that she had finally given up work, having fallen victim to some ailment she had not wanted to discuss. Though this was certain evidence that she was succumbing to something fatal, Seraph had failed to make her way across the Atlantic for a visit before it was too late.

Eyeing the mini-gym in the corner of her bedroom, Seraph decided she couldn't face it that morning. Her perpetual anger had subsided at the news of Eve's death, and she felt frail all of a sudden. It was official – she didn't have anybody left in the world now. Dragging herself out of bed, she padded slowly along the polished wooden floor toward the en suite bathroom to get showered. As the automatic illumination spread across the high-ceilinged, sloping room, she leaned against a huge white plastic bath in the centre. As she stared at the white floor tiles and glossy white-painted walls, the artificial light made her feel nauseous and she realised there was no other option but to get over to England as quickly as she could. The tight knot of angst and remorse that had formed in her gut made her realise she owed it to Eve. For the first time in years, work didn't seem to matter so much.

After showering and air-drying in the corner cubicle, she pulled on whatever her hand touched in the closet and scraped back her long red hair into a bun. In the mirrors of her sliding wardrobes, amidst the spacious but almost desolate surroundings of her master bedroom, she saw that her fair skin looked even paler than usual – but she had no time for make-up. She grabbed some stuff from the bathroom, along with a few items of clothing, and chucked them into a bag. She braved the call to Francesca, who had actually been surprisingly sympathetic, before slurping her coffee down and preparing to leave.

Under normal circumstances, missing a day of work was a heinous crime in her book, and the thought of all the responsibilities she would be neglecting made her feel nauseous. She had a hotel room booked for later that day at the Four Seasons, right next door to that of an NYPD commissioner she knew would be there to close some very shady foreign business deal – but she would have to forgo that, he would keep. Dedicated to her job at the *Chronicle*, she couldn't bear to leave it in the hands of anyone else. Nevertheless, she had decided in the shower that this was a historic day, and nothing was going to stop her paying homage to her miraculous relative. She incinerated her trash in the custom-built furnace she'd had erected in the middle of her lounge, ensuring nobody could work out her habits or steal anything incriminating. She grabbed her stuff and looked back on her clinical, generically white apartment, checking she had left nothing damaging lying around in the living room or kitchen diner. She set the security system on high alert for the duration of her absence, before slamming the huge, solid metal door of her apartment, which clunked with a sharp thud before slotting various locking mechanisms into place. Striding out into the lush, wood-panelled, carpeted corridor outside, she headed to an elevator to take her the eight floors down to street level.

As she walked out onto W 72nd Street, she was almost deafened by the conflicting sounds of horns tooting, distant protestors yelling outside yet another building threatened with demolition, the low hum of vehicles and the traipsing vagrants echoing their vitriol around the tall housing blocks. The grandiose Dakota building – with its gables, spandrels, balconies and light brickwork – still resembled some sort of grand residence, but only because of a thick electric fence around its perimeter, and a number of other high-security measures that had needed to be implemented to protect its period magnificence. Many other apartment buildings in the vicinity could easily be misplaced as dosshouses, crack dens, makeshift supermarkets or simply an opportunity for one of the city's numerous graffiti artists, many of whom plastered the streets with cartoonish interpretations of the unexplained disease that had devastated the world all those years ago. The trees and foliage of old were left to waste and the age of the doorman was a thing of the past. Very few owned their own vehicles, while bulky yellow hover-cabs scuttled along the severely potholed streets.

Stood on the sidewalk on the corner of Central Park West, Seraph hailed a hover-cab with her Unicus, got in the vehicle and keyed her destination into the cabbie computer – JFK. Heading east, she watched the unkempt tower blocks of the city pass her by: structures that had deteriorated with the battering elements of frequent storms, as well as the dust and filth of pollution. As she got towards the outskirts of the island, she cringed (as she always did) at the sight of the sixty-foot concrete wall that surrounded the city. Rising sea levels were to blame. It was decided years ago that there was no option but to build the barrier. Mayor Fitzpatrick just couldn't risk flood damage to any part of the metropolis, even if it meant a garish grey boundary blocking out what little light managed to stream through the clouds – and cutting off people's view of the sludge-ridden Hudson and East River. Ironically, trying to protect the city had meant many parks, streets, houses and public buildings were crudely swept out of the way to make way for the terrible Manhattan Dam, as it had become known. Seraph knew in reality that the structure's actual purpose was to enable greater population control – and surveillance. So many had flooded the city in the wake of 2023's tragedy, and the place exploded into a hotbed for crime. It had become Officium's main sphere of business, and was now their HQ, from which they felt they could run the world.

The cab took her through the colossal iron gates of the U-Card checkpoint on Manhattan Bridge, and across to Brooklyn. Through the window, she saw busloads of citizens being transported out to New Jersey to continue their lives of drudgery in the various factories and power stations struggling to keep the city alive. With families and marriage a thing of the past, few really cared about putting down roots, and she saw dozens upon dozens of hobos still asleep on the sidewalks – people who laid their hat wherever they found themselves come nightfall.

When she arrived at the gigantic, automated reception of the airport, Seraph scanned her U-Card above the ticket machine and the computerised voice of the self-serve kiosk rang out: *Good morning Seraph Maddon. Would you like to travel today?*

Seraph was impatient, almost shouting, 'Yes.'

What is your destination?

'Manchester, England.'

Please choose a ticket from the following options.

On the screen, Seraph saw one seat left on a flight about to leave in fifteen minutes so she would have to be quick. She selected the flight, not willing to wait around for hours to hop on another one. *This ticket will require us to take 3,545 E-Dollars from your available funds of 6,348 E-Dollars, do you wish to proceed?*

She wasn't delighted by the price – almost four months' salary – but again this was negligible in order for her to do Eve's memory justice. She said, 'Proceed,' and saw the funds drain from her account, almost forgetting to grab her U-Card back from the top of the machine as she went. She ran to the security point and chucked her baggage on the conveyer belt, before stepping through the X-ray machine. She passed through the decontamination chamber, standing in it for about half a minute while it blasted tiny particles of antibacterial matter all around her. Scanning her U-Card at the embarkation point, she barely heard the greeting, *Good day Seraph Maddon, your identity has been verified, have a pleasant journey to Manchester,* before running through the turnstile, down a tunnel and toward the plane.

Having made it just in time, thirty minutes later she was flying 45,000 feet somewhere above the Atlantic, crammed like a sardine in a can on a Sky Jet 1287, at a speed of 1,500mph. She got out her Unicus and began cancelling the various meetings she had set up for that day with colleagues, snitches and undercovers, hoping to avoid any small-talk with fellow passengers as she put on a busy demeanour.

CHAPTER 2

Around two hours later, Seraph disembarked the jet and was hurled into a completely different world as she navigated her way through the vast, heavily populated corridors of Manchester Airport. She was absorbed by the masses streaming their way along a suspended bridge walkway, and as she reached the packed, glass-roofed train station, the smell of public toilets and greasy food outlets hit her like a brick wall and nearly made her heave, having skipped breakfast and refused the plastic airline food.

She boarded a double-decker train on the speedline from Manchester to York, and as the journey got underway, she saw things had vastly degenerated since she last visited her parent's homeland, some twenty years ago. Whizzing past her eyes at 120mph through the carriage window were sheltered farms – miles upon miles of clustered white poly-tunnels – covering whatever fertile land was left in an attempt to protect crops from weather damage. Elsewhere, wind turbines had been squeezed in wherever possible. Her eye also clocked what appeared to be endless numbers of recycling plants and power stations dotted across the landscape of Lancashire and then Yorkshire. She had always romanticised about the exotic-seeming country of her family's descent, having rarely ventured far from the concrete-laden metropolis her mother and father had left England for four decades previously. However, those romantic notions were about to be tarnished.

She spotted many small towns and villages that had been completely abandoned and left to decay. Seraph had held on to some photographs her grandmother had developed from negatives, chronicling family holidays in the countryside and days out in some of England's oldest cities. It seemed like sacrilege to transfer the images to digital format, and she had kept the archive shots stored safely away. The pictures Seraph treasured in particular were those of York centre; its narrow, cobbled streets burgeoning with obscure shops, the ancient Roman wall, market stalls, tearooms, throngs of tourists, and green riverbanks littered with families enjoying precious days out.

Halfway through the train journey, the Global Health Organisation's daily announcement infiltrated every screen in the carriage. She checked her Unicus and realised it was already three o'clock in the afternoon. A representative for GHO appeared on the screen – a woman with almost unbelievably perfect skin, hair and teeth. She spoke in a cosmopolitan European accent, 'Good day citizens. Please ensure you make frequent use of anti-bacterial detergents, hand wash, sprays, wipes and decontamination chambers. Perform regular deep-cleans in your homes. Avoid unprotected sex at all costs, and keep your distance from anyone you believe might be falling ill. Have a safe and pleasant day.'

Seraph ignored every word of the patronising, imbecilic message, having heard the same warnings several hundred times before. *Why wouldn't people already know these things?* There hadn't been an outbreak for some decades – but these brainwashing techniques kept the threat of another attack at the forefront of people's minds.

When she stepped off the train at her destination, she was disappointed to see the Victorian building that had once housed the platforms had been replaced by a gigantic, hideous plastic, see-through cube with escalators crisscrossing over themselves with one purpose – to see masses of bodies as efficiently as possible on their journey. Even in Manhattan, a heaving grey monster with almost twenty-one million inhabitants, thousands of protestors had camped out on the streets to protect Grand Central, ensuring the station retained its original features. To developers it probably seemed easier to just get rid of old buildings and start again, rather than transpose anachronistic structures into an age of over-population, high-demand and low-culture. Square-pegs, round holes.

Once out of York Railway Station, high-rise apartment blocks and office buildings dominated the view. She imagined it was the same there as in New York – workers crammed into tiny cubicles, labouring over renewable energy research and marketing. Back home and in York it was obvious that nobody had much time, energy or money for entertainment and the huge advertisement billboards on Times Square – plus the stock markets – were dominated by pharmaceuticals and the latest in renewable energy technology. The world was panicky about resources running out, and many were employed under the heavy-duty contracts of Officium to make headway in developing alternative fuels. The invention of the all-encompassing Unicus in the 2030s meant computing, communication, navigation, Internet use – various multi-media – could all be handled by these relatively small devices with gigantic amounts of RAM. Made to the owner's exact specifications, the unit could be ordered in varying colours, designs and size of processing capability. The gadget was guaranteed to last a lifetime and could be hooked up to the Internet at any time, or charged up in virtually any shop, café or restaurant. The pinnacle of information technology had been achieved.

The streets of York were disturbingly quiet, with lone citizens shuffling around, the entire city centre pedestrianised and only the clunking of trains moving in the distance breaking the silence. As Seraph reached Low Ousegate, she noticed that the river had been hidden beneath gigantic, thick concrete tunnels, presumably to protect the city from the swelling waters. Walking further into the conurbation, she saw crude extensions had been added to many of the old buildings. Nearly all the boutique shops of the past had been eradicated to make way for huge blocks of flats, and grey concrete, glass and black metal obliterated the once architecturally diverse city, no longer the tourist hotspot of old. Seraph realised the power of the recycling industry was great, as she spotted a cylindrical grey-green plant lurking furtively in the distance, rising up from the mound on which used to stand Clifford's Tower. The rise and fall of an arm that allowed vapours and steam to escape from a hatch in the roof, perhaps some fifteen storeys up, was the only other sound that invaded Seraph's ears. Other than that, the silence was deafening, and it made Seraph's skin crawl. It seemed unholy, somehow. Inhuman. Unedifying.

Winding through the streets amongst the lowly inhabitants, Seraph felt totally out of place. With her leather gear on, people would no doubt be able to tell she had some money, while they wandered around in their worn-out canvas plimsolls, boiler suits and other assorted rags. She strode along at her full height, assessing everyone with a critical eye. She felt a fraud and a phoney, and was pre-empting an attack from some poor low-level worker who wanted to start educating her on what the real world was like. She felt as though she were doing these people an injustice by not getting on with her investigations back home.

She followed the rusting signs for the Shambles, which she remembered seeing in photographs – with its curious, overhanging buildings. After picking her way between various people sat or sleeping on the narrow side-streets, she arrived at the antiquated cobbled lane and her jaw dropped. She had never seen anything like it, and had not realised her aunt's place of business was so vast. It was the last remaining Tudor-era building on the street, and it looked as though three or four units had been melded together somehow to create the large bridal house. Situated on the corner of an extremely narrow lane which had been renamed *Eve's Place* a long time ago, the bridal house dominated the view. It was immense.

Its medieval black beams remained and the pristine white stone walls glistened against the crude buildings surrounding it. The wooden frames of the main front windows were painted a romantic off-white and were surrounded by dainty fairy lights, beckoning visitors in. Meanwhile, the tiny windows of the numerous rooms upstairs retained their misty plate glass. The whole place seemed shining, welcoming and magical, offering solace amongst the madness, just as Eve had done for Seraph. The three-storey bridal house also still held on to its slight tilt. Seraph stood outside the main window admiring a dress on display. Hanging on an extremely lifelike mannequin, the gown was extravagantly delicate and had not an inch of fabric untouched by Eve's magic; it was pristine, glistening, and showcased high workmanship. It looked so extraordinary against the background of this mad alley of various fast-food stations, virtual cafes, express nail bars and self-service salons.

Standing outside the front door, Seraph looked up at the relatively small, unassuming silver lettering above which read: *Eve Maddon Bridal Designs*. There were people inside the shop, but a notice warned:

Due to bereavement, we are closed for the foreseeable future. We hope you are not too inconvenienced. Our re-opening will be announced within due course.

Seraph knocked nevertheless and hoped someone inside would answer. Camille opened the door and spoke, pointing at the sign, but barely looking Seraph in the face.

'I'm sorry, but as you can see, we are closed.'

Seraph noticed the stick-thin woman was dressed quite stylishly in a long grey belted cardigan, white shirt, skinny black jeans and grey suede ankle boots, unlike many of the drones walking the streets. Camille must have been about fifty years old, and yet she carried herself in such a way to make her seem younger. She was as graceful as a ballerina.

Jetlagged and ratty, Seraph's no-nonsense attitude was bursting out of its seams, but she tried to be as calm as possible in her response, even though the woman was already closing the door on her face before she had time to say anything. She shouted, 'I'm Seraph, Eve's great-niece!'

Camille's pronounced cheekbones and small pointed nose came to life and she stopped in her tracks, changing appearance instantaneously. 'Oh, well, of course you are! I'm Camille. I didn't expect you so soon!'

The woman's height almost equalled Seraph's own, and her high forehead seemed to suggest a quiet intelligence. As Camille peered over her slim reading glasses to observe Seraph, the reporter spotted something hiding behind the woman's enquiring, unwavering stare – a vibrant spirit that didn't seem to truly belong in such surroundings. The Frenchwoman exclaimed, 'I should have known who you were, look at you, you're so much like her! Please, come in.'

Seraph had to duck to enter the front door, the supporting beam was so low. The décor inside was a subtle pink, and a gigantic, custom-made digital picture-board covered an entire wall, shining with an abundance of customers' constantly smiling faces as you walked in. Soon a swarm of predominantly middle-aged employees dressed in black surrounded her, welcoming her in to the long, narrow reception area and asking if she wanted any tea, whether she'd had a good journey and telling her how nice it was to finally meet someone actually related to Eve. And an American… they hadn't had one round those parts for a while, apparently. The new arrival was soon feeling slightly overwhelmed and claustrophobic. Through the chatter, it soon became clear that the shop's founder had been idolised and worshipped by her employees, and by many who knew her.

The niceness of Eve's erstwhile colleagues made Seraph uncomfortable because she was accustomed to dealing with harangued professionals, nefarious characters and assorted rogues. She felt a little out of place in Eve's world, and simply didn't know how to behave around genuine kinds of people.

She sat down on a wide, oatmeal-coloured chenille couch opposite the sizeable, curved, white-wooden reception desk, sipping tea out of a china cup and saucer, when she decided to ask Camille about various preparations and such.

'Eve wanted to be buried. I know nobody goes for that anymore, but you know her. She was eighty after all, and embodied all the old ways… if you know what I mean. It was confirmed earlier, it'll take place the day after tomorrow. Then we will hear the will. We all want to know where our livelihoods stand.'

'Oh god, of course. I never even thought… I just felt I had to come here, to say goodbye, but also to be here for her. Formalities didn't even cross my mind. I mean, god, yeah. I'm her only relative, aren't I? But people mostly end up leaving their money to conservation projects these days!'

'That's perfectly understandable… Oh, and if you'd like to see her, I can arrange…'

Seraph had seen one too many dead bodies in her lifetime already, deciding, 'No, I don't need to see her.'

'I really wish I could give you some time Seraph, but I've got a lot to attend to.'

'Say no more Camille, I'll get a hotel and come back tomorrow, shall I?'

After exchanging pleasantries with other members of the staff, and having a quick look around the vast dressing rooms at the back, Seraph was instructed by Camille on where to find a place to stay and to call her if she needed anything.

CHAPTER 3

Seraph had found a crummy Bed4theNite hotel in York. She swiped her U-Card at the entrance to let herself in and made her way straight upstairs to a room that the computerised voice had told her was available and had a double bed and en suite. Despite the extras, the room was petite. It had everything that was necessary, but limited space meant limited luxury. From the bed linen to the walls, and the carpets to the curtains, everything was white with an artless navy stripe running through it. The bed had about six inches of space all the way around and the bathroom just about housed a lavatory – but the user was required to stand over that while showering. She had been in worse though. At least such hotels had self-cleaning filtration systems and a Delta6 maid service. The worst hotels simply came with a box of recyclable bedding you had to make up yourself.

After dumping her bag on the floor before falling on the bed, Seraph wondered what she was doing there. She had acted on impulse, boarded a plane and had ended up stuck in one of those soulless chain hotels she detested. She never gave in to emotions, but maybe there was some other deep-seated reason she needed to be there.

The only daughter of Vivienne and Hamish Maddon, both of whom worked at Mount Sinai Hospital, she never shared a sibling bond with anyone. Her parents were both married to their work, on call 24/7, never having time for those all-important chats during her formative years. She had always believed they were the strait-laced and extremely predictable types, until after they died...

Seraph remembers the day. She had not long been working for the *Chronicle* as a crime reporter when she had gotten the news. Aaron King, an elderly hulk of a man who was a close friend of her parents, had turned up at her lowly junior writer's desk. King was a man of few words, so Seraph knew immediately that something was wrong.

'I don't know how to tell you… I'm so sorry Seraph. I'm just going to come out with it. Your parents were both killed on their way to work. They were both mown down by a bank robber being pursued by the cops. They were killed instantly. The bastard left his stolen vehicle on Madison Avenue and made his escape. I'm so sorry.' Aaron had a tear in his eye.

Seraph had sat there unable to move. She saw the man waiting for a reply, but she couldn't give one. He asked, 'Seraph, did you hear what I said?'

She looked at him blankly, squeaking out, 'Where are they?'

'Mount Sinai morgue. I can come with you if you want.'

She shook her head, and said, 'No, I'll be okay. Who was there at the scene? I mean which officer? I want to speak to them.'

'Bainbridge, he was going to come here, but I decided it might be better for you to hear it from me.'

'Dr King, I'd like you to go now please.'

He simply said, 'I'm here if you need me Seraph,' turned away and sloped off.

Seraph had gone to the toilets and sat with her head in her hands. For some reason, she just couldn't absorb the news. She had lived such a privileged life, had been given so many opportunities, and yet there had always been something missing. Their love. That day, she felt as though she was an imbecile, having previously felt assured that her whole world was untouchable, and that nothing bad ever happened to her because hers was a sphere she had control over. She had always hated predictability, but she suddenly wanted it back.

She went to see their lifeless bodies, and had felt absolutely nothing. She felt numb, and had stayed that way ever since. She wished someone could tell a twenty-five-year-old woman who had lost both her parents how to feel, because she didn't have a clue. She had never dealt with her bereavement, because she never knew who those people were that brought her into the world. They had spent so much time seemingly occupied by their work that she never got to know them properly. Even at a young age, Seraph knew there were issues between her parents, things too raw to bring to the fore. Before moving to New York, they had obviously seen and done things back home in Ravage-torn Britain that they never felt able to talk about. Teetering constantly on the edge, but always maintaining perfect balance, presumably nothing could be said in fear of tipping the scales, ruining their existence. As long as they all kept going, they were okay.

Then she had discovered the truth.

Francesca, her frizzy blonde hair spiking with the realisation that she hadn't been that tactful in asking Seraph of all people, had said in her twenty-cigarettes-a-day, Brisbane accent, 'I thought nothing of it when it came in… but then I realised the name rang a bell. This fella, Stephan Dulwich, he's the father of Nobel Prize-winning virologist Mara Dulwich. Don't know what he was doing in New York but as he left his suite at the Plaza early this morning, he seemed to step right out in front of a speeding delivery truck, which the driver abandoned and has no plates or identity markings. If you want me to pass this on to someone else darl, I can… but nobody works like you do.'

Seraph hadn't deliberated for a second, agreeing to do her best to get the ins and outs of what had happened. As she put the pieces together, she couldn't ignore the facts before her. It was not uncommon for people to end up dead on a street corner somewhere, but for the father of the world's most prominent virologist to be knocked down and killed in a similar manner as her parents, only weeks after them – it seemed to be too much of a coincidence. Scientists and their loved ones would often turn up dead if they had upset the mysterious figureheads of Officium, but she had no idea what her parents had done to warrant suspicion. They were just workaholics, that's all she had ever known about them.

That day, she looked up at the skyscraper she worked in on West 40th Street after visiting the scene of the crime, and her vertigo seemed to hit her like never before. The top of the building suddenly felt as if it were falling toward her very fast, and the ground seemed to shake beneath her as she felt certain the tip of the structure would collapse right on top of her. She somehow made it to the Cafe4U on the third floor of the gigantic, forty-storey Bed4theNite on Times Square, staring out at the crowds below. The personality-less white walls of the shop seemed to be closing in on her as she drank endless mugs of black coffee refilled by a pump at the side of her table. It was only when her bladder started to call out that she realised she had been sat there for so long that it had gotten dark. She wandered home in a daze and felt the anger rising up from deep down inside of her as she began to feel certain that someone had deliberately killed her parents. It just seemed too staged somehow.

Ever since that day, she had worked tirelessly to find out the truth about the group she suspected were behind her parent's deaths. Patrolling the streets of New York, she picked out people from the masses she knew could be of help, and paid many of them to provide her with the information she required. Ulrich, an old friend from NYU, worked at one of Officium's laboratories and had become a great source of information. Not long after their last meeting in January, however, his naked, battered body turned up mysteriously on the trash-ridden banks of the Hudson. That was one of the rare times she had actually cried, because she knew she had been directly or indirectly responsible for him, and she discovered his girlfriend was left bereaved… and pregnant.

The only reason Seraph had survived all these years, she figured, was because soon after her parents died, an unknown source had started sending her information about the city's officials, many of whom were involved in underground activities, including drug running, trafficking and tax evasion. This was a world where immorality was the only thing that could guarantee you a return. Virtue made you suspicious in the eyes of Officium. She had kept back all manner of strategic titbits about such people's personal lives, including their sexual preferences, secret affairs they would rather keep hidden and children they didn't want anyone to know were theirs. This kind of information was the only kind they really cared about – the sensitive sort – and the only stuff she knew she could bargain with. People, no matter how seemingly ruthless or cold, still always had a sore spot somewhere along the line. She subtly spread the word amongst her circle that she had images, videos, voice recordings and signed confessions (made under duress, she imagined) that incriminated a lot of those in the thick of the city's criminality, therefore protecting herself with the threat of being able to drag them through the mud and make their lives impossible if she needed to.

She had never found any solid evidence about her parent's deaths, however, but there were so many connections. She used to call up Eve late at night for a vis-call to talk manically about it all, and Eve would listen, trying to encourage Seraph to move on and get on with her life. She would sit patiently as Seraph ran everything by her, and still Eve would pass no judgement or opinion, simply encouraging Seraph to leave it all behind and move on, even suggesting she leave New York and move in with her. But that was not a possibility for Seraph, it never had been.

Amidst all the hurt and despair, Eve had always been there for her – the one constant in her chaotic life. Seraph had viewed her aunt as an almost superhuman being; infallible and untainted by the rankness of this world. Knowing Eve was out there emitting light amongst the darkness gave Seraph hope, comfort and renewed vigour. The emptiness she felt because of this latest loss could not even be comprehended. She would just have to continue as she always had done, and accept that Eve was gone.

Seraph knew her and Eve's similarities would probably extend to their chosen lifestyles; that is, remaining happily and steadfastly single. At thirty-six, she had never had a long-term relationship. She occasionally got the urge to take herself to a bar and pick up a date, but after she slept with them, more often than not she never saw them afterward – even if they did want to see her again. She felt the responsibility to her job outweighed everything else in her life.

She was around seven years old when she had first met Eve, who had flown out to visit them in Manhattan. Despite being in her fifties, her aunt still had the wit and spark of a twenty-one-year-old. She often shocked members of the public by stopping to talk to them on the streets, asking them where they got their apparel from if she saw something she liked. She was without prejudice and had the rare ability to look at people and appreciate their individuality. It was clear she had worked incredibly hard for what she had got, but she had such enthusiasm for life, she never let anything get her down. She never let anyone knock her positivity, and that's perhaps why she never gave in and sold the shop she had received so many lucrative offers for re-development, or as she liked to say, "the crude re-fashioning of". No doubt when the tides began turning, Eve had bought up nearly the entire Shambles to protect it.

The two of them had sat in Central Park eating sandwiches on a bench. In the distance, they could hear trees being torn down and the reservoir being filled. However, the beauty of an autumn day was not diminished entirely, with flame-red leaves tingeing the dull sky and bright yellow blooms attracting the park-goers' line of sight. Eve, with her multi-coloured smock dress and long red-grey locks, had sea-green eyes that had the ability to stare right through to your soul.

'Do you like school Seraphina?' her aunt asked.

'I love it. I never want to come home at the end of the day.'

Eve turned to examine her great-niece's face incredulously. 'Why don't you want to come home?'

'Mommy and Daddy go behind closed doors and whisper things I can't hear. It makes me frightened.'

'Oh, my dear, they do love you though, you know that.'

'I don't know that! I'm never allowed to go anywhere or do anything. I'm kept under lock and key.'

'Seraphina, they are just trying to protect you. There are people in this world who don't think of you as the precious angel that I and your parents do.'

The child frowned, unconvinced by her aunt's molly-coddling. 'Aunt Eve, can we go to the playground?'

'Okay. Just this once. I don't want your parents to think I'm going soft.'

'I won't tell,' Seraph giggled.

Seraph and her aunt reached the playground and the youngster jumped on one of the swings as Eve pushed. After a while, the elder of the two tired and sat beside her niece.

'You know. There is something I always tell the people that come through the doors of my shop. Something you might do well to always remember, Seraphina. I tell them that if they're okay in themselves, it doesn't matter what is going on around them, they will still be alright.'

Seraph had seen her aunt in person only twice since, but Eve had ended up becoming a close confidante, with the pair frequently exchanging lengthy emails and vis-calls. Though she was only seven at the time, those words in the park stayed with her and had gained more meaning as the years rolled by. Seraph had grown up reminding herself that she was okay, even if everyone around her wasn't. She began to see that she could try to escape the shackles her parents had been bound by, instead choosing a life of variety as a reporter. Their deaths, however, had thrown her whole ideal system into chaos, and she had busied herself with her work ever since, burying her feelings deep down to survive. She was a bubbling pot of anger, ready to bite back or leap on someone in defence of herself at any moment. Not knowing what had really happened to them had nearly driven her mad.

She had come to accept that she couldn't share her life with anyone, it just wasn't for her. She had foregone even having close friends, because she only ended up disappointing them too, unable to meet up with them because of her busy schedule and inability to take off her work-hat. She couldn't do with the questions either, about why she does what she does. She was a lone she-wolf, as she liked to think of herself, prowling the grey streets of New York for new leads, trying to decipher the real reason behind why the world had ended up so corrupt and morally polluted. She had taken her job to new heights, become notorious even, unrelenting in her pursuit of the truth. She wanted to know why people had become so gullible, so weakened by their fears and so easily led by anyone who shouted up about their beliefs. Her job was an obsession, one which she wouldn't be able to let go of easily, and one which she relished every day for the way it raised her adrenalin levels and put fire in her belly.

*   *   *

Yeah, thanks, it's recording. Err, video diary entry zero-zero-one. Hi there, I'm Tom Bradbury, professor of zoology at Cambridge University. Today is Saturday, November the tenth, 2012. I've just arrived in New Guinea on an expedition to seek out some more of the previously undocumented species here. We arrived in Jayapura yesterday before helicoptering out to camp a few miles from the Mamberamo river basin. It's 6pm but the temperature is still at least a hundred degrees. Even continually drinking water doesn't seem to cut the amount we're sweating out constantly. The giant bugs around here are having a field day with my flesh. You can probably hear them trying to batter their way through the tent. I've had to throw at least four nets around the thing to protect myself. We have to remain vigilant in case the conditions take a turn for the worse. The tropical storms have been known to cause extreme devastation. It will be a treacherous hike up into the rainforest but my colleagues Simpson and Harley are expert mountaineers and assure me we will be okay. We're waiting for a day when we can guarantee no rain for us to be able to get safely up into a lower-lying part of the Foja Mountains and see what we can find. We are going to erect a few canopies and try to smoke out whatever we can find.

Two native ecologists have agreed to accompany us.

I find it hard to see how anything could survive here. It's an impossible environment for crops and livestock to thrive in. It's not only thick with vegetation, but the weather is unruly and the conditions in the mountains are quite often freezing. The flora and fauna have had to adapt to their environment over the millennia and seem to be highly evolved, having been left to their own devices for so long. Hopefully we will be able to venture into the wilderness tomorrow to see what we can find. I'm expected to hold a seminar on Wednesday so I'm due to fly back home on Monday night. If nothing turns up by then, that's it. I'll hopefully have some findings soon, so until then...

CHAPTER 4

It was getting toward dusk when Seraph decided to explore the streets of York. Swirls of pinks and oranges flooded the skies overhead, slightly dulled by the thick clouds of smoke and steam emitting from a nearby power station. She walked out of the hotel onto the street and a realisation suddenly hit her. *This is where the Cedars Court Hotel once stood.* She remembered seeing the Edwardian building in a photograph, with its redbrick outer walls, tall chimneys, plate glass windows, spectacular gardens and men in white gloves welcoming guests in through huge oak doors. It had evidently been knocked down to make way for the thirty-storey Bed4theNite, a synthetic skyscraper housing as many cubicle-sized rooms as possible.

She walked through the streets and was struck by the various odours tingeing the evening air. Though she was used to city living and the aromas that went with that, York seemed to have a special kind of stench that was unique: sewerage and plastic. It was extremely odd. Perhaps the recycling plant that lurked in the distance was creating the strange concoction of aromas. Seraph wondered how someone like Eve could stand to live there. She should have retired years ago and gone to live somewhere warmer, cleaner and sunnier, but she had stayed in the capital of Yorkshire, a region which had sadly decreased in size as the sea levels had risen.

The people filing past her on the pavements seemed to be like Seraph, walking about alone, and without a specific destination. Like her, they were probably just wandering the streets so they didn't have to sit facing the bland, cramped four walls back home. Spotting an automated food dispensary, she stopped to get a cheeseburger, paying way over the odds for the privilege of eating mostly reconstituted offal, before finding a bench nearby to sit on.

Devouring the rancid offerings she had just bought, which she was used to living off in her line of work, her mind once again turned to Eve. It was true, she had always thought her aunt would live forever, and had never imagined she would one day be gone. It was ironic that Seraph only realised after she was dead, how much Eve had meant to her. It is the eternal tragedy; that you don't realise what you had until it's gone. This is why she had been spurred to travel at the drop of a hat that morning, she admitted to herself.

Having finished the food, Seraph explored the High Street, surveying the large automated retail units, very few of which were actually independent stores. Everything was usually part of the "4U" chain, such as Clothes4U, Shoes4U and Underwear Village. Peering through the windows of one such establishment, she saw rails of bland garments in various shades but in much the same styles. As customers made their choices, the item would be instantly replaced on the rack by a robotic arm reaching up through the floor. It was simply a case of taking your intended purchase to one of the multiple scanners dotted around the place to swipe your U-Card and pay. Monotony and convenience became the way of the world after everything was monopolised by Officium. Only the very elite could afford high-end fashion, while most were forced to purchase clothes mass-produced in factories – garments made for practicality more than style. Even back in New York, one of the world's fashion capitals, the thrift stores of the Villages had been closed decades ago to make way for supermarkets, while the famous department stores – Macy's, Bloomingdale's and Barneys – were overrun by squatters and vanguards amidst the chaos of 2023, and authorities had never managed to clear them out.

Seraph's own wardrobe consisted of mostly black slacks, t-shirts, sweaters, biker boots and her trusty short leather jacket. She had given up years ago on trying to be fashionable, she just didn't have time, and so she had stuck with a simple colour scheme for convenience. Just as in New York, Seraph also noticed York's population consisted of very few young people. She was dismayed not to see children walking around with their parents, as in the archive pictures, and even sadder to so many old folks hobbling around alone, having been left single by the Ravage. She was usually one of a minority wherever she went – young, nubile and unafraid.

She was accustomed to being unaccompanied, but she wasn't used to having nothing to do, and she was quickly feeling unable to escape her own, terrifying thoughts. Her job as a crime reporter came with a lifestyle that kept very unsociable hours. She saw herself as more of a detective really, but operating under her own jurisdiction gave her the edge. She worked constantly; eating, washing and shopping when she could. There would always be places to stake out, detectives to hang around, leads to follow, whistleblowers to chase, coffee shops to be seen in and people to "coax" submissions out of. She worked for one of the last online papers in the world that actually carried out investigative journalism, attempting to delve into the various conspiracies that were thrown about but could never really be proved – because most were too scared to dig deeper. Libel laws were so strict, and nowhere had imposed them more resolutely than the country she was visiting. Those who trod too close to the truth knew what they were risking. Whenever she actually managed to scrape enough details together to write up an article, the Internet would suddenly become abuzz with her findings. It wasn't very often that she was able to give her audience anything, but when she did, they lapped it up with eagerness. Those few subscriptions were what kept the paper going, and somehow, it remained. Her wage was a pitiful one, but she didn't really care, her job afforded her all the excitement she needed – and the estate her parents had bequeathed to her had helped.

To achieve her reputation, Seraph had to ensure she never once displayed even an ounce of weakness to her colleagues or contacts. She maintained a rigorous fitness regime; cross-training, swimming and regularly playing hockey with a bunch of girls in the vast basement gym of the *Chronicle*'s offices. She had been encouraged by her parents to take self-defence classes from a very early age, and didn't drink unless the situation required it, didn't smoke, take drugs or use collagen to improve her self-esteem. Her body was a clean fighting machine, disciplined both in mind and spirit, and very tightly wound. Being an immovable object in an easily-manipulated world made her a force of nature – a danger to those who believed they could literally get away with murder. People feared her because she seemed unnatural; thriving in such a crooked society without turning to vice herself. She had spent years building up professional relationships all over NYC, and had finally been rewarded with the title of Deputy Editor two years ago, although she never really had much time to do very much writing, or editing, for that matter. For years, she had been on the trail of one particular theory – that the Ravage of 2023 was an orchestrated catastrophe. The disease was never explained due to the swift devastation it caused and the way in which it seemed to affect its victims in different ways. Officium had used the tragedy to their advantage so soon afterward, and that was something that had never sat right with her. She recognised from a young age that a lot of people knew deep down that the way the world was being organised was wrong. That people were aware of this, but weren't willing to do anything about it, made her furious. A feeling in her gut told her there was something deep in the heart of Officium that needed to be uncovered.

Seraph had decided long ago that nobody had the right to choose how another person should live, it was something she felt very passionate about, and she had always been on the side of those trying to live their lives honourably. However, it didn't seem achievable in these times of fierce competition – where only ruthless business acumen or corrupt leanings guaranteed you a place in the world. The gap between the rich and the poor became so stark following the Ravage, an event that made those in power who survived believe that they were the chosen ones to take society forward. Hope and faith needed to be restored somehow to bring back life into the world. The most dumbfounding thing to her was that the Ravage happened forty years ago, and yet the world had still not moved on. Nobody ever considered going back into the countryside, and people wondered why they had such little space and felt as though they might go stir-crazy at any moment.

Looking at the sad faces of the pedestrians passing her on the streets of York, she envied them. They were ignorant, perhaps a little browbeaten, but they could not imagine the things she had seen and done in her relatively short lifetime. She had seen mangled corpses beaten almost to a pulp – left in apartments sometimes for days before being discovered – because most people had no family left to find them. She had met terrified women raped to within an inch of their lives by the agents of Officium, and had been unable to convince any of them to sign statements, such was their fear of being killed if they spoke up. She had slept rough with the hobos to get the word on the street, and had spent days tailing corrupt businessman around town – from one shady residence to another. Worst of all, she had been forced to flirt with hideous excuses for human beings, and in some cases sleep with them, and had completely rescinded any form of private life for herself. As they walked past her, she could tell the residents existed without ever having turned their minds to serious contemplation, simply going from one place to another on the way to the grave. She had really seen and done some things, but she knew it was an extreme way of living that she couldn't keep up forever. She sometimes wished she was a simple person with petty troubles, but she knew that her lot in life was not to simply while away the years quietly. Her career was her only addiction; one that she couldn't get away from. Her work kept her busy, occupied, offered her a sense of achievement and pride. It was both a blessing and a curse. She would end up just like her parents if she wasn't careful – dead before her time. But she neither cared about herself, nor had anyone to care about, so she would keep living that way.

Suddenly, it had got dark, and after deciding she had bore enough of York's unique aromas, she started heading back to the hotel. Just as she was letting herself in at the entrance, a man with a shifty look about him and scruffy clothes grabbed her arm and said, 'There are many of us who read your work, and we all thank you for what you're trying to do.' Seraph was pleasantly surprised to hear that she had reached people even there, but just as she was about to say thanks to the guy, he scampered off briskly back to wherever he came from, seemingly not wanting to draw attention.

Seraph wondered whether he was part of one of the resistance groups that were trying to rid the world of Officium's network. She had heard that what few of them there were had often been undone in their attempts to finally catch out Officium, because so many of their members were easily bought by bribes or blackmailed to become moles. She had never been able to find out much about one such group that was meant to be based in Europe, and was said to have tens of thousands of members. She had never considered affiliating herself with one of these organisations because everyone knew her face, so she would never be able to work covertly. She had thought it best to simply make her presence felt and demonstrate that she would not be bought, and would continue to relentlessly pursue the truth until the bitter end.

Smiling to herself she headed back to her room, deciding to spend the rest of the evening checking her messages, reading the latest news reports on the *Chronicle* site and eating trash from the refreshment tray in her room. She wondered what tomorrow might bring, and suspected Eve had a few surprises in store.

*   *   *

The milliner had been given only two hours to deal with her target. She had arranged it so that he would come to her. It was imperative she got in, and got out. She couldn't risk her identity. As far as the authorities knew, she wasn't even in the country, so being caught would spell certain catastrophe for not only her – but the cause too.

She was dressed casually, and with her hair pulled back into a tight bun, she looked just like any other library frequenter – except for the black ballet pumps laced firmly around her ankles – easier to perform in. No-one would presume that she was one of the deadliest creatures on the planet.

She sat at the end of a long, wide wooden desk, reading Balzac quietly, with a polystyrene cup containing her espresso to hand. Even though she could barely see her surroundings, she resisted the temptation to switch on one of the desk lights, knowing the dim lighting would allow her more of the element of surprise. This part of the New York Public Library, the rare books section – with its crowded shelves but few visitors – was deserted save for her.

Like clockwork, he appeared. Smart navy-striped suit, possibly Saville Row. Grey hair, broad shoulders, bulky physique. There were three desks between hers and the one he had chosen to sit at.

As far as he was concerned, he was finally getting to meet a representative of the group he had risked so much for. He had sold out some good people to finally get his fingers in a few pies. This was everything he had ever wanted. Money, power, success. He could smell it, taste it almost, and he wore his best suit for the occasion. That morning, when he got the message to meet, he had not thought for a second that he would be placing himself in danger. He was not even concerned that the message came from an unknown source. He was simply overtaken by excitement at finally getting what he deserved. Status.

He had joined the resistance to get knowledge of their inner workings, hoping it would gain him respect from Officium if he could find out enough about their enemy. He was fed up of being an underachiever, a mediocre excuse for a man, and a disappointment to his wife and son. He'd never been fit and strong enough to become an agent, since a childhood illness left him without his left foot. He needed more than to be a simple tailor, in a dwindling and dying market. When a client of his, Hamish Maddon, told him about a resistance group he knew of, he had leapt on the opportunity to get in on it. He made promises about using his clientele to gather information. But he had secretly had a very sinister, ulterior motive. He had unwittingly given up Maddon, who had died along with his wife, after he had revealed the location of RAO's meetings in New York. However, he had not carried out the act, so as far as he was concerned, he was without sin or recrimination. He simply knew he needed more from life, that's all, and now he was there – deliriously expectant.

A mildly attractive woman suddenly appeared before him, standing with a book in hand. She smiled sweetly and asked, 'Excuse me, but do you have the time? I can't seem to find a single clock in this place.'

'Of course,' looking down at his watch, he said, 'It's a quarter to two.'

'Thanks so much, that's very kind of you.' She continued smiling at him and stayed standing there. He felt it would be too rude to ask her if there was anything else, but his contact could arrive at any moment, and he became anxious.

She noted, 'I hear the police are making headway into finally getting hold of the person responsible for the Maddon killings. You know, the heart surgeons? Apparently their loss will now mean at least four dozen people will have to wait six months longer for bypasses.'

He looked up at her face, shock spreading across his. He wondered, but it couldn't possibly be… He had been so careful… hadn't he? He nervously stood up. He looked into her eyes, but he struggled to gauge what was behind them. She stood there with hardly any expression whatsoever. That scared him more than anything.

'Who are you?' he asked.

'I'm a friend of the dressmaker. You might have heard of her?'

He wanted to bolt out of the place. He was desperate to just start running.

'Yes, it was a grave shame about the Maddons. Their daughter is without both her parents now. Imagine that, a young woman without her mum and dad. Being without one would certainly be bad enough, but without both…'

She didn't seem intimidating, standing there casually holding her book between both hands in front of her. However, her words almost shocked the life out of him. He started to move away from behind the desk to make his escape. However, her book suddenly fell and he was drawn by its flight toward the floor.

Out of the corner of his eye, he saw an almost inhuman shadow move with incredible velocity. She leapt up onto the desk he had moved away from, suddenly threw her body in the air and expertly sent a foot crashing into his chest to ensure he had taken his last breath. Then there was nothing. His mass fell to the floor, and she walked toward the exit to the stairwell.

CHAPTER 5

THE "RAVAGE" IS AT AN END
5 December, 2023
By Rick Jeffries, Editor, *London Chronicle*

Over the past few weeks, the world's population has been decimated from ten billion to around seven billion. At least three billion are believed to have died, but that figure is unverifiable. There have been no deaths for the past four days, and so it seems, the only thing to do now is take stock, and bury the dead. The mysterious illness, which has become known globally as the "Ravage", seemed to appear from nowhere and disappear almost instantaneously, as if an unknown force swept it down upon humanity and took it away again. It is thought to have originated from Manchester, but that is not an absolute certainty. As the dust settles, many debate whether some powerful, deliberate force was at work, following last year's sudden and unexpected population explosion.

Most of the victims are the infirm, children, and people with pre-existing medical conditions. Only the fittest and strongest have survived. The disease persisted without prejudice, attacking people everywhere, and taking lives within twenty-four hours of infection in some cases. Scientists across the country and throughout the rest of the world are working around the clock, trying to determine what the world has been dealing with, where it came from, and whether a vaccine can be developed. The virus appears to be an extremely aggressive strain of flu, but according to scientific sources it is taking time to analyse. Symptoms vary but include a high fever, severe cough, migraine, nausea, wheezing and cramps. Citizens are being advised to follow all the procedures and guidelines suggested by the Global Health Organisation. The advice is to be aware and be vigilant. If you experience any of these, call your doctor or head to your nearest medical centre for advice. Otherwise, stay at home, please don't go out. Try to keep your distance from members of your household.

The GHO is warning against coming into close contact with anyone unless absolutely necessary. The "Ravage" is still yet to be explained and all are advised to exercise caution until it is determined what this disease was exactly and how it was transferred so quickly. Panicky citizens have flooded the nearest cities to receive treatment, and have been instructed not to return to the countryside until further notice, in case some trace of the disease still lurks out in the unknown.

With so many world leaders having been struck down, a number of former politicians and intelligence analysts are setting up a global support network called Officium, offering their services to help rebuild the world. The organisation is also promising to work to guard nations from any possible outbreaks in the future. The FBI, CIA and NSA have been broken up. Similarly, here in the UK, MI5 and MI6 have also been declassified, allowing Officium to take control of intelligence and security. Russian, French and German intelligence will also allow Officium unprecedented access to their systems and databases, and it is believed many other countries will follow suit.

It seems uncertain that the world will recover from this catastrophe, and if ever, it will be a long time from now. Flocking to cities and towns everywhere are families without loved ones, and people without hope.

CHAPTER 6

The next day Seraph decided to head back to the bridal shop. The sky was tinged grey, but it was mild, as it always was. Around midmorning, as she left her hotel wearing plain black jeans, leather jacket, grey granddad shirt and habitual shoulder bag, she took a moment to survey the city Eve had lived in for so many years. Just outside the Bed4theNite, she climbed up a small incline to step onto a few bricks, presumably some remains of the Roman wall. Having to steady herself as the loose pile she stood on threatened to crumble beneath her, she looked down on the inhabitants with her hands dug deep in her jacket pockets, and felt there was something she was missing. She saw the poor inhabitants, and yet Eve's business had remained amidst the crumbling, industrialised surroundings. She couldn't understand how a bridal shop, of all businesses, could have thrived so well in not only this ruined city, but in these times of few marriages. She leapt down and began walking through the empty streets toward the Shambles.

Her hair loose for a change, she pulled her hands through it to shake it out as she marched around. As she hit a pocket of inhabitants on Parliament Street, she couldn't help but notice every single one of them seemed to be glaring in her direction. She daren't make any kind of facial gesture in return, but they started smiling at her. She continued onwards, and as they separated to allow her passage through, she felt they were probably startled by her extraordinary appearance. However, as she continued through the crowds of admirers, she spotted two figures standing behind them who seemed out of place. There was a man and a woman both dressed similarly in blue jeans, black military jackets and cream t-shirts. They both had blank, expressionless faces, and looked as if they could handle themselves, with thick necks and solid stances. The inhabitants continued to swarm around her as she neared Eve's shop, and the two figures followed behind the masses in the direction she moved. As she reached the front door of the shop after swiftly turning off Market Street, the crowds and the two shadowy figures dispersed almost immediately, and Seraph quickly made her way inside. Reeling from her encounter, she had a few questions to ask of Camille.

Entering the deserted shop, she was welcomed by Camille, who exclaimed casually, 'Seraph, so nice to see you again! I was just going to have some tea, would you care to join me?'

Seraph was knocked off course, smiling and nodding at the Frenchwoman's beguiling friendliness. She followed Camille into an office behind the reception desk and sat at a small, round, wooden table positioned against a net-curtained window looking out onto the Shambles. The office was bland in comparison to the rest of the shop, with rows of filing systems, numerous sketch pads and fabric swatches, all piled high on a large heavy desk pushed up against the wall at the other end of the room.

Seraph started to peer out behind the curtains when Camille immediately stood up to roughly grab her arm, replacing the drapes quickly. Seraph was not only shocked by the contact, but by the suddenness and almost reptilian response Camille had exhibited. The women assessed each other as if they were preparing for a contest of some sort. The reporter yanked her arm out of the Frenchwoman's solid grip.

Seraph paced about and asked, 'Camille, what the fuck is going on? Something is not right here.' Pointing back in the direction she had just come from, she continued, 'I was just out on the streets and everyone was practically creating a barricade between me and two strange characters stood in the distance.'

'I apologise for being so brusque, but you can never be too careful sometimes. You of all people should know that.'

Seraph sat down, removing her shoulder bag and jacket. She refused to sit forward at the table, as if doing so would condone Camille's treatment of her.

'I knew there was something about you Camille, the moment I met you, I could tell there was more to you.' Seraph lifted her foot and rested it on her other knee, sitting bolt upright to impose her frame on the woman sat opposite. 'Now tell me, what is the meaning of this?'

Camille stood up and asked, 'Where did you see those people?'

'They were following me from near Parliament Street, and seemed to disappear into thin air as soon as I arrived here.'

Eve's manager stood there, holding a hand to her mouth in contemplation, with the other hand propping up the elbow of that arm. 'They know you're here…'

An unspoken knowledge passed between the two women.

'They're agents?'

Camille nodded and Seraph tried to absorb the revelation. 'But, why would they be after me here? They never dare come anywhere near me in New York.'

'I don't know my love, but it doesn't bear thinking about.'

Seraph stood up and grabbed Camille by the shoulders, demanding, 'Tell me everything. I need to know exactly what we're dealing with here.'

The elder woman paced about before sitting back down at the table and motioning for Seraph to rejoin her. She looked troubled and the expression on her face turned stony. She seemed to be fighting an internal battle, scratching her hair and shaking her head from side to side, as well as muttering something under her breath in French.

'Camille!' Seraph shot the woman an exasperated glance.

'Okay Seraph, but Eve would not have been happy about this.' Camille's contorted features spoke volumes.

Seraph's eyes narrowed and shock flooded her body at the mention of her aunt's name in such a context. She stumbled on her words, responding, 'No Camille, no, it can't be. No, I won't believe it god dammit!' Seraph stood up and turned her back to the other woman in the room. She held her head in her hands and felt her mouth go dry as she remained looking away from the Frenchwoman.

'Seraph, she would have done anything to protect you, including holding back the truth.'

'I can't handle this Camille. She can't have been…'

'Yes. She was… she was *the dressmaker.*' On that last word, Camille's French dialect strengthened.

Seraph fell to her knees and clenched her fists. She looked at the floor saying, 'No, she of all people can't have been involved. No. I can't believe this. I can't accept she was this other person. If only I'd known!'

Camille stood waiting for Seraph to return to her seat, preparing herself for a barrage of questions. However, Seraph saw no point in interrogation as her mind swirled with anger. 'She was an old lady, how could it have fallen on her, of all people? How could she have wanted this? How could she have? I don't understand!' Seraph stood up to kick the wall out of frustration. She pulled her fingers through her hair, twisting at it from the roots. Then she had a thought. She could see no other course of action.

Camille waited to see what Seraph would do next, but hardly had time to react as the door of the office was flung open and the headstrong American strode out of the room toward the front door. Quickly, Camille grabbed a small electron-pulse stun gun from a drawer in her desk, and ran out after Seraph.

As Camille reached the front door, she looked from side to side to see which direction Seraph had run off in. She spotted flaming locks billowing out from behind a black figure chasing down the bottom of the street, and started running after her. Tucking the gun in the back of her jeans, Camille sprinted with everything she had. She ran with expert poise, back bolt straight, and her arms resembled scissors slicing through silk. She barely breathed as she shifted her body into a mode of clear purpose. She soon caught up with Seraph, and grabbed the back of her jeans to hinder her progress. Seraph fell back with a jolt, falling flat on her back onto the cobbled, empty lane. Camille hovered over Seraph on the ground, and pulled her to sit up. She knelt down to reprimand Eve's niece, who looked mad with fury. 'My girl, you don't know what they are capable of. This is why we kept things from you.'

'I'm not some little girl Camille, I just want the truth.' Seraph couldn't help but feel she had acted like a child, however, reacting as she had to the revelation about her aunt.

However, they realised they weren't alone on the street. Camille looked behind her after she noticed Seraph's attention had been drawn. The agents appeared to have just emerged from Swinegate. Seraph glanced at Camille and appeared as if she wanted to leap into action. However, Camille swung her weapon out from behind her back and tucked it into the front of her jeans instead. She whispered to Seraph, 'Stay here.' She winked in understanding, and remained on the ground while Camille wandered in the direction of the two agents.

Then Seraph witnessed something quite incredible. The Frenchwoman reached the pair and seemed to hold court with them for a few seconds, before the female of the duo lunged toward Camille, who responded by grabbing the woman's arm swiftly and knocking her to the ground with a swift jab to her victim's throat. Camille stepped back a few paces from the altercation, and the man started to move toward her, with a menacing grin across his face. However, she was not deterred. She readied herself, adopting a pose belonging to some sort of martial art, Seraph guessed. As the male agent neared Camille, she screeched and seemed to lift her entire body off the ground, suspending herself in mid-air, before performing an inch-perfect roundhouse kick on the agent and landing deftly before the man as he fell next to his partner. Camille walked back toward Seraph with a gait that Eve's niece now recognised was due to her physical discipline. Camille took a small tubular device from her pocket. Speaking into it, she said, 'I have two shadows down on Stonegate that need to be dealt with immediately.'

Camille held a hand out for Seraph to grab hold of, and she pulled her up, motioning for them to head back to the shop.

'You're a woman after my own heart Camille.'

The Frenchwoman smiled, 'We have a lot to discuss, chérie.'

*   *   *

Video diary entry zero-zero-two. (Coughing). I'm laid up in my camp bed and I've no idea what day it is, only I know I should have been back in the UK a long time ago. We ventured up into the mountains the day after my last entry. The weather was quite fine really, if a little cool the further up into Foja we got (breathless). I think it must have been around 5:30am when we set off and we reached our destination at about noon. (Rolling about to get comfortable). All five of us reached a plateau and surveyed the scene below us. The lush green forest and active, diverse wildlife were a sight to see. It really did feel as though we had reached a lost world. The knowing nature of the place suggested an evolutionary strength beyond anything of any other country. We didn't find anything new, but one of my colleagues overheard one of the guides panicking as they realised we were in the vicinity of the "Poison Fowl." However, we were so inquisitive, we insisted they show us the way to this mysterious creature's habitat. I don't know if it was the thin air, but I could have wept when we discovered it was a bird of unparalleled beauty. The size of a chicken, but much slimmer, its feathers were as white and fluffy as a chick's, tinged grey-black at the ends. It had an elegant long neck with a black patch of velvet fluff on top of its head. Its pink feet and claws were small in comparison, while its wings were built for the purpose of short flight. It crowed a sensational rhythmic cry almost resembling birdsong but exhibited vicious tendencies as soon as we went anywhere near it. (More coughing and spluttering). We took some samples of feathers and faeces but the creature wouldn't let us get anywhere near it and we didn't want to risk infringing on its environment any more than we had to, such was its apparent rarity. We came back down the mountain that evening, and arrived back at camp at around 6:30pm, sound as a pound.

However, the next morning… (spluttering, wipes face with a cloth), where was I? Oh yes, the next day my colleagues and I woke up feeling as if we'd each been hit by a truck. While I exhibited symptoms of a chest infection, Ed Harley had a terrible stomach upset… possibly gastroenteritis I think… and Hal Simpson had something akin to glandular fever. I think I remember us saying to each other that we'd suffered similar ailments as youngsters, but for us all to get them again, all at the same time, it was too strange. We thought we would be able to shake off our maladies but we were soon all bedridden. Our guides fled and left us to it, not wanting to catch whatever it was we'd caught. We've all spent the past few days hanging by a thread, delirious and barely able to function. We ran out of water and had to use the satellite phone to call for emergency aid. It only came after about three more calls for help, but someone merely dumped a medical kit along with a few barrels of water, plus tins of rice and beans. They left them a few metres away from our tents. I somehow slithered along the ground to retrieve the supplies but I slept for about four hours afterwards, such was the energy I'd had to exert to get there and back. I injected myself with a penicillin shot but honestly felt worse off for having had it. Harley also felt worse off for it, while poor Simpson's allergy to the stuff meant he couldn't have anything anyway. (Catches his breath). We got the feeling that the locals knew of some terror hiding in those mountains and were afraid that we'd caught it and would pass it on to them. However, for the two guides not to have been struck down like we were, they must have had some sort of immunity. I honestly don't know how I've gotten through the past few days. I'm sure I've suffered palpitations, and my mind has been so troubled I've been hallucinating, waking up in pools of sweat and having to talk myself into trying to beat whatever it is we've been plagued with. I feel like my skin is hanging off me, having had no appetite. It must still be well over a hundred degrees out there and yet sometimes I feel as though I could have easily been in Siberia one minute, and the Attacama desert the next. I've often felt as if some virulent creature has been gnawing away at my bones and tissue. My lungs have strained to take in oxygen and even my eyesight seems to have suffered. The worst off of us all was Ed. With all the trips to the toilet, he's suffered extreme dehydration and he passed out a few times. Harley was so weak he couldn't even lift himself out of bed, but he had to keep trying to keep liquids down. It seems we are recovering slightly now, God help us. (Falling back onto the camp bed into a coughing fit).

CHAPTER 7

Five years ago, Seraph had asked Eve to visit her during fashion week. She hadn't told her aunt, but there was a designer she had been quietly investigating. If she turned up at the event, the world would wonder why New York's most notorious crime reporter was loitering around. Francesca had got the VIP passes for her, but she needed a cover to be able to attend and interrogate.

Eve had taken some convincing. She didn't like to leave her shop, and only travelled for purposeful business meetings, if she had to travel at all. However, a number of late night vis-calls later, and Eve had finally relented. She would come to NYC if Seraph admitted why she really wanted her to attend. Seraph had explained, 'I'm attending fashion week and I need somebody with me to confuse the masses. If you turn up as my companion, maybe they won't be so suspicious. They'll be wondering who the hell this old lady is with me, rather than thinking, "Shit, Seraph Maddon's here?" If you did this for me Eve, I'd be so grateful.'

It was a Tuesday. Seraph had told Francesca she would be busy all week with her aunt – if she caught her drift – and had left work early to meet Eve at the Plaza. Eve had only landed a few hours ago and was in one of the most exuberant suites in the hotel. Two-and-a-half-thousand square feet of opulence. Two bedrooms with their own en suite bathrooms, outrageous amounts of closet space and a huge living and dining room. Seraph walked into the lounge to be greeted by the old dressmaker, who said in a broad Yorkshire accent, 'Seraph, how nice to see you again. My, you've changed. You look luminous. And how awful this suite is.' Of course, Eve was being sarcastic. The surroundings could have easily belonged in the Élyseé Palace with stately furnishings including silk rugs, crisp white walls, gold cornicing, marble fireplaces, extravagant chandeliers, luxurious drapes, damask-upholstered sofas, huge velvet cushions scattered in every room, a painstakingly carved antique dining set, tall Venetian lamps and gilded mirrors.

'Aunt Eve, you haven't changed at all! How are you still looking this good at your age?' Seraph kissed her aunt's cheek and gestured toward Eve's long, platinum hair, which was tucked back into an old-fashioned but graceful style. She was also wearing a royal blue, silk kimono of sorts with matching pumps and fine, delicate plastic bangles and matching earrings.

'What do you mean at my age? You're only as old as you feel.'

'How did you manage to get a suite here?'

Eve began to speak with an air of superiority. 'Oh, I thought seeing as though I don't do this very often, I might as well treat myself. I pulled some strings, my dear.'

Eve assessed her great-niece, before asking, 'So, what am I in for this week then? Just tell me what you've really dragged me here for. I keep up with your reports you know, some of them are very interesting, but this job must take up a lot of your time and energy?' A concerned-looking Eve motioned for Seraph to join her for some tea at a terrace outside, and they sat at a white metal garden table with matching chairs. All around them were tubs of fake conifers and dwarf rose bushes, amidst a background of smog, traffic and the bustling park.

Seraph responded, 'Yeah, I'm kept pretty busy, but that's the way I like it. And I don't need a lecture on that subject... Look, you've heard of London-based designer Melina James, haven't you? She flits between here and there quite a lot.'

Eve scoffed, 'Yes, the one who creates those dresses in the shapes of houses, yes? As if in homage to the buildings that were torn down all over the world...' Eve's face was contorted in disgust; she had never understood people who didn't actually make clothes that were wearable.

'Yes, her. Well, I have been tracking her movements for months. One of the main resistance groups is said to be run by someone codenamed the dressmaker. They are thought to be even more careful than Officium.'

'Seraph, don't mention their name. You know they have eyes and ears everywhere. I even heard they are starting to make U-Cards with built-in microphone chips!'

'Surely we are safe to speak freely here though?'

'Yes, but even still, I don't like to hear them mentioned.'

'Okay, well I have a hunch she is part of this resistance group, which I'm told goes by the name React Against Officium, or RAO. They are based somewhere in Europe, apparently, but have members all over the world.'

'What led to this hunch?' Eve was looking at her niece with quiet interest, with a hand held to her face to offset her inquisitiveness, as she awaited her rapturous niece's response.

Smugly, Seraph replied, 'I have this unknown source, who has been feeding me bits and pieces of information over the years. A few months ago, this contact told me to watch James closely. I asked if they knew whether she was the dressmaker, and when they gave me an ambiguous reply, I made the assumption that perhaps she is.'

'How do you know you can trust this source?'

Seraph eyed her aunt, realising she was no pushover either. 'I just know that they have given me some very beneficial information over the years, so it would be absurd not to trust them.'

'Nobody can be trusted in this world anymore, nobody. You know that.'

'I think I realise that more than most. However, this is the way I have to work. I have to take whatever bones are thrown my way. My reputation isn't going to uphold itself.'

'Why do you need to get information about this resistance anyway? Perhaps they remain so secretive for a reason. You could be risking their safety by delving too deep.'

'This so-called dressmaker walks amongst the people as if she were one of them, though she is rumoured to be the head of a secretive spy-ring. Melina's been spotted meeting some well-known officials, some of whom are thought to belong to Officium. I think if she is this dressmaker, perhaps she has been turned, if my source has warned me to watch her. It is purported that she wants to move to New York permanently and go for candidacy.'

A noticeable frown formed on Eve's forehead. She appeared troubled, and seemed to veer into deep thought, before resurfacing out of her mode of concentration to smile broadly at her niece.

'What is it?'

'The thing is Seraph, I've heard about this dressmaker too, and I hear she doesn't let just anyone meet her. She exists completely surrounded by secrecy, and only the most trustworthy know who she really is.'

'Like I said, I'll take whatever I can get. There's no harm in trying sometimes, is there?' Seraph winked.

Eve chuckled at her niece, won over by her enthusiasm. 'I wouldn't have come here for anyone else. You know I hate leaving the shop.'

Seraph couldn't help but smile. 'Oh, I'm sorry Aunt Eve. Have I dragged you out here to this luxurious pad against your will? You might enjoy yourself, you never know.'

Eve couldn't help but produce a wry smile and Seraph went over to hug her, giving her a tight squeeze and a pat on the back. 'You can't be that unhappy about being here, look at you, all dressed up! You don't fool me.'

'Well, I couldn't just turn up here of all places, looking like I'd been dragged through a bush backwards.'

'You're such a paradox, Eve. Never change, will you?'

'I don't think there's any chance of that now, at my age, is there?'

Seraph and Eve had taken in more shows that week than they could count, and Eve's outfit changes outnumbered the shows even. Her aunt really should have modelled; she could literally hang anything off her and make it look good, despite her advanced years. Seraph would have preferred to be less curvy and more straight up and down like her aunt, but Eve would whack her posterior cheekily, saying, 'God I wish I had been given an arse like yours!'

Lincoln Center was not what it used to be, but the event had carried on, using what bits of it were left as well as various other venues across the city, including a public lavatory in Grand Central once. Seraph's seventy-five-year-old English relative kept her reaction to everything hidden behind her orb-shaped sunglasses, ignoring the whisperers who wondered who the heck she was. A rumour had soon spread that she must be some vague, indistinct member of the Royal Family, for her to have gotten into the event. The gossip had miraculously diverted the attention completely away from Seraph. The designs they had viewed that week ranged from the fantastic to the absurd, but Seraph could tell that Eve had in actual fact relished seeing so many creations, even if some were made from recycled plastic bags and fishing nets.

Seraph remained in the background but made the most of any opportunity to drag lowly assistants behind a dressing room curtain and force them to spill everything they knew about Melina and her contacts. Seraph really had no qualms about taking targets to task. Even the NYPD knew they couldn't touch her. She loved getting in on the action and highly anticipated getting her hands on the ultimate prize – information.

And finally, she had got what she wanted. A name. A well-known, married official, who Seraph suspected was also a member of Officium. Melina had been having an affair with him. The truth was plastered all over the Internet the next day, and Melina went back to designing dresses in the shapes of houses, realising that was all she could really hope to expect from life. Her political life was over before it had even begun, and no doubt the resistance had realised that one of their own was a fraud, and had therefore ostracised her from their group.

That week, Seraph and Eve had so much fun. They spent their evenings having meals at the Plaza, one of the last places not to have automated service. Seraph had shared Eve's suite with her and they stayed up late every night, talking and reminiscing. One night they had ended up trying out O'Neill's, a scruffy Irish pub hidden in a quiet corner of Midtown West, and it turned out to be the best time they had ever had. The watering hole had dark wood-panelling on every wall, real beer pumps and an open kitchen enabling its clientele to see the food being prepared. They had eaten various delicacies such as white pudding and stew. They danced to folk music, and Seraph had discovered her love of Guinness that night, although it no longer tasted quite like it used to, so she was told. They had an absolute scream, and Seraph realised how much fun her aunt could be. She never even viewed her as a seventy-five-year-old woman, more of a best friend who had seen and done things, but was still so willing to give anything a go.

Eve had left a number of bizarre and retro outfits behind for Seraph to keep, most of which had sadly remained hanging in the closet. The pair had bade their farewells with a hint of regret at not having got together sooner. They promised each other that they would each try their best to meet again soon, but life had got in the way, and that was the last time she ever saw her aunt in person.

CHAPTER 8

Back at the bridal house, Camille hurried Seraph in and locked the front door. She went behind the reception desk and pressed a button underneath, dropping the iron shutters outside and initiating an infrared detection system. 'We'll soon know if anyone tries to break in, but I don't think they would dare now anyway.'

'Camille, even I wouldn't dare touch you!' They smirked at one another, but they each knew there were things still to be said, and a lot to sort through.

Camille led Seraph through to the back, past the dressing rooms to check nobody had snuck in, before testing the industrial backdoors that were only ever opened to take deliveries. 'I think we are safe, Seraph. Let's go down and I'll show you where we carry out our work.'

They walked past a gallery room containing several mannequins on which hung various bridal designs, all lit up against some expert backlighting and yet more pink wall decoration. There were gowns of varying colours, lengths, styles and sumptuousness. Huge glass windows shielded the dresses from harm, and Seraph recognised her aunt must have erected such a space to showcase her work as well as give people something to come and see for free.

Once through the gallery, they went through another door to enter a cold, windowless workshop of sorts. The brickwork was exposed, and the floor was covered in thick terracotta tiles. Camille flicked a switch and large spotlights overhead sizzled into life. The room housed dozens of boxes of materials stacked up on high metal shelves, along with various heavy-set worktables, on which sat industrial-sized sewing machines covered up while not in use. At the end of the room, a grey metal door carried the sign *Fire Exit* above it. Camille moved toward it, and Seraph followed, eyeing the woman curiously as she leaned forward to the retinal scanner. *ID verified.*

Welcome Camille Honoré.

The door clunked as it unlocked and after Camille heaved the entrance open, the pair entered a dark corridor. As the door closed with a thud behind them, hidden lights illuminated the brick tunnel they were in.

'It was either a stroke of genius or pure luck that Eve obtained these buildings, which used to be butchers shops many years ago. Because of this, they all have underground cellars, and we've set up our headquarters in them. We also have rooms like these in many other cities across the world, quietly watching those who think they are beyond surveillance. All the staff here live in the flats upstairs.'

Seraph felt pure excitement as she prepared to enter her aunt's secretive HQ. Her heart pounded in her chest, and she tried to prepare herself for what she was about to see. As she followed Camille along the corridor and down a set of well-worn stone steps, she could hear hushed voices in the distance, and tapping on keyboards. They rounded the corner and found themselves in a vast underground facility. The walls were covered in digital whiteboards with profile shots and various documents overlaying each other. Members of staff would bounce up to touch the screens and shift things about as they went about their work. There were three long rows of desks and each had piles of papers, equipment and garbage littered all over them. It seemed the team had probably been on high alert, eating whatever they could as they worked all hours. Presumably because of her arrival, Seraph realised guiltily. She recognised most of the workers as being members of the bridal shop staff she had met the day before. There were a few male faces too, however, that she couldn't recall meeting.

Camille walked over to a woman sat at a control panel, a wall covered by several screens featuring images produced by CCTV cameras. She asked, 'Are they dealt with?'

'Yes, Alpha Team took them to our safe house and are keeping them there until further notice.'

'Good. I don't want their employers to know we've got them. Get their chips removed, put the safe house on high alert, and begin implementing "Re-civilise". Those two could be handy once they've had all the rubbish pumped out of them.'

Camille turned to Seraph. 'Officium use drugs on their agents to make them more pliable. On the odd occasion we come across these creatures, we try to normalise them and give them a chance to start afresh. It's not always their fault that they ended up leading such lives.' Seraph nodded in understanding, secretly wowed by the facility that had been set up. She peered at the screens and saw the two agents tied up in an empty room, seemingly knocked out by sedatives or perhaps still reeling from the effects of Camille's handiwork.

Camille clapped her hands, and everyone in the room, perhaps around twenty people in total, stopped whatever they were doing and stared in her direction. 'Everyone, you all know Seraph, Eve's niece. Two agents were following her, so we all need to pull together to ensure they don't get a second chance at pulling her in. From Birmingham to Glasgow, get word out to everyone on the street, and I mean everyone. Our efforts need to be concentrated here, especially for tomorrow.' The team looked at Seraph, and Camille reiterated, 'Snap to it, get to work. Monitor the perimeter of this building.'

Camille went to speak to some members of her staff quietly, leaving Seraph to observe the scene. The intelligence team all had their highly-sophisticated Unicuses hooked up to enormous monitors in front of them, and their devices had scrambling sticks hanging out of them to prevent Officium tracking their communications. A lot of the staff also had tiny earpieces in to be able to talk to not only each other, but anybody they decided to call up with the touch of a button. As each person flicked between audio hack-ware, documents, messaging, GPS tracking and websites on their screens, Seraph felt dizzy. It would probably take her years to work out their practices.

'Seraph, we need to talk. Now you've seen in here, let's go up to Eve's flat.' She nodded and followed Camille as she led them back out, gesturing to the operatives that she was going upstairs if they needed her.

Seraph and Camille climbed the rickety spiral staircase up to the top floor of the bridal house. Eve's living quarters were exactly as Seraph had imagined. Humble but tasteful. Dark, solid wood beams punctuated the mostly white ceilings and walls. The rickety wooden doors had old-fashioned metal latches and the ceilings were so low Seraph almost had to stoop. The furnishings were antique, but very well-kept. The living room was a mixture of block pastels and flowery prints. At its centre sat a large, cream, high-backed Victorian sofa with brass feet, covered in large cushions. The furniture, most of it solid oak, was tasteful and elegant – pieces not easily found so readily – the collection of a true fanatic. In front of the sofa sat a chunky coffee table made from railway sleepers, with coasters from all over the world laid on top of it in linear patterns. Eve had visited many countries and always tried to bring a coaster back with her, even fashioning her own from materials she had found on her travels, it appeared. Seraph saw no television, but it was clear to see how Eve had entertained herself. There were rows and rows of books, and literally every space of wall available was used to hold a bookcase full of reading material against it. A huge oak writing desk resembling an accountant's workstation was also pushed up against one wall under the room's windowsill. Bits and pieces of paper littered it and poked out of multiple drawers both on top of the desk and underneath it.

The bedroom was decorated by white wallpaper with subtle patterns of pink, blue and silver flowers. An iron-framed bed was positioned at one end while at the other there were great big, huge wardrobes stretching across the entire length of the L-shaped room. An oval vanity mirror perched on a small white dressing table positioned under the window with a vase of pink carnations on the sill. The curtains were pink and a solid rocking chair sat in one corner. The spare room was similarly decorated, with a simple single bed and more flowers in the window. Seraph hadn't seen fresh-cut flowers for years.

In the kitchen, a great surprise awaited Seraph. This was one part of Eve's flat that was modern, with completely white units, white tiled walls and flooring. Everything about it was generic, in keeping with people's way of living. Not even Eve could keep a kitchen spic and span for decades without having to have it replaced, and this style is probably all she could find from Kitchens&Bathrooms4U. Eve hadn't managed to keep the new world out of her home entirely.

Seraph sat in Eve's sturdy studded-leather desk chair and eyed the living room as Camille handed her a glass of water she had just retrieved from the kitchen.

The Frenchwoman sat on the sofa, and waited for Seraph to start asking her all the questions she knew were probably buzzing around her journalistic brain. However, Seraph was stunned by everything she had just witnessed. For once in her life, she was totally shocked into silence. All of a sudden, she just started laughing in disbelief and shook her head from side to side.

Camille asked, 'What is it?'

'I just remembered the time she came to New York for fashion week. I should have known then. She looked so sheepish when I mentioned the dressmaker, but I could never have imagined she was that person. I mean, it never entered my mind. I always viewed her as a sort of simple spinster who had somehow managed to make a success of herself. How wrong was I?'

'I know, Seraph, I know.' Camille looked down at the floor, and clasped her hands together. Seraph sensed there were a few stones left unturned.

'I hardly know what questions to start with Camille, perhaps you ought to just tell me everything you know about my aunt. About how she could have ended up doing what she did?'

Camille stood up and looked out of the window. She avoided Seraph's gaze and revealed, 'Eve would have preferred you never to know about her secret life. And if she ever thought you needed to know, she would have wanted to be the one to tell you herself.'

'So, what does that mean?'

'She made provisions to bring the truth to your attention. I believe the will might reveal more.'

'I can't wait for that Camille. You'll just have to tell me yourself. I'm going out of my mind here. I loved her more than anyone else I've ever known!'

'I loved her too, Seraph. She was my best friend. But there were things she never even disclosed to me. There was a reason behind her role as the dressmaker, quite a devastating reason, and it will not be easy for you to hear.'

Seraph's mind drew a few conclusions, and she felt sick all of a sudden, unable to hold the bile down. She rushed into the kitchen and heaved into the ceramic sink, the acid burning the back of her throat as it spluttered out of her mouth. Camille followed her in, and held Seraph's hair back. Camille rubbed her back, and waited for her to finish, passing over a towel when she had done.

Seraph turned to look at Camille, resting against the counter as she dabbed her mouth. Her face was red, her eyes bloodshot and her mouth trembling. She struggled to speak as dread washed over her, and she spoke two words very quietly, 'My parents.'

Camille nodded reluctantly, but Seraph sensed there was more to it than that. She just didn't know if she was braced for anything else.

'I need a drink Camille, a very stiff one in fact.'

Camille led Seraph to the couch, and offered, 'I'll go downstairs to retrieve some sherry. Wait here.'

Seraph listened as Camille descended the stairs, and she realised her entire body was shaking. Whether it was because she had just thrown up, or the shock of everything, she wasn't sure. She grabbed a woollen blanket draped over the back of the couch and pulled it around herself. She wanted to start crying. She could cry forever if she allowed her emotions to get the better of her, and she tried unsuccessfully to convince herself that she was above this. Cloaking the blanket around herself, her thoughts turned to memories of Eve and her parents, and the surroundings of the room seemed to vanish as she lost herself in deep thought. Without realising it, Camille had arrived back in the flat and had brought her a tumbler from the kitchen with a large shot of sherry in it. Camille had to snap Seraph out of her thoughts, practically shouting, 'Seraph, here you are. Take this, but drink slowly.'

Seraph saw the comforting liquid swilling about in the glass, and swallowed it in one go. She held the glass back out toward Camille, gesturing for more.

Camille shot her a disapproving glance, but Seraph didn't look as though she would take no for an answer. Camille refilled the receptacle, and Seraph took a sip, before asking, 'How did you meet Eve?'

'It's a long story…'

Seraph fell back on the sofa, trying to get herself comfortable as she recovered.

'Do I look like I'm going anywhere Camille?'

'Okay, I will tell you, but you must listen and not ask questions.'

'I'm listening. Tell me everything, and leave nothing out.'

CHAPTER 9

Camille paced about the flat as she spoke, while Seraph lay on the sofa as if she were undergoing a session with her psychiatrist.

'You may have heard my codename whispered about just as much as Eve's was. I am the milliner.

'I was raised in an orphanage on the outskirts of Paris after my parents died in the Ravage. Like you, I had no brothers or sisters, and so I became a creature of solitude, preferring not to entangle myself emotionally. What happened in 2023 was terrifying, but for the children, even more so. Some lost their siblings, some their parents, most their grandparents. I had not a single person left in the world. It seemed as if we had all been born merely to suffer and to try and survive as best we could with what we were left with.'

Seraph saw Camille try to shake off some fraught remembrance, before she continued:

'At the orphanage, I realised my forte for sewing and it's something I went on to pursue. And so at age eighteen I left the suburbs behind after winning a scholarship to attend the Parisian School of Art and Design, graduating in 2034. After that, I spent years travelling the world, making garments to sell on the streets, randomly moving from one place to another. I begged, borrowed and sometimes even stole to keep food in my stomach and clothes on my back. I fell in with a street gang in Budapest and we moved from one place to another together, doing whatever we needed to in order to overcome the noose Officium had hung around the world. For at least five years, I had no fixed address whatsoever. It didn't bother me sleeping on the streets, or in alleyways, or on someone's cold floor. I'd never known comfort, and so, it was normal to me. I woke up every day knowing that the search for food came second to my need for excitement. I'd grown extremely tough and people back then knew me as

51

something of a scrapper. Looking back, I realise I was desperately seeking my place in the world. I always knew that there was only one person I could rely on and soon friendships broke down, loyalties became divided and I broke free. An attempt to spring a group of factory workers from their bonds went wrong and I decided it was time to put some distance between myself and Europe, taking myself off to the Orient.'

Camille glanced at Seraph with animation as she turned her mind to the next chapter of her life.

'In Japan, I found my second home. There, I appreciated the culture, the society and their way of living. It was even more cramped than in Paris but that didn't matter to me. Living in a pod was luxury compared to my previous habitations! I developed a friendship with a sensei, after he bought up some of my silk dresses for his daughters. He was a tiny, unassuming man, devoted to his wife and family. His clan were brave enough to live in some abandoned farmland just outside Tokyo and one day he invited me to his humble abode for dinner. I was struck not only by his generous hospitality, but also by his family's skills in Shotokan Karate. There were literally hundreds of trophies dotted around their shack, dating from as far back as the Seventies. At that time, he was the only person in the world to have reached his eleventh Dan, a grandmaster of unparalleled skill, agility, strength and speed – but something of a pariah. I asked one of his daughters to show me her skills, and she nearly broke my back as she grappled me to the ground with one fell swoop. I was so impressed, I begged him to teach me everything he knew. He refused at first, but I was persistent. For weeks, I laboriously cycled from the city to his home every day, turning up with more gifts for his daughters. Each time he turned me away, I refused to be dissuaded. Then one day, he relented, and my tutelage began in the boggy rice fields at the back of his home.

'The fertile green surroundings and the prolonged and unforgiving rain became the backdrop and the dojo of my lessons – and my enemy. Barefoot and dressed sparingly, I took a lot of blows at the will of his hand. He nearly knocked the life out of me as my face was continually pushed into the cold, life-draining, damp mud. While the family ate their meals together inside, I was left out in the cold in my makeshift bamboo shelter to survive on decaying vegetables and dried fish. I nearly gave up so many times. But that would have been the easy way, and that had never been an option for me. I knew that as long as I had breath and strength left in me, I would never break.

'I still remember so clearly the relentless circuit training in the unforgiving earth of those fields, and performing press-ups while he stood on my back taunting me with abuse, saying I was just another pathetic woman who would break against his will. Each taunt made me more determined, more resistant to failure, and I began to feel invincible. I rose above the idea of being weakened by my human form. After mastering the basics, I had grown so physically and mentally strong that when it came to combat, the process wasn't a conscious experience for me. My very first attempt to smash through a wooden plank was successful, easy even. Until you actually participate in the disciplines of martial arts with a humble approach, an open mind and a full heart, you can never understand the mentality it enables you to develop. Once the mind has been broken, and rebuilt, you can become whatever you want to be. If you will something to be so, it must be. My body became a highly-tuned force of rigidity, and I was no longer a creature of reaction, more one of calm and serenity, allowing the world to wash over my being. The key is not to react, merely to retain strength. Unless it was really necessary to perform, only then would I execute myself, and if so, only absolute exhibition of one's skills would suffice. Sensei Toshiro entered me into some national competitions, and I won every single one. He and I formed a bond that went beyond the one he shared with his family even. We were equal souls existing on a level plane, and even a whisper of breath from one of us revealed to the other what we were thinking or feeling; we were so in tune with one another.

'However, knocking my opponents out soon became too easy, and I tired of my life in Japan. I began to yearn for the streets of Paris back home, and I returned there in 2041 after several years of living from hand to mouth, from country to country.

'I maintain my discipline and still spar and meditate every day even now. It was something that I knew would never leave me. Many members of RAO have been taught by me, and I've now reached my eighth Dan, something I never asked for nor brag about, because it is simply a testament to all the wonders that martial arts have enabled me to enjoy – friendship, discipline and freedom from fear.

'After returning home from Japan, I got by selling millinery on the streets of Montmartre, until one day an elegant Englishwoman turned up and bought everything on my table. She noticed my shabby clothes and unwashed appearance, declaring, "How can someone of your talent be so undervalued?"

'At first I was reluctant to latch on to her friendliness, but she wouldn't take no for an answer when she insisted on buying me dinner that night. She offered me a job at the bridal house then and there, and I asked, "What makes you think I want to work for you?" She gave me that stern look of hers, and simply said, "Because I know a woman of your calibre will be indispensable and instrumental to my cause." I was instantly intrigued, and she began to explain how she'd heard from Sensei Toshiro that I'd left Japan and come back to Europe. He was part of the resistance and had not stopped exclaiming to her about how good a combatant I had become. Then she had some revelations that I wasn't expecting. She informed me that my mother and father had been in the French Secret Service, a fact I knew nothing about until she disclosed it to me. She placed a file on the restaurant table, and I looked it over with interest and horror. However, I began to get some sense of my identity and I realised my similar pursuit of thrills and adventure was something I'd undoubtedly got from them. They were not killed by the Ravage, but by Officium, and I knew as clearly as I see you now, that my lot was to join Eve's efforts. I moved to York and settled for a quiet but purposeful life, helping her make this place more successful than either of us could have ever imagined. Many of our members met and married through the work they carried out for Eve, and the women became clients at the shop. However, don't let that overshadow her success Seraph. She still had dozens and dozens of customers who came from the farthest corners of the globe to have their wedding dresses made by her. I suppose it was the romance of this building that drew them here, but also the relatively small fee she charged for them to have a gown made from scratch, and to their exact specifications. Her decision to remain open amidst a world of declining craftsmanship somehow paid dividends, and for once, refusing to follow a trend proved unbelievably canny. There were still a lot of people who had managed to find happy lives for themselves, but they were very few and far between after the Ravage.'

Camille took a deep breath and continued, 'Now she's gone, I have no idea how I will carry on without her. She was the bedrock of this place, and it simply won't be the same without her. I loved her dearly, and I never expected to feel so sad about her loss. I never in my wildest dreams ever thought anyone could be as good a friend to me as she was. I never thought such kindness existed in the world until I met her. She was the ultimate person, ultimate woman, ultimate warrior even.

'She never mentioned him by name, but I knew she'd known great love during her lifetime. It was written all over her face sometimes. A woman who has been loved truly has a certain look about her, one of heightened knowledge and undeniable mystery. She lost that great love, and it is that which made her what she was. But I cannot tell you anymore than that.'

When Camille had finished her explanation, she fell on the coffee table in front of Seraph. Her head bowed, she began to cry, sniffing and dripping with tears. Seraph got up off the sofa and knelt down, taking Camille in her arms. They played mother and daughter to one another, and Seraph's mind turned to one thing – when had this love affair taken place, what happened to him and also to her own parents? She didn't want to launch a barrage of questions at Camille, who was obviously grieving and was just as forlorn as she over Eve's passing. She decided she would find out for herself what had happened, even if it killed her, and she would finally lay all this to rest. She didn't care what it took, she would do it. It was time.

CHAPTER 10

Later that day, Seraph and Camille left the bridal shop and headed for a late lunch in the centre of York. The surveillance team seemed to have managed to lock down York, and anyway, they each felt they could take on anything together. As they wandered the streets, Camille linked her arm through Seraph's. The pair had suddenly become great friends, and they shared a bond that would perhaps never be broken.

Camille noted, 'Eve lived here long before this place was ruined. She used to tell me how devastating it was to see it degenerate so much.'

'I know. My grandmother had tons of photographs of how it was before. I kept most of them, and was struck by the unique culture and history of the place. It always seemed so exotic to a New Yorker like me.'

'And yet, your homeland seems exotic to me!'

'But, you've travelled all over the world…?'

The pair chuckled.

'Yes, but America was one place I never really got to. It's still on my list.'

'Well, you must visit me as soon as you can, once I get back that is. Only, New York is not what it once was either.'

Camille said, 'I can imagine, but I'm sure we'd still have fun.'

They were going to one of the few places left not to have automated service, the world-renowned tearooms known as Bettys. They arrived to see a queue extending right round the corner and further back down Stonegate, and Seraph felt deflated, sure they wouldn't be able to get in very easily. However, as soon as the maitre d' saw Camille, a broad smile crossed her face, and the impeccably uniformed woman beckoned the pair over.

'Hi Camille, table for two?'

'Oui,' she said, 'For me and Eve's great-niece here.'

'Oh my god, you're her niece?! Such a pleasure to meet you.' The female attendant gestured for the women to head inside, after shaking Seraph's hand rigorously.

A waiter showed them to some seating with a reserved sign on it. The small, square table was covered in crisp white linen, stainless steel cutlery and a small bunch of fresh tulips, and was situated in a quiet corner at the back of the bustling restaurant. The huge glass windows allowed them a panoramic view of the world outside, and the pale-yellow wallpaper along with brass fittings made the place seem light and airy.

The two women sat down and Camille explained, 'Eve had this table constantly reserved for her. She used to bring clients here to discuss what they wanted for their big day. She was a shrewd judge of character, and never took on a bride who she didn't think was worthy. However, we only turned away two women in all the years I knew her, so you can imagine we were pretty inundated with requests.'

'I don't know how she managed it all Camille. She was such a paradox, wasn't she?'

'Yes, and yet at heart, she was a simple woman with simple tastes. She relished patterns. I'm sure if she'd undergone psychometric tests, they would have confirmed that she was a genius beyond compare. I'd studied in Paris, and yet sometimes even I didn't know how she could simply look at a pattern for a few seconds, and then know it off by heart. She had a photographic memory, and could see all the pieces of a dress slotting together as if they were part of a puzzle shifting into place inside her mind.'

'So, how did she end up in dressmaking? She never told me exactly. In fact, there were so many things about her I never questioned, but perhaps should have done.'

'Oh, I think it was something she was destined to do, but I've no doubt she will explain more about that to you in her own way, when the time is right.'

'That sounds ominous…'

The pair smiled at one another, and their waiter came back to get their drinks orders. His uniform was a tailored white shirt, navy bow tie and black slacks with a prominent crease running down the middle.

Seraph asked, 'What coffee do you recommend?'

The waiter, an attractive middle-aged man with dark brown hair, pale complexion and slim physique seemed to blush across the cheeks at Seraph's interest.

'Urm, well, it depends on what you usually go for?' he said, looking down at his notepad to avoid her gaze.

'I'm definitely a very strong coffee type. New York journalist, you see.' Camille smiled at Seraph, who felt she had probably ventured too far with the enthusiastic waiter.

The man's face tinged with more blushes, and he dared to say, 'Yes, you're not our usual kind of customer. If you're after something very strong, then I'd suggest the Brazilian rainforest blend. Strongest stuff on Earth.'

'Thanks, I'll have steamed milk with that.'

'Very well, and what can I get you Ms Honoré?'

Camille looked at him with a wry smile, and said, 'A pot of Earl Grey, Julian, and less of the flirting with my friend here.'

The waiter rushed off, desperately embarrassed, and Seraph shot Camille an unimpressed look.

'What? What did I say?'

'Poor guy, he was only being friendly. You forget, I don't get this kind of service very often where I come from. I never have time to queue to get into any of the respectable places. The last time I tried to get into Pastis in New York, I was told by some surly bitch in no uncertain terms that I'd be waiting a decade for a table.'

'Well... he was flirting outrageously! I don't blame him though.' Camille winked at Seraph slightly.

'I don't know what you mean Camille.' Seraph looked indifferent.

'Oh come on, as if you haven't had dozens of men after you? What with that hair, those eyes, that figure?' Camille's eyes danced as she purposefully tried to rile Seraph up.

Seraph leaned forward to whisper in Camille's direction, 'Fuck off, before I start flirting with you.'

'Ha ha. Seriously though, not even a little romance?'

Seraph breathed deeply and sank bank in her seat. 'Most of the time, the prospect doesn't even cross my mind. The only person I could have made it with is now dead. And that was probably my fault.'

'Aah you must mean Ulrich? Eve told me about him...'

'Yeah, I'd rather not talk about him,' Seraph said, looking out of the window. 'It was probably never meant to be between us, but I still cared for him. It's still not really sunk in that he's gone.'

Camille bravely ventured, 'So, maybe you resist getting close to someone to protect yourself?'

'For me, it's not even that Camille. I'm married to my work. I can't imagine ever loving anything more. No man could compete. I have this terrible gnawing in my brain and until I nail those assholes, I'll never be able to concentrate on anything else.'

'Umm, I bet if someone tall, dark and mysterious did come along, you'd be slightly tempted.'

'I don't know Camille, a lot of the men I've come across in my world aren't worth my time. They're all obsessed with their egos and someone like me only serves to either pump it up, or flatten it.'

The women guffawed at one another, but quickly quietened down as Julian returned with their drinks. He nervously placed them on the table, clanking the crockery. Seraph tried to avoid eye contact, while Camille goaded her with knowing smiles.

'Thanks Julian. We'll have two cream teas too, but one without the tea for my exotic friend here.'

'Right you are, Ms Honoré.'

Seraph lifted her eyes slightly to glance at the waiter, and she realised the poor man was totally smitten. Feeling terrible, she turned back to Camille once he had gone, 'I don't know why you think you can get away without telling me why you're still single too!'

They each sipped from their cups, before Camille made a response with a confident air. 'I do okay for myself Seraph, but I'm simply not built for partnership. My life is the cause. And besides, you're more my type than the likes of our waiter there.' Camille nonchalantly held a hand to her chin, pursing her lips, as Seraph absorbed the revelation.

She was slightly surprised. 'Oh, okay, but you do know I'm not...'

'Zut alors! Oh my stars.' Camille chuckled to herself, trying not to fall off her chair.

'What?'

'Oh, my dear, you're so straight, it's painful.'

Seraph spoke sarcastically, 'Oh god, sor-ry!'

The women couldn't help but continue to giggle. For each of them, it was a relief and a pleasure to finally have someone on their own level to talk to for a change. As their food was brought over on tiered trays, Seraph gasped at the quality. They each had a stack of small triangular sandwiches, as well as a trio of miniature cakes, one of which was a mini scone. Seraph headed for this treat first, biting through it voraciously. Through mouthfuls of food, she exclaimed at Camille, 'Oh my god, this is divine. I've not eaten like this before... ever!' Every chew she made produced a satisfying sensation on her palate. She detected thick gooey cream, ripe sultanas, crusty scone and fruity jam. The food in most establishments was tasteless, mass-produced and flash-cooked. She devoured the whole lot, and Camille seemed totally amused by the whole scene.

Seraph said, 'What's next?'

'Oh god, not you as well? Eve was a bottomless pit too!'

'I like my food, Camille, what can I say?'

CHAPTER 11

The pair spent a couple of hours in the tearooms, with Seraph scoffing literally everything in sight. She had a few more cups of coffee, along with a huge ice-cream sundae and a giant baguette sandwich with thick Yorkshire ham. As she gobbled the lot down, Camille sat back in disbelief. Her own appetite was small, and as each year passed, it got smaller.

It was early evening, and as they stood outside Bettys and breathed in the oddly-comforting warm scent of the soup factory in the distance, Camille asked, 'Did you leave anything in your hotel room?'

'No, I never leave a trail. Why?'

'Why don't you just stay in Eve's flat tonight? It's homelier and safer.'

Seraph had a nervous disposition toward ghosts, but she realised Camille probably wouldn't take no for an answer. 'That would be lovely.'

As they passed the tall windows of the tearooms, Seraph waved at Julian as they wandered off, and he smiled back gingerly with his cheeks turning red. Seraph and Camille laughed at each other, but as they wandered through the streets towards the shop, the real world hit them smack in the face. The recycling centre workers had just starting pouring out into the streets, and Seraph and Camille held on to each other for safety as they were carried along by the crowds of people. Covered in dirt, and smelling unsavoury, the poor inhabitants looked down at the ground in a bid to hide their sad demeanours. Seraph and Camille looked at each other in mutual despair, and carried on walking. When they finally got back to the Shambles, Camille got out her keys and let them in rapidly, slamming the door behind them before setting the security barriers up again.

'I'd better get back to my team, otherwise they may forget who's in charge. Go up to the flat and make yourself at home. If I don't see you later tonight, I'll see you in the morning for the funeral.'

The mention of the f-word also brought reality back to the two women.

A look of dread passed between them, and they knew it wasn't going to be an easy day.

'Okay, I'll see you later then.'

'Oh by the way Seraph, she didn't want anyone wearing black.' Camille seemed to be hinting at Seraph's perennial choice of clothing.

'Erm, actually, I don't have anything that isn't,' Seraph admitted.

'If you look in Eve's closets, I'm sure you'll find something colourful.'

'I will do, thanks Camille. I had a great time this afternoon.'

Camille winked slightly, 'Me too.'

Seraph went up to the flat and into Eve's bedroom, throwing open the sliding oak wardrobes that stretched across the entire length of the room. She eyed the huge closets, saying out loud to herself, 'God, what a collection.' There was not one hint of black clothing in sight, and indeed, everything seemed to be vibrant, multi-coloured and patterned. There were various sizes of dresses, hats, shawls, scarves, wraps, skirts, jumpers, shoes, boots, cardigans, evening gowns, slippers, pyjamas; everything you could possibly imagine. Some still had the labels on, and Seraph was impressed to see the names of several world-famous designers, except Melina James of course. Seraph was overwhelmed and didn't know where to start, deciding she would find something in the morning.

Instead, she began to explore the rest of Eve's flat. She assessed the thousands of thank-you cards in the desk, and found there was nothing out of the ordinary in there. The two bedrooms were impeccably tidy and didn't reveal anything more either. However, she had a thought as she noticed a loft cover in the hall. She pulled it and a set of stairs tumbled down. Climbing the steps, Seraph felt sure she was on the right track. Turning on the light, however, she was disappointed to discover the loft contained only a few old boxes. *Still, there might be something interesting in these.* She discovered deeds to the shop, bank statements from decades ago, old employee records and receipts. It all seemed pretty mundane and tedious. However, there was a box pushed right to the back of the loft, draped in a blanket that had been perishing for years. She discovered old photos in this one. There were pictures of a young Eve. She was once a very attractive woman, with red hair that was brighter than Seraph's flowing down her back. Her face without make-up revealed a multitude of freckles and her features were not that dissimilar to Seraph's own. She must have been young in the photos, perhaps in her early thirties, and what sprang to mind was who took them. Photo after photo showed Eve happy and smiling, in different poses, but looking much the same in each of them. At the bottom of the pile was one of her with a man. It looked like he had taken the photo at arm's length, because their faces filled the frame. He looked about the same age as Eve and had dark hair, strangely handsome features and a gentle look about him. The pair of them looked very much in love. Seraph would have to keep some for posterity, she decided. Her long-hidden romantic side was intrigued.

Sifting through box after box, Seraph found no other evidence of Eve's love interest. There were just boxes full of more business papers. Frustrated, Seraph moved to the steps to descend back down. As her booted foot fell heavily on a floorboard at the bottom, she heard a creak and a crunch, before the floor seemed to cave underneath her and her foot fell through the wood. A slat had broken in two, and Seraph had been forced to cling on to the steps to prevent herself falling on her back. After she wiggled her foot free, she took a step back and peered down at the floor. Dropping on one knee, she picked the splintered shards of floor out of the hole they had fallen in, and she threw them to one side after she spotted a wad of papers hidden beneath. She retrieved the packet, wrapped in an A4 cardboard sleeve bound by an elastic band, and realised it probably contained documents that she wasn't meant to find. She held the discovery in one hand, testing its weight on her palm, and she knew there was something in there that would no doubt reveal some of Eve's secrets. Seraph wondered whether she could handle anything more, and contemplated calling Camille up to look over it with her. However, her curiosity was piqued.

She quickly stood up and moved back to the sitting room, slamming the pile on the solid coffee table as she sat on the Victorian sofa. She ripped off the elastic band and pulled open the file.

The first thing she came to was a marriage certificate. As soon as Seraph saw the words *Eve Marie Maddon* in the first column of the document, shock flooded her body. As far as Seraph had known, Eve had been eternally single and happy about that status. *Camille was right, there was a man.* She eagerly examined the rest of the information and discovered Eve had married a Thomas David Bradbury at York Register Office on Saturday 10th August, 2013. Eve was thirty at the time, and he was almost thirty-three. *Shit. Oh god, what happened to him?*

She turned over the document and looked at what was underneath it. There was a birth certificate, but it was only Eve's, revealing she was born in York on 20th January, 1983. Her parents were Valerie and Frank, twenty-three and thirty-five at the time. *Quite a large age gap,* Seraph thought, but then she remembered that Frank had been married before he met Valerie, and that previous marriage had produced Harry, Seraph's grandfather and Eve's half-brother.

The next item she arrived at was a photograph. It was Eve and Tom on their wedding day, stood outside an ordinary brick building that Seraph presumed was the register office. They were both tall and slim, and he held her hand against his chest while they laughed in the direction of the camera. He wore a grey suit with a red tie and a matching rose buttonhole. He had dark-brown, crew-cut hair, dark eyes and an extremely proud grin. Meanwhile Eve cut a most magical figure. Her bright red, almost orange hair was pulled up into a beehive-style, with delicate strands framing her face. Her huge smile revealed large white teeth. She had blood-red lipstick on, while her other make-up was understated. Her dress was a short, Sixties-style pinafore in white, worn with matching laced-up platform shoes. She held a small bouquet of pink carnations wrapped with white ribbon.

Seraph's heart beat wildly in her chest and it felt as though Eve herself had just reached down from heaven to touch her heart. She couldn't hold the emotion in, because the photograph spoke volumes. It showed that Eve had truly loved somebody, and that for them to have been separated, something terrible must have happened. She couldn't take it anymore. *How could Eve have kept so much from me?* She stared at the photograph and her heart broke in two looking at the scene of happiness before her. She madly searched the other documents for more photos, but there were none. This was the only one it seemed. She wanted to scream. Tears started to well in her eyes, when something drew her attention. Amongst the items she had just spread across the table was a small, fragile-looking notebook with the words, *Diary of Eve Maddon, 2013, The Year My Life Began,* written on the front. She picked up the diary and held it in both her hands, trying to steady herself as she realised this would prove to be a sacred window into Eve's secretive life. She gathered herself, and pulled the woollen blanket around her shoulders, as she began to read.

CHAPTER 12

20th January, 2013

I used to stand on the riverbank sometimes to escape the scenes back home. With the green grass beneath my feet and the elements battering my body about, I'd feel as though my pain was eradicated to a certain extent. I would wonder what I'd done to deserve such a fate as mine, and I would close my eyes and try to imagine myself somewhere else. I would look across the water at the lights on the other side, and I would imagine happy families sat there enjoying their evenings in front of the TV, without the arguments, tears and violence that I constantly endure.

Today I turned thirty and I suddenly realised, my life up until this point has been totally wasted. I've foregone friends, a career, happiness – to look after my embittered alcoholic mother, a manic depressive who made me believe from a very early age that I was worthless, a total nothing, a dot on this Earth that was insignificant and unworthy of being alive. Reaching this milestone in my life, I realised something as I woke up this morning. I realised I had a choice. I could continue to share in her misery, or I could leave. I knew I could never really solve all her issues. Cleaning up her mess would not help her. Holding her as she cried would not help her. Feeding her and clothing her and washing her would not help her. She needed to help herself. There had been so many occasions when she would do something nice for me, like have dinner ready on the table for me when I'd arrive home from work, and for an instant I'd believe that she was better than she was. I'd believe she was capable of such good, and I'd doubt myself. I'd wonder whether I was the one in the wrong. I'd doubt that I was a good person, and that I was mistaken in thinking badly of her. I'd doubt that I was in my right mind. But every time I had those doubts, she would soon revert back to her normal self, asking for money to go out down the local pub and slapping me when I refused, or throwing vile verbal abuse at me, such as, 'I wish I'd got rid of you when I'd had the chance. You're just like that father of yours, much use he proved to be.' Every time she did something nice, she'd soon do a dozen hurtful things in return when she knew she wouldn't get what she wanted out of me. The worst thing was that I'd always get my hopes up, and she'd shatter them just as quickly. She'd scared off so many boyfriends, made the inhabitants of our town pity me and had disgraced herself in the street on a number of occasions.

My birthday present to myself was to therefore pack a case, walk out the front door and keep walking. I didn't look back, and I don't think I ever will. So, I've left the small Yorkshire town of Selby behind to move to the capital of our county, York.

30th January, 2013

The fresh, free air has never smelt or tasted better. More has happened in just ten days than my previous thirty years on this planet. I stayed in a crappy B&B for the first few nights, before securing myself a flat. It's so nice to be able to walk to work now, and not to have to think about rushing to the train station in the evening to get back home and discover what new messes she had created for me to clean up.

My job at Anne Marie's bridal shop is in danger, however. It is due to shut down because of falling sales. It's the same everywhere. Nobody wants to buy anything because they're all either skint, or can get it cheaper online. Frankly, I've always thought Anne Marie overcharges, and she never listens to a thing I suggest. Her window displays never showcase enough designs, and merely put the customer off with the prices on display more proudly than the gowns. I no longer care so much about my job anyway, after some news I received earlier today. My father is dead.

My mother called to say that she wanted me to come home. She begged, pleaded even, for me to return. But I would not, I said. She cried, sobbed and screamed at me. However, I'd decided I could no longer help her, and I stuck to my guns. She ranted on and on, and proudly revealed that my Dad had died of cancer years ago, but she decided not to tell me because he'd left me a lot of money, and she didn't want me to have any of it. She said it was probably too late now, and that she was glad he was dead, and that she was happy I would get nothing. I hung up on her instantly, and went to a bridge overlooking the River Ouse, throwing my mobile phone in so that she could no longer get in touch with me.

I got on the computer at work and searched for Harry Maddon, my half-brother. I don't know why I hadn't tried to get in touch with him before, but I knew I really needed to now. I found his name on a Google search, knowing he had a thriving plumbing business somewhere in Doncaster, so I'd heard anyway. I found a number and dialled. I asked,

'Hello, can I speak to Harry Maddon?'

He replied in a deep voice, 'Yes, speaking.'

I said, 'Harry, it's Eve, your sister.'

He paused for several seconds, and replied in a softer, excited tone, 'Eve, bloody hell, I've tried for so many years to find you.'

'I know, but it seems my mother has spent a lot of time and energy trying to prevent that.'

'Jesus, what kind of person…?'

'I know Harry. How are you anyway?'

'I'm great, how are you?'

'I only just found out Dad's dead. She didn't tell me that either. But listen, she said he had left me some money…?'

'Yes, he did. They are holding it still in the hope that you might get in touch, but your mother always maintained you'd gone to live abroad. In about two months' time, they were going to release it to me unless you claimed it.'

'Shit, Harry, oh my god.'

'Listen, Eve, why don't we meet? Where are you living now?'

'York. Do you want to visit?'

'Yes. How about I bring Susan and my son Hamish with me? He's fifteen now and has Dad's looks.'

I'd started crying down the phone as I realised I did have a family. We arranged to meet at the weekend, and he's put me in touch with the solicitors that our father dealt with. I rang them and they revealed he left me around £250,000. Harry and I were given the same, and he used his share to start up his own business. It seems Dad started property developing after he left Mum, and he had done very well for himself. He never remarried, and once he had been diagnosed with cancer, he had made a will for his estate to be shared equally between the two of us. I can't wait to meet my brother again, having not seen him for some twenty-odd years. I arrived home this evening and cried with the realisation that Mum prevented me seeing Dad over the years, and now it was too late. He was gone. Despite the things he had done, he was still my dad. I daren't even contemplate the thought processes she must have had to do that to her own daughter.

3rd February, 2013

My brother is an incredibly handsome man. He has rugged good looks, combined with a stature that would turn a lot of women's heads. His blue eyes remind me of Dad's, but it is his son who is the spit of our father, with his light-brown hair, freckles, green eyes and gangly frame. He is going to be at least seven feet tall I'd say. I'm so happy I can't stop crying all the time. We ate at Oscar's and spent hours catching up, while Hamish looked bored in the background, bless him.

When I'd seen my brother standing outside the restaurant, my eyes instantly filled with tears, and they were falling even before I got to him. He moved toward me with open arms, and grabbed me in a huge bear hug, holding me whilst I cried. Through bleary eyes, I saw Susan crying behind him, and after I removed myself from his arms, I went to hug her too. We all tried to tidy ourselves up a bit before heading inside, but people could tell some longed-for family reunion had just taken place.

I tried to avoid questions about Mum, but I knew they were unavoidable. However, Harry and Susan were incredibly understanding, knowing I didn't need their pity or sympathy.

14th February, 2013
On this day, of all days, I bought up a dilapidated old building on a corner of the Shambles, and I decided I will turn it into a bridal shop. I handed in my notice at Anne Marie's, swooping in and out of the place with a spring in my step. I could envisage the *Closing Down* signs she would soon be putting up. I'm finally going to put those years at design school to good use. I took the assistant's job at Anne Marie's when I was at a low ebb, and for some reason, I'd never thought I could get anything better. However, after years and years of watching her doing everything wrong, I decided I was going to do it right.

9th March, 2013
Something wondrous happened yesterday. No sooner had my name gone above the door, when a knock came around midmorning. There was a tall, slim man with dark hair and a familiar face. He was dressed in a long, tweed double-breasted coat, white shirt, light blue jeans and grey leather lace-ups. I didn't recognise him at first, he was so debonair. I was sat on the carpet-less stone floor with my body turned away from him as I continued to paint a wall while peering behind me through my peripheral vision. He stood in the empty room, which would become my shop floor, surveying the crumbling surroundings. As soon as he said, 'Eve Maddon, here you are,' I knew the voice immediately. I dropped the brush in its pot with a thud, and turned my body around on the floor to eye him carefully. It was Tom Bradbury.

'Tom… oh my god!'

I stood up quickly and practically ran over to him. I was just about to hug him when I realised my overalls would probably cover his smart clobber in paint. So, instead, I lent a hand on his shoulder and kissed his cheek. He placed a hand behind my back to give me a slight hug, and we both seemed to colour-up. We eyed each other carefully, and I realised he was still lovely, even if a little more worn around the edges.

'I found out from someone in Selby that you'd bought a place here.'

I smiled a friendly grin, and he stood with his hands behind his back, as if he were a country gent enquiring of the lady of the manor.

'News travels fast. I'm going to turn it into a bridal shop.' As I studied him, I sensed he was preoccupied by some thought or other, but I continued the small talk. 'It's so good to see you. What are you up to these days?'

He shifted about on the spot. 'Didn't you see the news before Christmas?'

I frowned, shaking my head, 'I never watch television. I certainly don't believe anything I hear on the radio either. I've had enough drama to last me a lifetime.' The look on my face betrayed my anguish, and I could see he had spotted it.

'She's still no better?'

'Not as far as I know. And to be honest, I don't want to know anymore.' I was desperate to avoid his gaze by that point. I could see my pain reflected on his face.

'I'm staying with Mum and Dad while I take some time out from my career. So, I was hoping we could catch up?'

'Yeah, that'd be great.' However, he must have sensed my struggle to seem enthusiastic, after being reminded of my past troubles.

He ventured, 'Mum said Valerie was ranting in the pub about your dad…'

'Tom, don't…'

He grabbed my hand, and said very quietly, 'I'm so sorry.'

I tried to hide my face, and said, 'I was never one to dwell. I just want to get on with my life. One good thing came out of it, anyway. I got some money from him to buy up this place.'

I was struggling to hide my emotions from him, avoiding his eyes, but almost shaking with the effort it took not to cry. He moved toward me and took me in his arms before I had chance to register that my childhood sweetheart had somehow just been flung back into my life. He held me purposefully, despite my dirty gear, and I nestled into his neck. A contented feeling started to overwhelm me as I smelt his fresh aftershave and tea tree shampoo. I whispered, 'Why were you on the news?'

'I'll tell you later. My only concern at present is making sure you're alright.'

As we continued to hold one another, I felt myself begin to relax in his proximity, and our bodies seemed to slot together perfectly. He began to stroke my hair and I felt a shiver down my spine. 'Tom…'

'Eve...'

He pulled away to study my face without flinching and the wistful look in his eyes made my heart lurch. He stroked my cheek with the back of a hand and when he brushed his mouth against mine, a pulse of energy rocketed through my system. My heart was pounding in my chest and my arms went underneath his coat. His grip around my back tightened and we held each other very close, almost squeezing the life out of one another. 'Oh god Tom, I missed you.'

'I missed you too. I should never have let you go.'

My mouth caressed his neck and I heard him take a sharp intake of breath. We held each other fiercely and I ran a hand over the short hair of his head. I moved back round to his face and went towards him to playfully nip his bottom lip. Our noses rubbed together and we breathed each other in. Suddenly it felt like the most natural thing in the world for us to be together again. He kissed my cheeks, eyelids and neck, and our heavy breathing echoed around the walls of the shop when we started kissing passionately. As his tongue massaged mine, I tasted coffee and toast and his thin lips got lost between my more ample mouth. My insides were on fire, and my pelvic floor quaked. We pulled away to smile broadly at one another before continuing to kiss. His hands were in my messy, pinned-up hair and he was breathless as he whispered between kisses, 'You mean so much to me.'

There was only one thing we both wanted to do. Luckily the front windows were still covered in old sheets of taped-on newspaper, otherwise people passing by might have thought they had stumbled on a peepshow. I ripped off his woollen outerwear and as it fell to the ground, he said, 'Rosie is not going to be happy.'

I looked at him suspiciously, and he explained with a smile, 'My dry cleaner.'

I prodded him hard in the stomach and he grabbed me to continue kissing me ardently. We wrapped our arms around each other so tightly, so happy to be back together again. When I'd decided in my mind what was going to happen next, I went over to the front door and locked it. I pulled Tom in the bare, windowless backroom with me, and he pushed my body up against a whitewashed wall. He pulled off my splattered vest, and I unbuttoned his shirt. He inexpertly tried to undo the fastenings of my rolled-down painter's trousers. I took the matter in hand and pulled them off, pulling his off too after he kicked his shoes away. He undid my bra, I pulled down his Y-fronts and he yanked my knickers off. We fell, and he made love to me on the concrete. The cold floor didn't manage to quell our heat, however. My heart and soul burned for him, but it all happened so quickly, I just didn't know whether it was real or not. Suddenly a longed-for fantasy had become reality. I was in a lustful trance, overtaken by him. I let myself go, losing myself beneath him. He didn't hold back and I relished him using my body voraciously. It was pretty amazing. He was extremely attentive, a much more confident lover than before, and I came god knows how many times. It was so erotic, perhaps the most erotic moment of my life, and the scene only made us feel more adventurous. Scuffed knees and grazed shoulder blades didn't matter a jot. He made love to me better than I'd ever known before. I couldn't get enough of him, and I bit, scratched and kissed his flesh, whatever I could grab hold of. Our chemistry was fraught, desperate and heightened by our history. He constantly smiled at me, until he groaned as he neared ejaculation. I pulled him toward me very tightly, and we laughed loudly when it was all over. He fell on top of my body, and I held him there. He said, 'I never forgot you. I knew I never would.'

I smiled and said, 'Do me again you randy old Yorkshire bugger.' He laughed and bit my nose. We streaked back through the shop and ran upstairs to my flat, where we continued in bed together for the rest of the day and all through the night. In my bed, he kissed me so tenderly, so longingly, that I fell in love with him all over again. We talked, and ate, and screwed, and howled with laughter, using my bed as the pedestal of our reunion. Life experience made us appreciate it all the more this time round. And for some strange reason, it felt like we had never been apart. No time seemed to have passed between the last time we were together and now, and all those sensations I associated with being with him were not forgotten after all. I realised one thing as I watched him leave my flat this morning with paint marks on his crumpled clothes and a look of pure happiness across his face. Tom was the man I wanted to marry and be the father of my children. We had loved each other as teenagers, but now as adults, it was much more passionate, much more meaningful. He was everything I'd ever wanted… and more. He was my soul mate.

When he was nineteen and I was seventeen, he spotted me in a shabby pub with some friends (one Mum didn't frequent) and he came over to start talking to me. He said he was drawn by my outrageous dress sense. For me, it was his dark eyes and broad smile. He was on a gap year, working to save up money before studying zoology at Cambridge. I was so intimidated by his intelligence, but he was so funny. He would reel off joke after joke, and before I knew it, I'd abandoned my friends and we'd found a quiet corner to hide ourselves in as he tentatively kissed me. We'd do that week after week, turning up with our friends at the Red Lion before breaking off to kiss and cuddle in a hidden nook of the pub. One night, he'd whispered, 'Eve, I love you.' I'd seen the look in his eye and I knew he was being completely truthful. I'd snuck him into my bedroom while Mum was passed out on the sofa, and I became a fully-fledged woman. I didn't expect to, but the naïve young girl I was back then fell completely in love with him, and we'd have sex in secret whenever we could. We were crazy for each other.

However, six months later he was due to start at university, and things got very tense between us. I was beside myself, knowing he'd be gone for long periods of time. We'd argued and fought, and his dad had found out about us. He warned Tom off me, and he went to Cambridge. I'd only ever seen him in passing since, in the distance across a street or something, and I would always try to avoid him. I was desperately unhappy that he had chosen something else over me, and I couldn't get over it. I cried myself to sleep for months after that, and the worst thing was I could never speak to Mum about it. She would not have listened, and she would not have cared.

To have him back now is so surreal. We are very different people, and yet, there must be some fundamental part of ourselves that bonded so tightly all those years ago, it never really left either of us. He's taking me out for dinner tonight, and I cannot wait. I just hope we can make it through the meal without having to rip each other's clothes off. I'll write more soon.

CHAPTER 13

It was dark outside the bridal shop and Seraph had been so shocked by Eve's revelations, she called Camille up to the flat to join her.

Camille rushed up the stairs like a bat out of hell, and saw Seraph in a crumpled mess on the sofa. 'Oh my god, I thought something terrible had happened to you when you said come quickly! Where's the fire?'

Seraph could barely breathe from the grief, and she struggled to get out her words. 'Look at this stuff, Camille.'

Camille sat next to her and saw the wedding photo first. 'Mon dieu, mon dieu! Look at her. Wasn't she beautiful?'

'I know,' Seraph spluttered out.

The elder of the two examined Seraph with a stern but gentle look and said, 'My dear, I thought you were tougher than this.'

'I thought so too, but look how beautiful she was. Look how happy they were. I just don't understand why she didn't tell me about him!'

Camille took Seraph's hand as she looked over some of the other things in the folder. Seraph pointed out the bit in the diary where Eve and Tom had made love on the floor of the shop. 'Ooh la la, she was a lively one. It doesn't surprise me though my darling, she would always make jokes loaded with innuendo. She had such a filthy sense of humour. She was a real woman, your aunt!'

Seraph sniffed into a bit of tissue and spluttered out, 'I know.'

'Come here,' Camille said, pulling a distraught Seraph into her arms as she rested back against the sofa.

'What I can't get over Camille, is that she wasn't the person I thought she was. I always used to view her as this untouchable being – the one person out there in the world untarnished by desire, or greed, or want. And for me, that kept me going. I aspired to be like her, and knew that even if I was just a little bit like her, I would be okay.'

'She was real though, Seraph, just like you or I. I think we always look to our elders for support and succour, but at the end of the day, we're all just human. We all have foibles, issues, troubles, pasts and quirks of our own.'

Seraph sat forward and tried to gather herself. 'I thought I was stronger than this but I'm a total fucking mess. What's wrong with me?'

'You've just had your heart broken, my love.'

Seraph could have spiralled into another round of crying at that comment, but she stood up and attempted to walk off her pain. 'Do you know what happened to Tom?'

'I never even knew his name until I saw this. By the way, where did you find it?'

'Underneath the floorboards as I came down from the loft.'

'I never used to like going up in that loft for her, it always gave me the creeps. Was there nothing of interest up there?'

'Nothing much. Only this stuff under the floor. There is more in that diary, but I daren't read it. I don't know if I can handle any more.'

'Then take it back to New York with you, and read it there when you're ready to.'

Seraph shook her head, 'I can't not read it, but I don't want to face the reality of it either. Will you read the rest to me?' she pleaded.

'I don't know. It would feel like an invasion of privacy. You're a relative, but I was just a friend of hers. I'm not sure if I want to read the words either.'

Camille got up off the sofa and went into the kitchen to press for a cup of tea for each of them from the drinks unit. She came back seconds later and handed Seraph hers.

'Thanks. Could you read it, please? I would appreciate it so much if you were here with me.'

Camille seemed to have relented, but warned, 'If there are any big, fancy words, you'll have to read instead!'

'Okay.'

With that, Seraph clung on to her tea as Camille prepared to recite the rest.

CHAPTER 14

10th March, 2013

My love sleeps in my bed as I write to you from my dressing table at the window of my bedroom. His slender, white body is laid face-down tangled up in the sheets, and a slight bit of leg is poking out. I can hear his breathing, in and out, and he occasionally grunts a little. I can't stop smiling as I watch him sleep, and feel as though I'm the luckiest woman in the world. I have Tom back.

Last night, he arrived to pick me up for our first proper date together. He was wearing a black, long-sleeved shirt tucked into cream chinos, teamed with a smart tan leather jacket and brown leather loafers. He was clean-shaven, smelling great – and so hot. I could hardly contain myself. I was wearing a plunging, bright orange maxi dress with huge flowery prints, red velvet jacket and matching wedges. I met him at the side door of my shop in a narrow alleyway, and he joined me on the step to kiss me. He looked dazzled by the sight of me, and I thought, *Oh lord, please let us make it out tonight!* He said, 'You look amazing,' before sliding a hand up inside my jacket and starting to kiss me. I felt the twinges in my groin, and he moved up against my body to impose himself on me. Earlier, I'd been to the salon for the occasion and my hair was loose and curly, and he ran his fingers through it. I could tell where our embrace was leading, and I stopped him, speaking through gritted teeth as his lips remained against mine. 'Tom, please let's have our first date, before we never get the chance again.' He laughed his loud, guttural snigger, and kissed me quickly before jumping off the step to hold his hand out for me to take.

Once out on the Shambles, we kept warm with our arms around each other and began wandering the streets. It was early evening and Tom said he had a surprise for me. I tried to get it out of him but he wouldn't succumb to any of my tricks. We sauntered through the city, which was quietening down after the usual Saturday hustle and bustle. I admired accomplished buskers playing and singing, various human statues, market stalls that were shutting up shop for the day, tourists enjoying the remnants of their jaunt and so many little boutiques selling unique items. I'd worked in this city for so many years, but now I was in love, it seemed all the more wonderful.

He led me towards the Cedars Court Hotel and I felt my face begin to shine with delight. A smartly-dressed doorman welcomed us in and Tom directed me to the award-winning French restaurant inside. My guts were churning, and I felt delirious.

We proceeded to eat the most epic, magical meal. I had a few non-alcoholic cocktails, which Tom ordered for me without my even realising it. That's the thing about him; he knows me without even saying, and we don't have to apologise to one another about anything. I'd never experienced such service in my life. The waiter explained each course in depth, replenished our drinks without us even noticing and scraped our crumbs off the crisp white table linen with a golden rod at the end of each course. It was unbelievable. The most I'd ever experienced before was ordering a 2-4-1 meal from the local pub, and having to get my own condiments and cutlery from a greasy trolley. I felt a little uncomfortable really, but Tom was a constant reassurance, smiling and repeatedly asking if everything was okay for me. We ate the same food; Parma ham, escargot, sorbet, beef bourguignon and chocolate torte for dessert. Everything was cooked to perfection, served on large, white porcelain plates. We decided to go the whole hog, and had coffee and chocolate truffles afterward. The lighting was dim and romantic, and mellow music played quietly in the background. We held each other's hands over the table and he would often reach over and kiss mine. Midway through the meal, he rolled his sleeves up and I joked that he must have been getting a little hot under the collar. But I too was secretly feeling the heat. He was a boy I once knew, now a gorgeous professor, who I daren't let myself believe was really into me. He is so manly and yet not arrogant, the epitome of gentlemanliness, of manners and respect. If I wasn't desperate for him before, I was after that.

We left our table at about 11pm, and went to sit in a quiet part of the hotel lounge, which was furnished in a manner much resembling a gentleman's club. He had half a lager, and I had an orange juice. We sat on a luxurious little green velvet sofa, cuddled up in each other's arms, trying to digest some of the meal we'd just gorged on. He smelt my hair and asked, 'Do you believe in fate?'

'Maybe.' I paused and said, 'Perhaps I do. It certainly seems fateful that within the space of a few weeks of leaving Selby, I've got myself a shop, a new family and a man.'

He said, 'It's quite incredible, isn't it? But I knew you were the sort of person who didn't do things by halves!'

I giggled and brushed my lips against his. I noticed his expression had turned serious though, and he said, 'I came to find you because I nearly died last year, and you were all I could think about when I was at death's door.'

I held a hand over my mouth, shocked and almost tearful. He held me closer and said, 'Please don't be sad. It brought me back to you. I want to tell you about it, but not now.'

I kissed him fiercely and held my arms around him tightly. 'I never stopped loving you Tom, not really. Over the years, there were some weeks where I'd think about you every day. I'd wonder where you were, whether you were happy and healthy. I don't know how I'd have reacted to finding out you were dead. You were the only one who had ever really given me any comfort.'

He grimaced and said, 'I should have been there for you.'

I said, 'You're here now, and I hope to god you're not going anywhere.'

He grabbed my cheek and stared into my eyes, saying, 'Wild horses, wild horses…' He kissed me passionately, and we realised we needed to take it elsewhere.

We left the hotel and practically ran back to my place. We got inside and slammed the door. He was kissing me in the hallway, and he pulled off my jacket in desperation. We'd started to go up the stairs when we fell back, and he yanked up my dress and undid his belt. I pulled his chinos down and he was inside me within a flash. I screamed with pleasure. I held his head in my hands and stared into his soul. I wanted to own him, to possess him absolutely, and I would do anything to achieve that. He had his way with me rapidly and I honestly thought I saw white light as he and I reached orgasm in ecstatic, bittersweet unison. He said as he rested against my chest afterward, 'Will you marry me, Eve? My one and only love, will you make me the happiest man alive and be my wife?'

I thought I'd soared above myself into the clouds, looking down on an unreal, impossible situation. I paused for a moment as he looked at me for a response. I smiled and said, 'I'll be with you forever Tom, forever and a day. Yes, I'll marry you.' I started crying uncontrollably, shivering and shaking with happiness, and he held me so tightly. He cried too, and we rushed up to the flat to get warm.

Dear diary, I feared I would need you during these few months, but as it turns out, I don't need you so much after all. I have Tom to take care of me now, but I thank you all the same for your company.

My life has truly begun, and I'm never going to look back.

CHAPTER 15

When Camille finished reading, she and Seraph sat back in total shock. The diary was replaced on the coffee table, and Camille nestled into the cushions of the sofa to take it all in. She looked across at Seraph and the pair began laughing hysterically. They were in absolute disbelief. Hiding behind the squeals however, there were tears and exasperation.

After they finished, Seraph squeaked out, 'She was so passionate wasn't she, Camille? I just can't comprehend any of that diary. It's not her at all, not the Eve I knew.'

'It's incredible, but I believe it.'

'She spoke of my grandfather, you know, and my father Hamish. She met him when he was a teenager and said he would grow to seven feet tall. Her estimation wasn't far off. And the way she felt so locked up all those years with her mom, that was so sad. There are still so many gaps in the story.'

Camille took a few moments for contemplation, and decided, 'For now Seraph, you should feel very lucky. She was an immense spirit, and you should feel extremely grateful to have been so close to her, to have known her even. We both know there are terrible things to come, if we are ever to right a few wrongs in this world, and we must remember that there was once love, and family, and righteousness. Your heritage is a rich one, chérie.'

Seraph nodded and fought back the tears. She stood up to look outside. 'What now Camille? What do I do?'

'We say goodbye, and we hope that more answers are forthcoming.'

With that, Camille left the flat and went back down to the control room. She told Seraph she would be in the flat next door if she needed anything later that night. Seraph retrieved a One4U meal from the kitchen, and sat eating it as she tried to soak up everything she had learnt. She felt empty and numb, and wondered whether it was the shock of it all. *It might all look better in the morning*, she decided. She crawled into Eve's bed fully clothed, wrapping the covers around her, trying to absorb some of her aunt's presence. She needed to feel a connection to someone, or something, which might give her comfort. Closing her eyes, she pictured Eve and Tom so happy on their wedding day, and fell into an instant deep sleep.

CHAPTER 16

Eve had lived a long life and there was nothing to be sad about, hence the no-black rule she had been intent on Camille implementing.

Seraph's great-aunt had not been very religious but for some reason she wanted her departure from the world to be overseen by someone of the cloth. It was to be held at the grand, but crumbling, York Minster – one of the few relics of the past still standing – a gargantuan Gothic, medieval marvel that looked unreal against the background of the ruined city.

Seraph had slept so deeply that when she woke, she shot up in bed with a start, wondering where the hell she was, having entirely forgotten that she had crawled into bed there the previous night. Everything looked different that morning, and she was comforted seeing Eve's surroundings staring back at her. As if telepathically, Camille knocked on the door holding coffee and toast in her hands. Passing them to Seraph, she asked, 'Morning. Feel better today?'

'Much, much better, thanks.' Seraph even managed a smile.

Camille was dressed in a bright pink fitted dress that showcased an impressive figure for a woman of her age. She wore slender, black patent court shoes and went barelegged. After she sat down at Eve's dressing table in the corner, Camille produced her Unicus and appeared to be engrossed by something. Seraph noticed the Frenchwoman's device with admiration – it resembled a cute little black Chanel handbag. However, the journalist still preferred her own one in the shape of a large purple bow. Camille's sleeveless dress revealed extremely defined muscles in her arms, and she had full make-up on, with her hair loose and straightened.

'I don't have to make an effort too, do I? I think I could just about manage jeans and a t-shirt today.'

Camille shot her a look of unacceptability. 'You are the niece of Eve Maddon. Plus, we need to show the world what we are made of, remember?'

Seraph groaned and relented, 'Fine. I'll throw something on then.'

'We'd better leave soon Seraph, it starts in an hour. Hop in the shower and I'll get some items from the wardrobe for you that should fit. I'll leave them out and you can meet me downstairs when you're ready.'

'Yes, ma'am.' Seraph saluted in Camille's direction, before heading off to the bathroom.

Around an hour later, Seraph and Camille clung to each other as they made their way into the Minster. Some of the shop staff trailed behind them, but a lot of them had been forced to stay behind to keep guard.

Camille had thrown on a little matching jacket to go with her dress, and said as they arrived at the venue, 'I'm giving the eulogy. Remember, as far as the world is concerned, she was Eve Maddon, bridal designer.' She warned, whispering under her breath, 'Our enemies are not beyond us, even in here.' Seraph smiled and nodded in understanding.

Having found a seat near the front of the packed-out Minster, she noticed almost every seat was taken and several hundred people were also stood in the aisles, corridors and wings of the venue. She also saw literally every shade of every colour of the rainbow amongst the congregation – most of whom, she thought, are probably RAO or former clients of Eve's. Seraph was wearing a delicate cream lace vest underneath a violet-purple ensemble of cotton pencil skirt and matching collarless jacket, with brown suede kitten heels. Camille had chosen well, and miraculously everything fitted perfectly. Looking around, it seemed as if the few creative people left in the world were all sat in that place, saying goodbye to the owner of one of the last bridal couture houses. The funeral guests' whispers, rustling and breathing was deafening; the house of worship was that full. Even the sun had broken out, shining through the ancient stained-glass windows so that magnificent rainbows fell across Eve's casket at the front.

The protestant minister began the service by welcoming Eve's guests, and remarking on the fact that the Minster had not seen so many people in attendance in decades. No hymns were sung – but there was one lengthy reading from the bible about love: 1 Corinthians 13, vv1-13. The words moved Seraph greatly. She had never heard anything biblical recited in such impressive surroundings before, and the acoustics inside seemed to reverberate and accentuate its meaning for her. Suddenly, she sensed Eve was sending a message from beyond the grave. A sense of dread washed over her, and Seraph knew that something terrible must have happened to Tom for Eve to have been separated from him. He was obviously a man of substance and decency, and Eve would not have let him go that easily. That meant the truth would probably be difficult to bear, and Seraph didn't have the stomach to face that yet. In particular, the first few lines of the reading stood out to her.

Camille was asked to say a few words afterwards, and so she took to the pulpit with a typed bit of paper in her hands:

'Friends of Eve... I hope that my words express what we're all feeling today. Sad, but thankful. As you know, she didn't have much family. Her only remaining relative is Seraphina, sitting at the front there, who is her great-niece.'

As Camille pointed at Seraph, she sank in her seat as the congregation tried to get a look at her. *Thanks Camille.*

'However, despite her lack of blood relatives, she always felt that the people who came through the doors of her shop became members of her family. Eve wasn't married herself, but she loved the idea of marriage and along with creating dream wedding gowns, she provided many of her customers with sage advice. She treated all her clients on an individual basis, and this made her a special dressmaker. She would go the extra mile to get to know her customers personally, and would know soon enough what kind of gown would suit a lady within minutes of meeting them.'

Seraph noticed a woman sitting next to her, who was nodding in agreement with everything Camille said. The eulogy continued, 'The only thing I feel sad about today is that I wish I'd known Eve longer. The past twenty years under her tutelage have been remarkable, but another twenty wouldn't have gone amiss. Despite this, we should celebrate Eve's long life. She was eternally happy, sometimes temperamental, but always of good humour!' A few laughs were raised among the congregation at that statement.

'Many people who knew her as a young woman have passed, and one thing I've always wondered is, what was she like? I would love to have known her then. She was still so vibrant in later life, who knows what prowess she had back then as a younger woman? I imagine she began life fighting, as she certainly went out fighting, refusing to give in to old age until she ultimately had to.

'She wasn't someone who boasted about her abilities. She didn't go to a renowned design school or study underneath the world's great designers. She was a self-taught oddity, someone who was born to be great, someone who had an eye for detail. She had an extraordinarily steady hand, a massive heart and a God-given way with a sewing machine. I will always remember the time we were up all night altering this one particular gown.

'I had only just started working for Eve and thought her practices were a bit strange, but I soon cottoned on to her dedication. The client was getting married the next day, but she needed some adjustments to her dress at the last minute. Eve was flapping around because it was a dress of exceedingly intricate design. She had challenged herself as she always did, trying to attempt a new method of lace-making introduced by my fellow country people. It was like a tapestry almost, and if one bit was out of place, the whole thing looked wrong. Eve got so frustrated, pinning bits together, pulling bits apart, and it was around 3am when I saw her madly scurrying about, throwing her hands in the air, cursing to herself and chucking bits of material off tables in a bid to find something. I demanded to know what she was doing and she spitted, "Looking for some damned pins!" I couldn't contain myself with laughter. I was overwrought with exhaustion, as was she. I fell about on the floor, until I finally found some breath to say, "Eve, look at your dress!" She looked down to see her own clothes littered with dozens of pins! She was so tired and so exasperated she didn't know what she was doing! Once she realised, she collapsed on the floor in hysterics too. We worked until 7am the next morning, and the client got married on time! That is how I will always remember Eve – so hard-working, dedicated and full of humour. She knew exactly how important a woman's wedding day was. She got it right every time. She touched so many people's lives, and that is what she called her life's work. Working with her was like embarking on the greatest ride of your life, and never wanting to get off. I only have one thing left to say... thank you for being you Eve.' With that, Camille wiped a few tears from her eyes, and was helped from the stand by a member of her staff. And then everyone got up to applaud.

Seraph felt a little tear creeping into her eye, even though she had held it together pretty well until that moment. She daren't stand up for fear of falling back down. How did this woman dedicate her life to the institution of marriage when she herself had once found such great love, only to lose it? Seraph could see so many gaps in Eve's story. She had so many questions still to be answered.

CHAPTER 17

Without pomp or ceremony, Eve's wicker casket was quietly interred at the local VIP cemetery, which charged an astronomical fee per plot due to the lack of space. Seraph and Camille were the only ones in attendance, along with a couple of members of the bridal house, and the foursome had quietly and sombrely acknowledged the old lady's passing. Seraph wanted to bawl her eyes out, but she restrained herself. She remembered Camille's words earlier, and she tried to maintain some dignity and grace for the sake of her aunt and the cause.

The funeral guests arrived at the Shambles to be welcomed by a variety of musicians lining the street. Pianists, violinists, fiddlers, guitarists and trumpeters played upbeat music. Dozens of tables had been erected since Seraph was last there that morning, and piles of cakes and sandwiches were covering them. Camille noticed the shocked look on Seraph's face as she walked by, 'I know, and what's even more amazing is that Eve organised everything herself a few months ago.'

Seraph sat on the doorstep of the bridal shop and surveyed the scene. Hundreds of women and men larked about, dancing to the music and drinking the abundance of cheap horrible wine that someone had brought along.

Seraph sat with a paper plate full of sandwiches and other delightful snacks that had been brought over from Bettys. However, she could only pick at it all; her appetite had died all of a sudden. For some reason she noticed all the staff of the shop were wearing pink like Camille had been that morning, and she remembered it had been Eve's favourite colour.

Seraph sat wondering what could have possibly happened to tear Tom and Eve apart. Whatever occurred must have affected Eve greatly, only she obviously never let on that anything had happened and certainly never mentioned Tom to her. Perhaps whatever nearly killed him that time had reared its head once more. The conjecture was hurting her brain so much she could barely concentrate on anything else.

'Seraph! Seraph!' It was Camille, followed by her entourage and a serious woman dressed in a stuffy smart suit. Seraph stood up to find out what was going on.

'We're going inside to hear the will. This is Eve's solicitor, so shall we get on with business?'

'Sure,' replied Seraph, 'Let's get it over with.'

In Camille's office, around the worktable, sat Seraph, Camille, Eve's middle-aged solicitor and her almost identical young assistant.

'I'm going to dictate Eve's exact words. She was very clear about wanting the will to be from her own hand, or mouth, so to speak…'

Seraph thought, *Just spit it out.*

The solicitor cleared her throat and looked as though she was breaking out in a sweat. Camille shot Seraph a concerned look before asking the woman, 'Miss, are you okay? Do you need a glass of water?'

Holding her hand to her forehead, the solicitor replied: 'Oh, I'm fine really, it's just that… well, this is a rather unusual one… I just need to gather myself.'

A few moments later, she began:

'This is the last will and testament of Eve Marie Maddon, born in York, North Yorkshire, January the twentieth, 1983.'

'I, Eve Maddon, bequeath my bridal shop in York to Camille Honoré. The deeds and assets of the shop I give entirely to her. I know she will continue our work just as well as ever, and I trust that she will not give in to the predatory property developers, as I didn't. Just to say, as well, thanks Camille for looking after me in my latter years, and thanks for being a really great colleague – and friend. You know without me saying anyway. I'll save you a place in heaven my guardian angel.'

The solicitor relayed the message with a bit of awkwardness, but it was obvious that she had been instructed by Eve to dictate it word-for-word. Meanwhile, Camille took a hanky out and was wiping her eyes gently, trying not to draw attention to herself. The solicitor looked up embarrassedly before continuing:

'On the matter of the rest of my estate. I leave 200,000ED to Camille, to help her with the continuing running costs of the shop, and to give it that minor makeover she has been planning for so long. And I stress – minor.'

Camille took an intake of breath at this and blew into her hanky, before whispering quietly to herself, 'Merci beaucoup, mon amie.'

The solicitor made a funny sound in her throat again and Camille realised there was yet more to come, recomposing herself immediately.

'I also leave 100,000ED to the Restoration of York Charity. I'm not sure they will appreciate it much, or be able to do much with it, but it'll ease my passing knowing that I gave something back to this once brilliant city.

'Now, to Seraphina Grace Maddon, my great-niece. I know you will be there Seraph listening to this. Despite not seeing each other for some time, we knew our feelings for one another, didn't we? Life just got in the way.'

Seraph sat there not moving, and one cold, solitary drop fell from her eye without any encouragement or provocation. Camille saw her face and covered Seraph's hand with her own. The solicitor noticed too and asked if she needed a moment, but Seraph shook her hand in defiance.

'Therefore, it is to you Seraph, that I leave the remainder of my estate. It will probably add up to the sum of around 1.8million E-Dollars or so, but you'd better ask the solicitor about that.'

Seraph frowned and blurted out disbelievingly, 'Eh?'

The solicitor spoke in her own tone of voice this time. 'Now you understand my nervousness. Only, the thing is, her fortune actually amounts to around about 2.5million ED, given inflation and interest accrued on various investments and such.'

Camille sat there with her hand over her mouth, wide-eyed.

Seraph stood up, and moved behind her chair, holding on to the back of it in disbelief. She shrieked, 'From dresses?! You must have got it wrong. She couldn't possibly have had that much dough. No. No. Can't you just give me a vintage handbag and send me on my way?'

'She had quite a long career, remember?'

The solicitor's words aggravated her and Seraph began to react to everything that had just transpired. Gesticulating widely she almost growled, 'I just cannot believe that she's left me all this money! I mean, it's too much, too much responsibility. I don't even know I want it, and what would I do with it? I don't understand how she could have had so much wealth and have stayed in this shit hole!' Towards the end, she was almost screeching. Camille shot her a look, and Seraph threw her an apologising one in return.

'Your aunt was an enigma that's for sure. There's more in the will, actually, if you will bear with me.'

'Do I need a drink before I hear the rest?' Seraph felt the only way to get through this now was a bit of humour… and liquor.

The solicitor continued, 'No, the only other thing is this letter, which she left for you Miss Maddon.'

The solicitor searched for the item in her briefcase and handed it to Seraph. The envelope was luxurious, made from some sort of thick recycled paper, and it had been sealed with a strange wax seal, probably to ensure Seraph would know whether anyone had peeked or not.

'I can assure you she gave strict instructions for no-one to ever open that, and none of us have. She scared us all into believing that Armageddon would fall across the Earth if any of us were to ever delve into its contents, and we never did. Plus, she paid us handsomely not to!'

Slightly distasteful, thought Seraph.

The solicitor began shuffling papers, shifting about in her chair, re-reading everything to make sure there was nothing left to go over.

'That's it, then, I think. That was all that was in the will. All I need to do now is take your contact details, both of you, and we will be in touch with you shortly.' And as if in a dream, Camille and Seraph handed over their Unicus IDs.

Confused and still disbelieving, Seraph spoke almost hysterically, asking, 'That's it then, I just get all this green and I'm sent on my way? There must be more to deal with? More to say?' She continued hanging onto the chair she was stood behind. She started to take stock and said, 'Look, I'm sorry, but I'm in shock. What will happen to all the money? I don't know where I will put it!'

The solicitor gave her assistant a knowing look, as if to say, *Oh it's one of those is it?* As if speaking to a child, the solicitor replied quite slowly and concisely, 'Miss Maddon, our accountant is trained to deal with such cases. She will advise you on what accounts you will need to set up and so forth. Your aunt had organised everything so that you would just get the funds. She instructed us to sell all her assets bar the bridal shop before her passing. There is nothing for you to do but wait for the money to be put into your possession. It's all yours and we cannot tell you what to do with it. I advise you to read the letter, Miss, perhaps it will provide you with some assurances from Eve. Hopefully it will provide answers, an explanation perhaps, of how someone could have accrued so much money from such a dwindling business…' The solicitor collected herself, before continuing, 'Anyway, I digress, it's not my job to question my clients' business dealings or anything, but I will say this, in my twenty-five years of doing this job, I've never met anyone as unique or dumbfounding as Eve Maddon. She was truly a one-off, a strong character and a special human being.' Gathering her things together, she nodded to her assistant for them to leave. Within seconds, they were down the street and gone.

Camille and Seraph sat speechless, trying to deal with what they had just been told. They both looked and felt as if they had been done an injustice, as if money and bricks and mortar, and security for the rest of their lives, was no recompense for the fact that Eve was actually gone. She'd had time to prepare for her departure from this world, but nobody else had. No-one could have realised how her death would affect them, least of all Seraph. She wanted to know more, to learn everything, to have more than just a load of money and an inexplicably annoying diary! She felt the letter in her hands. *There has to be more in here.* Thinking quickly, she turned to Camille.

'Are you going to be alright? It's just that, I think I might go up to the flat and read this letter. I think I might need to be alone to do that.'

'Of course, you go up.'

The shop girls came rushing in with bottles of cava and streamers, whistles and hats. Seraph noticed the wake had turned into a full-on party out on the street. As they engulfed Camille and beckoned her to join them, Seraph watched on as Camille nodded in reply to each person who asked whether she had been given the shop or not in Eve's will. It seemed no surprise to the staff, though, that she had been left in charge. Suddenly it occurred to Seraph that she didn't want anyone to know about her windfall, and as soon as the notion had crept into her mind, Camille came back into the office and said, 'Don't worry, I won't tell anyone... If you feel like it later, come and enjoy the party with us. Eve would have wanted you to.'

And with that, Camille went to the door, turned back, smiled at Seraph, and was gone. The reporter went upstairs, lifting her legs up each step as if they weighed several tonnes each.

CHAPTER 18

Seraph's heart was pumping, she was sweating and feeling extremely nervous. She knew the contents of the letter might be difficult to stomach. Pouring a shot of disgusting sherry into a glass, she sat on the sofa and tried to relax. She felt like the moment had to be savoured and she didn't want to rush it. She wanted to be relaxed in order to be able to take in every word Eve wrote down for her. She drank the liquid and hoped it would do the trick.

However, one figure kept whirling around her head. *2.5million. 2.5million. 2.5million.* That kind of figure could buy her as much property and security as she could ever need, and any lifestyle she could envisage. It just didn't seem right somehow. True, it wasn't worth as much now as it would have been when Eve was starting her bridal business, back when each country still had its own currency, but it was still a life-changing, jaw-dropping amount of hard cash.

She had watched terrible game shows and always secretly imagined how she would spend the prize money if she were ever so lucky. Everyone does it, hoping one day they might hit the jackpot. But now Seraph was almost sitting on all this, she resented the responsibility. She felt as if she hadn't earned it. Those daydreams about winning the lottery were always broken by the thought that Seraph loved her job, and that it challenged her enough not to need huge amounts of money like that. That, in reality, wealth doesn't really make us happy. Seraph had been lucky enough to never have to work to survive, she had lived to work because she had enjoyed her job so much, and therefore the fantasy of winning all that money was purely that. A fantasy. A what-if. A daydream of possibilities, no actualities, but which she was now faced with.

The desire not to rush the situation was being overshadowed by the promise of revelations in the letter, but Seraph still felt she needed more time to calm down. She tried taking deep breaths, but that didn't work, so she lay back and attempted to picture herself on some far-flung tropical island. Calmness and serenity.

Another drink later and she decided she was good to go. She carefully pulled open the seal on the envelope, not wanting to tear even a millimetre of paper, such was its importance. She pulled out the contents and discovered several sheets of thin, almost weightless writing paper. Seraph took out the sheets, which were folded in half. *Okay, this is probably about to get weirder...*

As she opened the pages, however, she found most of them were blank. Only the first page had anything on it – a few words and only one message:

Go back to New York straight after the funeral. Answers await you there. I love you. Eve x

CHAPTER 19

At an indistinguishable point in time and space...
The sounds of a clear blue stream trickling by in the distance and exotic birds chirruping filled Eve's ears, while scents of petunia and lavender lingered in the air. She was laid amidst the long, green grass of a blossoming meadow and right next to her was Tom. The sun beamed down on their faces as they held hands and absorbed the rays. She wore a white summer dress with faint blue flowers and he a white flannel shirt with rolled-up sleeves and white linen trousers. He moved on top of her and they began kissing. He held his hand to her cheek and she started crying. He brushed the tears off her face and bundled her up in his arms. She entwined her legs and arms about him and tried to breathe as much of him in as she could.

Suddenly, she realised.

They both had the appearance of being in their early twenties. However, they somehow knew they were both dead. And one of them had lived for more than eighty years.

Eve remembered absolutely nothing of dying. She woke up and saw Tom's face hovering over her as the sun beat down on them – that's all she knew. Her subconscious knew she was dead, yet she told herself she had wandered into a beautiful dream, and that admitting the reality might erode the illusion.

Tom led her through the mature gardens of a country house nearby. He explained that he wanted her to watch a film with him. They entered a home cinema and he told her that he had once watched an interesting film in the same room.

At first, Eve wondered what was going on. Up on the screen was a woman giving birth. *Ugh, what is this?* Then, it dawned on her. It was her mother. She looked sweaty and red, bulbous even, but beautiful and serene too. The child was born and Eve knew she was witnessing herself being brought into the world. However, she watched the film as if detached from her former life. Since death, she had become a different entity. When people have the strange feeling of looking down on themselves as if their soul is floating above them in the air, they are foreseeing these moments in their afterlife, she reasoned.

Tom sat quietly next to her with a knowing smile as the film unfolded. Eve tried to ask him questions, to get a reaction from him, but he merely shook his head and pointed toward the screen. The strangest thing about the whole situation was that Eve had longed for Tom so much after his passing. She had missed him so much. He had haunted her dreams, her every waking hour and her life had never been the same again after he was gone. She wailed in the night when she knew nobody could hear her. She would push her face into the pillow and almost stop breathing because of the manic crying and sobbing. However, now she had him next to her, it was as if that grief never happened and nothing was ever wrong. In the real world, she would have jumped on him and never let him go upon seeing him again, but in this plane of existence she knew that he was back and that he was not going to leave her this time. She could relax and feel content in his presence. So, she decided to watch the film calmly, but knew they would be there for some time.

Watching the early years of her life, Eve saw the devastating truth about her mother and father's marriage unfold. Her parents seemed to have had an idyllic life in the small village of Carlton. Her mother was much younger than her father, who had already been previously married with a child, Harry. However, they appeared very much in love. That was, until, her father's used car business went bust and they had to move to Selby and downsize to a smaller house. They had massive debts and arguments filled the house. One day, Eve's dad just took off. This, in turn, led to her mother Valerie's increased drinking and depression, which she refused to seek help for. He was gone without a trace, leaving her alone with her alcoholic mother. Eve had been astonished to see that up until this point, she had been such a happy child. Nothing seemed to faze her and she had no concerns or worries or cares. She had forgotten that she had once been such a child, but she could not bring herself to cry for the little five-year-old girl she once was. She couldn't cry, because she knew there was much more to come yet. Much more hardship, pain and suffering. And she knew that life had made her a very different person to the one she started out as.

Then followed the years that her mother struggled in vain to hide her secret. While she went to school, her mother went to work as a receptionist in the mornings, and came home to drink all afternoon. As a child, Eve would desperately use any excuse not to have to go straight home after school, in the hope that by teatime her mum may have sobered up a bit, and might be easier to handle.

Soon, on the screen, she saw a nineteen-year-old Tom sat next to the seventeen-year-old version of herself. In that moment, her heart almost broke in two, watching the pair of them. *If only we knew then*, she thought.

Peppering her memories were also shots of Tom darting in and out of her life on street corners or at the back of a pub somewhere. She would always try to circumvent him, and avoid getting hurt. Her heart leapt when she saw those moments. She wanted to reach into the screen and grab her younger self, shake some sense into her and make her realise Tom was the only one for her. But that is the bitter irony of life, she resolved – that we must unconsciously make those mistakes – knowing deep down they needed to be made, knowing there was a time for everything.

An intermission. Eve and Tom had reached her thirtieth birthday and it was now time to consolidate before watching the next instalment.

Tom asked, 'What do you think so far?'

'I think you know me well enough to know what I think and feel. You and I were once practically one and the same person.'

A wry smile crept across his face, 'When I watched my life as it had happened, when I was in the same predicament as you are now, one thing struck me more than any other. It was that, my life never really began until we did, as a couple I mean.'

Eve felt like that thirty-year-old woman again, desperately in love and aching for him. Those first few months in York with Tom had moulded the person she would be for the rest of her life.

'I know exactly what you mean, my darling. I found it so hard to go on without you, as if it was pointless. But I decided that I would see you again one day, and that until that time I needed to do the best I could with what I had left. I felt I owed it to the love we shared, which not many people experience in a whole lifetime. Feeling lucky to have had you at all kept me going.' Eve took a few moments and reiterated her sentiment again, 'It is so strange, is it not? So strange that life, as wondrous as it is in all its various splendours, is so meaningless without that one great love? Whether it is a passion for someone or something, life without that is pretty much senseless!' The two of them laughed and giggled, as if they couldn't believe how surreal life really was. They sat back down and recommenced viewing.

CHAPTER 20

Video diary entry zero-zero-three. Hi, Tom Bradbury here. It's very important I record all my findings in New Guinea, so here goes…

It's now December the thirteenth and I've been stuck on this island for more than a month, despite only intending to stay here for a couple of days or so. My colleagues and I had to prop each other up as we battled the life-threatening illnesses we each came down the mountain with. We struggled to open the tins of food, and drinking water was painful. Between the insect bites, dehydration and hunger, each of us nearly gave up and died in that jungle. There was no help whatsoever and it was only two days ago that we felt strong enough again to pack up the camp and venture back into civilisation. Even then, the journey was tiring and the relentless rain drove us to despair almost. We somehow made it back to Jayapura yesterday after hitching a lift on the back of a wagon. We've checked into a hotel and we all feel much better thanks to some hot food, warm beds and a bath.

If we weren't all fit and healthy, I'm sure we would have all died out there of whatever it was that had stricken us down. The fact we survived in those conditions all that time is testament enough, but overcoming infection too, that was not easy. I still don't feel myself and I'm not sure I ever will. I feel as though something has eaten away at my very core and I will never be the same again. Out here, all I could keep thinking about was my first love, Eve Maddon. She was a beautiful, red-headed creature with a figure to die for. The memory of her has haunted me for years. I always regretted us breaking up and now I realise I still love her, I'm going to find her when I get back. Life is so precious, and I never realised it until now.

We've got the samples still that we took from the bird, along with a few images, and we will be flying back to the UK tomorrow. I'm sure there will be a lot of questions to answer and lot more to ask ourselves. Whatever this thing that struck us down was, it was a force of nature unlike anything anyone has ever seen the like of before Wish me luck getting back to some sort of normal life. Goodbye.

PART II
Vis Unita Fortior

CHAPTER 21

Seraph felt terrible for just leaving without saying a proper goodbye to Camille, but Eve's words seemed to be telling her to get back to New York as a matter of urgency. Seraph also decided she needed a change of scenery, having been so shaken by Eve's revelations. Her safety and the prowling agents didn't cross her mind. She simply needed to get back home, because that's what Eve had told her to do. She knew the resistance would be somehow looking after her anyway.

It was 5:17pm that same day when Seraph jumped off the train from York onto the platform in Manchester, only to discover all flights in and out of the UK had been cancelled. The news networks confirmed a freak hurricane was loitering around unpredictably in the East Atlantic and nothing and nobody would be going anywhere fast. *These storms are becoming more frequent*, thought Seraph, but this was just her luck.

She didn't want to check into a dreadful chain hotel again, so it seemed her only option was to wait it out in the airport lounge in case the situation did change. When it got to 9pm though, she was just about losing the will to live. She re-read Eve's diaries about ten times, desperately trying to hide the content from the other people trapped there with her who all looked about as psychotic as she felt. It was definitely time to head to a bar, where she could find a corner to hide in.

She found an imitation, old-fashioned pub tucked away in a quiet nook of the airport, and ordered herself a coffee and some kind of questionable meat pie from the selection screen at the side of her booth. The place was dank and dingy, with a lurking clientele and synth-jazz blaring in the background – it was just the right kind of establishment to disappear in.

Within minutes, she heard a low rumbling and the green light flickered above the hatch next to her. Retrieving her order from inside, she started downing her food, willing the storm to pass so she could be on her way.

Two coffees later, however, Seraph was just about out of her mind. She rested her head on the table in front of her and felt her eyes falling as soon as she did. It was no use, she would have to check in to one of those godforsaken hotels again.

She got up to leave, swiping her U-Card at the door of the pub to pay her bill as she exited. As she did so, a man caught her eye for a brief moment. He was entering just as she was walking out. He was much taller than her, at least by some six inches. She glanced at him and his dark brown eyes caught her off guard. He seemed familiar somehow, but she told herself it was nothing and headed in the direction of the hotel. However, she couldn't help but look back to see if he was watching her leave. He wasn't and she pretended not to care.

CHAPTER 22

The next day Seraph had even contemplated heading back to York, with the situation seeming very unlikely to change anytime soon. However, she decided to just stay put. She had spent hours lying on the bed trying to arrange her thoughts but nothing seemed to make sense to her anymore. She didn't want to face the reality that her parent's deaths were somehow linked to Eve and her cause. It was all too much to absorb, and would mean admitting everything she had ever perceived about them was wrong.

She had ravenously eaten everything in the mini-fridge, and had decided there was nothing for it. *Reality check.*

She took out her Unicus. Despite providing 2YB, it still ran very slowly with the amount of crap she kept on it, refusing to delete a single thing in case it came in handy for future use. She recoiled at the number of messages in her inbox. She answered some of the ones from Eve's accountants and lawyers. Work would be hell when she got back. *Too much to catch up on and not enough time to do it all.* She decided she may play the grieving card and claim she needed some time off for a while. The truth was of course, Eve's story had captured her imagination and she was desperate to put all the pieces together. She needed more time to assemble them, and she suspected there were more revelations to come.

Deciding to put her time to good use, she wondered whether she could find any details about Tom. She searched the births, marriages and deaths databases of Yorkshire. The search brought up hundreds of results, so she tried to narrow them down with a few key words. *Born 1980. Married 2013.* Three results presented themselves, all grouped together. The first was his birth certificate, the second was the marriage record she had already seen and the last was his death certificate. Seraph took a deep breath as she prepared to open the last file. On the screen, the details stared back at her. Eve had been the one to file his death, and had the term *Widow* beneath her name. On the certificate, it seemed that she had adopted his name and was called Eve Bradbury. However, she must have reverted back after his death perhaps. He died in December 2023 of heart failure. *Shit. They had 10 years together at least, thank god. But why did Eve keep it a secret…? Heart failure at 43? Maybe it was Ravage-related…?* All these questions she had, and yet there were still no real answers.

As she sat there, she heard her stomach grumble and realised it was getting toward evening again. Seraph decided she needed proper sustenance. She would have to face the pub again and hope that nobody there would bother her. Besides, she needed to take her mind off the whole business for a bit.

Maybe once she got back to New York, everything would become clear. It was just so frustrating to be trapped there, unable to carry out Eve's instruction. She checked the departure information on her Unicus as she made her way back through the corridors of the airport toward the pub but discovered there was no change; nothing was flying in or out still.

On entering the establishment, she tried not to make eye contact with anyone, but her attempt to float in without anyone noticing her failed. Everyone noticed her, as they always did, because of her red hair and gamine appearance. She sat down at a vacant booth and ordered something ridiculous-sounding called Sausage Surprise from the screen. *Whatever that is…* Then she thought, *What the heck, I am going to be a millionaire*, and also pressed for a pint of Guinness, perhaps the most expensive thing on the menu but also maybe the thing she needed most at that time.

After scoffing her meal in record time and drinking the Guinness like there was no tomorrow, Seraph selected another pint of the black stuff. Just as she had done so, she looked up to see a man staring at her from across the pub. He seemed to be giving her daggers. He was sat at the bar and once she managed to focus her eyes, she realised it was the guy from the other day whom she had passed on her way out. She looked away quickly and pretended not to have noticed him. She tried to be indifferent, not to have gone partially blush across the face and not to be slightly inebriated from the Guinness. The man seemed to have turned his attention back toward the direction of the automated bar service when Seraph suddenly realised who he was. This time, she decided to stare in his direction, but when he failed to notice, she made the brave decision to go over herself.

She cleared her throat to alert him to her presence and he swung round to meet her confident glare. He seemed startled to see her there before him, but she gave him little time to react. She tried but failed to seem bouncy when she asked, 'Doctor Ryken Hardy, isn't it?'

His struggling smile revealed a set of almost unbelievably straight teeth. 'Yes, and you are the infamous Seraph Maddon.' He turned back to the dimly-lit bar as if to give her the brush-off. However, she was persistent, nearly having to shout above the noise of the synth-jazz blaring out from the nearby speaker units.

'Would you like to join me at my table? Perhaps we could both do with some company?'

Unimpressed by the offer, he mused before turning back to her to say, 'That's mighty magnanimous of you, but I'll think about it.'

Furious, Seraph swiftly walked back to her booth, wishing she had never bothered. She pretended to occupy herself with the menu, but inside she was desperate to bolt out of the joint.

Two minutes later, however, he seemed to have changed his mind and was stood before her, looking cocky with his drink in hand. 'Sorry about before, I've just had a bad day that's all. I would like to join you, if that's okay?'

Seraph eyed him suspiciously, and nodded for him to sit down. *He's asked for this.* He had barely had time to arrange himself in his seat when she blatantly began her interrogation. 'So, I heard you got fired?'

A hint of fury crossed his features but he quickly recovered himself, smiling through gritted teeth. 'What a surprise the conversation turns to my career as soon as you get me sat down.'

She had succeeded in getting him back for his rudeness. 'Come, come, Doctor Hardy. Don't be such a shrinking violet. Yes, I want to know exactly why you got ditched from your position. Doesn't everyone want to know?' In that moment, she peered through slit eyes at his hulking frame. His shoulders were impressively wide and solid, filling his tailored navy blue velvet jacket right to the edges. His hands were large and veiny, with manicured nails and a large Rolex sitting on his brick of a wrist. The bit of neck that poked out of the top of his black polo neck was thick and tense, seeming to bulge with muscles every time he moved. His pronounced Adam's apple bobbed provokingly as he spoke in deep, cosmopolitan tones resounding of a British man who had travelled and seen something of the world. His form was giant, but his face and limbs were long and sophisticated. His chiselled cheekbones and jaw, large oval dark-brown eyes, tanned olive skin, short but side-parted straight jet black hair and sharp clothes were overpowering. His appearance didn't seem to fit the sartorial de rigueur of his profession.

'I was fired for lack of results in my sector, but of course we know the real reason. You ought to know. Seeing as though you're always writing drivel about me.'

Seraph knew she had got to him, and he was ready to pump for information. Sat opposite him, however, she could hardly do anything to escape having to look at him. He was gorgeous, unbelievably handsome, dashing even, but she didn't want to admit it. His Roman nose, full lips – almost purple in colour, along with a set of perfect large ivory teeth, were all of a sudden becoming a point of distraction to her. She nervously ran her tongue over her own front teeth, which were slightly crooked from years of playing hockey. Instead of turning into a gibbering wreck, she decided to get a hold of herself and take control of the situation.

'Well, if you agreed to give me an interview once in a while, I wouldn't need to dig stuff up on you, would I?' He smelt of something. Musky.

The hatch blinked into life, delivering Seraph's pint and raising Ryken's eyebrows. He seemed to be drinking a soda. He explained, 'I don't give interviews, because it wouldn't make any difference, the truth would only end up misconstrued as it always does.'

Insulted, Seraph sat as far back against her seat as possible, taking a gulp of her drink. She collected herself, and realised anything other than an air of serenity would make her seem affected. 'I deal in neither slander nor libellous conjecture. There's a distinction – but in my book, the truth is the truth. The *Chronicle* prides itself on writing investigative journalism, what little of it we manage to churn out. I would never write nor say anything that wasn't accurate, so stop skirting around the issue.'

He seemed to be taken aback, startled that he hadn't managed to overwhelm Seraph with his good looks and reputation. She wasn't the sort of woman who would be won over easily.

'Seraph, I can call you that can't I?' She put up no protest, so he continued, 'Look, let's start over shall we? We got off to a bad start. I apologise.'

She still wouldn't be won over, but she would be the modicum of polite company to prise what she wanted out of him. Sarcastically she began, with an index finger against her mouth, 'So, Ryken, I can call you that can't I? I'm having trouble placing that accent of yours. It's verging on Lancashire but there's a shred of something else in there, am I right?'

'I grew up in Manchester but I guess I've still not got rid of the Mancunian in me completely. I lived in Berkshire for ten years before moving to New York for work eight years ago. So you could say I've got a bit of a mongrelised dialect. And your family were from the UK too?' He noticed her accent seemed to dip a little talking to him, probably hoping that dulcet tones and mimicry would encourage him to surrender.

'Yes, I have very strong ties to Yorkshire. My parents met and married while studying medicine in Leeds, just before moving to New York. They both carried on their training at Columbus and became heart surgeons.'

He frowned, recognising they had more in common than he could have possibly imagined. 'Both of them? What must they think, having a reporter for a daughter?' He smiled teasingly, but she suddenly looked sullen-faced. She shifted uncomfortably in her seat before responding.

'They never saw me reach the peak of my career, but I'm sure they will be both rolling in their graves over the job I do.'

He smarted from her revelation, realising he had made a grievous error. She looked away, appearing to busy herself with taking in the surroundings; the faux-leather upholstery of the booths they were sat in, and the mock-wooden stools, floors, tables and bar that Ryken had just left. He didn't know what to say.

She spoke out of the corner of her mouth, still looking away from him. 'They were murdered.'

His tone turned softer and he asked, 'How?'

'Almost the same way as Mara Dulwich's father. Go figure.'

He wanted to tell her it was a silent "w", but he was too polite and sensitive.

'But why...?'

She shook her head, and kept avoiding his gaze. 'I don't fucking know. It's one of the things I've been chasing my entire career. But I'm almost certain it was the bastards of Officium who did it.'

He looked around to check nobody was within earshot, eyeing the few lone pub-goers that were in there with them. 'Bloody hell, we ought to go somewhere quieter if you're going to talk so candidly.'

She swigged the Guinness again, and looked at him directly in the eye with a stern look that could freeze ice. 'You obviously don't know who you're dealing with here. I don't give a damn who hears us. How do you think I get the stories I do?'

He seemed shocked by her bravado, asking tentatively, 'Why do you reckon they were responsible?'

She widened her eyes in his direction, and maintained a tight grip around the vessel containing her stout. 'I don't know for sure, but I've a pretty good feeling it was. I've covered some of the worst crimes imaginable, but most killers are more often than not just deadbeats who couldn't control their trigger fingers. The way my parents were killed was too contrived. Mown down in broad daylight by some robber who conveniently got away. Dulwich was also killed in nearly the exact same circumstances only weeks later – by a vehicle with no identification plates. I tried to get the satellite images of both incidents, but when I went to the NYPD's archives, I found they had been conveniently deleted – on both counts. The thing had Officium smeared all over it.'

She hastily turned to avoid his gaze, knowing he would certainly have drawn his own conclusions about her motives following her cutting admission.

'So, you know they control Dulwich Labs?'

She rolled her eyes, 'That knowledge became a triviality to me about... let's see, oh yes, the day they stopped being so secretive about their research centres and renamed them all Dulwich Labs. The bastards are that arrogant that they put Mara Dulwich's name to their shady clinical trials after she disappeared in the wake of her father's death.'

'I took that job thinking I'd be working for Mara, but Suranna soon put me straight on a few things.'

'I bet she did… I guess they tempted you with Mara's name then?'

'You could say that, yeah…'

'You ought to have known better.'

'How do you know so much anyway?' he enquired.

'Ulrich was my informant… 'til he washed up on the banks of the Hudson. He had been rotting there for days until a boat spotted him just in front of the Dam.'

He saw the remorseful look on her face, and held a hand to his forehead in disbelief. 'Shit. I didn't know about that. I've been off the radar for a bit.'

She almost croaked out, 'He had a baby on the way.'

Both of his hands were at his face, and he muttered, 'Fucking hell. He was a good bloke. I can't believe it. I'm gonna find out who did it.'

'You'll be lucky, they never get found out. Eleven years later I'm still waiting to discover who exactly murdered my parents – and why.'

He looked deeply troubled, as if his mind had wandered to a dark place. Her own mind was already plagued enough without him adding to her woes.

Seraph tried to change the subject. 'So, why have you ended up trapped here too, Ryken?' She swigged more Guinness, and played with a napkin while she awaited a reply.

'Oh, I was forced into attending a family gathering, but when I got here I found out there wasn't any sort of reunion taking place at all. It seems my invitation was a hoax. This has been a totally wasted trip.' He looked suitably pissed off, but as she waited for him to expand on that, he seemed unwilling to reveal anything more.

She spoke up, 'I travelled here to attend my great aunt's funeral,' before checking herself. She would never normally give out such personal information to strangers, but for some reason she couldn't help unleashing her need to chat on him.

He waited for her to say more but when she didn't, he asked, 'She must have been a pretty great aunt for you to have travelled all the way here? And to leave your investigations behind?'

Seraph looked down at the table while Ryken awaited an answer. She gave a wry smile, 'You've no idea how great. The funeral itself was pretty wild actually, so it was worth coming just for that.'

There was another silence but he seemed to have become accustomed to them. 'In fact, she was the only living relative I had left. But she was quite a unique individual, and that's why I flew out here in an instant. Crazy eh?'

'The only thing that's crazy at the moment is that we can't get out of here!'

'Tell me about it. It seems this cesspit is the only place in the airport you can find a bit of peace and quiet.' The pair smiled at each other. There was another slightly awkward silence, as they remembered who it was they were each sat across from.

'So, Ryken, are you ever going to answer my question? About what happened to your job?'

'You already know, so why ask?'

Seraph could tell she was getting more and more drunk, not used to the effects of Guinness. She was constantly fighting a losing battle, attempting to keep up a demeanour of indifference, when actually she was secretly delighted to have this man of all people fall across her path. She had been trying to get at him for ages. She simply decided to feign nonchalance, hoping silence would force him to speak, and it did.

'Look, Seraph, we're stuck in this place together, seemingly the only New Yorkers within a one-hundred-mile radius and we're both going out of our minds. Shall we share our troubles?'

'Why the hell not,' she said. 'But unless that soda's got bourbon in it, you're not a real New Yorker, Mister.'

CHAPTER 23

Ryken and Seraph had spent the entire evening talking. Before they knew, it was 11pm and the pair realised why they were both beginning to yawn in the soporific surroundings of the pub, despite the endless rounds of coffee they'd had.

Seraph had been careful not to reveal too much about her aunt to the delectable virologist. She had only gone so far as to reveal that Eve was not the eternal singleton she had previously believed her to have been. She described to Ryken everything she had seen in York (aside from the agents and her new best friend's karate skills), and how the city seemed before the Ravage had obliterated it. She spoke of her family's ties to Yorkshire, and how she had been so disappointed to see the place so changed. During all her talk, Ryken listened intently. He would sometimes appear dewy-eyed and almost glaze over, before checking himself and coming to as if out of a dream. In between bits of her story, he would recall an article of Seraph's and ask her about it. She underwent some sort of catharsis as she rambled on and on, but hardly noticed him staring at her so intently.

It had got to the point where Seraph was sick of hearing her own voice, and she was sure she had given away far too much. She decided to turn the conversation to Ryken. 'I've shared, like we agreed, but I don't think you have?'

'I guess I'm a better listener than a conversationalist.'

'You don't get out of it that easily. What have you been doing with your time since being out of employment?' She had taken her leather jacket off and was fiddling with the long sleeves of her black t-shirt, using anything to avoid having to look him in the eye. Every time she did, she felt mesmerised by his gaze.

Ryken went coy all of a sudden. He shifted in the booth and seemed a little defensive, crossing his arms before he spoke.

'I admit my trip here was not exactly boring.'

'Ulrich spoke highly of you, but he warned me to watch you, told me you were the one who could break this conspiracy.'

'He spoke highly of you too. He once said you were the woman he'd have married if you'd given him half a chance.' She frowned and tried to hold back her emotion, but he could see it cross her face. Regret. 'I thought he must have been mad, having heard about the way you mercilessly carry out your investigations.'

She lamented him describing her like that, after the revelations and events of the past few days. She raised a hand to her forehead, and tried to cover her reaction. He knew he had hit a nerve and was about to apologise, when she felt an impulse to explain herself. 'There was me thinking you were above the rumour mill! I've quite successfully given myself a persona that scares the living daylights out of the miscreants who believe they are untouchable. Perhaps what scares them the most is that they can't understand why someone like myself prowls the streets without fear. However, I like it that way. The less people really know about me, the better. But you ought to realise that sometimes we never really know ourselves or each other even, really and truly. Being a physician, you should recognise that the human condition is ever changing, ever evolving, and never unsurprising.'

Her words seemed to reach a place deep inside him, and he began to open up. 'If I asked you not to print a word of what I'm about to tell you, would you promise not to? As a friend, which I'm hoping you are now, could you take what I'm going to say off the record?'

'I don't know until I've heard what you've got to say though.' Seraph's interest was heightened now; she was sitting on the edge of her seat and leaning forward to see into Ryken's eyes. For an instant, she realised she had forgotten all about Eve, but she found herself being distracted by something much more troubling. The closer she got to the giant specimen of virile manhood sat before her, the more she recognised how attracted to him she was. She felt weak, stunned by his masculinity. She had never been quite so affected before. Everything seemed to fade into the background as she couldn't help but feel her senses drawn to him. He was not only attractive, but extremely intelligent, apparently decent and physically very imposing. His sonorous voice and accent were pleasing to her ear. She was just wondering how he got his body in such a shape, when he snapped her out of her reverie.

'Before Suranna died, she told me she had discovered some phials tucked away in a deep-freeze compartment that the team were told was off-limits. She'd accidentally ended up in there one day and found they were labelled H8K1-Z. She stayed late one night, taking one of the said containers out for testing.' He looked around and leaned further toward

Seraph to whisper, 'She thawed the stuff and analysed it. She couldn't believe what she'd found.'

'What? Tell me Ryken.' Her tone was urgent, and her heart began racing.

'Seemingly an inoculation unlike anything she'd ever seen before. I won't bore you with the scientific mumbo jumbo, but basically, a very probable cure for 2023. From Mara's research, we know that it was a constantly mutating strain of avian flu, attaching itself to its hosts' immunities and trying to break those down. A conscious and highly intelligent organism, so to speak, that could counteract antibodies and even aggravate past medical conditions. It invaded every cell and had learnt to be dominant to survive. But it was more than that. It was something that had seemingly never encountered humanity before. Something so raw, that the civilised world was unprepared and unable to cope with its evolutionary strength. Officium must have had the vaccine all that time, and yet, they've always claimed none could be created because of the way in which the infection seemed to fall across the Earth and evaporate just as quickly.

'Yes, it would have been immediately impossible to create enough injections for such a large global population and for something that had seemingly never come into contact with humanity before then. When all the fowl were destroyed in 2023, their eggs were too. Of course, we need fertilised eggs to develop vaccines. However, as Suranna discovered, they seem to have managed it somehow. How long they've had the thing in the deep-freeze, I don't know. I used to wonder why they needed virologists, when there was no chance of us ever carrying out more research on this strain. However, Suranna revealed to me that they are terrified something like this might rear its head again, and they keep people like us employed for that purpose. There were rumours that the disease was genetically engineered, but according to Mara's work, it was such a force of nature, it could have only come from an area uninhabited for decades. Without coming into contact with the infection for centuries, possibly even millennia, the human race had not been able to build up any immunity to it.'

He sat back almost breathless, and seemed to have unburdened himself of his troubles. Seraph sat back in her seat too, her eyes wide, and stamped her foot. 'Fuckers. I knew it. I always knew, and yet, most other people probably know too. But why is this world still in the shadow of this?'

'We weren't alive when it hit, so I guess we will never know the effect it really had. All we know is that we were born into this madness, and that nothing can move forward until the veil is lifted. Knowledge is freedom, and if the world knew the truth for a certainty, I'm sure people would rise up against Officium finally. But without definitive proof, we can't do anything. We need hard evidence otherwise anything else might send panic through the population again. I know one thing for sure at least, they will literally stop at nothing to keep the truth hidden. Suranna started to fear for her life after her discovery. She tried to destroy the evidence of her analysis of the disease, but they must have somehow found out... because two days later she was dead, and the cold storage those phials were in was taken elsewhere. I couldn't do anything, and then I got fired, presumably because they feared I knew something. So, I came to Manchester to return to the apparent source of the disease. The labs here didn't turn up anything either, so I can't prove anything.'

'This is truly amazing shit, truly. This is going to help me so much, you've no idea.' She was almost ecstatic with the possibilities whirling around her head.

'Seraph, for now this has to stay out of the public domain. Their agents have been following me. I've been hiding out here scared for my life.' She could tell from the tone in his voice, he was deadly serious. He suddenly looked almost boy-like with the fear she saw in his eyes.

'Okay, fine. There's one thing I don't understand though. They don't fire people, they kill them, so why are you still alive?'

'I could ask the same thing of you. I think if anyone was a threat to them, you were. Perhaps they see that we're more valuable alive than dead.'

She smiled disbelievingly, 'No, I have an invisible protection floating around with a security lock tighter than Fort Knox's. There must be more you're not telling me?'

A look of contemplation spread across his face, working out his response. But he simply said, 'You know about as much as I do, I'll hazard.'

She eyed him suspiciously. 'How do you know there aren't agents in here with us right now?'

He glanced sideways to eye the clientele, before explaining, 'No, none of these are.'

'How can you tell?'

'Agents don't loiter. All they know is how to kill.'

'Explain to me then, why didn't they grab you when you left your hotel room earlier? If you've taken a room up in the Bed4theNite, which I'm sure you have, surely they'd see your U-Card had been used?'

He thought quickly on his feet. 'I think I managed to escape from my hotel room without their notice. I climbed out of my window and scaled down the side of the building.'

That explains the physique, Seraph thought. 'You abseiled down?'

'Yeah, I got a taste for it when I was in the army.'

Seraph was twitchy even at the mention of heights. It was her biggest fear. 'Gawd, you must be insane! What floor are you on?'

'The fifteenth... it's nothing.' He watched her grimace, and remarked, 'So, the great Seraph Maddon does have an Achilles heel after all?'

'Umm, you can have that one, but that's your lot.' Seraph realised there was more to this man than the stereotypical elbow patches. 'So, you were in the army? When? In my job, I really ought to know…'

'Back home when I was much younger. I was trained as an officer in the medical corp and became a captain, but once I realised I wanted to spread my wings, so to speak, I left and came here for a change of career, and ended up in virology.'

Seraph processed the information, and recognised why he dressed so sharply, with his brown leather brogue ankle boots, cream jeans and delightful shoulder-hugging jacket. She pointed towards his clothes, 'That explains the get-up. You don't scream boring scientist who peers over a microscope all day long. The British Army know how to dress, don't they?'

He smiled and sat back in his seat, seemingly a bit more relaxed himself, 'They do indeed. I learnt more than you can possibly imagine during my time in the army. It made me who I am.'

'And yet, you left. It seems odd to me. I assumed most people got drawn into such institutions and never left?' Seraph wanted to get the measure of him.

'It's fitting you should choose the word institution. That's exactly why I sought a new career. It afforded me an extraordinary lifestyle, a world of opportunities and discipline, and yet I felt constrained by it. I left because of that, but also really because I felt my purpose in life lay elsewhere, and I was right. Now, I'm lumbered with this.'

'We're both lumbered with it, but I've been chasing this mystery for what feels like decades now, and no substantial evidence has come along in all that time.' She put her jacket on and got up to stretch the lethargy out of her legs before sitting back down. 'You know, I always knew I would choose either one of two professions – detective or reporter. And guess why I didn't become the former? I would have been too constrained, as you put it earlier. Too bound by jurisdiction.'

Ryken was deep in thought for a few moments before speaking with mild gesticulation. 'Look Seraph, it almost seems fated now that I should meet you here. You can help me, with all your contacts and whatnot. Now you know my predicament, we might as well see what we can turn up together. I'm in danger, there's no doubt about it, but my biggest concern is getting to the bottom of this. That is what you do, isn't it? Get to the bottom of things?'

'Exactly. But aren't the research teams constantly shifting around? Ulrich said they would sometimes leave one lab at short notice, to go to another secret location, just like that.' She snapped her fingers and he raised his eyebrows as if in agreement. Then she had a thought.

'Wait a moment, I have an idea.'

She took out her Unicus and opened it up. She sent a message to the rascal: *Call me ASAP*. Within seconds, the screen flashed with *UNKNOWN CALLER*. Ryken waited inquisitively, and she pressed the answer button.

On the screen, she saw the obscured silhouette of a man who wanted to conceal his identity. He asked in a thick Caribbean accent, 'Seraph, me beauty, what can I do for you?'

In the background, she saw a virtual beach bar packed with holographic images of people holding cocktails. *He could be anywhere in the world*, she thought. She got straight to the point. 'I need you to get me the last known location of Mara Dulwich. I'm praying you'll say it was somewhere in the UK.'

'Me dear, why you need this info, girl?'

'Darling, you should know better than to ask questions.'

'Who you with girl? You got a blush across your face, and I know it's not me who gave you dat.'

Irritated, she commanded, 'Atlas, just get me the info before I fucking leap through the screen and grab your balls off.'

'Okay, okay, I'll see what me can scrub up. Catch you later sugar.'

'Don't disappoint me.'

She hung up and turned her attention back to Ryken, who was sat there in rapture. 'That wasn't who I think it was, was it?'

'Yep.'

'How do you know all these people?'

Nonchalantly she said, 'I guess it sometimes helps having a great rack. The only thing worth anything in this world is who you know, not what you know. Look how much we've discovered since finally crossing each other's paths.'

He suddenly didn't know where to look, and felt completely intimidated by her. He hid behind his coffee cup, and drank eagerly.

She got the message within a few minutes, and it read: *Drake's Cottage, Waterside, Stratford-Upon-Avon.*

She replied, *Thanks, you sure on this one? When was she last there?*

From Atlas: *Bout three day ago probly, her Unicus were there for sure cos it spiked the whole area. She go by codename the apprentice. Would know her anywhere. She has the fastest machine on the planet! Can't fake the presence her device creates.*

'Okay, he says she was in Stratford three days ago. What do you think? Shall we head there and see what we can find? You never know.'

'I don't see why not.'

With that, the pair made their plan to visit Mara and had gone their separate ways, in a rather formal business-like manner. Ryken went into the gent's toilets, saying he was going to climb back up to his room from a window that went outside. However, once he thought she had probably gone – he went back through the pub and through the airport to get back to the hotel via all the normal routes. Once back in his room, he was severely troubled. As he laid on the bed with his legs hanging over the edge, all he could think about was Seraph. Despite wearing bland clothing, hardly any make-up and no jewellery, she was the most beautiful woman he had ever come across. Luscious, wavy chestnut hair, alabaster skin, bright blue glacial eyes, full pink mouth and magnificent Amazonian figure. Rounded cheekbones, beautiful elegant hands, purposeful long nose and elongated neck. She was tall, slim, and yet had curves. She was womanly, and yet strong, with a scent of powerful coconut shampoo and fresh linen. Ferociously intelligent, and yet extremely feminine. She was so unlike most women out there who primped and preened themselves to within an inch of their lives. She was a miraculous specimen of womanhood, and the way she seemed so unaware of her beauty fascinated him. She exuded a spirit of depth that seemed to tug at something deep down inside of him; a kind of liveliness that made her body seem irresistible, the way it moved and communicated. He felt the need for a cold shower. *Get a grip man.* He quickly quashed those thoughts, pushing them to the back of his mind as he remembered there was business at hand. There were matters to be dealt with. *Pull yourself together*, he insisted to himself. *She is just some arrogant reporter who thinks there are no consequences to what she writes.*

CHAPTER 24

S eraph was running out of clothes and had been forced to spray some deodorant over her granddad shirt to liven it up a bit. When she met Ryken the next morning at 11am outside the rent-a-vehicle point in the airport, he was also nearly wearing the same stuff as yesterday but he had put on a V-neck brown sweater instead of the polo neck. They had decided the day before that they would take a hydro-car instead of going via public transport. They would not be able to talk freely if they went by train. This way, they could travel at their own pace. Plus, if there were any authorities after them, they hopefully wouldn't have had chance to tamper with any of the rentable vehicles, they figured.

Once they were on their way, having tapped Stratford into the navigation system, they got to talking. With the road and poly-tunnel fields whizzing by them on the ten-lane motorway, Seraph wondered aloud, 'Don't you think it's strange, even dare I say more than just a little bit fateful, that we ran into each other like that in the airport?'

'What do you mean?' Ryken took his concentration away from the wheel, letting the auto-driver system take over as he turned to look at Seraph.

'You know, you being who you are, and me being a reporter, a very well-known one who works for the only paper in the world that dares to investigate Officium. It all seems eerily set-up.'

Ryken got a bit defensive. 'Well, I didn't arrange it. All I know is that we met and now we're off on what is probably going to be a wild goose chase.' He was secretly trying to hide the fact that he was sat in close confines next to a woman he was becoming absurdly attracted to. She looked even better in daylight, with her crinkly, fiery tresses almost brushing his hand as she shook them about. He couldn't stop thinking about what it would be like to kiss her. He needed to find out so that he could relax.

Hah. Typical man. Infuriating. She offered, 'For someone who constantly works on the assumptions of theory, you're pretty pragmatic aren't you?'

'I'm not a natural scientist, that's true. I'm more of a let's make a plan and stick to it kind of guy,' he replied.

'By the way, I didn't set this up either, if you were wondering...'

'Oh, don't worry. It didn't cross my mind for a second that a woman such as yourself would throw herself across my path like that.'

'Keep trying, you know I won't give you the satisfaction.' Seraph looked straight ahead and ignored his goading remark.

He raised his eyebrows and let a few minutes of silence pass before enquiring, 'What makes you think Mara will talk to us anyway?'

'I heard she has affiliations with certain people I have connections with. You're better off not knowing.'

'The plot thickens...' He mused, before bravely venturing with a query. 'So, how did you and Ulrich meet?'

She sensed something behind that enquiry, but obliged him anyway. 'We both minored in ethical studies at NYU.'

'Why ethical studies?'

'I dunno. I suppose I had this romantic notion that journalism could be ethical, should be ethical, and needed to be carried out ethically.'

'So you're not really the person who bribes, beats up and even cons her victims with false affection so that they spill their guts?'

She was tired and ratty, having been kept up all night with nervous excitement at finally getting closer to the truth. She had also spent several hours reading every news article ever written about Doctor Hardy, and had read about the various acts of bravery he had performed in the army and the George Cross he had won for saving fifteen people from a burning bus during one of the London riots of the early 2050s. *He had to be a goddamn hero, didn't he? Ugh.*

She avoided looking at him and sniffed, 'If you think you can possibly psychoanalyse me, be my guest. Believe what you want.' She didn't like the person he was insinuating she was, but she didn't want to be herself either.

He knew she was volatile. He had heard the rumours from many different people, of how she could turn at a moment's notice. Her beauty was agitating him, and he felt like he wanted to affect her in return. 'What was it with Ulrich then? Sex? Or just intimidation?'

She kept looking away from him, tapping her foot against the dashboard and sitting on her hands to avoid punching his lights out. He was picking too close to the bone. Ulrich was still a raw subject. 'If you want to keep your pretty face intact, you ought to shut the fuck up Doctor Hardy.' She practically spitted out his name.

She maintained her gaze looking out of the window at the road ahead, but he was brave enough to persist. 'Come on Seraph, it might help talking about it.'

She breathed deeply and tried to ignore him. But she could feel the anger simmering, and she continued to stare into space as it began to overflow. 'Talking is bullshit. I only know about acting, that's all I know – acting the hard bitch to get a story, playing tough to force people into submission or being so unapproachable that assholes like you just leave me the hell alone.'

He was shocked by her severity. One minute she could be so nice, and the next she could turn into a psychotic harridan, spilling her acidic bile all over the place. He went silent, cowering in his seat, and he prayed she might just leave it there. However, just as she seemed to have gone quiet, she turned her whole torso to face him, and roughly grabbed his stubbly chin in her hand so he couldn't escape. She maintained his gaze from close proximity, and shot him a look that could kill. Her gaze was steady, as was her hand, and she viewed him with complete disdain. He had hoped that the first time he would look into her eyes like this would be in a more amorous situation, but he could see no feeling behind the windows of her seemingly non-existent soul. Her eyes ablaze, she goaded him with contempt, 'I know what you want Ryken, but I'm never going to give it to you. You men are all the same. None of you could possibly understand what makes a woman like me tick.'

He maintained her gaze, undeterred, 'Try me.'

His persistence knocked her off course, and she didn't know how to respond. She just wanted to rid herself of his questions. She threw his chin away and looked at the road ahead. 'Would it make you feel better if I just fucked you too? Well, you can just keep dreaming.'

'No it wouldn't make me feel better actually.'

Oh god, those shoulders of his. Jesus. She couldn't think straight.

'I don't have to explain my methods to you. You think that being a heroic army doctor is honourable. Wow, let's all congratulate you. Let's pat you on the back and give you a juicy fat pension at the end of your career. You ought to get inside my head and see some of the things I've seen. My job puts me in the thick of it with the scum of all scum. Some things simply can't be healed with a band-aid.'

'Seraph, I'm not your enemy, trust me. I really do want to be your friend.'

She couldn't handle his obstinacy, and desperately needed to silence him. She overrode the seatbelt mechanism and the vehicle computer started beeping with a warning to reattach it. She ignored the noise and launched herself toward him to straddle his lap. He didn't have time to react, but he could feel his pulse quicken. She barely looked him in the eye, and grabbed his face with both hands. She kissed him hungrily, chewing his mouth and tearing away at his lips. Her tongue fought frantically with his and he eagerly responded to her kisses, running his hands through her loose tresses. She pulled away and grabbed his groin roughly. 'What exactly is it you want from me, Ryken?'

He sensed her sudden malice and turned his face away from her. 'Get off me, Seraph.'

She saw the pity cross his features and was absolutely boiling with anger all of a sudden. She grabbed his face so he would have to look at her, and she said, 'I may do things that upset your idea of what a woman like me should be doing with her life, but do you know what? Everything I do is for a cause, and a good one at that. Call me a whore, or whatever you like. At least I don't do anything that I know will keep me awake at night. And judging from the bags under your eyes, your bloodshot eyeballs and false air of cool, I'd say there was something keeping you up into the early hours.' She smiled menacingly. In the daylight, she had got the measure of him. 'I'd say there was something eating away at you, something so terrible, that you can't even admit it to yourself, let alone anyone else. If you care about yourself even a little, you won't ever question me again, because I am one ruthless bastard Ryken, I'll freely admit that. I'll admit whatever you have to throw at me. I do what I do because it simply has to be done. The rumours about me are every bit true… and now the big man has been brought down to where he belongs.'

When she had finished her rant, he lowered his eyes away from hers, and she saw the look of astonishment on his face. She got up off his lap and threw herself back into her own seat. She turned her back on him to look out of the passenger window, spending the rest of the journey in silence. He was absolutely shocked by her crude behaviour. He didn't know how someone so beautiful on the outside could be so vindictive and callous on the inside. Perhaps she sensed the smidgen of jealousy he felt over her dalliance with Ulrich, but it wasn't his intention to arouse the demon inside her. He knew that she was absolutely right about him, however, but he hadn't realised he was such a bad actor.

CHAPTER 25

An hour passed before they arrived at Stratford-Upon-Avon. It was a quiet town surrounded by miles of unkempt countryside, but it seemed to have survived against the odds, even after most people had moved to the bigger cities. As they got out of their air-conditioned vehicle in a gigantic multi-storey car park behind a Supermarket4U near the outskirts of town, their lungs had to adjust to the air outside once more. A tinge of sewerage was in the air, as well as the scents of burger vendors, vile public washhouses filled with layabouts and a familiar stench pulsing from a nearby recycling centre.

'Same smell as York,' she muttered. He heard the remark but ignored her. Like her aunt's home, the former tourist hotspot was now a struggling recycling centre, but it was still a gathering place for theatrical talent.

As they wound their way through the streets, they saw huge apartment blocks dotted all about, as well as office buildings, Bed4theNites and Cafe4Us. People on the streets seemed to scarper indoors at the sight of the two recognisable giants wandering around the place.

When Seraph and Ryken walked through the centre and saw that Shakespeare's birthplace was still stood intact, if a little renovated, they were absolutely in awe. They had never seen anything like it before; mud-coloured outer walls, plate glass windows and misshaped oak beams. A relic that seemed to have been lifted straight out of another time zone, with even the gardens still maintained behind a six-foot-tall metal fence that looked as if it could be electrified. The place was still used as a museum, and after all these years, people queued outside to get through its doors. Following their tiff back in the car, the pair seemed to have calmed down somewhat, and their eyes met at the mutual understanding that somewhere like that was sacrosanct. To knock this down surely would have been total sacrilege. There was an unspoken agreement that they would have to put their personal feelings aside to get the task done.

She spotted a dispensary selling falafels and stopped to retrieve one, swiping her U-Card as she opened a plastic collection chamber, before watching as Ryken then took two for himself before devouring them rapidly. As they munched silently, they walked. Afterward she swigged on a pouch of water from her bag, passing it to him without thinking or speaking after taking her share. He eagerly guzzled the remainder down.

Seraph and Ryken followed the river past the theatres, which stood on either side of the street and were also amazingly still in operation. Shakespeare was still required; an interpreter of humanity's plight and an eternal necessity. They came to a house that was unmistakably Mara's. It was very much like Eve's bridal house, in that it remained intact and untouched by the dreaded developers who loved to turn beautiful old houses into bastardized versions of themselves. Mara's was a lone stone cottage looking out onto the River Avon, which though uncovered unlike the Ouse in York perhaps should have been, to prevent the local inhabitants having to watch rotten bits of detritus and old mattresses float by their homes in almost black water. The building had a small garden at the front separated by a narrow footpath, two large bay windows and a wide, blue wooden door in the middle. It was a sizeable property surrounded by thick ivy and hanging baskets filled with geraniums of various colours. The smell of the flowers almost managed to mask the stench of the river. Almost.

Seraph looked about the house to assess the situation. It looked inviting enough, but she had never actually met Mara in person, so she wasn't sure how she would react to strangers banging on her door. Her eyes met Ryken's and he said, 'We've come all this way, let's just risk it.'

He marched forward purposefully and pressed the old-fashioned buzzer. Then he quickly darted behind Seraph to leave the rest to her. She shot him a look that said, *Thanks a bunch.* They waited for a few moments, but there was no answer. She rang the bell again, but there seemed to be no life inside the house.

'Fuck. Maybe we should have called ahead after all.'

'Maybe we should,' he said.

She pressed her nose up against a wood-framed bay window peeling with paint to peer through the net curtains, but couldn't get a clear picture of whether there was anyone home or not. She moved a few paces to her right to stand before a gate at the side of the house, a tall wooden barrier between a passageway to the backyard she assumed. She chucked off her shoulder bag and held it out for Ryken to take. 'Hold this.'

He took the item and remained silent as he watched her step on to a shallow sidewall before launching herself over with ease. After a minute or so, he heard an almighty crash as she kicked her way back out to him, splintering the lock on the gate.

She grabbed her bag back and he asked, 'Really, was there any need for that?'

Angrily, she replied, 'There's nobody home, and the whole place has been stripped bare. This has been a totally wasted trip.'

He breathed heavily with disappointment, and as they stood there trying to decide what to do next, Ryken saw something out of the corner of his eye. Over Seraph's shoulder, on the street behind her, there were four agents sat in a parked car. They seemed to have a certain look about them, generic clothing and a stony demeanour. Ryken instantly recognised what they were doing there. He moved toward the reporter and tried to penetrate her eyes with the fear in his. He whispered, 'Run when I do.'

She recognised he had seen something behind her, and started to turn around to have a look for herself. However, he grabbed one of her elbows tightly to bring her attention back to him, and said, 'If we don't run, we'll be dead.'

She saw the fear in his eyes but didn't understand it. She guessed at what he had spotted and said, 'How many?'

He held up four fingers in front of himself.

'I thought you'd seen an army with that look in your eye. I'm not afraid of them.'

'You ought to be, trust me.' He was growing increasingly anxious, and she glanced behind herself to get a look. He decided to take control of the situation and grabbed her arm, pulling her with him out of the front garden of Mara's house and back the way they had come.

She tried to release herself but there was no escaping his grip.

'Seraph, I'll carry you out of here if I have to, but it'd be easier if you just fucking run when I do.'

He saw the agents had got out of the car, and he yanked her arm harder as he started to speed off, pulling her along with him. As they heard rapid gunfire ring out behind them, she suddenly understood Ryken's panic and pelted off with him. They ducked and ran, and Ryken pulled her down a side street on the left. They continued running as fast as they could, weaving from one cobbled street to another as they ran for their lives. Once they found themselves back in the centre of town, behind an old tobacconist's, Ryken felt satisfied they had lost them, and he motioned to Seraph for them to take a breath for a minute.

'This really is serious shit, then?' she asked.

'Yeah, and we need to get back to our car before they do.'

'Well, let's just get back then. I can handle myself, you know? Don't think you have to protect me.'

He laughed. 'Oh believe me, I don't.'

Just as they were starting to relax, they heard pounding feet somewhere in the distance, and they knew they hadn't lost their shadows.

'Shit,' Ryken said, 'we're screwed now.' He motioned for Seraph to follow him, and they set off again at speed, their lungs beginning to burn from the constant stopping and starting. They went further toward the edge of Stratford, twisting and turning from one residential street to another. Seraph looked over at Ryken to see if he knew where they were going, but his eyes were darting about as if he were madly searching for something. Despair was slowly starting to creep into her mind, knowing he didn't have a clue where they were heading, and they hit a dead end.

Ryken assessed their situation, desperately seeking a way out, but his mind was going into overload. He was turning red, almost beetroot. Seraph felt a drain lid under foot, and an idea hit her. She pointed to the ground and he knew what she was suggesting. He immediately started grabbing at the corners to pull the cover up, and together, combining their strengths, they managed to heave the lid open. Within seconds, they had both dropped into the sewer, and had replaced the entrance as quietly as possible.

They stood in near darkness, waiting for their pursuers to catch up with them, and a few moments later they heard the expected voices and footsteps across the drain lid above. Ryken seemed more unnerved than Seraph at that point, so she punched his arm and shook her head to prevent him leaping into action once more. They waited, in silence, and after the foreign voices up above went quiet, and the heavy footsteps had marched into the distance, they caught their breaths against the walls of the sewer and collected themselves.

Seraph tried to gather her thoughts, asking, 'Why did they speak in a strange tongue?'

Stooping to avoid banging his head, he shifted about as he explained in whispers, 'They have their own language, a secret code that only their kind can decipher. They operate outside of the law, they can navigate their way around the world unchecked, and they are trained, ruthless killers with only one purpose – to prevent secrets leaking out that pose a threat to their employers. Before the Ravage even, Officium began recruiting the strongest men and women for their own global police force. Experimental drugs and stem cell experiments made the agents almost physically superhuman. However, there were side-effects. They became unthinking, amoral creatures of particularly dark habits that followed orders because they knew nothing else. They protect these secrets because if they were exposed, they believe unwaveringly it would certainly spell catastrophe for the world as we know it. Honestly, you are better off not knowing what I know. I wouldn't want you burdened with the knowledge I have on these people. Knowing would only endanger you further.'

Seraph glared at Ryken with suspicion, 'I wonder how you know so much? You talk as if you were one of them. You're not are you? It would make sense though, given your background and the way you maintain your physical fitness.' She pointed at his hulking physique.

He looked demonic all of a sudden and a dark cloud seemed to gather over his head as his voice turned to a harsh tone, 'Well, why haven't I killed you already then?' The sewer shook with the reverberations of his defiant exclamation.

She also felt hurt and wanted to leap back out of the drain. 'I'm not an emotional person, but I'm starting to wonder why I even fucking bother! Coming to Stratford was just the dumbest idea I ever had. I don't know how I ended up in this situation. I should have just stayed in New York.' She was almost shouting and shielded her face with a hand to avert Ryken's gaze. The adrenalin was wearing off and the severity of their predicament was kicking in.

He tried to reach over and put a hand on her shoulder but she shrugged it off. 'Look, Seraph, I apologise. But I'm just as frustrated as you are. Maybe we both just need to get back home, don't we?' She looked at him and a moment of lightning passed between them. He felt an urge to comfort her but was afraid of provoking the wrong reaction.

'Yes. That's what Eve told me to do.' She looked around the sewer, facing the bleakness of the surroundings. Thankfully there was no sewerage at their feet, and she reasoned that it must be pumped elsewhere – probably to the poly-tunnel fields. However, the drain still had an awful smell about it, a dank stench, and it was completely dark the further you looked down the tunnel. 'So how do you suggest we get out of here? Will they be roaming the streets for us now, along with a load of others they'll have probably called up?'

'We can't go back to the car now. I think we need to stay underground for a bit,' he decided. 'Let them tire themselves out looking for us. We both need to turn off our Unicuses in case they're tracking us, and any other devices that they may be able to trace.' They both turned off everything they had, and Seraph noticed Ryken's Unicus with admiration – it was a heavy rectangular slab with a metallic silver coating. It probably had the capability of a supercomputer. After he turned it off, he popped something out from a cavity underneath it – a small torch. 'I had this in the army, if you were wondering.' He spotted her eyeing up the device. For some people, a Unicus was the only piece of individuality they could have in this world – including Seraph.

'So, shall we just see where these tunnels lead us?' Seraph asked, and Ryken nodded, leading the way into the darkness, with the light of his emergency torch illuminating the way.

CHAPTER 26

Some time later Ryken and Seraph managed to navigate their way out of the sewers, toward the outskirts of Stratford, where they emerged from beneath the ground through a drain cover in a barren field of dead earth. It was drizzling with rain and the air seemed to be highly oxygenised all of a sudden, and they felt light-headed. It was pitch-black, and the pair of them had no idea where they were, only that the town seemed to be far away. They could see the lights of the RSC's rooftop restaurant in the distance, glittering against the swelling River Avon, protected by great concrete flood barriers set against the almost indestructible black waters. The pair of them decided to start walking from where they had emerged, neither of them willing to take rest.

Soon, they found themselves picking their way between white, unlit poly-tunnels that were just bright enough against the light of the moon to show them the way. The ground underneath their feet was damp and boggy, making it much harder for them to travel on foot. They were both beginning to get breathless when they left a poly-tunnel field and arrived at what seemed to be an old tractor trail. They decided to follow it, hoping it would lead them somewhere. Neither of them had the energy to talk, they simply knew they had to keep going. They couldn't stop. Stopping would mean certain defeat.

They must have followed the trail for a couple of miles, and they ended up at Warwick, now deserted. People had left the ancient town for the seeming safety of the bigger cities. The whole place was in complete darkness, thankfully sheltering them from any chance of detection. They walked along the tarmac road, full of potholes, mud, grass and bits of rubble. They passed empty houses that were falling into extreme disrepair through total neglect. Seraph spotted something very sad.

'Oh my god,' she said. It was the first time she had spoken since they had left the drain. Ryken saw the same thing; the shell of Warwick Castle. The place had fallen into total ruin, a shadow of its former self, unloved and uncared for. The turrets were crumbling, the main tower was moss-covered and the grounds, probably once immaculately kept, were full of weeds, wild animals and rubble. Vast, geometric gapes were visible right along the walls; presumably the huge stones of the castle had found a new purpose as flood defences nearby. The pair walked up to the ruins and felt as though they were at a graveyard. They explored what was left of the place sombrely, utterly shocked that something once so obviously historically significant, was in a complete wreck. They imagined medieval re-enactments had once taken place there, of princesses being rescued by knights. It had ended up disused and unloved; it was so tragic.

The pair came to what appeared to be some old stables situated within the grounds. They went in, fell on some mossy earth, and shivered into some semblance of sleep, both absolutely exhausted.

While Seraph almost fell into a coma from fatigue with her back to Ryken, he couldn't rest completely. His adrenalin levels refused to go down, despite his crippling exhaustion, and he seemed to drift in and out of sleep all night. He kept his gaze in Seraph's direction, watching her sleep and checking she was still there, still safe.

It had knocked him sideways in the sewers, seeing that even she had tendencies to despair. His mouth had gone dry, his legs weak and his heart thumped so hard in his chest he thought she could probably see it through his shirt. He realised that he was quickly falling in love with this woman, Seraph Maddon. His heart, mind and loins had never agreed more on anything else before. When they were running from the agents near Mara's, he noticed the strength in her limbs as she ran, and the determination on her face. He knew that she was a woman to be reckoned with. A woman of spirit, intelligence and breeding, and something that was gradually sending him increasingly crazy. He lay there, thinking about the way her mouth moved when she talked, how elegantly her fingers twirled when she played with her hair when deep in thought, and the way her eyes danced whenever she deigned to look into his. When she jumped him in the car, he thought he had strayed into a dream. He had this goddess sitting on his lap, devouring his face, and yet he knew deep down that she was unwilling to really give anything of herself up to him. It was different with her. For the first time in his life, he wanted sex to mean more, and he needed intimacy. He just wanted to reach across and hold her while she slept. But, he didn't know how to get through to her. *What the hell am I going to do?*

CHAPTER 27

Light was creeping through the cracks of the stable's shell, rousing Seraph from her sleep. She awoke feeling dehydrated, dizzy and still utterly drained. Every bone in her body ached, and she winced as she stood up. She went to look outside after noticing Ryken seemed to be fast asleep still. He looked scruffy with his three-day stubble, and appeared about as comfortable as a horse trying to sleep sat on a bicycle.

He seemed to stir when he heard Seraph rustling about, but he wasn't sure if he was awake or dreaming. He'd had the most terrible night's sleep imaginable. He could hardly open his eyes, because if he did, he knew the nightmare would start all over again. Seraph went over and shook his shoulder, and a gruff moan was all the response he could muster. She shook him again, asking, 'Ryken, we need to get moving, don't we?'

He sat up this time, his eyes still slits, trying to block out any light that was breaking its way between the wooden slats. His head was pounding. He needed coffee, or anything wet for that matter, fast. He stood up and surveyed the scene outside. The derelict castle looked even worse in daylight, screaming out of a long forgotten, bygone age. He went round the back of the shed to take a leak, and Seraph realised what he was doing after he started to unzip even before he was out of sight. She would wait for more civilised facilities, she decided.

They started walking toward what used to be the centre of town, hoping to find something that might help them on their way. Walking past modern as well as Tudor buildings, they trudged through the litter, the rubble scattered here and there, and eventually stumbled across a vehicle sat in the remnants of a garage. It was an old Nissan Aura, a puny and pathetic little shoebox of a vehicle for the likes of Seraph and Ryken to be squeezing themselves into. However, it didn't seem like they had any choice. And amazingly, there were sterile pouches of water in the back. Someone had obviously abandoned the car in a hurry. They each took one and drank with the thirst of thirty.

Ryken tried to hotwire the vehicle, but it didn't seem to be ticking over. Seraph didn't have much faith of getting out of there that easily, even if Ryken's skills extended to mechanics too. The tank seemed to have a decent amount of fuel in it, so Ryken decided to peer under the bonnet, and discovered that the battery had simply been disconnected. He tinkered with the wiring for a minute, got back in the car, started it up and gestured for Seraph to get in. He said, 'I've worked on these old engines, if you're wondering, and it's a good job too, don't you think?'

Unimpressed, she sat in the chair uncomfortably, allowing the seat belt to pass over her arm, but feeling almost certain the vehicle would be the death of her. It was certainly a relic of another time, a jalopy of destruction she decided!

Ryken opened a map he had retrieved from his bag, saying, 'And they thought I was an idiot for buying one of these old things. People just don't think they can survive without their Unicuses, but sometimes you have to.'

Seraph knew she definitely couldn't survive without her Unicus, it was her link to the world. She had a thought and asked, 'Do you think this death trap could take us as far as London?'

'I don't see why not. What have we got to lose? Why London?'

'My aunt used to say the Ritz was the best place in England to get a bit of anonymity. They don't let anyone disturb their guests. And I mean *anyone*.'

'But our U-Cards would still give away our location when we check in.'

Seraph resolved, 'We just need to get there, that's all. I can't think of anything else.'

'Okay, but there's just one thing. After I bought my return ticket from New York, I had about 100ED left, so I'm broke. I'm clinging on by a financial thread.'

She looked smug all of a sudden and he asked, 'What? What is it?'

Seraph hadn't told him yet, but she decided this was probably as good a time as any. 'I'm going to be a millionaire thanks to my aunt, so don't worry yourself.'

Ryken eyed her curiously, trying to gauge whether she was shitting him. She looked at him with all seriousness, explaining, 'I'll have to find out when the funds are going to go through, but I'm sure I can hurry the probate along. Then we'll have no problem getting out of the country. But I think it'll be safer to call the lawyers from the hotel once we arrive there.'

'Err, yeah, agreed, okay then, let's get going.' He had to pause a few moments longer before driving off. 'Millions? From wedding dresses? No... fuck off.'

'It's taken me about three days to get used to the idea too. Welcome to my bizarre world.'

With that, Ryken drove off in a daze, using only deserted country roads and farm tracks. He would often look across at her still in disbelief, and she would nod, reminding him that she was indeed going to be someone worth knowing.

CHAPTER 28

They had spent most of the journey toward London inching across the landscape without having to hit a motorway. In this shed of a vehicle, they'd have no chance on a cruise-controlled motorway. They would be dead within seconds. They had just about made it to the outskirts of the London suburb of Watford, when the car spluttered and died. Ryken had not the energy to try to fix it. They could see the outskirts of the town anyway.

On the walk there, they realised they looked a bit too dishevelled and might draw unwanted attention to themselves if they didn't clean up a bit. Their shoes were filthy, their hair had bits of earth encrusted in it and their trousers were splattered with mud up to their knees. They snuck into the public loos to get washed and scrub down their clothes. Seraph went in the more private disabled cubicle and stripped off, splashing water on her face, underneath her arms and across her chest. She felt half-dead from walking through sewers, sleeping rough and traversing the landscape for miles and miles in darkness. She remembered having the funeral clothes in her bag still, and pulled on the cream lacy vest. After wiping the muck off her leather jacket, she chucked it back on. She knew there was nothing for it and discarded her black jeans before teaming the purple skirt with her slightly improved biker boots. The combination seemed to work.

After freshening up and smoothing down her clean-ish clothes, she went outside to see Ryken there already waiting impatiently. He noticed her new garb and smiled, but she pretended to ignore him. Feeling slightly improved the pair started heading towards the rail terminal in the town. It was a greyish, to-the-point kind of place, but it hadn't been as badly ruined as York had. A lot of the houses nearby had managed to stay intact, although even more had been packed in crudely wherever there seemed to have existed a bit of land spare.

Arriving at the station, Seraph decided whichever way they looked at it, they would have to risk using a U-Card. She got out hers and looked at Ryken, 'Look, we have no choice, we'll have to risk it.'

He reasoned, 'Yeah, but once we get into King's Cross, no doubt there will be agents waiting to pounce on us. It's futile. We could try to hide amongst the crowds, but we can't risk it. If we get caught, there really will be no chance of escape. No chance of getting out alive, even.'

Seraph paced about outside the station, wracking her brain for a safe course of action when a thought hit her. She had a scrambling device in her purse that the rascal had developed for her. She quickly began searching for it, and slipped it into her Unicus. 'They'll never trace this,' she smiled.

She had luckily memorised Camille's ID, so she keyed it in and pressed call. After several seconds, the bridal shop manager answered, appearing nervous on the screen, 'Hello?'

'Camille, it's me.' There was a blackout for a few moments, and Seraph asked, 'Are you still there?'

There was rustling on the other end, clunking about and then she came into focus and spoke, 'Seraph, I had to just go somewhere private. Your picture is plastered all over the news. They're after you and Doctor Hardy. You need to get somewhere safe and stay there.'

Seraph's hand went to her forehead in shock, and she asked, 'I don't understand, what are they saying we've done?'

'They are saying you're wanted for murder.'

Horror spread across Seraph's face. Ryken couldn't quite hear the conversation over the din of the crowds passing by them, and he impatiently waited for an explanation.

'Camille, you know…'

'Of course, you've done nothing. Where are you now?'

'Fucking Watford.'

Ryken sniggered at hearing her speak so dead-pan.

'Listen, I need the money and I need for you to call ahead to the Ritz for us. We're heading there now and need some special treatment, if you know what I mean?'

'Okay, I'll arrange everything. Get to the Green Park tube station. We'll be watching. Just be careful Seraph.'

After hanging up, Seraph told Ryken they were wanted. He reacted by hitting the wall and breaking the skin of his knuckles. He was so angry; he turned a violent purple colour. He exclaimed, 'We haven't done anything wrong!'

She tried to calm him down. Grabbing his arms and pulling them down by his sides, she looked him straight in the eye as if to betray her similar despair. 'We're basically done for, aren't we? We might as well risk the card,' she reasoned.

They checked the timetables, and found that there was a train to King's Cross in five minutes. That would be enough time to get their tickets and get to the platform. They went to the kiosk and as Seraph scanned her card, she did so very precariously, knowing such a simple action would have far-reaching consequences. She bought two day-passes, and a couple of tickets to other locations in the hope of confusing their pursuers. As soon as the tickets came out of the machine, they ran down to the platform. When the train turned up seconds later, they boarded, punching their tickets in as they went on. Ryken gestured for them to head to the back of a carriage, and they tried to look as inconspicuous as possible.

They held their breaths and kept a watch on the carriage doors throughout the journey; their hearts racing each time the train stopped at a station along the way. When a suspicious-looking character started wandering toward them, Ryken turned his body towards Seraph's in her window seat and said, 'Play along.' His knees touched hers and her eyes widened at his proximity. He grabbed her cheek and began kissing her intently before she had time to put up any protest. Before she knew it, his tongue was in her mouth and his other hand had slid its way under her skirt to grab her thigh. They both had terrible breath and his stubble grated. However, her blood started pumping around her body faster than ever before. He heard a slight whisper of a sigh as she relaxed and put her arms around his shoulders, allowing him to continue kissing her passionately. When he slowed down to plant a delicate butterfly kiss on her bottom lip, they eyed each other closely and she felt a tremor shudder through her. He suddenly pulled away, looking around to assess whether there was any danger.

She whispered under her breath, 'What the hell?'

He spoke gently as he looked ahead, saying, 'Thanks. I just needed to do that in case we wind up dead.'

She looked out of the window and muttered, 'Asshole.'

However, he smiled to himself, so happy to have found out that she really wanted him too.

As soon as they heard over the tannoy that the next stop was King's Cross, their thoughts turned to what they would face next...

London was the expected heaving metropolis of sweaty, agitated bodies crammed into as many tight spaces as possible. There was absolutely no population control there. The skyline was littered with dozens and dozens of tower blocks, skyscrapers and multiple recycling plants. Every other building seemed to be a food outlet, and most others looked like run-down washhouses. Room was so tight, that people could no longer afford bathrooms of their own, and had ended up having to use public baths to cleanse themselves. However, most of the establishments had turned into centres for drug-runners and small-time hoodlums to doss about in. Traffic jams were never-ending, black smog left the place in perpetual darkness, and the river clung to itself in a congealed cesspit of excrement and fly-tipping. *This was hell itself*, Seraph thought. They would be lucky to escape. Lucky to survive the radioactive abyss.

CHAPTER 29

It was late afternoon when they arrived at King's Cross. Ryken and Seraph headed swiftly to the Underground, praying nobody would be there waiting to pounce on them, and that none of their fellow travellers would recognise them from their mug shots.

They got to the escalators and filed to the right, keeping their heads bowed as they travelled down the white tunnel. Ryken had insisted Seraph stand in front of him, and he had a protective hand resting on her shoulder. Ryken suddenly couldn't resist the temptation to look behind them to see if they were being followed. Thankfully, he didn't see any appropriately suspicious-looking characters. Near the bottom, however, as they were just about to move off toward the platform to get on another train, he felt a looming presence behind him. The shadow of the person suddenly eclipsed his own, which was a rarity, and Ryken could almost feel the breath of the person on his neck. People on the Underground knew to keep their distance, there was escalator etiquette, and yet this figure was continuing to move in. For a split second, Ryken looked down at the step he was stood on and up at the one behind him, and he saw the feet of a man millimetres from his own, standing right on the edge. They were seconds away from the bottom, and he had to act fast. There was a train coming, and he saw his opportunity. He realised there was a shadow in front of Seraph too. A woman with an almost invisible ear-piece in, his twenty-twenty vision noticed. Ryken quickly positioned his elbow in place, concentrated his energies, and dealt a severe blow to the man's abdomen. Ryken swirled around instantly, catching the man as he was about to fall. They caught each other's eyes for a second, and Ryken knew for certain the man he had just winded was an agent. He could see the killer's senses going into overdrive in a bid to overcome his current predicament. However, Ryken was too quick, dealing another severe blow to the agent's groin with his knee, and draping the guy's crumpled body over the rubber handrail, gesturing to passengers behind them that he had probably had too much to drink. He turned back to Seraph, sending shivers down her spine as he pulled her hair away from her ear to whisper in it, 'Knock out that bitch in front of you once we get to the bottom.'

She turned to eye him, raised an eyebrow, then looked back at the woman and saw the female agent looking from side to side as she prepared for action. Seraph winked at Ryken and said, 'With pleasure.'

Once Seraph was about to step off the escalator she noticed the woman turn and look stupefied by the sight of her partner in a crumpled mess. Seraph took advantage of this brief moment of confusion, grabbed the woman by the shoulders, and forced her into the throngs of people swarming the platform as another train neared. She head-butted the woman in such close proximity and so fast that nobody would have seen it if they had tried, and as the woman began to fall unconscious, Seraph saw her being carried by the crowds in the direction of the exit at the end of the platform. Seraph felt Ryken's large hand grab her own, and the pair were pushed onto a train.

Once the carriage doors closed and they felt safe, Seraph and Ryken faced each other in close confines. They were pushed up against each other in the packed surroundings of the train. Ever so subtly, Seraph put one arm around Ryken's body and rested her head against him, relieved they had managed to escape. He took a deep breath as she did, feeling calmed as he went to cradle her with both arms wrapped tightly behind her back. He suddenly felt so protective of her and realised that being near her was all he needed.

Five minutes later, the two of them were spilling out of the carriage along with everyone else. They knew they weren't far from their destination; the Green Park tube station was only spitting distance from the Ritz once they were out of the Underground. This time on the escalator, they both ran all the way up, past dozens of passengers that were politely filed to the right hand side. They continued to use the crowds to their advantage once they were out into the open air, but it didn't appear as though they were being followed. Ryken had an idea. He stopped to talk to a naïve-looking young Rail Guard and asked her for directions to the Ritz, which was clearly just in the distance. She gave him the route generously, along with a warm smile that Seraph didn't fail to notice. When the crowds had pushed them all together, though, neither woman had noticed Ryken steal off with a tech-taser and stun gun. The woman officer had obviously been far too distracted by Ryken's smile.

Setting off in the direction of the imposing cream building, which they could see up ahead on the right, Ryken caught Seraph's hand and pulled her through the crowds with him. The smell of body odour, fast-food vendors, pungent sewers, warm diesel from the Underground – topped off with the scent of freshly-fallen metallic rain – proved an unpleasant distraction from the danger they faced. They weaved their way toward their destination as fast as they could through the throngs of people, not caring that they could be observed by anyone. A man even taller and wider than Ryken suddenly presented himself in front of them, blocking their way, but they continued to move toward him. Ryken's forthrightness assured Seraph that he had a plan, and that he wasn't afraid made her fearless too. Ryken loosened his grip on her hand and got out the tech-taser, using it on his opponent. Seconds later they swerved around the juddering body of the agent, and Ryken took the weapon back to set to recharge, ready to use again if they needed it. He gave Seraph the stun gun and instructed her to just aim and fire. She seemed only too willing to take the device, happy to get in on the action.

They were yards from the hotel entrance, and could see it all lit up ahead. They could see several opponents lining the entrance, perhaps a dozen in total, but they themselves had not been spotted. They obstructed the crowds as they stopped to look at each other in despair. There was no chance they could get past all of them. They had no idea what to do and stood there defeated, their chests heaving, bellies empty, heads dizzy with adrenalin. They were exhausted; emotionally and mentally drained.

Somewhere in the distance, Seraph heard her name being yelled out.

'Miss Maddon, Miss Maddon!'

Back towards the way they had just come, on the other side of the street, a large steel door had been opened in the alleyway next to a windowless, brick building. Seraph saw the voice was coming from a woman dressed in a uniform. She put two and two together, grabbed Ryken's hand and started bashing through the swarms of people to head for seeming safety. They had no other choice, and she was willing to take any chance she was given at that moment. They launched across the treacherously uneven road without even checking for black hover-cabs or hydro-cars. They rushed inside the door, and it was just slamming shut when they heard heavy footsteps running determinedly their way. The door closed with a reverberating thud, and a number of deadlocks automatically clunked.

Ryken and Seraph fell against the white walls of the corridor they found themselves in, breathing heavily with relief. Their minds were trying to catch up with their bodies, which had been running on a fight or flight instinct for the past twenty-four hours.

The woman, a petite blonde with doll-like features, went over to Seraph and helped her up. 'Seraph Maddon?' Seraph nodded weakly in response to the question. 'Kimberley Buck, assistant manager here at the Ritz. My husband Carl is the manager but he's a bit preoccupied at the moment. Can I just say, what a pleasure it is to meet a relative of Eve's, she was the most amazing woman, I can't tell you.'

'Uh-huh, I know you can't tell me… Listen Kimberley, right? We need to rest, we need somewhere to get changed and washed. We've been through hell to get here.'

'Well, it may not seem it but you're at the Ritz alright. You're in the private wing. Only our most distinguished guests get in through this entrance. You don't have to worry, those people following you have no knowledge of this part of the hotel. You're safe now. Anything you want or need is yours.'

Seraph seemed to have caught her breath and forced her heart to finally slow down. She looked over at Ryken who was just about coming to as well. They followed Kimberley as she led them down the dimly-lit tunnel. When Ryken pressed his hand against her lower back as they made their way through the maze, Seraph felt a jolt of electricity shoot through her system. She realised she was becoming powerless against it. After a few turns, they found themselves at an elevator. Kimberley gestured for the two of them to get in, and she followed. She took them to the fifth floor, and out of the lift into a richly-decorated corridor, with deep-pile green carpets and cream damask wallpaper. They were inside the private wing of the hotel, they reasoned. They reached a room with *King William Suite* written in gold lettering on the door and felt as though they were being accorded the greatest of luxuries. Kimberley pressed her thumb against a wall panel to open the door, and a computerised voice rang out, *Kimberley Buck, welcome.* The door opened and she led Seraph and Ryken in.

If only their minds and bodies hadn't been shot to bits, Ryken and Seraph might have actually been able to enjoy the lavish surroundings. They walked into a spacious drawing room with gold carpet, delicate glass chandeliers, an elegant writing desk sat in the far corner, two high-backed flap chairs at the bay window with sky-blue paisley upholstery, plus an impeccably polished mahogany furniture set of coffee table, side-tables and a tall semicircular console table on which stood a colossal porcelain vase containing a huge bunch of pink roses. Surrounding the coffee table in the centre were four smaller tub chairs matching those near the windows. The walls of the room were pure white with silver cornicing, and on a light-grey marble fireplace stood granite statues of a naked Greek goddess and her lover, suspended on one foot each as they pointed at the other from either end of the mantel piece, above which hung a grand mirror with a thick, gold-gilt frame. A sleek Reid-Sohn piano in dark maple sat just behind them in another corner of the room, open and beckoning someone to play it. In the background, there was classical music filtering through the rooms.

There seemed to be something strange about the windows and Seraph went over to find out they were fake – an image of a serene, active garden on a large flat screen made to look like a window. They must really be tucked away somewhere secret, Seraph decided.

Kimberley spoke, snapping Seraph out of her observations. 'There are clean clothes in the dressing room, fresh towels, a freshly-run bath, a small buffet in the dining room, and anything else you need can be requested with a call to me. Just say my name into the wall panel over there. Enjoy, and really, nothing is too much.' Kimberley left the pair, sensing they needed their own time. She closed the door, and then there was silence.

Seraph went into a dining room next door and found a gigantic oval-shaped mahogany table big enough to seat at least a dozen people. As she said, 'Wow,' her voice echoed around the room. She ran her hand over the crisp white cotton table linen, and saw there were two places set next to what was actually a rather large buffet. There were trays and trays of food covered by silver hoods. Behind the antique dining table were matching cabinets full of crystal glassware, plus a full dinner service of blue china with an intricate pink pattern. There was a cutlery case left open on a side-table, and some items had already been set on the table for them. There was also a large oak fireplace, set against a chimney breast covered in dainty floral wallpaper, with the rest of the walls having cream panelling. The material on the cushioned surfaces of the dining chairs matched the wallpaper, as did the curtains hanging in front of yet another fake bay window. Underneath the dining table lay what seemed to be a peach-coloured Persian rug, and sat on the fireplace was a solid gold, antique wind-up clock in a glass case that looked as though it was worth as much as a house. It was old-fashioned decadence. Seraph realised they would probably have no time to enjoy the luxury, though; they simply wanted to get out of their clothes and ultimately get out of there. She just needed time to think, and being there made their situation seem all the more extraordinary.

Seraph went back through the dining room door, then to the drawing room, and through there found the bedroom next to that. She found Ryken crashed out in the foetal position on a settee – a luxurious deep-filled, cream-coloured object that was pushed up against yet another fake window. He moaned as his body relaxed against the furniture. She watched him, and as his body fell, he slipped into an easy sleep. *Great, what am I meant to do now?* She sat on the queen-sized bed, and admired the carvings around the edges of the heavy bed frame – scenes of a garden party imprinted on the hand-carved mahogany wood, painted ivory. The decoration of the room was simply neutral, with lemon-coloured curtains and a shaggy cream rug covering the highly polished wood flooring. In the corner sat an antique French dressing table made from similar materials to the bedstead, with roses carved into the wood around the black metal handles of three drawers. On top of the item sat a triple vanity mirror so tall it looked as though it threatened to topple the whole thing, while underneath laid a leather-upholstered stool with more intricate rose carvings. The bedside lampshades were made of pleated silk in the same bright colour as the curtains. Seraph realised she had only ever encountered luxury like this once before – the Plaza. But this was something else. She felt the pure cotton comforter under her hands and realised it was also matching the other furnishings of the room – lemon with a fine pattern of blue daisies running through it.

She felt the urge to wake Ryken up and start bothering him, but she knew she needed a bath. She was desperate for one, so headed through to the en suite bathroom. The sizeable porcelain corner bath was opulently brimming with bubbles, and she could tell smelling salts had also been added. The room was completely tiled in Aztec patterns of sea blue, turquoise and silver, with intricate ornamental glass lights in similar patterns and colours suspended from the ceiling to light up the room and make it feel much like a cool, Mediterranean bathhouse. It seemed to be the perfect watery haven.

She closed the door and locked it, stripped off and submerged herself. Her body practically caved in on itself with the sensations of warmth, weightlessness and cleanliness. She leant back and tried to relax, but her head was full of the scenes of the past few days. She replayed everything over and over again in her head. She could hardly remember the kisses she had shared with Ryken, because every time their mouths met, she seemed to veer outside of herself. She treated him badly to spite herself; she was just so afraid of how he made her feel. She recalled being so overtaken the moment she had moved toward him on the train, drawn by the need to feel safe. She cringed as feelings stirred inside her, and she dunked her head underwater. Emerging from the depths with her hair sodden, she felt able to think more clearly.

There was a silver compliment basket by the bath, full of toiletries, so Seraph decided to go to town on herself. Once she felt her skin had been cleansed of the filth of the past few days, she emerged from the bath with bright skin, fresh hair and a purged soul.

Putting on an oversized robe and wrapping a towel around her head, she went back into the bedroom and saw Ryken still asleep on the settee, snoozing away happily like a child. She was starving, so went to the dining room and filled a plate with triangular sandwiches, tiny decorated cakes, savoury snacks and fruit salad. She also poured herself a large glass of white wine. After everything she had been through, she decided she deserved it. Sitting on a large antique dining chair at the head of the huge table she felt a little lonely and insignificant. Seraph had a penchant for woodwork, but these items of furniture spoke of a time gone by, a period of high skills and craftsmanship that had faded away.

Having wolfed down the food and drink, Seraph went for more. She picked at the food as she put it on her plate, and surveyed the scene out the window. Instead of the perfect garden, she tried to picture the real one it had substituted. She got lost, imagining looking out on a city covered by smog, a place so once full of culture that had ended up so burdened by making whatever it could of the few industries left in the world. It was so pitiful. This capital city would once have been so special to so many people, but was now just a slum to survive rather than live in. It was a crammed metropolis to merely exist in, to work in and feel lonely in. The only royal residence left was Buckingham Palace; all the others had been bulldozed for high-rises. Even so, the place was surrounded by a gigantic defensive wall, making it difficult to really see the building anymore. King William and his family were under constant protection from the threat of flu after Officium had decreed it so. No doubt, it was another of their ploys to keep hope at bay. The Parliament buildings were a shadow of their former selves, and the London Eye was at the bottom of the North Sea somewhere. Parks, gardens and lakes had been substituted for real estate developments, and the West End was more known for its gaudy comedic productions, rather than political drama, which people just couldn't stomach any longer. The Royal Albert Hall had been utilised in the same way as Radio City in New York, and had never been able to recover as a gathering place for musical and theatrical talent. It was used to host vast conferences of doctors and professors from across the world who gathered to discuss the latest developments in virus control.

Jolting her from her thoughts, Ryken was up and noticed Seraph had bathed. She asked, swinging a bottle in his direction, with a mouthful of food still, 'You want wine? You look like you need wine.' His face was grey with exhaustion, and a little rest seemed to have done him no good at all.

He shook his head. 'I don't drink. How's the food?'

She replied, 'Good, want some?' He nodded.

She went back over to the buffet and piled a plate high for him, playing mother. She took it over and he started devouring it.

'You slept then?' she asked him.

'Yeah, I didn't really get any kip at all last night. But I think my gurgling stomach just woke me up.'

'I emptied the tub. You'd have to run it again if you want a soak.'

'I'll have a hot shower when I'm done here.'

He devoured the food, and went up for more. After he finished, he rubbed his belly saying, 'I think maybe I might have just had a bit too much.'

She looked contemplative before offering, 'I'm sorry I treated you so badly in the car yesterday. But I have just buried my aunt.'

He thought he was hearing things but when he looked up to see her face had softened slightly, he believed it. 'I guess I shouldn't have pushed you so much.'

'Yes, you really should have known better.' She shot him a wry smile and looked almost shy even.

He looked down at the plate, and said, 'I'm sorry, you know, for dragging you into this. I didn't mean to rope you in or anything.'

She stared down at the table as she made her admission. 'Listen, Ryken, there's something I didn't mention to you… They came after me when I was in York.'

'Who did?' He looked up at her with concern, his eyelids peeled back.

'A couple of agents. I didn't mention it because I didn't know whether I could trust you.'

'How did you escape them?'

'A friend of mine took care of them. But that's not important. What matters is that they're after us both. We're both a significant threat to them, so we need to stick together.'

He nodded but seemed troubled by her revelation. He asked, 'Is there anything else I should know?'

She winked, 'All in good time, all in good time.'

He grunted and headed off in the direction of the bedroom. She heard the shower go on, and decided to find some clothes in the dressing room, a rather large antechamber to house a few rows of hangers. She found some plain white bedclothes and quickly threw them on. She went back into the dining room, sank a full bottle of water and double locked the hotel room door. She went into the bedroom and dimmed the fake windows. Intending to have a little rest, she got under the covers and exhaustion crashed down over her entire body as she fell into a deep, deep slumber.

CHAPTER 30

Seraph opened her eyes and an earth-shattering realisation hit her. She lay on her side with the covers pulled up right round her ears, and she dare not move for fear of having to face reality. In that waking moment, she felt so certain that Eve hadn't died. It was as if her aunt's spirit had still not left her.

Unfortunately though, she couldn't stop herself, because the more she woke, the more she remembered. They were stuck in London with seemingly no way back home. She hadn't really dreamt it all. Eve was still dead and buried, and she struggled to shake off the pain and disappointment that made her feel so bereft.

She tried to shift her body under the covers but there was a heavy weight on top of the blanket blocking her movements. She struggled to release herself from the bed, and she heard his breathing right behind her. It was Ryken, laid next to her. She whispered, 'Ryken, wake up… wake up.'

He shifted slightly, but only to tighten his arm around her body. His head also trapped her hair, and she was powerless to move. He breathed in the scent of her deeply and muttered dreamily, 'Seraph.'

Frustrated, she said loudly, 'Ryken, get off my hair!'

He lifted his head, pulled her hair from under it, and slammed his cheek back down on the pillow. He groaned and squeezed her tight again, gesturing for her to stay in bed with him. *How the hell did we end up like this? Was I drunk?* She checked and discovered she was still wearing pyjamas.

Ryken didn't seem to want to shift at all, and his vice grip around her torso wouldn't be released that easily. She decided to do the only thing she knew would definitely wake him up properly. She said in a mock-sultry voice, 'Ryken, I want you naked, I want you butt naked right now.'

He was immediately roused from sleep, and as he started to release her, she shook herself roughly from his grip and jumped out of bed, exclaiming,

'You're pushing your luck Hardy!'

She stood in her bedclothes, with dishevelled hair and grey bags under her eyes. Unimpressed, she flailed her arms around demanding an answer. The groggy but lusty look across his face only served to incense her even more. He sat up and she was so happy to see he was wearing pyjama bottoms. However, she was disarmed by the sight of his chest and abdomen, rippling with muscles and covered in luxuriously downy body hair.

'I just sort of crashed here thinking you wouldn't mind me sleeping in a bed next to you, given that we slept next to each other in a stable the other night. I thought in more convivial surroundings, you probably wouldn't mind.' Ryken shook out his own bed-hair and rubbed his forehead, trying to get rid of his headache. He asked, 'What time is it anyway?'

'Don't think you get out of this so easily.' She shot him another look, but stole across the room to look at her Unicus. 'It's 7:30. We've slept for fourteen hours. Shit.'

'Jeez, I don't think I've slept as long as that in my whole life.'

She sat on the edge of the bed, and he joked with a wry smile across his face, 'I can still get naked for you if you like?'

Standing back up, she said, 'Shut up Ryken,' and marched over to the bathroom and slammed the door.

A few minutes later, she came out of the bathroom in a robe to get a selection of clothes from the dressing room, and noticed Ryken was amusing himself with the buffet, apparently trying to discover whether there was anything edible left. He saw her on her way back to the bathroom and asked, 'Shall I order breakfast?'

She shouted, 'Sure, just get everything. I'm starving!'

Fifteen minutes later, she came out dressed in black leather trousers, brand new knee-high biker boots with multiple buckles and straps, and a grey polo neck jumper. She had let her hair hang loose and put a minimal amount of make-up on. She walked into the room indifferent to Ryken's impressed reaction to her appearance, and immediately headed for the food that had just been brought to the room.

Ryken was dressed already too. He was wearing dark green corduroy trousers, a black V-neck jumper and brown leather walking boots loosely laced. She eyed the corduroy, winked and nodded at him. 'I see they chose the type of clothes they imagine you wear.' He ignored her remark about his "middle-aged scientist" clothing.

They sat at the large table to eat, and he remarked, 'The food turned up pretty quick. And the clothes. They somehow seemed to get our sizes pretty spot-on.'

Pouring herself coffee, she pierced a sausage with her fork and bit through it as she nodded indifferently in response. She walked over to the coffee table and retrieved her Unicus. Switching it on, she continued to eat and navigate the news networks.

Her eyes lit up and she looked across at Ryken, who didn't seem surprised when she said, 'The jets are off the ground?'

'I know. I checked the news earlier.'

'Why didn't you say? We can get back now.'

'And how might we do that? Given we're the country's two most-wanted people, and as soon as we get within five miles of an airport, we're more than likely to get caught!'

She grabbed her coffee cup and stood up to stare out of the hotel room windows, just as she would do in her own apartment if she were there that morning. She glanced over at Ryken, grinning as she said, 'Oh ye of little faith.'

He still didn't know about her connections...

She sat back down at the table, took a slice of toast and ate a corner of it, speaking once she had swallowed. 'We got here didn't we? Stop being so defeatist *Mr I Need a Plan*. Look, I need to make a call, forgot all about it last night. Let's not panic until I've spoken to my friend.'

Seraph went into the bedroom for some privacy and dialled the number. Camille answered, 'Hi Seraph, did everything work out alright at the Ritz?'

'Yes, we're still here but we need a way out. Do you know anything about the funds going through yet?'

'Oh, yes, I got them to hurry things along. The money should be going through today, it might even be in your account already.'

'Oh, terrific! That's great. That's fabulous. Thanks Camille.'

'Listen, Seraph, just get back to New York won't you? Get back and stay low if you can. I can only help so much, my hands are tied if you know what I mean.'

'Yeah, I will call you once this is all over.' And just as she was about to hang up, Seraph said in a serious voice, 'Camille, sorry I left York without a proper goodbye. And thanks, thanks so much for everything.'

'No problem. Oh, and Seraph, have you finally found that tall, dark mystery man we were talking about?'

'Oh hell, Camille, if I have to come back up there just to shut you up...'

Camille could barely contain her giggles. 'I can see it written all over your face.'

'Goodbye Camille. I'll deal with you later...'

Seraph and Ryken had polished off toast, fruit, coffee, orange juice, tomatoes, bacon and sausage. With their stomachs full, they were ready to make a plan of action. Seraph had picked up the message from the accountants, informing her funds amounting to 2,565,001 ED had been deposited in her designated bank account. Seraph checked her account, and showed the balance to Ryken. He asked, 'So how do you suggest we get back home Richie Rich?'

'I have an idea…'

She headed to the wall panel and spoke directly. She asked Kimberley to come to their room if she could, and in less than two minutes she was stood there with them.

'So, what can I do for you? And may I say, you both look so much better this morning. I hope everything was to your satisfaction?'

Seraph got straight to the point. 'Everything was perfect, thanks. But we have quite a large request to make now. We need a private jet chartering for the two of us to get back to New York. As you've probably realised, we're in a bit of a fix and we need some help getting to the airport too.'

Kimberley seemed to flush slightly in the face, pursed her lips and began, 'Miss Maddon, there are a lot of complimentary services we would extend to you, but I'm not sure…'

Seraph sensed it might be a matter of money. 'I have funds Kimberley. Money is no object here, whatsoever. I just need you to get us out of here safely, in any manner possible, and charter a jet for us. Can you do that for me?'

Kimberley seemed to be weighing things up in her mind for a few moments, and then decided, 'I don't see why I can't accomplish all those things. I'll just need you to transfer some funds for me when I've found you some transport.'

'That's marvellous, no problem at all. That will be fantastic Kimberley.'

The hotel worker turned to walk back out of the room, and said before leaving, 'Can one of you handle a motorcycle?'

Ryken perked up, and waited for Seraph to reply, but when she didn't, he proudly said, 'Yeah, I can.'

'Great. I'll get a member of staff to get my husband's out of the garage for you. It'll be the fastest way to get out of here. You will be able to leave via a secure exit and get to the airport within ten minutes.'

Ryken finally felt he had a part in their escape, what with Seraph and her massive bank balance calling most of the shots. He would have the important job of getting them to their flight and hopefully back home to some sort of safety.

CHAPTER 31

Having spent the past couple of hours trying to use their time as wisely as possible, with Seraph going through the vast amounts of messages in her inbox, and Ryken planning the route to Thames Airport, they were sat there expectantly – waiting for Kimberley to give them the news they were desperate for – that they could finally get out of there. Seraph had fired off a few memos to colleagues, as well as her lawyer in New York and her boss, but she knew that once she got back, that's when she would really have to deal with everything. Meanwhile, Ryken had loaded up the navigation centre on his Unicus to determine which of the various routes to the airport would be quickest, safest and least likely to bring them anywhere near Officium's reach.

Seraph was sat on the bed propped up with various cushions, while Ryken sat with his arms stretched across the back of the sofa. They felt uncomfortable in the other rooms, certain they might break something if they stayed in there.

'So, are you sure you know which way we are going? Recite it to me again.'

Ryken rolled his eyes. 'Seraph, have you forgotten what I used to do for a living? I know okay, don't worry. You can leave one thing to me, alright?'

'Sorry, yeah, okay.' She got up to pace about. 'It's just that, I feel a total fish out of water in this country. In New York, I feel secure. I mean, my life is pretty crazy there, but I still feel like I have some sort of control. Here, I feel totally ill at ease, and that was even before those freak-shows started chasing us.'

'I got the feeling you have some issues with control.'

'Pardon me?' She gave him that look again, a glare that warned if he said the wrong thing that was another cross against his name in her book.

Apprehensively, he said, 'You know what I mean. Unless you're in charge, you're not interested.'

She grew defensive, but more than anything, she realised she had started to care what he thought of her. 'I can't churn out the stuff I do without going it alone most of the time. I'm self-sufficient, independent and totally untrusting of everything and everyone but myself. It's how I survive. I can't suddenly change overnight.'

She walked to the window, looking out intently with her arms folded. He got the feeling he had touched a raw nerve, but this was something he wanted to pursue. He wanted to get under her skin and find out what really made her tick. He looked up at her stood near him and asked in a deliberately and annoyingly nonchalant tone, 'Surviving? Is that what you call it?'

She turned to look at him, saying, 'I know what you're doing. I warned you before about testing me. I'm trained to know what you're thinking even before you do.' She pointed at him, continuing, 'Listen to me, I see everything around me in perfect clarity, and that's why I live like this. It's because there is no happy ending, there is no fairytale in this world, and there is only the truth. And that is what I spend my time trying to find. I think it's time spent very wisely, actually, and I'll do whatever it takes to get to it. I'm the one given this responsibility, because no-one else can do what I do.' She stopped, almost breathless from speed-talking, and crossed her arms again in defence. He didn't seem to have any reaction to what she had just said. He was sat there motionless just taking it all in apparently. She sat back down on the edge of the bed, arms still folded, and looked down at her lap to avoid his gaze. She didn't want to give herself away too much, but she feared she already had. Looking him in the eye would spell certain doom for the hard exterior she cloaked around herself daily. She bit her lip to stop it trembling, and she willed herself to fight the emotions creeping across her face.

Ryken started to get up to move toward her, but she raised a hand and turned her face away from him. She warned, 'Ryken, you saw what I did to that woman yesterday, I don't think you want that for yourself, do you? Don't come any closer.'

He desperately wanted to get close to her, to comfort her, show her how he felt, but it seemed like this definitely wasn't the time. He sat back down, but decided to let her know he would not be completely defeated. 'I see you better than you see yourself too, Seraph. I think you are the most extraordinary person I've ever met. And as of a few days ago, I decided that I'll be here as long as necessary, waiting until you decide you do need someone. I'll wait as long as it takes, and I'll be in your life in whatever capacity you want me.' He spoke passionately and with vigour, rapping his fist against his knee, but she continued looking away. She smiled inside, but her cold exterior didn't give her away. She wasn't about to waste years and years of surviving on her own, just to give it all up to some man who would no doubt let her down in the end. Once all this drama was over, he would soon realise his feelings had been conjured up by the extreme nature of the situation they were facing. She couldn't risk letting her coping mechanisms slide, only for him to decide one day, that he didn't really want her.

Seraph stood up sharply and went into the bathroom, slammed the door, and fought the mixture of emotions washing over her, holding her head in her hands as she sat on the closed toilet lid. Everything was starting to catch up with her, and he was only making things worse. Her mind was a junkyard of jagged memories and cracked reflections that revealed the person she really was, the person she was continually burying deep down inside of herself all the time. The person who was so lonely, so heavy with the weight of responsibility she carried, and secretly so unhappy at not having someone there to pick up the slack when she needed them.

Ryken's presence alone made her heart beat faster, her mind cloud over and her soul soar. She was frightened of what she felt, but she was beginning to realise more and more, that she couldn't be without him. They hadn't talked about what they had been through as such, but they could see it on each other's faces, and it bonded them more than anything else ever could. She would have to face her feelings sooner or later, but that would mean having to admit so many other things simultaneously.

Ten minutes later there was a knock at the door. Ryken got up to answer it, while Seraph made herself presentable in the bathroom. It was Kimberley. She walked in without pleasantries, and Seraph jumped back in the room within a flash, ready to get out of London as soon as possible. She avoided Ryken's eyes, knowing that a simple glance gave her away far too easily. She would prefer to deal with all the agents in the world, if it meant not having to face his steely stare.

Kimberley was holding her Unicus, and had it open and ready. Seraph noticed her gadget was a red number in the shape of a sea shell, with magnetic pearls as the fastening. *Nice*. Kimberley explained, 'I've managed to acquire you a jet. They are preparing it for you now at Thames Airport. You need to be at hangar thirteen, on the south side. You'll just have to wing it when you get to the security barrier.' With that Ryken began highlighting on his map to Seraph where that was, and nodded at Kimberley, who continued, 'The bike is ready in the delivery area. I have to warn you though, there are agents surrounding the entire hotel and all buildings in the vicinity. They know you are here somewhere and they are not prepared to give up easily. My husband and I have done all we can to keep your whereabouts secret, but as the managers of this place, we can't protect you once you're out of here. Now listen… Seraph, I need you to just key in your bank details here so I can arrange the funds for your flight.'

Seraph was highly impressed by Kimberley's logistical skills and reasoned that being the manager of such a hotel must require such organisation and resources. She stood up to take Kimberley's Unicus, and keyed in her details, watching as 166,013ED was transferred from her account. 'Thanks Kimberley, that's a bargain for passengers like us. Listen, this is really good of you. I just wanted to ask you one thing, you and your husband, how did you meet?'

Kimberley's look said it all, but to confirm Seraph's suspicions she said, 'Eve.'

The pieces of the puzzle were falling into place, but Seraph didn't have time to arrange them all yet. She needed to get back to Manhattan first.

Kimberley took back her Unicus and waited for the transaction to clear, before motioning for Ryken and Seraph to get themselves ready. They put what few belongings they had in their bags and slung them over their shoulders. Ryken and Seraph gave each other a look to say, *Let's get this over with*, and followed Kimberley out of the room. 'I'll take you down to the delivery point and you can make your escape from there.' Locking the door behind her, Kimberley looked each of them in the eye and said, 'Once you get out of here, don't stop until you're on that jet.'

CHAPTER 32

They piled in the elevator, all three of them, in complete silence. With Kimberley stood in front, Seraph linked her fingers through Ryken's, and he squeezed her hand in return. She saw a small smile creep across his face as she glanced at him sideways. The lift doors opened and they entered the tunnel they had been in yesterday. This time, however, Kimberley took them further under ground and when they heard vehicles whooshing across the roads above them, they assumed they were heading toward the main building of the hotel. After making a few more turns and taking a flight of stairs upwards, they were in a small warehouse of sorts, housing foodstuffs, linen, uniforms and all manner of housekeeping equipment. Kimberley led them unnoticed through a throng of busy workers rushing about, and they arrived at a semicircular loading bay, where a couple of large vans were parked up. The bike was there too, parked up in all its glory between the two delivery trucks. It was a Hellion Inferno, possibly the fastest, most dangerous domestic bike in the world, running on super-electricity and petrol, with a recorded top speed of 300mph, 12,000cc and an infamous booster button. The bodywork was black with purple flames running along the main cavity. The tyres looked brand new and ready to burn. The carburettor was the size of an elephant's trunk, and the triple exhaust glistened against the lights overhead. Ryken could hardly contain his joy, mouthing *Fuck me*. He had always wanted to ride one but had never had the money or the time to. Then he suddenly realised, *I'm going to have to do this now, aren't I?* And Seraph would be there with him if he mucked it up. *Shit.* The adrenalin began pumping around his body, and he tried to place himself in a robotic mode of thinking, of simply acting and reacting. *This can be done*, he thought, *we can outrun anyone or anything on this. And like Seraph said, we are being protected somehow. Somewhere, someone is looking after us.*

He grabbed a jacket from the bike, threw it on, along with gloves and helmet. He took it off the stand and felt the weight of it. It was a beast. He got on and started up the engine. He revved it several times, and acquainted himself with the controls as he heard it growl and purr at his touch. He really did feel like he was dreaming all of a sudden, as if he had strayed into the craziest possible scenario his mind could fathom.

When he was ready, he gestured for Seraph to get on too. He watched her hug and kiss Kimberley and the pair say their farewells, and was struck by her hidden affectionate side. Seraph tucked her wild mane underneath her jacket, zipped up, gloves on, helmet on and positioned herself behind Ryken on the bike. She had once vowed never to get on one of these death-traps, but there was no choice. Ryken showed her where to put her feet and gestured to the hand holds at the back. She motioned when she was ready, and Ryken revved the engine. Kimberley nodded at them as she took the controls for the warehouse doors to open, and he sped right up to them as they were being raised. Seconds later, they were out of the loading bay, down a very narrow empty street that led out on to a main road – a one-way carriageway. They stopped at a junction up ahead, and Ryken kept his eyes flickering from mirror to mirror while they waited for the traffic lights to change. Meanwhile, Seraph curiously eyed passers-by who must have never seen a bike like this before because they were staring intently. However, they weren't distracted by them…

Willing the lights to change, Ryken kept peering around to catch sight of any possible followers. As he turned his head slightly to check his blind spot, he caught sight of the passengers in the vehicle that had just pulled up next to him. There were two of them, each dressed in full bullet-proof clothing, each holding guns. They were looking right at him. *Bollocks*.

He quickly checked the road ahead, saw the lights were still red, but decided to hit the acceleration. Seraph hadn't expected him to shoot off like that and knocked against the backrest with a blow, before slamming her chest right up against Ryken's back as he changed gears rapidly. She threw her arms around him for stability, and they shot off even faster down a dual carriageway. He weaved in and out of vehicles, braking hard, accelerating harder, hitting the clutch over and over as he madly tried to steer the bike – and themselves – away from danger.

Seraph looked back and saw the white hydro-car chasing them, which had a siren screeching on the roof. She saw the people inside – their blank faces – and knew instantly who they were. She turned to grab hold of Ryken tighter, and she closed her eyes. She couldn't deal with this. She just needed to trust he was going to get them to safety, but closing her eyes only made her feel sick with the power of velocity.

They jumped several red lights, left several old ladies shouting when they failed to stop at crossings, and caused two vehicles to collide when they swerved to avoid their bike. Ever still, Ryken twisted the acceleration to its full capacity, forcing the engine to its limits, pulling the handle as fast and as hard as possible. He worked the bike to its maximum, but still couldn't get to a stretch of road where they could really see what the machine could do.

Then he saw the signs for the Thames Airport Ring Road and breathed a small sigh of relief. They weren't too far away. However, there wasn't just one car following them now, there were three or four, including two official police cars. There was traffic up ahead, blocking their way to the ring road, and Ryken could see only one solution. He rammed the pavement, sending the bike into shock, and shot off past a gang of youths loitering on the curb. They didn't even have time to get a look at the object that had just whizzed by them.

Ryken pressed the horn, alerting people to move out of the way. He constantly had to brake, accelerate, brake, and accelerate, and there was smoke from the tyres billowing out from underneath them. Looking behind them again, though, Seraph saw that the cars were trapped behind the traffic and had no way of getting through. She squeezed Ryken's waist and he looked behind to see the same thing. The pair smiled at each other through their helmets.

Coming to the end of the pavement, they reached the junction for the ring road and zoomed off, neglecting to check for oncoming traffic as they headed east. They left the swollen, graffiti-ridden neighbourhoods behind, knowing they had to simply keep going. Ryken sped up a suspended ramp towards the motorway, revving the engine repeatedly to ensure it was warmed up enough for what he was about to do next. They saw the ten-lane road was heaving, but that wouldn't matter to them on their chosen vehicle. They swerved in between cars that were queuing to join the jam-packed highway, weaving their way in and out. Ryken headed towards the hard shoulder, and checked the path up ahead. It was clear. He did something he had always wanted to. He hit the booster button and they screamed off, as the bike immediately changed up to eighth gear by itself. Within seconds, they were travelling at 180mph. Ryken still needed to be able to brake within a good distance just in case an obstruction presented itself. Seraph held on to Ryken, scared out of her wits, feeling as though she was going to perish at any second.

Within minutes, they pulled off the motorway and took a single-carriageway bypass to the airport. It was empty, presumably because the Sky Jets had only just started flying again. And so, they sped along at a steady 70mph down the road, sure they had lost their tails. Just when they had dared to entertain that thought, a light helicopter came flying overhead. Menacingly, it hovered right above them, and a gunman opened a door of the craft to aim directly at them. This time, Ryken would definitely need to open up the bike to its fullest. He shouted back at Seraph, 'Hold on,' and as she gripped his body tightly, he hit the button again and accelerated, accelerated, accelerated, until they hit 272mph. Seraph shielded her body behind Ryken's, which she imagined was taking a huge battering from the G-force. They weren't wearing full leathers, but it hadn't seemed that important earlier, they'd had more pressing things to worry about. Ryken's strength was being tested to its fullest, as he tried to hold the bike as steady as possible with the pair of them on it together. It took every muscle in his body to maintain control. Thankfully, the helicopter struggled to match their acceleration.

Soon, he saw the airport in the distance. It spurred him on to keep going. When they were seconds away from their destination, he slowed the bike down, and it seemed to whirr unhappily at being forced to decelerate from its maximum speed. As they approached the barriers of a checkpoint, Ryken shifted his weight back dramatically while Seraph desperately tried to cling on as he applied a blast of acceleration and flicked up the front wheel to send them crashing through. A guard stood at his post hardly had time to react to them screeching by, while Seraph's heart pounded in her chest with shock and amazement as they touched down again. Ryken headed for their hangar, which he knew was the third one along on the south side. The place was eerily deserted. They came to a halt outside a small jet, which was already fired up and ready to go. The stairs up to it beckoned them to board, and Seraph leapt off the bike, which Ryken parked up quickly. He dumped his helmet on the seat, as did Seraph, and just as he was about to make off to the jet, he turned back to kiss the motorcycle on its front, saying, 'Thanks.' The pair of them ran the few yards towards the jet, still in their leather jackets and gloves, and jumped the few steps as quickly as possible. A flight attendant was there, and shouted over the engines, 'Ryken and Seraph I presume?' They nodded and got on, helping to pull the aircraft door shut. The cabin assistant, a man of about twenty, shouted loudly in the direction of the cockpit, 'Go!'

The plane started moving, and Seraph and Ryken remained standing as they looked out of the cabin windows to see where the helicopter was. They couldn't see it, but they could hear it, even over the jet's engines. It must be right above them, they realised.

The young attendant ordered them to sit down and strap in, as did he, and the plane made a turn towards the runway. The pilot took the aircraft to the top of the runway, ready to jet off, but the helicopter landed in its way. Figures jumped from the helicopter and started walking in the direction of the aircraft, holding Harbinger-class bazookas in their hands. Seraph and Ryken saw dozens of cars with sirens all speeding up toward them too. They felt sure that they were facing total defeat.

Outside, however, the shadows seemed confused all of a sudden, looking around wildly, trying to determine where the craft had gone, it seemed. The cars all stopped too, and people got out, looking madly to see where the plane had disappeared to. It seemed that it had vanished into thin air.

Inside the craft, Ryken and Seraph were unsure what was going on, but they were happy to see the plane slowly and quietly navigate its way around the helicopter, squeezing past it, so that it was pointed down the runway again. They heard the engines roar, louder and louder, until the pilot released the brakes and the craft sped off down the runway. Seconds later, they were soaring up in to the sky, higher and higher.

Sat back with their eyes closed, relieved to finally be getting back to New York, Ryken and Seraph breathed deeply, trying to calm themselves down. The seatbelt lights went off, and the flight attendant got up to fetch them a glass of water each. He offered them, and they were taken gladly. He spoke in a brilliantly eloquent British accent, 'We should be safe now. Safe all the way to New York.'

When the aircraft seemed to level off, having reached its desired height in the sky, the door of the cockpit started to unlock, and the pilot stepped out. Ryken saw her first, and then Seraph, who blinked several times to see whether her eyes were deceiving her. They knew her instantly from her website pictures. It was Mara.

CHAPTER 33

Mara stood just outside the cockpit door looking at Seraph and Ryken. She said in a rather educated tone, 'May I introduce you to my son Lucius? Lucius, this is Seraph and Ryken, as you may have gathered. We're at 48,000 feet now, and we should reach New York in about one hour, fifty minutes' time.'

Lucius, a gentlemanly looking fellow with dark features similar to his mother's, simply saluted the pair. Mara nodded for Lucius to go up front to the cockpit.

Seraph stared at the woman, a lady of about forty-five or fifty, and realised there was something about her she had never spotted before. She was wearing pink leather sandals, and an ornately embroidered purple kaftan over white linen trousers. She had long hair, black in colour, brown eyes, a tall athletic physique and a slight patch of freckles across her nose and cheeks. She stood confidently, with her hands clasped around each of her elbows. Then, as she smiled at Seraph's observations of her, the younger of the pair saw it. Eve's smile.

Seraph stood up out of her seat, and she began to shake, while her stomach seemed to have been left behind on the ground. It was as if she were looking at a ghost. She held one hand over her mouth, and Ryken remained in the background wondering what the heck was going on.

'Why do they call you *the apprentice*?' Seraph asked, almost choking on her own words.

Mara smiled confidently. 'I think you know. Camille taught me everything she knows. In my line of work, I learnt long ago that the only person I could rely on for protection was myself.'

Seraph walked up to the woman and paced around her, surveying her as if she were a waxwork model. She walked over to her seat to rummage in her journalist's bag and retrieve the wedding photo. Mara continued smiling as Seraph held the photo up to compare the faces, before handing the image to the lady.

Mara said, 'Didn't Mum look lovely?'

'Oh my god, you're my cousin?'

'Yes!'

Seraph covered her face with her hands in shock. Her eyes were already stinging with tears when Mara held out her arms for her. The women threw their arms around each other and held one another tightly, while Seraph cried loudly and unashamedly, saying, 'You're the mirror image of your father.'

Mara spluttered out, 'I know,' before continuing to cry herself.

Ryken observed the touching scene and could have almost shed a tear or two himself. Mara pulled away from Seraph to hold her cheeks in her hands, 'I always wanted red hair like Mum, but you seem to have been gifted with the recessive gene.'

The pair laughed at each other through bleary eyes, before continuing to hold one another.

Seraph asked, 'Why, why did we never meet before? Why did Eve never tell me about you? About your father?'

The two women stood back from one another, but Mara continued holding Seraph's hand. She began, 'There is so much to talk about my love, a lot to talk about indeed.'

Ryken suddenly piped up, 'Erm, ladies, I'm still here.' He waved at them, and Mara left Seraph's side to walk over to him. He stood up and she held out a hand for him, eyeing him up with a regard of respect.

'Doctor Hardy, we finally meet.'

'Professor Dulwich, a pleasure. So, what was all that on the runway then? How did we get out of there so easily?'

'Oh that,' Mara said, 'We have mirrors hidden within the hangar. The agents couldn't see us once they'd been turned in place, making us seem invisible all of a sudden. It's an old trick really. Listen Ryken, Seraph and I have a lot to discuss. Perhaps you might give us some time to speak alone?'

'He's okay Mara, he can stay, I trust him. We may as well just tell him that your mom was the dressmaker.'

At this mention, Ryken's eyes widened and he seemed to go into shock, trying to cover his reddening cheeks with his hands. He sat back down and absorbed the revelation, knowing what it meant. He asked, 'The head of RAO?'

Mara nodded and shot him a knowing look, while Seraph remained on the periphery, totally unaware of the knowledge they shared. Everything was suddenly slotting into place for him.

Seraph sat back down next to Ryken, while Mara sat in one of the two seats opposite them, and began to explain.

'Seraph, my father was known as Stephan Dulwich, but his real name was Tom Bradbury. In 2023, my mother signed his death certificate, but the body was not my father's. It was his colleague's Stephan's. In the ensuing chaos of the flu, Mum and Dad used the confusion so that he could assume a new identity. I was nine years old at the time, and I have some vivid recollections of what happened. The devastation is imprinted on my brain. Unless you went through it, you could never really understand. The looting, panic buying and gang wars. The bodies lining the streets, the doctors struggling to treat hundreds of thousands of patients, hospitals crammed full of victims, a country and a world weeping and wailing over a seemingly unexplainable tragedy. But there are a select few of us who know what really happened. The best person to explain is my father.'

Astonished looks passed between Seraph and Ryken, when Mara started to pull a memory stick out from a pocket in her trousers. She held it up and said, 'Listen to what he has to say very carefully.'

She took the stick and plugged it into her own Unicus, a large pink leather-bound device with a sizeable screen. The contraption's chunkiness suggested that the amount of RAM it possessed was enormous. Once she loaded up the viewer, she passed it over to Seraph, who held it on her lap, with Ryken eagerly peering over her shoulder to look at the screen.

Tom's dark features were frozen in an image, and it was just possible to see his shoulders covered by a plain sky-blue t-shirt. He appeared to be sat in a small, dimly-lit tent. As Seraph said, 'Play', the video diary automatically began...

The image disappeared for a few seconds, before it re-emerged with Tom's face again. This time, he was laid down on a camp bed with a blanket pulled up around him, and he looked very worse for wear, with a drawn face, purple bags under his eyes and an unshaven face. Seraph and Ryken looked at each other as they prepared for what they might hear next. This next message began with a lot of coughing...

Another transmission crackled into focus after that, and this time Tom seemed to be sat in a pokey hotel room with bland furnishings and decoration...

CHAPTER 34

A fter viewing the three video diaries, Seraph passed the Unicus back to Mara and remained standing. She shook her hands out to try to rid herself of the shock she felt.

'I think I know what this means Mara, but I want you to still tell us.'

'Sit down, Seraph, and I will explain.'

'I can't. This is all too much for me. I just don't know how she could have lied to me for so many years. Fuck.'

'She didn't want to, but she had to.'

'Tell me everything Mara. Let's get this over with.'

Ryken got up to pull Seraph toward him to sit back down, rubbing her arm in a bid to comfort her.

Mara began, 'My father went to New Guinea on that expedition when they were still finding all kinds of new species out there, having been previously unable to tackle the treacherous and uninhabitable environment. When he returned to England after that trip, he took some time off and found Mum again. I'm sure you know the rest Seraph. They married quickly and had me not so long afterward. His near-death experience is, I'm sure, what made him realise what he really wanted out of life.

'He took a job at Durham University and used to travel up there for work three days a week. When he would come back after that time away, I'd always be sent off with some babysitter or other, leaving Mum and Dad to have their alone time together. They couldn't be without each other, you see, they were so passionate, so in love. I realised that from a very early age, and it both bewildered me and left me in awe of their bond. They both worked very hard at their marriage. I think if Mum hadn't suffered complications during my birth, they would have had several more children!'

Seraph sniffled slightly at the revelation, and Ryken grabbed her hand to hold it while Mara continued.

'He tried to forget his experience in New Guinea, but there were always people emailing or phoning – wanting to question him about the infection he had suffered. He and his colleagues didn't want to dwell on it whatsoever, and indeed each of them was determined not to talk about what they had been through. They wanted to get on with their lives and leave it all behind. Tests carried out on the bird's samples didn't reveal much, but its DNA did seem to suggest it had developed an immune system beyond anything any other creature on the planet had at that time. Having suffered so terribly at the hands of the disease, neither Dad nor his colleagues wanted to even contemplate encouraging research of it any further. Having nearly met death, they simply wanted to ignore its existence and hopefully protect humanity by not revealing much about it.

'In 2022, a British team brought back one of those rare birds from the Foja Mountains. You might have heard it mentioned – it was termed the "Indonesian Mocking Fowl."'

'Anyway, specialists at a secretive laboratory somewhere in Manchester were carrying out research on this bird when a lot of the nearby chicken and turkey farms were overrun with sick animals. Obviously those scientists did not contain the creature and its deadly virus as well as they thought they had. Either that, or it was purposely released. It was around March 2023 when hundreds of thousands of fowl all over the country were culled out of a fear that quickly spread across the rest of the world. This greatly devastated the food chain. Between the spring of that year and the winter, the flu had time to develop and mutate. It soon became so pathogenic that it was easily passed from person to person, and as if overnight, billions of people were struck down.

'Mum and Dad were holed up with me at the shop at the time. He instantly knew what was going on and we hid indoors, only going outside if absolutely necessary. When Dad heard one of his Durham colleagues who lived in York had been struck down with the disease, he left us and went to nurse him. He knew he would certainly have some immunity having had it before, and didn't worry about suffering from the mutated strain so much. His colleague Stephan had an underlying heart condition, and even though he was only in his forties like Dad, he succumbed to the disease and died. Dad returned home to Mum after Stephan's death, leaving the body in the man's house, unable to do anything with it because of the overrun hospitals and funeral homes. Stephan was an eternal bachelor and had no family. While Dad had been away nursing his friend, some men had visited the bridal shop looking for him. They were dreadful-looking, suited men who aroused Mum's suspicions straight away, and she sent them packing with a story about Dad having gone missing on hearing about the outbreak. Dad was terrified when he heard what had transpired and phoned his former colleagues, Harley and Simpson, but was unable to get hold of them. Then it was on the news that the two men had both been branded criminals and shot dead… probably because they posed a threat, having suffered the flu at its source. Looking back now, it's clear that Officium acted so rashly because they were so guilt-ridden and intent on taking control. Mum and Dad had Stephan's body, and they passed it off as Dad's. In the chaos of the flu, nobody dared question whether it was Dad or not, and that kept the agents of Officium at bay. Yes… even back then Officium were already scrambling their security forces around the world. The fear of a pandemic brought so many to their group because they promised to guard against any future outbreaks. However, we knew that it was really them who let loose the virus. Instead of leaving it out there in the jungle, they couldn't resist bringing it back to the UK for testing. Whether intentionally or not, they enabled it to spread across the globe, seemingly with ease. The population explosion of 2022 may have helped its spread.

'Dad as good as died in Officium's eyes, saving him from interrogation, or worse yet, certain death. But it meant the loss of our lives as we knew it. I went with my father to live in that cottage in Stratford – the real Stephan's holiday home. My parents decided I would be safer there than at the shop. Though she had declared Dad dead, people followed Mum's movements for months after that, until they finally gave up and left her alone – convinced she knew nothing and wasn't a threat. Once things had calmed down, she used to visit us at weekends, and whenever she could, but we always knew we had to maintain a cloak of secrecy. It was difficult, but we felt lucky to still be alive, to have survived such a traumatic event. So many people died during 2023, that nobody asked Mum what had happened to me and Dad. They just assumed we'd passed away like so many others, and she adopted the guise of the single dressmaker. I was schooled at home by Dad, and Mum threw herself into her work at the shop, using one of her trusted contacts to authenticate our new identities.

'I studied medicine at King's College before pursuing a PhD in virology at Manchester University, feeling as though that was my calling. I saw what it did to my father having to hide for all those years, and I knew I had a responsibility to get to the truth. He grew a beard and long hair, but even then, he feared for his life whenever he walked out on to the street. Mum saw the change in him too and it devastated us both to see it. Before that, he was such a jolly kind of person, laughing and telling jokes, always playful and chatty.

'Being the daughter of Tom Bradbury, I had some insider knowledge of the virus that attacked humanity in 2023, and I used that to my advantage. I gathered people about me and made headway into viral research, but it was so difficult to achieve anything. Officium were very careful to remove all trace of their own research, and if the virus hadn't managed to kill its victim, all it seemed to do was cancel itself out so there was nothing to work with. The organisation tried to recruit me for their employment, but I refused a number of times, knowing I'd be risking Mum. The swines were calculating enough to take my name for their own gain when I too was forced into hiding after Dad's death. They were desperate to keep their secret hidden, and even more anxious to keep the world trapped beneath a blanket of fear – seeing to it that anyone who came close to investigating that particular strain was dealt with.

'Now, you may be asking, how does the shop tie in with all this? When Mum and Dad married, they hadn't expected the business to take off as it did. It seemed Mum's decision to do something unheard of and create bespoke gowns at relatively low prices earned her a reputation, and people flocked to her doors. I remember being very little, and often waking up in the middle of the night to find Mum sat in a corner on a chair, having fallen asleep over some creation or other she'd been working on while overseeing my own sleep. She was so dedicated, and she used to tell me it was because marriage had saved her and given her so much, that she felt an overwhelming desire to help other women achieve that. She wasn't a romantic, no, she wasn't a romantic at all. She saw the practical benefits of partnership and love, of security and solidity. Both of my parents survived and overcame terrible trials in their lives, and that made them appreciate what they had, every day.

'Mum had built up so many acquaintances through her work at the shop, that she saw an opportunity to quietly make enquiries about Officium. So many felt, as we did, that the new way of the world was wrong and that something had to be done to bring the truth to the fore and reassure people that they need not live in fear. Trying to prove Officium's culpability always seemed impossible. They used the aftermath to their advantage, despite knowing they would arouse suspicion in anyone who knew about their secretive laboratories across the world. Taking over surveillance, intelligence services, even food and clothing chains, the world was at their mercy, and Officium did whatever it took to hide their part in the catastrophe.

'RAO had to operate in absolute secrecy to prevent Officium finding out about its existence. We're only one of many resistance groups, but I suppose the success of ours was down to Mum's curious profession. They never suspected her because she was a simple spinster as far as they were concerned, and I think you'll agree she carried off the ruse quite well.

'We all undertook courses and training to maximise our skills, for the benefit of the cause. Mum's ultimate skill was literally as a weaver of webs, a networker. She brought people together in the correct way, and was able to see what skills they could bring, as well as how they could be used. But our work is a constant waiting game, a test of faith requiring extreme patience, a task we knew would only be accomplished if we could realise how to operate within the realms of seeming impossibility. It is only in recent years that Mum allowed her codename, the dressmaker, to be leaked out, to instil an element of fear into their cold hearts following Dad's death.

'She spread the word amongst her customers that a resistance group indeed existed trying to change things, and they would be sent on their way with contact details if they wanted to join. They never knew it was her running the show. Only if they proved their worth would they get to meet her. With Camille's help, they expanded the building and set up a surveillance team beneath the shop. So many people offered donations to the cause, but she and Dad were so careful with money over the years, and they invested in renewable energies – ironically the thing that Officium are so desperate to make developments in. She constantly battled to protect him, but nobody could stop the evil bastards killing my father in broad daylight, all because Officium found out that the Plaza was a known meeting place of RAO. They had seen him leaving it one day and had most probably killed him because of his connection to me. The same thing happened to your parents, Seraph, they were spotted there – and paid with their lives. They were RAO too. Eve learnt that someone had betrayed the cause, and she sent Camille after them. The milliner killed the man with one fatal blow. She spared no mercy for the person who betrayed both your parents and my father, the most brilliant man I've ever known.'

While Mara looked down at her lap in silence, Ryken started to feel Seraph's hand shaking within his own. He lifted up the armrest that was separating them and pulled her toward him. He grabbed her body tightly to his own, and she hid her face in his shoulder, crying at all the revelations. Ryken looked over at Mara, who was sat there staring at him with a sad look on her face at the sight of the pair hugging. He continued to hold a tearful Seraph, rubbing her back and holding her hair in his hands. He knew this might be the last time she would ever let him touch her. He kissed the side of her head, and made the most of his chance to be close to her. Seraph pulled away from him eventually and saw the look of fear in his eyes. She looked at Mara and saw her foreboding countenance too.

'What is it? Why are you two looking at each other like that?! Tell me!'

He remained silent as he saw her expression, one of hurt and disbelief that there could be anything else. He tried to wipe the tears from her face but she pushed him away as she waited to find out what was going on.

Mara appeared uncomfortable, as if she were plucking up the courage to say whatever it was she still had to impart. 'Seraph, this won't be easy for you… Ryken is an undercover agent.'

Seraph went into shock and felt sure all the blood had just drained from her body. Her head swam and she couldn't help but feel unbelievably let down.

Mara suggested, 'Perhaps you should spend the rest of the flight in the cargo hold Ryken.'

Mara had gone back to the cockpit to give them time alone. Seraph was shaking. She stood up to move away from him. Her jaw was clenched in anger, and she felt like she could probably punch her way through the fuselage. She tried to walk off the feeling of having her trust betrayed, but it was engulfing her thoughts, and her face burned red with fury. He moved toward her, turning her around by the shoulders to look at him. 'Seraph, I was going to tell you.'

She shook herself away from him, trying to avoid admitting his existence even. 'Don't touch me.'

'I... I... was trying to protect you.' He held his hands limply by his side, and his whole body looked dejected.

She wiped away the tears from her eyes, and suddenly she felt only rage. Her vitriolic rant began, 'I knew there was something about you, right from the start, something untrustworthy, and yet I trusted you, probably more than I've ever trusted anyone. I should have listened to my instincts. How could you lie to me all this time? After everything I've been through this week, I didn't think it could get any worse!'

He bowed his head to look at the floor. 'I'm so sorry.'

She turned to look the other way, avoiding his face, reiterating, 'If you don't get out of my sight, I will literally break your neck. Get in the cargo hold before I do something I probably won't regret. You may as well have killed Ulrich yourself.' She kicked one of the chairs violently and punched the air, screaming through clenched teeth.

He fell to his knees behind her and held his hands around her legs, begging for forgiveness. 'You don't mean that, please let me explain. I can't bear this, Seraph.' He wanted to weep with despair.

She swivelled around and started to swing an arm out towards him. However, he caught it quickly. He pulled her down to the floor with him, and held her wrists in his hands. While her eyes burned with fury, his pupils dilated with wild desperation as he tried to authenticate his emotion. 'I love you, I loved you from the moment I met you. I'll never leave you. I'd never hurt you.' He tried to pull her into his arms, to kiss her, but she suddenly jolted herself from his embrace. Then she let out her anger on his cheek. The sound of the collision shook them both to the core. She saw the suffering behind his eyes, but she was boiling inside, she couldn't control it. She sat back down in her seat, and held her chin in her hand as she faced away from him, seemingly lost in her own thoughts – and having done with him.

He was defeated, and he got up and walked away. He realised it wasn't the time, but he hoped she would come around.

Seraph sat alone, looking out of the window at the clouds rushing by. She was so furious with herself, so unbelievably disappointed at being taken in so easily by Ryken, only to have her faith crushed once again by an inferior man. Her face contorted in a mixture of emotions: hatred, disappointment and heartbreak. *How could he do this?* She just wanted to block out everything that had happened over the past few days, and forget about him entirely. She went into the bathroom and locked the door. She sat on the toilet lid and tried to gather herself, but her emotions were spiralling out of control. She kicked the door, stood up and shook the sink, punched a crack in the mirror and shouted, 'Bastard,' at the top of her lungs. She was so incandescent, but when she caught sight of herself looking manic in the mirror, she stopped to look into her own eyes. She took a few deep breaths to calm herself down. Recovering quickly, she pulled herself together and went back out to her seat. She decided that this revelation actually made things so much simpler. She never wanted to see him again.

CHAPTER 35

Not long after, Seraph saw the familiar skyline of New York out of the cabin window and was instantly relieved. She was nearly back home, and felt everything would be alright. It was morning again. How strange and wondrous everything looked, even the smog clouds. She started to belt up as Mara announced they would soon be landing, and she heard someone buckling up a few seats behind her, presumably Ryken. But she wouldn't grace him with a glance. He must have sensed she still didn't want him anywhere near her, so he kept his distance, even after they landed.

She jumped up out of her seat after they stopped in a private hangar, and spoke with Mara in the cockpit.

'Why didn't anyone tell me about him?'

'We needed to test his loyalty.'

'Is there nobody capable of telling me the truth? I'm going out of my mind here. What am I going to do?'

'What Mum told you to do Seraph, go home.'

'And what after that? Am I meant to forget everything I've been through with that man?' When Mara didn't react to Seraph's desperate pleas, she became even more frustrated. 'How can you be so cool? How can you people live like this, lying and deceiving and pretending everything is alright when it's clearly not? I mean, you couldn't even attend your own mom's funeral!'

Mara remained steadfast and spoke coolly, 'I know it's hard Seraph, but this is what we have to do. None of us have ever known any different, and we've had to become hardened to get through it all. Listen, you may need him yet. He can help our cause. Maybe you should hear him out. I don't think he would have stuck with you if they'd managed to turn him.'

'I want to kill him Mara, I really do. He lied to me. He's hurt me so badly.'

Seraph fought her emotions yet again, and Mara sensed talking like this was doing her no good. 'Look, Seraph, we've organised a car to take you and Ryken back to your respective apartments. You need to go home and wait. We'll be in touch.'

'I can't go back in a car with him.'

'You really have no say in the matter. There is so much more at stake than just your pride.'

Mara's words practically pushed Seraph out of the cockpit and back into the cabin, where Ryken was waiting shiftily. 'Ryken, you and Seraph are getting back to the city in that hover-sine out there, okay? Go back to your apartments and stay there until further notice, both of you.'

Ryken nodded, grabbing his stuff in readiness.

Lucius pushed the aircraft door open and Mara bade farewell to Seraph with a clumsy hug. 'See you again sometime my love, I'm sure of it. And goodbye Ryken, off you go.'

With that, the pair were out of the craft and into the vehicle that would take them back to the city. They didn't know how Mara had managed to wing it so that they could evade U-Card control, as well as the dozens of other security checks necessary to get back in the country, but they weren't about to ask any questions.

Seraph got in the hover-sine first, and sat as far away from Ryken as possible, immediately pouring herself a double whiskey from the mini-bar. The vehicle pulled off and the pair remained in silence, avoiding each other's glances or even the fact that any other person was in the vehicle. However, when the driver asked for both their addresses, it brought reality back to them.

Ryken ventured bravely, starting to explain, 'After Suranna died, I spotted an opportunity to finish this once and for all and I got myself a new job, as an agent. I was trying to do the same thing you've spent your life doing, only I had to sacrifice a lot more of myself, believe me.'

She slugged the liquor, unimpressed and indifferent at his attempt at an explanation. 'Go to hell.'

'It doesn't matter what you say or do, I'm past the point of no return. We both are. The only reason you're so angry is because you realise that you and I are the same. We've both had to adopt personas that aren't us to achieve what we need to.'

She threw him another look of disgust and twisted her lip as she battled her urge to start shouting at him again. Calmly she spoke, 'I don't deal with people like you. I don't even bother pissing on people like you when they're on fire. Do you know what I do with them?'

Her face was animated, waiting to see if he could make a comeback after mocking him into submission.

'What do you do with people like me then, Seraph?'

'I erase them from my life and never see them again. I can cut you off as easily as look at you.'

'You can't just blot me out after what we went through, and who knows what else lies out there awaiting us.'

'What we went through? You mean, what you put me through? I'd rather deal with a dozen agents right now, than look at your ugly mug.'

'And I would rather die than see you suffer one more moment of this, Seraph. This is childishness. Please, don't hate me. Please hear me out.' He slapped his knee hard while a vein in his neck seemed to be bulging with fear, panic and desperation.

She turned to him, slurring her words slightly from the whiskey. 'Don't ever underestimate me okay? Don't antagonise me anymore than you already have. I can survive alone quite well. I don't need anyone, especially you. I thought you were protecting me, and all that time I had an agent under my very nose. I don't know why I trusted you.'

She was starting to give herself away again, seeming to tremble with every protestation she made. He made a bold move and went to sit on the seat she was on a few spaces away from his. She tried to grab him and push him away, but when she was forced to look him in the eye, she seemed to weaken against her impulse to smack him. He quickly pulled her body close to his, tightly holding her against him, and after a few moments she relaxed and let her forehead fall on his chest. He had succeeded in saving her from herself. He spoke slowly, explaining, 'I know I was wrong in what I did, but not long after meeting you, I was frightened you wouldn't like the truth, especially after you told me about your parents. I was scared I would lose you if you knew about what I'd done in the past. I was petrified that you wouldn't want to be anywhere near me, and so I kept a few things back. But I didn't do that maliciously. I was trying to protect you. I just hope that one day you will let me explain why I went undercover and why I did the things I did. I had just about forgotten who I really was, when I bumped into you and remembered. None of us are born evil Seraph, but some of us end up in such situations, we just get caught up. I was almost lost until you rescued me.'

She shrugged herself out of his grasp and tried to push him away again. 'I can handle the truth Ryken, as long as I know about it. You insulted my intelligence, that's the worst thing. We may not have a lot in this world, but we can have honesty. Don't claim you were trying to protect me, I don't buy that whatsoever. Look at you, you're more than capable of killing a whole bunch of agents, but you dragged me into that sewer knowing that you'd be found out otherwise.'

'No, I didn't have any weaponry on me. They would have killed us, believe me, I know.'

'Whatever.'

Deep down, she was fighting the urge to be with him with every atom of her body. She was so unbelievably torn inside, she couldn't reconcile one part of herself with the other. The unforgiving side was battling the newly ripened heart that Eve had blown to pieces. Slowly, Ryken was putting those pieces back in place, but she didn't trust any of this at all. It was foreign to her. As she pushed, he pulled.

He had faith that she would come around eventually, but his mind turned to what was ahead. 'Is your apartment safe? Do you have any security measures in place?'

'Yes, I'm in the gods. I have the works.' She looked confident as she continued, 'And I have my back-up, remember.'

'That's good, but be careful still.'

'What about your apartment building?'

'I don't have the safety of the Dakota, but I have my climbing gear...'

'Don't go back there if it's not safe.'

'I'll be fine as long as you are.'

When they got to the checkpoint at the Manhattan Bridge, Seraph and Ryken had slipped underneath the wide seats in the hover-sine, covering themselves with the curtains hanging beneath the chairs. Laid there side-by-side, she turned her head away from him, while he was pensive alongside her, feeling sure that the woman next to him was the love of his life – but at that moment he could do nothing about it. Thankfully, the guards seemed too pressed that day to have a good snoop around the vehicle, and had simply let their driver go on his way.

When they stopped at Seraph's apartment block, Ryken looked on in awe at the rather grand exhibition of German renaissance masonry, one of the few period housing blocks left in the city. He wondered how she had afforded it on her wages, but he remembered her parents were probably loaded – and she had some serious connections. She had left the vehicle quickly, saying goodbye to Ryken and promising to keep in touch. He couldn't expect anything more from her really, he was lucky she was even talking to him. He asked the driver to drop him around the corner from his apartment block, attempting to outwit any loitering agents. He waited until no-one was looking, and strapped on his climbing gear, heading up an iron column on the glass building, toward his apartment.

CHAPTER 36

Ryken climbed the six storeys to his Tribeca apartment, pressing the fingerprint key to unlock the window before leaping into his cube-shaped black-and-brown-decorated abode. He sat on a leather couch with his head in his hands, and he had no idea how his life had got to this point. He had been carried off on this journey somehow, and he knew he was in deep trouble. He was desperately and achingly in love, and he knew where he would rather be at that moment in time, and it wasn't sat alone in his bachelor pad.

At the mention of the dressmaker, he knew that Mara must be part of the resistance, and he knew that they knew who he was. Deep down, he had known Seraph would one day find out, but he had hoped it would be in better circumstances. He never thought in his wildest dreams that he would one day regret his actions of the past because of a woman.

As a young man, he had been desperate for adventure. He had become one of the rare few given the opportunity to serve as an officer in the British Army. Rare because their numbers had been constantly dwindling since 2023, no longer needed in times of medical warfare.

In 2055, he was thirty and on a career break, taking three months holiday to reassess his life. He had trained in the medical corp and had done as much as he could within the bounds of his job there, and he began pining for bigger and better challenges. It was during this break that he was scaling the heights of Red Rock Canyon in Nevada. There was nothing more wonderful to him than climbing, pushing himself to his very limits in terms of both mental and physical ability. He had reached the summit, breathing heavily and sweating profusely from the exertion he'd had to exercise to get his huge frame up the mountain. He took a bottle of water out of his climbing bag, and had started glugging it, when he felt a tap on his shoulder.

'Hello Ryken.'

He swung round, unaware there was anyone within a fifty-mile radius. The person was dressed in the same manner as him and had seemingly come up the other side of the rock.

'How do you know my name?'

'I know a lot of things about you, actually. I've been searching for you everywhere and here you are.'

'Who are you?'

'My name is not important. I'm here because I hear you're taking time out from your career? Tut tut. There must be something missing from your life for you to be out here all on your own in the middle of the desert.'

'Go on…'

'I work for an organisation that is very interested in people like you who want to further their careers beyond the realms of anything they thought possible. I am here to ask you to join us, and everything you ever wanted will be yours. Money, success, power. We have it in abundance.'

'What makes you think I care about money?'

'Don't we all Ryken? Don't we all? Here is our card, think about it and let me know.'

The person began walking away, saying. 'We'll be hearing from you. Call the number if you want a new challenge.'

Ryken had looked at the card and saw at the top, *Dulwich Laboratories*. He could hardly believe his eyes. He had certainly heard of Nobel Prize-winner Mara Dulwich and was immediately flattered – and intrigued. He thought she had disappeared off the face of the Earth since her father's death, but he assumed she had decided to re-emerge. He looked up, shouting, 'Hey wait!' But the figure had disappeared out of sight. He called the number the next day, saying he was interested in a job, and was invited to interview.

That's how it had all started. He had been drawn in by a name. He had been asked where he would like to be stationed and New York was one place he had always wanted to live, so he had started a new life, progressing through his studies rapidly and soon becoming a qualified virologist rather than just a lowly army doctor. For some reason, he was drawn to virology. Research into stem cells, cloning, growth hormones, cancer and artificial organs just didn't cut it. To him, getting the low-down on 2023 was the ultimate prize. He wanted to pursue Mara's ideas on total viral immunisation. Her theory was that because the 2023 virus had the ability to attack the immunities in its hosts, perhaps its antithesis would encourage immunity in humans to any and all future viral attacks. However, he was never able to turn up anything substantial enough. It had been too long since the disease had made its impression on the world, and it seemed like achieving her theory was a pipedream.

He ended up having a fling with his unit's head researcher Suranna. It didn't last long, but he learnt a great deal from her. He found out that their employer was in actual fact Officium. He was horrified to discover the truth; that the people he suspected were responsible for killing half his family, were paying him. He was shocked to learn there wasn't even one level of society they hadn't managed to infiltrate.

He had been sucked in and he knew that there was no way of getting out easily, especially after Suranna turned up dead. He had noticed she was becoming more distracted at work, more weighed down with something, and had started letting herself go. Her blonde hair had thick black roots showing through, she had stopped wearing make-up and her previously stylish wardrobe seemed to have been abandoned. He had taken her to one side for a quiet chat. She had a look of fear in her eyes, and she said, 'Ryken, I made a discovery that I think is going to get me killed. They have vaccines for the 2023 virus.'

He was absolutely furious, but there was nothing that could be done after the cold storage was mysteriously moved. Two days later, she was dead. He knew that would be his fate too unless he did something radical. So, he let the world believe he had been fired – when he had actually taken on another job. In actual fact, he had arrogantly offered himself up as an agent to his employers, telling them he knew what their organisation really was and that he wanted to get back out in the field. He made a lot of promises, claiming he simply wanted the adrenalin of being back out there. They had been sceptical at first, suspicious even, but he had undergone the training and passed with flying colours, excelling beyond anything any other agent ever had done. He hadn't needed to undergo any of the enhancement trials, and had therefore retained some sense of humanity. However, he had still sacrificed a lot of his beliefs, and wasn't very proud of some of the things he had seen and done in training.

A week ago, he was sat in his apartment when he received a vis-call from an unknown number. He answered it, and recognised the person on the screen. He had seen her at Red Rock all those years ago. She was a mousy looking woman, but you could tell she knew how to hold her own.

'I hear you've managed to get yourself quite high up in the game, Ryken,' she said, in an English accent mixed with a slight bit of French.

He was unsure what was going on, asking, 'What do you mean?'

'You took the bait, but you didn't realise who had really thrown it to you.'

RAO was present everywhere you went, and yet just as Officium was, neither of them was ever mentioned, never talked about, only whispered amongst the people. They both existed silently, but eerily.

'You represent the resistance?'

'Of course. We hear you've just completed your training, and now we need you to attend a family gathering in Manchester, can you make it?'

'I will try…'

'You won't try, you will be there. We need you to see what you can find in their labs there…'

'Okay. How will I get out of work?'

'Tell your employer you're taking a holiday for a family matter.'

'I'll see what I can do. How do I get in touch?'

'Oh, we'll be in touch Ryken, don't worry. Just get on the next available flight. We'll know when you're coming. Just don't disappoint us.'

He snuck in to the labs in Manchester but had found nothing there. Frustratingly, he had travelled all that way to get nothing, and had become an enemy of Officium in the process. They realised he had betrayed them by breaking into the Manchester labs. Scared for his life, he decided he would fly to Africa on a fake U-Card and get himself lost in the wilds of Kenya somewhere. Then he bumped into Seraph at the airport when all flights were grounded. He recognised her from the paper, and had scorned her when they first came into contact, knowing how ruthlessly she worked. Then he realised why she paraded the streets of New York as she did. She didn't know that he was also trying to get to the truth, but in a different manner. And within minutes of talking to her, he was smitten. Her womanliness was so appealing to him. She was so innately beautiful and she didn't even know it. She was also a woman's woman, fiercely loyal, affectionate to those of her own sex and subtly maternal. He was absolutely raving mad for her.

Still sat there on his brown leather couch, he received a message on one of his Unicuses. It was from his contact. *Seraph is being followed. She needs you.*

He got up to go out, saying out loud to himself, 'And so it begins…'

CHAPTER 37

Seraph was outside the door of her apartment after leaving Ryken in the hover-sine. She keyed in a code before saying her name into the voice recognition entry system, and the screen seemed to flicker for a few minutes. An automated tone communicated, *DNA analysis also required.* That meant someone had tried to break into her place while she had been gone, and so a tiny robotic arm popped out of the wall offering her a swab to wipe inside her cheek. She followed protocol, and dropped the swab in a little chute just next to where the arm had popped out. Seconds later, several deadlocks released along with the greeting, *Welcome home Seraph Maddon.*

Once inside, she looked at herself in the hallway mirror and tried to rub away the blushes on her cheeks. She instantly recognised how she looked and quickly moved away from the mirror to distract herself with other things. However, as she stood in the kitchen making herself a coffee, thoughts of his scent, his mouth and the look in his eyes were haunting her, invading every other process going on in her mind. But she couldn't get over his betrayal. It hurt so badly, because she had unconsciously given up so much of herself to him already.

Grabbing her Unicus, she slung it on the coffee table, loaded it up and waited for the messages to come crashing in. However, there was nothing really of note, apart from the ones from the lawyers she had received yesterday. That was another thing she had forgotten about; all that money she had no idea what to do with.

Scrolling down the list even further, though, she was surprised to find something from Camille that she had so far overlooked. It was sent the day she had left York. All she found were the words: *Check your pockets. No need to thank me.*

Seraph started rummaging through her handbag. No other item she

170

owned had pockets so it must be that. The compact black leather handbag had pockets upon pockets for everything a journalist possessed to be stored in. She tried the front four pockets, the two side pockets, the three inside pockets – and nothing! Shaking the bag, she could tell it still contained some sort of item even though she believed she had emptied it. Then she remembered a back pocket under a flap. In there... something... A ceramic hand gun with a pouch full of bullets. She could have used it all this time, and yet she didn't realise.

Thoughts were whizzing around her head. She remembered the letter Eve had left for her. She looked at the first page, and re-read: *Answers await you there.*

Where are these answers?

Seraph flicked through the other pages and wondered why Eve had needed to include so many other blank sheets for just one small message.

Jolting her out of her jumbled musings, a vis-call came through. It was Francesca.

'Hi boss.'

'I heard the planes were taking off again?' The ferocious, fast-talking Australian would be your best friend as long as you were straight with her.

'Yes, I got back first thing.'

'Thought you might have. So, when's my best journo coming back in?'

Seraph bit her fingers as she proceeded, 'Err, well, umm, I was hoping I could have some time, to, you know. I mean, you know I wouldn't unless absolutely necessary.'

'Say no more, hon, I know a thing or two about loss too. Look, when do you think you might come back in? Next week?' Seraph knew she would need longer than that, but Francesca might think she was pushing her luck.

'Francesca, I'm really sorry, but I just don't know. I have a lot of affairs to tie up. My aunt left me some money, quite a lot actually.'

'Oh, I see, that's it then?'

'No, I mean, god no. No, I'm not quitting, no. Never. I mean, there is a lot of admin. Plus, I have a lot to follow up. Turns out she had a whole other life nobody ever knew about. It might make a story yet!'

'You nearly had me worried then. Couldn't find another one like you anytime soon. Well, let's say, you call me first thing next week and let me know what's what. I need you back though, don't forget that. And if you need anything, just let me know.'

'Thanks Francesca. Oh, by the way, I may have something else in the pipeline. Something big. Ryken Hardy finally talked. But it'll have to simmer a bit first. Will get back to you on that one.'

'Stone me, darl. I knew you would not take off your journalist hat even though you've been out of the city. Good girl. Speak to you soon.'

Later that day, Seraph had been out to get groceries, stopped off for a coffee and come back. She unpacked, set the filtration systems to perform a deep clean and decided it was time to relax. Everything could wait until tomorrow, she decided. She needed to catch up and take stock. So much had happened in the past few days, she felt as if she didn't know whether she was coming or going. She lit candles around the bath and was just about to dive in when she heard her Unicus sound off in the other room. She discovered it was a message from Ryken, and was just about to delete it when a pang forced her to read it: *Forgive me? I miss you. Ryken x*

She couldn't help but smile, really. She felt alone without him near. He had been indispensable the past few days when she needed someone to talk to, someone to protect her. Someone to help. Someone to hold onto on the back of an insanely fast motorbike. Although, in her subconscious, he was much more to her, but she hadn't realised it fully yet.

She replied very formally: *I'll call you tomorrow. Get some rest, this isn't over.*

He replied within seconds: *I'm here whenever you need me. Night or day. R x*

Seraph got into bed that night and slept deeply, unaware of the agents who had followed her to the supermarket and back, but had been hampered by Ryken tackling them both with his fists.

CHAPTER 38

When Seraph woke the next day, she had spent about half an hour lying in bed, just trying to figure out what she was going to do about Ryken. She knew what she felt in reality for him, she knew the first time she had looked into his eyes, but she didn't want to face up to it. She had spent most of her adult life thinking she would never meet anyone who would fulfil her expectations, and so she just gave up years ago, and was happy to concentrate on her work instead. However, she could hardly ignore what her heart, mind and body were telling her. Her stomach lurched every time she found those dark, searching eyes on her. His whole being was electric and it made her feel alive being near him. Deprived of his presence, she felt the withdrawal and didn't like it. She felt like a crazy, needy woman, and that's why she had always avoided situations like this before. He had more respect for her than she felt she deserved, and it only made her want him more — and feel sick for having carelessly flaunted herself for so many years.

However, today was a new day and she needed to get up and on with it. After struggling to settle her thoughts, she decided to get out of bed and get on with things. All she could hope is that Eve might have something for her today to take her mind off all the wild scenarios whizzing around her head.

She got some coffee from the kitchen, turned on the holographic TV pad on the coffee table, switched on her Unicus, opened the blinds to look out onto the city and felt that mind over matter was the order of the day. If she willed Eve to talk to her from beyond the grave, maybe it would happen. If she willed a great big sign to appear outside her window, maybe it might tell her exactly what she needed to know. If only...

She checked her Unicus and found no missed calls or messages. *Damn, I'm not very popular.*

Two hours later, Seraph had endured about as much trashy TV and GHO updates as she could manage. After showering and eating a couple of doughnuts, she looked at the clock and saw it was 11:30am. *What to do? What to do?*

Suddenly there was a thud behind Seraph's door. She shouted, 'Who is it?'

'It's me. Let me in.'

'What the hell are you doing here?' she exclaimed.

'Just open up!' After he spoke, she heard him wince behind the door, and as she peered through her peephole, curiosity got the better of her. Opening the door, she discovered a battered and bloodied Ryken before her, clutching at his arm in pain. Her immediate reaction was to get him inside, so as not to attract attention from her neighbours. She pulled him in, and slammed the door. Once he was in her apartment, she looked him up and down and the sight of him tugged at her heart strings... and yet. His shoulder bag fell to the floor as soon as he was inside, and she motioned for him to move to the sitting area and sit down on a rectangular white leather couch.

'How the hell did you get in my building?'

'It wasn't too difficult.' He reached inside his jacket and slammed a PPK on the table.

'What happened?'

'I should have had better security. I barely got out alive. I had to hijack a car to get here.' He started to take off his jacket, but pain engulfed him and he slipped on his side against the couch. Seraph went over at once, to pull him back up and help him get his jacket off.

'Oh Jesus, oh god, look at your shoulder.' She helped him off with his jacket, and discovered his arm was dislocated.

'You're going to have to push it back in for me. I've done it loads of times. Just lift it back, don't be afraid of hurting me. Just do it Seraph, please, I'm in agony.'

His eyes were bloodshot and pleading, and every capillary on his face seemed to be tinged purple. Despite his protestations, she didn't want the responsibility of having to help him of all people. But when he winced in pain again, she smoothed down her purple velveteen tracksuit as she nervously readied herself for the task at hand.

'Ryken, I'm going to do my best for you. Just don't move okay.'

She stood behind the back of the couch, holding the palm of one of her hands on his back to steady herself, and sliding the other underneath his armpit to feel where she needed to pull. He pleaded with her to do it. 'Seraph, just yank it hard. Do it.'

'Okay.' And with that, she pulled his shoulder back with a shove, and heard what sounded like the cracking of several bones shifting back into place – somehow. He stood up and shouted, 'Fuck! Fucking hell! Bastard! Fucker!' He held his arm, pacing back and forth in agony, before seeming to relax. He flopped back on the sofa and fell back into the cold leather, saying, 'Thanks. Thank you Seraph.'

Biting her fingers, Seraph didn't know what to do with herself. There was a large elephant in the room, and she didn't know how to react to its presence. One part of her wanted to kill him, and the other had felt compassion upon seeing him in such a state. She sat on a couch identical to his, positioned opposite, and looked out of the full-length balcony window overlooking Central Park.

He seemed to come back to life and asked, 'Have you got an ice pack or something? And painkillers.'

'Err, yeah, I'll have a look.' She left him in the seating area and went over to the white marble kitchen diner to retrieve the items.

He pulled his shirt off with some effort, revealing his torso underneath. He took the ice pack and held it to his shoulder. Seraph recoiled at the sight of him; he was badly littered with bruises. She handed him a glass of water and cocodamol. 'What the hell happened? Look at the state of you. Jesus.' She fetched several more ice packs while he explained.

'I got back to my apartment yesterday with no hindrance, but after I'd been out to get groceries and came back this morning, they were waiting for me. I shouldn't have used the front entrance, I guess. One of them crushed my shoulder between the front door, hence the dislocation.'

'I told you. You should never have gone back home. Why didn't you fucking listen? You always know what's best, don't you?'

'I just didn't reckon on them outnumbering me so greatly. I thought I could handle a confrontation, and maybe get some information out of them.'

'How many were there?'

'Three towering bastards, all as big as me, it was no mean feat getting out of there. Luckily I left a few ropes rigged up near a window, otherwise I wouldn't have got away. The thing was, they wanted to take me in, they didn't want to kill me. But there's no catching this dog.' He was speaking out of breath, and started coughing, still getting over the ordeal. 'I didn't know where else to go, but here.'

'Ryken, calm down okay, you're here now. They can't get you. Just relax. The bathroom is through the bedroom, go and clean yourself up alright?' He nodded, pleased that she was instructing him in a course of action. Meanwhile, she went to the security panel near the front door to set the electrified door to stun if anyone were to attempt entry. She closed the wooden shutters in every room.

He came back out after a few minutes, but still looked the worse for wear. She got him a blanket out of the closet and laid it out on the couch for him. 'Take it easy for a minute Ryken, while I think.' He didn't have the energy to argue, simply wrapping the blanket around himself and falling down on the sofa. He breathed a deep sigh of relief, and closed his eyes for a few moments, but his mind was racing so much he needed to open them again and stare into space in an attempt to soothe his troubled brain. Seraph was pottering about in the kitchen, trying to look busy while she considered their situation.

Laid there on the couch, he looked at the sheets of paper on the plastic white coffee table in front of him. 'What's this?'

She moved over toward him and sat on the coffee table. 'It's what Eve left for me. Only, it seems she only wrote on the first sheet.'

He lifted his head slightly, and said, 'Pass it here.'

He looked at the sheets, turning onto his back to get more comfortable as he held them between his hands and turned them over.

'You know what kind of paper this is, don't you?'

'No, what? What is it?'

'Pass me my Unicus from inside my bag over there.'

She quickly rummaged around and found what he was after, passing it over to him. He took out the miniature torch, and switched it to UV lighting. 'It's translucent printer paper. Spies used to use this kind of stuff.'

As he shone the torch on the pages, she saw letters appear. 'Oh my god Ryken… all this time.'

She grabbed the papers from him and flicked the torch over them all, madly checking there were words plastered over each page. She arranged them in page order and eyed Ryken. He had a serious look on his face as he pulled the blanket back up around him. She dare not believe in resolution, she was so wrung out of hope, but she knew the words within that letter needed to be read.

'I don't know if I can handle what's in this,' she said, deciding another emotional battering from Eve might just about finish her off. This would mean, once she read it, her connection to Eve would be broken. It would all be over and her beloved aunt would be lost to her forever. There would be no more late-night conversations when one of them got lonely or upset and needed to just feel that connection to someone who understood them. No more messages or greetings cards. No way of reaching her. It was a hard reality to face.

'You don't know what she was like Ryken. She was the deepest, truest person I ever knew.'

'It might be best to just get it over with.'

'You're right. I know you are.'

'I'm here if you need me.'

'I'm gonna go through and read it in there.'

He groaned out, 'Okay', shifting his huge bulk on the sofa in a bid to get himself comfortable.

Seraph was sat on her bed, behind the partition wall separating her and Ryken. She propped herself up with several pillows and proceeded to read whatever words Eve had left for her. Holding the torch, she began.

CHAPTER 39

My darling Seraphina,
I hope you're sat comfortably. I'm sure by now you will have uncovered the truth about me. Officium wouldn't imagine their greatest enemy writing a pathetic little letter on paper, so I've no doubt this will have found you safely. But, this is not going to be an easy read. There are a lot of things you need to know, and I'm sorry they have to be revealed in this manner, but it's the only way. By now, I will be gone and there is so much you need to know.

You know I always regarded you more as a granddaughter, and I hope you thought of me somewhat as a grandmother. I let you believe so many things, but I will tell you the truth now, even if you've already found it out for yourself.

I hardly know where to start, but I guess at the beginning might be best. I married Tom Bradbury in 2013, the best year of my life. I was so, so content with him, you cannot imagine. Our love was a kind rarely found. We shared so many laughs, so many happy times. There was non-stop laughter between us, and there was hardly a tense moment. We loved each other, pure and simple. There were no hidden motives, no agenda, just love. We had each suffered our own hardships since we were teenagers, and that only made us appreciate what we had, and cling on to it. Tom nearly lost his life, and he had changed because of that. I suppose that's why he transformed from that sweet teenager I once knew to a very contemplative, intense soul, who realised that when a good thing came along, you couldn't ignore it. We married so quickly but neither of us ever doubted what was between us. It was instantaneous, unquestionable chemistry, so strong that our beings were intrinsically connected. On our wedding day, my life became complete as he slipped that ring on my finger. I was so happy. We honeymooned in Antigua for two weeks, and we bared our souls to one another. It was a very passionate love between us, extremely so sometimes, and I became pregnant not long after we were married. I was shocked by the discovery at first, it was unexpected, but we prepared to become parents with such enthusiasm. Tom sold his bachelor pad and we used the money to renovate the flat above the shop, preparing it for our new arrival. We could have bought ourselves something bigger, but we loved the romance of the Shambles. The beams, low ceilings, barn doors and stone walls. Tom's love for me grew even more after I became pregnant, and it was the greatest experience of my life. I bore a child on 15th May, 2014, and we named her Imogen Samara Bradbury, 8lb 13oz. She was the most beautiful thing I'd ever set eyes on, and I suddenly realised what life was really all about. I suffered terribly during the delivery, but Tom was such a wonderful support, and we got through it together. He was my rock.

Though I'd become a mother, I continued my work at the shop, and for some reason my business thrived. People started coming from all over the world to have me make them their wedding dresses. I gained a sort of cult following, because I made to order – at bargain prices, for the workmanship they were getting anyway. I started to take on more staff to balance my work life with motherhood.

Tom was sure he had left the trauma of his illness behind, but in 2023 it caught up with him. When we heard Stephan had taken ill, Tom went to his house and nursed him, and I signed the death certificate as if my husband had died. It was easy. Amidst the chaos and panic, Tom took his friend's identity, and went into hiding with our daughter. He needed to be dead, otherwise he knew he would never be able to escape Officium's clutches. I reverted back to my maiden name to protect myself. The world collapsed, and Officium took advantage of the situation to infiltrate every level of society. They not only bought up the 4U chain, but they gained a monopoly over a huge number of the world's doctors and professors.

Now, on to the most difficult subject. Your father Hamish never told you, but he attended our wedding with his parents, and we saw him quite often as they would visit me in York frequently. He turned out to be a very gifted physician, but Vivienne was just as talented, as I'm sure you well know. As a young woman, she was just like you – ferocious and feisty. She survived a tough council estate upbringing only to gain herself a place at Leeds to study medicine. She was wild but Hamish tamed her, loving her possibly more than any man ever could. They just couldn't risk you finding out the truth, and they distanced themselves because of that. You gave them such joy, Seraph, but they felt such a responsibility to make this world a better place for you. They couldn't risk your safety, and they never wanted you to pursue your career for fear you might get hurt. They themselves had lived during some terrible times, the worst of times even, and they spent their lives trying to protect you. When we found out that Officium had set up their headquarters in New York to further their business interests, your parents offered themselves up. They finished their medical training at Columbia and both excelled in cardiology. Their day job was working as heart surgeons. However, they were also in with Officium's crowd, and would leak information to me about the organisation's members and activities, especially in medical circles. We tried to get evidence of the group's culpability but it always seemed impossible. We knew that digging up bits of dirt on them wouldn't be enough. We needed evidence of what really happened to cause 2023, but we could never get it. They were so secretive, and their agents would stop at nothing to protect the truth. It's the only thing they know to do. We never managed to get anywhere, but we knew we couldn't just stand by and do nothing either. The world would only be free if we could get hard proof.

I used my contacts from the shop to build up a group of people who felt as we did, that something needed to be done. It was agonising not being able to live a proper family life with Tom, but we knew it had to be done. The love we shared meant that we had to do whatever it took for him to survive. However, after your parents died, he couldn't hold back his anger. He travelled to New York to meet with members of RAO there, but he paid with his life. For so many years I'd known it was coming, but nothing could have prepared me for the loss. I couldn't really say goodbye to him properly because it would have meant risking my identity. The only thing I knew to do was to carry on. He was seventy-two, but for me he had still always been that same teenager I fell in love with all those years ago, and it tore my heart to bits. It was then that I really started to make headway into making my organisation as strong as it could be. I really needed to make our intelligence work after that, and we began reinforcing our surveillance teams across the world. Camille was there for me throughout everything, and without her, I wouldn't have been able to achieve what I have. She made so many contacts across the world during her travels. She had the skills, the tenacity and the strength our cause needed. She was the key to making RAO work.

Mara is not so dissimilar to you, Seraph. But she grew up in the wake of 2023 and she is incredibly tough because of it. She was always her father's daughter, and we knew from a very early age she would pursue some sort of scientific career. Her husband Richard, Lucius's father, was killed by Officium. He was a fellow virologist who stepped on the toes of the wrong people. She was only thirty-five when she lost him. I hope that once this is all over, Mara will find herself a quiet place to hide away and finally find some peace.

I'm so sorry that we did, but we kept the truth from you because it was your protection. We couldn't risk you, my darling. We all felt that if you knew nothing from an early age, you would never need to be burdened by it all. But none of us expected you to go chasing after the truth as you have, and I took it upon myself to protect you after your parents died. It was I who fed you information on all the power players of New York City, and a lot of people paid with their lives to get you that information. There are only a few of us strong enough and dedicated enough in this world to fight for justice. We've suffered some terrible losses, but we must have faith.

We amassed thousands of members all over the world, and to aid our cause, our group purchased grand hotels for our meetings. The Plaza, Ritz, George V, Lido, etc. They would have gone to wrack and ruin, or been transformed into Bed4theNites, if we had not taken them on. All the people who run those places belong to RAO, all working and gathering information, using their jobs as the perfect guise, as have I over the years. We all knew the risks, the danger, the severity of our situations if we were discovered, and yet we stayed true to the cause, knowing we were acting for good, for the restoration of this world back to something akin to normality. Tom and I also bought up half the Shambles as the *For Sale* signs went up, knowing the entire street would have been knocked down otherwise.

I would travel all over the world, to Moscow, Bangkok, Tokyo, Rio de Janeiro, Hong Kong, Cape Town and New York, under the pretence of buying up materials and meeting clients. However, my real motive was to meet prospective members. In recent years, Camille would travel as my bodyguard. She was the perfect companion, never attracting attention, but ready to demonstrate her skills if necessary. If there is one person in this world you can rely on without the shadow of a doubt, it is Camille. I'm sure she has plenty of stories to tell you. I foresee you and she forging a lasting, life-long friendship.

Many of my clients at the shop were members of RAO who had met their partners at our meetings, or working with Mara. I was simply someone who brought people together, and it is the people who believed in me that made me the dressmaker. They pushed me to be great, to act for them in their stead, and utilise my resources to the best of my abilities. I simply became what I did because of situation and circumstance. At the end of everything, I'm still only a woman who loved a man and lost him. He was never the same after 2023.

Mara and her family are sufficiently provided for from her father's will, don't worry about that, so I've chosen you to take the majority of my estate. And I want you to continue my legacy, which I will now explain.

You need to get into their labs in Brooklyn, where I believe they have those vaccines they've always denied knowledge of. You need to get in and bring them to justice, once and for all. I need you to do it for me, and Tom. Use that money and do whatever it takes to end this once and for all. Afterwards, start a new life, be happy and help the world rebuild itself.

You know I love you. You will find what you're looking for, I'm sure, if you haven't already. When this is all over, my girl, seek some sort of happiness for yourself. In the next life we will see each other again.

All my love, ever yours, Auntie Eve x

CHAPTER 40

Seraph turned over the last page of the letter, just to make sure there was nothing else, but there wasn't. She sat trying to comprehend everything she had read. She could so easily have started to cry, but suddenly her mind had become so clear. The end was in sight. She took a few deep breaths and composed herself.

She walked back through to the living room and saw Ryken dozing on the couch. The blanket had fallen down and his chest was bare. She went to cover him back up, smiling to herself at the sight of such a beautiful man laid up in her apartment. She sat by his side, squeezing herself onto a patch of seat he hadn't managed to occupy. She took a large, warm hand of his into hers, and kissed the grazes on his knuckles. She pulled it up to her cheek and held it there, closing her eyes. He stirred, shifting about with his eyes still closed. She knelt on the floor and went closer to him, studying his face. She whispered, 'Ryken.'

His eyes flickered open and he saw her hovering above him. For the first time since he had met her, he noticed she had dropped the veil of coldness that hid the warm spirit behind her eyes. She gently stroked his injured face with her fingertips, and he put both of his hands behind her back, lifting himself up slightly to say, 'Come here.'

She got up to lay next to him on the large couch as he made room for her. She rested on his chest, snuggling into his warm and furry body, feeling so comforted as his arms went tightly around her torso. She took a deep breath and shivered as she relaxed against him.

'Seraph, everything is going to be alright.'

She heard the words that every woman wants to hear, and yet still don't quite believe.

'My name is Seraphina.'

He repeated in a quiet, dulcet tone, 'Seraphina.'

Hearing him say her name like that, and feeling his warm breath right next to her, Seraph was overtaken by the urge to kiss Ryken. He was a broken man, a tortured soul and just a fellow human being in that moment, and she needed him. She stroked his hair, feeling its silkiness between her fingers. His cheeks were dewy and taut as she held her hands against them, but his lips were soft and plump as she pressed her mouth gently to his for what felt like an eternity. She pulled away to look at his face again, eyeing him to gauge his response. His long black eyelashes fluttered apart and her stomach flipped, as she realised fully that this man was her own self, staring right back at her. They saw in each other a person who understood them completely. Their greatest affinity, they recognised, was the sheer and utter need for some sort of passion in life, and now it was each other.

The room became non-existent all of a sudden and they viewed each other through a mist of wantonness. Everything about him was sending her rocketing toward the realisation that being with him was the only thing that made perfect sense. He waited patiently for her to return to him, closing his eyes to invite her to do with him what she willed. He could barely contain himself and wanted to savour their first moments of intimacy. She held one hand to the base of his trunk of a neck and the other she used to hold her body up on the couch. The tip of her tongue licked the satiny underside of his top lip, and he strengthened his grip around her back. She planted tantalizing kisses all around his mouth before gently pushing deeper to find his tongue. Beneath her she felt his arousal, and he surveyed her with a look of unequivocal lust as he pulled the zip of her hooded sweater down, urgently whipping it off her arms, desperate to get a feel of her skin. Soon they were kissing wildly, madly, writhing against each other. They both sighed and sucked in breaths between lengthy kisses. The taste of him was like catnip to her. She moved from his mouth to bite his earlobe, before exploring his neck and moving down to his chest. She bit the downy, rough skin there and suddenly, he couldn't take it any longer. He grabbed her wrists, and sat against the backrest with her on his lap. She wrapped her arms behind his head, ruffling his hair eagerly with her hands. He grabbed her buttocks, kneading them and squeezing them as he kissed her deeply. They were furious, anxious, desperate lovers. She pulled her mouth away from his to catch her breath and shoved his face into her breasts, letting her head fall back as he licked her cleavage, before unhooking her bra. As he slid her straps down, he kissed the bare skin of her shoulders delicately, and saw her nakedness before him as the garment fell to the floor. He smiled, astonished at the sight of her pale womanliness, and she smiled back, feeling as though he was the only man in the universe who deserved her entirely, and she was ready to give herself up. His fingertips glided along the velvety skin of her back as he examined her, before diving beneath her clothes to grab the flesh of her rear possessively, pulling her hips toward him so she tipped back slightly. She trembled as she awaited his touch elsewhere, and his mouth found one of her upturned nipples. Her womb contracted and she yelped. Every ounce of feeling in her body flooded to her pelvis. She watched him curiously as he reverently kissed and sucked the membranous pink flesh, before elatedly burying himself in her bosom. He came back to kiss her mouth and tore away at her lips so much she could hardly breathe. They were completely lost in ecstasy – all pain and suffering flying out of the window.

He suddenly stood up with her in his arms and laid her down on the long coffee table, sweeping everything off it as he did so. He knelt down and urgently pulled her remaining clothing off, throwing it behind him. Before she knew it, his arms wrapped themselves around her naked thighs and his mouth was against her delicate flesh.

She cried out with shock and delight. She looked up at him and saw his eyes were black with fervour. Her knees fell and she widened her hips, willing him to take as much of her as he could. His tongue sought its way to her hidden depths. He lifted her whole pelvis up to bring her further toward him still. She felt as though she were undergoing a transformation from mere mortal to heightened being of paradisiacal knowledge. He determined to bring her to climax, expertly rubbing his tongue against the nub of flesh at the crest of her womanhood. She groaned loudly and couldn't control herself, wrapping her legs behind his head tightly to affix him to her. 'Don't stop Ryken. Don't stop. Oh god.'

He kept going, absolutely relishing giving her such pleasure, and his slow movement prolonged her excitement. She tried to encourage his quickness but he held back, wanting to give her as much enjoyment as possible. She looked up at him and the sight of his black hair between her legs sent a quiver through her, so strong, she could barely contain herself. She was almost delirious with delayed, climactic jubilation, crying out, 'I love you Ryken. I love you so much, it hurts.'

He growled and really let himself loose on her. She panted, 'Don't stop, please don't stop. Please. Oh god, oh god.'

Her whole being was alighted by the spark between them and the fount of her pleasure was suspended in exquisite, existential rigidity by his continuous contact. She needed to hurl herself over the edge and she grabbed her breasts, rubbing them and squeezing them, lifting her pelvis up off the coffee table into his face. She started to orgasm, and he kept going. She screamed and shrieked, and his chivalric perseverance produced a tantric response from her that lasted longer than she thought conceivable. Her whole body pulsated with intense euphoria; the warmth spreading from the pits of her womb to the ends of her fingers and toes. Lifting her arms above her head, she saw stars before falling into a paroxysm of juddering revelations. She breathed heavily as she relaxed and let her limbs hang off the cold plastic surface she was laid on, completely exhausted.

He brought himself up and looked down on her sprawled-out body with a look of achievement, having conquered the seemingly insurmountable. He laughed slightly but soon thought better of it.

She peered at the mischievous look on his face and grinned, groaning, 'That was amazing, but I'm not done with you yet, sweetheart.'

His teeth shone back at her. 'I certainly hope not.' He pulled her weary body to sit up again and kissed her stomach, burying himself in the cushioned expanse of her midriff. His mouth started to explore the rest of her body and she trembled, still sensitive from his previous endeavours.

'Stand up, Doctor Hardy,' she said, teasingly.

He stood up immediately, anxiously standing in front of her with his body towering over hers. In his jeans, his hips were slim and sculpted in comparison to his mountainous shoulders and chest. She held her arms around him and kissed his solid stomach before commanding, 'Drop them.' He did as he was told, and she soon saw his glistening manhood standing there before her. She eyed his magnificent figure with rapture and said, 'Your body is sublime.' She saw the proud but loving grin on his face as he looked down on her and awaited her next instruction with baited breath.

She put a hand behind one of his huge thighs and pulled him toward her. She kissed him tenderly and he clenched his fists. She stood up and he grasped her flank, pulling her toward him in a warm, easy embrace. He tugged the band out of her hair and spread the locks out behind her, kissing and smelling them.

'Seraph, I love you.'

She smiled at hearing the tremor in his voice, but she was more confident, spreading her hands and mouth across his chest before saying, 'Make love to me, Ryken. Take me to bed.'

He saw the soft look of love in her eyes and felt absolutely mad with desire; testosterone and blood pumping around his body outrageously. His nostrils were engulfed by her scent and he needed to be inside her more than anything else he had ever wanted.

He swept her up in his arms and carried her toward the bedroom. She smiled at him as he did, holding her arms behind his back steadfastly. She rubbed her nose against his and appeared coy as she declared, 'I love you, Ryken.'

'I'll never love another woman.'

He reached the bed and their bodies cascaded across the mattress. He kissed her extremely tenderly and she guided him toward her as their groins throbbed with anticipation.

At the point of their union everything stopped, and they felt as though they were standing on a precipice, ready to throw themselves into complete and tranquil oblivion.

She took a deep breath and welcomed him further into the realms of total bliss. They held their arms around each other securely, moving together in exaltation. He muttered something indecipherable; sure he had floated up out of himself to look down on a life-changing moment. He had finally found the solace he had been looking for his whole life, and a sense of unbelievable wellbeing overcame them both. As they rocked rhythmically together, he had to exercise great control to withstand her efforts to draw forth his delight.

She kissed his wounds and held her arm around his shoulder to ease his burden. She breathlessly repeated his name as his mouth rampantly pressed itself against her throat. She could hear the pain in his voice when he said, 'Seraphina, you're so beautiful.'

His weight above her was unbelievably comforting, and she girdled herself about him, absolutely overcome with her need to possess him. She was wholly in awe of his masterfulness, and she gnawed on his shoulders to contain her screams. As they reached the peak of their enjoyment, they stared into each other's eyes and he groaned loudly as his thrusts became more rapid and determined. He shivered and trembled, sweat dripping down his back as he gripped on to her for dear life, no longer in control of his impulses. She grabbed his buttocks, encouraging him to forget consideration and make use of her.

'I'm coming Ryken!'

They maintained it for several moments until Seraph bowed to his art and went into spasm, violently shaking against him as she cried out.

Afterward, they held each other in a sweaty embrace, breathing heavily in each other's ears. She needed to bury herself in his neck, refusing to believe it was all over. He rolled on his back, pulling her across his body with him. He felt infinite relief, while she felt painful abandonment. He showered her with affection and covered their entwined bodies with the duvet. She gripped his torso and he kissed the back of one of her hands as he felt her warm, silent tears start to run over his chest.

He asked, 'Was I that bad?'

'Ryken, hold me, please. I need you so much. I was so ignorant, so blind. I never thought I could feel this happy.'

'Me either, my angel.'

She pulled herself up to look down on him, smiling and sniffing through tears as she reiterated, 'I love you, Ryken. I always have.'

He grabbed her, bringing her into his arms very tightly. She could hear his heart pounding in his chest as he declared, 'I am never, ever going to let you go.'

He knew that meant more to them than the obligatory three words of old.

CHAPTER 41

It was early evening and Ryken was sleeping in Seraph's bed, while she sat in the other room on the couch, re-reading Eve's letter over and over again. She was trying to commit it to memory, realising she would need every word of it to get her through what lay ahead. There was a lot still to achieve, she realised.

Outside, the sun was starting to go down. She and Ryken would be safe there for the night, but they would need to make a plan of action for tomorrow. No doubt, by daybreak, there would be swarms of agents surrounding her whole building. But for tonight, she would close the blinds, block out the world, and gather herself for the fight ahead.

She sat there, with hot blushes across her face from her and Ryken's lovemaking. She recalled every minute of it, smiling to herself, even embarrassed by her actions. He was an incredible lover, but it was more than that between them. It felt as if they were meant for each other, a perfect fit almost. She felt something in her stomach she had never felt before. She knew he had done questionable things in the past, but she didn't care. Seraph wanted to believe that he was only out for her. He made her feel alive and as if she could take on the world. She needed and wanted him so badly, she couldn't help herself. Every inch of his body was magical to her, every breath he made so precious, every kiss bewitching and every look between them... lightning. She loved him with every atom of her being.

He popped his head around the door of her bedroom, with a look on his face she had never seen before. It was soft, lusty and misty-eyed. He beckoned her back to the bedroom, and she obeyed. She walked over to where he stood and wrapped her arms around his neck, falling to pieces as soon as she got near him.

'Ryken, I was going to make you dinner,' she pleaded, as he teased her neck with his kisses. He was ready for her again.

'Fuck it. I need your ass back in that bed.'

She groaned and as she jumped into his arms he gasped, and they laughed at one another before French kissing with a familiar but passionate ferocity. He had slipped off her black silk nightgown before he made it back to the bed with her, and they made love through the night, exploring every inch of one another, desperate to make the most of whatever time they had left. For who knows what tomorrow might bring.

PART III
Veritas Praevalebit

CHAPTER 42

It was dawn the next morning and Ryken was cradling Seraph against his naked body, under the covers. They hadn't really slept much at all, between feeding each other snacks from the kitchen, and falling on top of one another whenever the mood took them. He didn't think he could love her anymore, but when he woke up that morning with his arms around her and her face nestled in his chest, his heart almost broke in two. He knew what lay ahead, but she had no idea…

They were talking quietly, with him holding her as streaks of light began to break through the cracks in the wooden blinds. She was finally opening up to him after letting him read the contents of the letter.

'My mother and father met in the wake of the Ravage. They never used to speak about what they went through, but I knew there were issues, things that they never dared bring to the fore. I knew they loved each other, and yet, there was some kind of doom looming over their marriage. I learnt to cope by throwing myself into everything at school and college. I ceaselessly aimed higher and higher, and could have made a career for myself in any field. But I realised long ago I had an innate predilection to become a reporter. It is almost as if it's in my DNA to chase stories, get to the bottom of cases and find the truth. That coupled with my need to find out why the world had become so changed, put me where I am today. But I've taken my profession to the extreme Ryken, such that I can't escape it now. People stop me in the street and offer me a knowing wink, thanking me for the work I do, knowing the constant battle I'm up against to get to the bottom of all this. Even in York, a man stopped to tell me he read my stuff. That keeps me going, knowing there are people out there who want the truth as much as I do. And I keep going for them. I'm their representative, their soldier. I'm not proud of the way I've had to work but I'll do whatever it takes, believe me. I've been fighting this for so long, it's time to act now.

It's time to really take action. I can't get anywhere else without proof. I need you to get me in. We have to do this for so many people, but mostly, for ourselves. There is so much at stake here.'

She turned to look at him with all seriousness, pleading for him to help her finally get to the bottom of her life's work. He was powerless to resist her.

'Seraph, can't we just leave, go somewhere safe and stay there, the two of us? I only want you now, nothing else. Just you and a peaceful place to live out our days.'

Seraph sat up to turn around and look down on him laying there, holding a sheet against her skin to cover herself. 'I want that too Ryken, but you know we have to do this. You know we can't go on knowing we could have done something and didn't. This is not just about us. We can't find a peaceful place until we finish this. You and I were destined to bring Officium to justice.'

He held a huge bear paw against her cheek, and eyed her with a look of pure love. Deep down, he was terrified – knowing what needed to happen next. 'I've seen what these people are really capable of. They killed people I cared about too. They will not stop until we are both dead now. I've seen and done things I hope you never have to know about. I don't know if I've got any strength left to fight them.'

'Then take my strength, I've got enough for both us.' She kissed him on the mouth, and grabbed him in a fierce embrace, her heart and her lungs pounding against him. But he seemed past consolation, releasing himself from her arms and getting up out of bed to put his boxer shorts back on. He paced the room, and looked behind the blinds at the city outside.

'We have to go to Brooklyn then? I'm not even sure the labs will still be up and running there. I haven't been there in years, since I began working at the Manhattan branch.'

'We have to give it a shot. Eve wouldn't lead us into danger on a fool's hope. She must have felt sure that is the location of the phials.'

He sat on the edge of the bed with his head in his hands. She moved up behind him to put her arms around his torso, running her hands through his long, silken chest hair. 'Look at the state of me Seraph, how am I meant to face them again?'

His body was badly bruised still, his perfect face was mangled, and he would appear suspicious as soon as he stepped out on the street.

'You've got me Ryken, and a woman in love is more dangerous than anything else on this planet.' He turned toward her with a helpless look in his eye and he lifted her to sit on his lap, pulling her towards him tightly, stroking the soft skin of her back gently. He buried his face in her wavy red locks and breathed in her scent deeply. He was so relieved to have her near him. She looked at him and as he smiled, she smoothed the creases around his eyes.

'Okay, but we need coffee before we even think about figuring this out.' He kissed her before shifting her back onto the bed and heading toward the kitchen. As he did so, he grabbed a Unicus from his jacket on the sofa and quickly sent a message to a contact before Seraph came into the room. *We're heading to the lab today. I have her love. I'm ready to do this now.*

Within seconds he got a message back. *Tomorrow we end this.*

Seraph and Ryken gathered in the sitting area, opposite each other on the two identical white leather sofas. She was in her dressing gown, and he still in his underwear. They each grasped their coffee mugs, drinking the life-giving liquid eagerly. He offered, 'It's a great place you've got here. Must have cost a bomb.'

'Mom and Dad bought this for me when I started out on my career because of the security of this building. I never knew until now why they were so bothered about my safety and hated the job I had chosen for myself.'

'Are you one of those insanely tidy people? Everything is so white.'

'Ha. You and I both know I don't really live here. I don't have time to make a mess or choose colour schemes while I'm out prowling the streets down there.' She pointed to the full-length windows beside them, and he acknowledged her meaning.

'Where did you get those pieces in the kitchen? The wooden ones. They look slightly out of place.'

He gestured generally at a teak fruit bowl, a wooden drainer resembling the bare bones of a pirate ship, a mug holder carved in the shape of an acorn tree and a huge wine rack affixed to the wall that had miniature bottles of wine decorating the edges all the way around.

Seraph revealed, 'I made them.'

He looked astonished, asking, 'Really? I mean...'

'They are probably the only things in this apartment that are really me. I took one of those virtual carpentry courses and found I have a flair for it. I really love wood, always have. The smell, the texture, the way it can be manipulated and yet still have its own personality, its own kinks and imperfections. Craftsmanship is in my genes. A lot of my ancestors were designers, weavers, builders and so forth. They make me feel sort of insignificant really, because they were all so talented. None more so than Eve, but this is my own little way of carrying on the tradition. I'm never happier than when I'm in a workshop tinkering away, but the materials are so difficult to get hold of. It's a creative outlet for me.'

'I'm really surprised you're into this kind of thing, those are really remarkable pieces. You could do this for a living instead, if you ever decided to give up reporting.'

'Thanks,' she replied, slightly embarrassed.

'I bet there are plenty of other surprises you have yet to reveal to me, aren't there?' He smiled a smile that made her heart leap, saying, 'I like that about you.'

'Ryken, you have no idea.' They grinned at each other, trying to ignore the impending fight that awaited them.

She was the first to put forth thoughts on how they should tackle the task ahead. 'We need to get out of this building before we do anything else, don't we? We've got to figure that out before even contemplating how we are going to make it to the lab in Brooklyn.'

He asked, 'Have you got a vehicle?'

She raised her eyes slowly, and he encouraged, 'Tell me.'

'I've got a VW Isis in the garage downstairs. It was Dad's. But I never drive it.'

'Is it still in working order?'

'I guess we'll just have to give it a shot.'

'Great, so all we need to figure out now is how we're going to get downstairs.'

'What do you mean?'

'Look outside the front door.'

Seraph went to look out of the peephole in her door, and saw what she hoped wouldn't be there but knew ultimately would. 'There are four of them out in the corridor, waiting patiently for us. Guns, full armour, weaponry galore. How did they get in?'

'Same way I did. We've had the training of all training remember.'

'Shit.'

'There's only one thing for it, Seraph. You are going to have to conquer your fear of heights.'

'For some reason, I knew you were going to say that. Fuck.' She went to the kitchen to pour more coffee, and he came up behind her to wrap his arms around her torso as he watched her spread cream cheese across four bagel halves. He took a couple and devoured them within seconds.

They guzzled the rest of their coffee down, and headed to the shower together. They both stood under the water, cleansing the filth of the past few days off their skin. They washed and talked quickly, making a plan, drying off afterwards with the fan system turned up to full blast.

Seraph sutured the gash on his cheek and taped up his shoulder, noticing he was impressed by her skill. 'You can't put that bloodstained thing back on. I've got some old clothes of my father's I kept, if you want some? He was about the same size as you, give or take.'

'And I thought you weren't sentimental... I'll take whatever you've got.' He grinned.

She produced a few clean shirts from her closet, and laid them out on the bed for him to choose from. He selected a crisp white number with sky-blue edging around the collar and sleeves, and he teamed it with his dark blue jeans. She put her arms around his neck, saying, 'My Mom and Dad would have loved you. And you would have loved them.' He kissed her so gently and held her tight in response, knowing what she had lost, and feeling so proud that she thought of him in that way. Their hearts ached as they remembered it would never be a simple case of being able to be together. Just because they had realised their love, it didn't mean the whole world was fixed. However, holding their arms around each other for those few moments, they absorbed as much of each other as they could.

He pulled his hands through her luxurious mane, 'Just wait until you meet my mother. She's a very passionate Greek woman, with a tongue as sharp as yours. You will get on, I'm sure, and she is going to be bowled over by your beauty, I know she will.' She smiled, but each of them knew the enormity of what lay ahead of them, and who it was they were fighting for.

There was something she still wanted to address; some subject she knew had to be broached before they set out into dangerous territory once again. They were fitting years of getting to know one another into just a few hours. She sat down on the bed in her silk dressing gown, and grabbed his hand for him to sit next to her, keeping hold of it as she asked gently, 'What happened to them Ryken? What happened to your family? Tell me.'

The vein in his neck started protruding again and she could see the torment cross his face. He took a deep breath and she awaited his response patiently. He began, looking down at the floor, 'My paternal grandparents and great grandparents all died in 2023. My father was twenty-two at the time and he struggled to get over it. He married my mother two years later and as far as I know they were happy at first. He became a highly respected detective superintendent in the Manchester Met. I only found out recently that Officium got to him and made him do unscrupulous things. I'm not sure whether he had any choice. He drank heavily and hit me and my mother. The older I got, the more I fought back, and he eventually left me and Mum alone. I don't know what became of him. I've not heard anything from him in twenty-three years.' He held his forehead and added, 'They used him, Seraph.'

The lump in Seraph's throat would not be swallowed, and she wanted to cry for him. But she had to be strong. 'I'm so, so sorry Ryken. I was so wrong to ever doubt you.' His pain and suffering only made her love him more. He stayed silent, looking at his feet, trying to hold his emotions in. She pulled his hand toward her mouth and kissed the back of it, before holding it to her chest. She said, 'You're the most wonderful man I've ever known. You're nothing like him.'

He wiped tears from his eyes with his thumb and forefinger, and she could feel him shaking. His chin fell to his chest and he couldn't see in front of himself for the acidic globules of pain pouring from his eye sockets. She pulled his head toward her chest, and held him in her arms while he shuddered with the relief of unburdening himself. She stroked his black hair and spoke soothingly, 'I'm here, Ryken. I love you so much. Don't ever forget that, my darling.'

When he quietened down, she moved further up the bed, and pulled him up with her. Propped up by cushions, she held his head against her chest, and he grasped her tightly. He wasn't a giant of a man in those few moments and they lay still for what felt like ages. He nuzzled his head against her soft body and relaxed at the sound of her heart beating. He could have stayed like that forever, but he knew what needed to be done.

'Ryken, if I could have one more minute with my parents, I'd do anything for that. To be able to tell them that I understand now, that I love them, and that there is no need for forgiveness because of that. My father was fair, strapping and built like a rhino just like you, while my mother was a raven-haired powerhouse of a woman. I grew up in awe of them, even though we were never as close as we should have been. They were murdered by those bastards, who robbed us of two great people. They were us Ryken, only ten years ago, but something is pushing you and I on now, I know it. The fates have aligned to make this possible, I feel certain. We can do this.'

'We really do have to end this then, don't we?'

She breathed heavily, saying, 'Yes.'

Seemingly recovered, he kissed her quickly, twice, before moving out of the room. He came back with his bag, and emptied his climbing gear out on to the bed.

'I'd better get to work. Have you got a drill?'

She winced at the thought of holes being drilled and heights being conquered. 'In the hallway cupboard.'

She sensed this was what he needed to do – get up and on with the task.

CHAPTER 43

Ryken had a couple of ropes rigged up on Seraph's balcony that he had drilled into the small patio, and they were both getting ready to go. Seraph took only what she needed, leaving her bag behind, as did Ryken. She wore a thin purple sweater underneath her leather jacket, along with the biker boots she picked up from the Ritz in London pulled over a pair of black jeans. Her Unicus slotted in an inside pocket of her jacket, while he tried to hide the myriad devices he carried in his own worn-out brown leather jacket. After tightening his own harness, he fastened hers, asking, 'Are you ready?'

'As ready as I'll ever be,' and they both pulled on their chafe-resistant gloves.

'Don't think about the height okay, just think of it as a minor obstacle, not a danger. Take a deep breath, and descend. I'll be here with you every step of the way.'

She nodded in response, but felt sick to her stomach with nerves. The idea of going over the edge made every inch of her want to run out into the corridor and face those agents instead. She felt the coffee she had drank earlier rising up from her gut along with a fair bit of bile. She was fighting the urge to throw up, and had to use every ounce of concentration to counteract her natural instinct to run. Ryken kissed her quickly on the mouth and tried to lift her spirits, 'Imagine yourself at the end of this task, and it will be done. I love you, and I'm not going to let anything happen to you.'

She wasn't comforted, however. All she could think about was trying to escape her current predicament. She nodded and tried to focus, gathering her thoughts together. She followed him out to the balcony and the full-length window locked automatically behind her. His hands were as steady as steel, but as he beckoned Seraph over, he saw she was trembling. He could see the fear in her eyes and honestly didn't know whether she would be able to go through with the task at hand.

'You are going to be alright,' he reassured her. She nodded, swallowing the bile in her throat again. He knotted the rope through the carabiners of her harness, before sliding the pulley mechanism into place. He tightened his own before testing each of them with all the strength he had. He looked over the edge to judge the drop and threw over the ropes. Suddenly, she felt so sick, she had to reach over to a decaying plant pot and throw up in it.

She turned back to Ryken after wiping her mouth. 'I can't do this.'

'You can.'

She moved back against the building and held her palms out to steady herself. 'No, I can't. I fell in a ravine when I was little and broke my collarbone.'

'You're not a little girl now, you're my woman. I need you to get over that ledge for me.' His tone was harsh and unforgiving but he grabbed her body in his and held her tight, kissing her forehead hard.

'Right, Seraph, we're going to climb over the wall together, and I want you to hang so you can feel your own weight. Keep your eyes on me, don't look down. I'm here with you.'

Seraph looked at the mechanisms Ryken had just tightened up, but still honestly felt like she was going to die. She started shaking her head in protestation, but he somehow sensed that agents would be swarming the place soon if they didn't get a move on. He climbed over alone and held out his arms for her with his feet wedged in the gaps between the columns of the wall. The sound of the metal on her harness clunking about in the wind almost drove her to despair.

'Please my angel, just climb over and keep your eyes on me. Now, Seraph!'

He held out his hand for her and she walked slowly toward him, still gripped by fear. As soon as she got near, he grabbed her and pulled her over. They fell back and were left hanging. He kept hold of her body tightly, pulling her into his chest as they swung in mid-air. She was trembling head-to-toe, so badly she could hardly feel her fingers.

'The ropes are holding our weight, Seraph, so nothing is going to happen. Just don't look down. I'm going to release you and you're going to grab the slack bit of the rope in your left hand and the other in your right. Grab them!'

She did as he said, no longer able to feel a single part of herself. She swung about and closed her eyes.

'Feed the rope through, feed it through, do it now. I'm here with you.'

She slowly started feeding it through, and felt herself dropping very gradually. She bravely kicked her legs out toward the building and he said, 'Good, very good, keep doing that.'

Once she decided it wasn't that bad, and that she had done the hard part by making it over, she started feeding the rope through quicker. Ryken noticed and instantly responded, following her as they descended past people's windows quicker and quicker. She opened her eyes and couldn't help but look down. There were about five floors to go. Her head swam with fear.

'Fuck.' She took a deep breath, and let the slack go very quickly. He followed immediately.

Once they were on the ground, he grabbed her for a quick, reassuring embrace, saying, 'Well done.'

They released their harnesses but had no time to waste. They ran around the corner and through the iron gates of the Dakota car park, Seraph swiping her U-Card as they went. They knew they would have barely seconds to get out of there. They ran down a ramp and toward her car. It was an old-fashioned hybrid vehicle with metallic red bodywork and large windows. She unlocked it and they got in, before the seat belts passed over their arms automatically.

Once in the vehicle, Seraph put her head against the steering wheel and took a few deep breaths. He rubbed her back and smiled, 'You did it, Seraph.'

Seraph pressed the ignition button and said, 'You can direct me Ryken. Which way would be best?'

'Why don't I just drive?'

'Trust me, this piece of crap requires a woman's touch. Now we're on the ground, I'm in charge from now on, okay? You can't drive with that shoulder anyway, can you?' He was happy to be the one being told what to do, after the scene they had just left behind. They switched between roles effortlessly, and she was the instigator once more.

She put the car into reverse and started to back out. However, she broke suddenly when they saw him. An agent had popped out from nowhere and was stood just across the car park. As soon as the agent saw them, he talked into a small device to no doubt tell his colleagues about their whereabouts. This place would be swarming with them within minutes.

'Honey, you're about to see what else I can do.' Seraph shot a menacing glance at her lover. Holding her hand behind his headrest, she reversed speedily, before heading for the exit at pace with her palm against the wheel. Launching out of the car park, she swung out on to Central Park West, narrowly avoiding at least three hover-cabs as their vehicle almost toppled over with the way they had careered out. As they saw the green of Central Park whizzing by outside the window, she checked her mirrors and saw no cars were chasing them – yet – but she knew they couldn't be complacent. She slammed her foot on the accelerator and sped off, tooting her horn for people to get out of the way. At best, the vehicle could travel

50mph, but the normally quiet engine was roaring under her harsh command. She didn't care if they had the entire police force after them, as far as she was concerned, everyone was an enemy. She just needed to get to that lab.

'Seraph, keep heading south.'

She didn't speak, she just kept the pedal to the metal, racing between vehicles and bicycles. Leaving devastation in her wake, she continued without flinching, with Ryken a shocked passenger in the driver's seat. He could only sit there and wait to see what she would do next.

'Ryken, look up ahead.'

A barricade containing dozens of police officers and agents along with traffic cones and metal barriers had been erected just before the jam-packed concrete of Columbus Circle. A number of angry people were getting out of their cars to see what the hold-up was.

'Through the park it is,' he said.

'Shit, hold on.'

She looked behind her and swung into the outside lane, before seeing her opportunity and turning the wheel dramatically to get across the other side of the road before it was filled with traffic. She slammed the accelerator down to get them across. Turning into the park, they clattered about as they rammed over the sidewalk, across paths and grass, between trees and people. When they saw the entrance to Seventh on Central Park South, Seraph screeched off and clattered back onto the road, miraculously avoiding collisions with several vehicles. Hitting the vehicle's top speed, she took it through whatever gaps she could find. They clunked about as she mercilessly took the vehicle over bumps and potholes.

'I don't know if we can make it all the way to Brooklyn in this beat-up old thing, Ryken. It's too far if they're gonna chase us all the way.'

They were coming up to what used to be Macy's on the left, when they saw the sirens behind them. A number of vehicles were chasing their way.

'If only we had that bike, nothing could beat that thing,' she joked.

'I know. That's my next birthday present my angel.'

She answered jokingly, through gritted teeth, 'Hint taken and noted *my sweet*, now what the fuck are we going to do next?'

'Take Sixth. I have an idea.' He looked behind at the chasing vehicles but felt they could still do this.

'Okay.'

At the corner of Macy's, she suddenly lifted the handbrake and veered around onto W 34th, before screeching again as they rounded another corner to take Sixth. She continually pushed the vehicle to its limits, smashing and crunching the brakes and accelerator.

'God I love you,' he said, reaching over to kiss her cheek.

She shot off down Sixth, and sped along the relatively empty, straight road as fast as possible, reaching top speed at the quieter points.

'Do you know Broome Street?'

'Yeah, why?'

'We're going there to get my bike.'

'Okay.'

'Pull down Dominick, and we'll run round the back.'

'Sure thing.'

Seraph's arms were aching from having to hold the steering wheel tight over all the bumps in the road. She could sense the old car wasn't going to last much longer, and tried to hold out on damaging it anymore than it already been if they were to make it to Ryken's place.

'Take your next right Seraph, and pull up just in front of the shoeshine booth.'

She did as he said and screeched to a halt as they pulled up. She locked the vehicle and thought, *What the heck!* She threw the keys at the shoeshine guy and said, 'Take good care of her buddy.'

She and Ryken started running down a back-alley toward his apartment block. They reached the entrance of the underground parking facility of his building when a van full of agents pulled to a halt up ahead, getting out to face them. Seraph and Ryken slowed down to look at the group, counting six in total, before looking at each other.

They knew it wasn't going to be that easy for them to escape the clutches of Officium after all. Ryken started walking toward them, ready to face whatever they had to throw at him. Seraph put her arm out to stop him. 'Ryken, don't be idiotic, let me deal with them. They won't kill me, remember.'

'Seraph, I'm not going to let them take you.' He was confused, misunderstanding her meaning.

'Who said anything about them taking me?'

She turned to Ryken and stroked his cheek, before roughly swiping the weapons she knew he had hidden under his belt. She cocked the ceramic gun she had hidden in her boot and he winked, watching her as she replaced it. She caught the look in his eye, one of love and fear, and she shot him one in return to reassure him she knew what she was doing. Before moving off in the direction of the agents, she looked back at her lover and smiled, reassuring him yet again that she was confident. She bounced off on her feline paws and sucked in the love Ryken and she shared, breathing it into every vein in her body. She felt a shiver run down her spine, and shook it out, knowing she was more dangerous than she had ever been. She felt the rush of adrenalin in her body more than ever before, and her love for that man gave her the supreme strength she had never realised was in her. His energy was the most powerful catalyst she had ever encountered and her limbs pulsated with it. In the darkness of the

H

underground facility, she became that other side of herself.

She tucked the stun gun and taser into the back of her own belt, before taking off her jacket and discarding it behind her. She ripped off her jumper, revealing a thin vest underneath. Seraph could sense Ryken was about to leap into action, but she looked back again to warn him to stay put, and she carried on walking in the direction of the agents. When she was only yards away from them, and out of Ryken's earshot, she dragged a hand through her long hair seductively and said, 'Hello boys, what exactly can I do for you?' She flashed her smile, appearing totally unthreatened. Stood in V-formation, they looked at each other out of confusion, and in that split second she used the chink in their armour to her advantage. She broke out the stun gun and aimed it at the two men directly in front of her, shooting one and then the other, before dropping the used-up weapon to the ground. The agents sprang into action immediately, and she could hear Ryken running towards her in the background. Two agents came at her from either side, but she jabbed one of them with the taser, and reached behind her to kick the other one in the groin with the heel of her shoe, before smashing both of their already dizzy heads together. She regained her stance as she saw another about to lunge at her, and she retrieved her ceramic gun from her boot to shoot him in the foot. She dropped her weapon to the ground, and as the last one started to move towards her, she readied herself. He tried to throw a punch in her direction, but she ducked to avoid him, and sent a blow to his body with her own fist instead. Regaining her composure, she eyed the agent she had just winded, and pivoted her body back to kick him right across the temple. He fell to the floor in a crumpled mess. Surveying the pile of squirming bodies before her, she picked her gun back off the ground.

Ryken got to her just as she dealt with the last of the agents, and looked at her in absolute disbelief. 'These boneheads obviously haven't had it in a while,' she purred in his ear.

'Obviously not.' He surveyed the carnage, and grabbed her for a passionate kiss, running his hands across her back and over her behind. He was rampant with desire, eyeing his warrior woman with a lust he hadn't believed could get any more fervent.

She said, 'Come on, let's go before this place is crawling with them.' And with that, Seraph picked up her clothes off the floor, and Ryken swiped a few guns off the wounded agents that lay around them. He led her to where his Kawasaki Ignis was parked up, and the pair leapt on. Seraph threw her arms around him and kissed the back of his neck before they shot off toward the Battery Tunnel.

CHAPTER 44

Ryken and Seraph had made it to the Battery Tunnel, and had used his fake U-Card to get them through, swiping it quickly as they went past an unmanned booth. They whizzed along the dimly-lit tunnel and Seraph felt sure they were capable of accomplishing anything together. She held his body tightly and he rode one-handed to hold her hands between one of his.

When they reached Brooklyn, their thoughts turned to what needed to happen next. He took the bike to Prospect Heights and stopped just around the corner from an old Polytechnic. He got off and she followed as they assessed the place from a distance.

'Is that it?' she asked.

'No, it's that apartment building next to it there with the blue windows. It's covert.'

'Yeah, it doesn't look like much, but then they never really cared about where, did they? How are we getting in?'

'Umm, I'm not sure... I guess we didn't think about that before leaving your apartment.'

'I suppose ringing the front doorbell's outta the question?'

'There is something, one avenue you probably wouldn't agree to though...'

'Yes?'

'The apartment building right next door is roughly the same height, and only a few yards away from that one. We could jump from the top of one to the other.'

She chewed her lip, considering the prospect of facing her fear again. She thought it through logically, 'And what then? After we get to the roof? How will you get in?'

He pulled out the Clever-Grip pads that were stowed in his inside pockets, and she took a deep breath. 'It will mean some free climbing.'

She weighed up everything in her mind. 'Only one of us can use those, though, can't they?' She gestured at the pads. He nodded, and soon it became clear to her what had to be done.

'Ryken, don't argue with me on this one. I will go in from the bottom, and you from the top. I can distract them, okay? You can get the stuff and I'll find you.'

He looked unwilling to agree to this plan of hers, grabbing her cheek with his hand. 'I can't let you do that, Seraph, I can't risk losing you.' He looked pained at the thought of being separated from her again.

'There's no other way Ryken. I will be fine, you know I will.'

He knew they needed to get a move on so he relented and took Seraph's hand, pulling her across the street in the direction of a narrow backstreet behind Officium's lab. He suddenly pulled her in a doorway, and held her body to his, grabbing her at her lower back. 'Oh god, Seraph.' He kissed her ardently, pulling the back of her head toward him so that her mouth went smashing into his. They wanted each other again, so badly. 'If I don't get out of this my angel…'

'Ryken, don't. That is not an option.'

He held on to her, and lowered his deep voice to an even more sonorous tone, 'I love you.'

She grabbed his wrists and shoved him back against the door. She pressed her body up against his, squeezing his hands tightly with her own. She kissed him back passionately, and they shook themselves from their vigorous clinch with breathlessness. He smiled as if he couldn't believe he had found such a woman.

'Ryken, don't worry about me, I have a plan. Go.'

And with that, he went down the street and around the corner, and they were once again separated.

CHAPTER 45

After Ryken had left her, Seraph ventured from her hiding place and went to scout the laboratory building. She was careful to move slowly down the alley, and once she reached the end, she peered around the corner to get a feel for the place. Sure enough, she spotted people in suits entering and leaving the building. She watched people's movements for a few minutes, and spotted her victim.

The young woman was about her height, and seemed an easy target. Seraph crossed the road and followed the girl, who was probably heading home from work. She saw her opportunity a few yards away and ran up behind the woman, pulling her into an alleyway sharply. Seraph pushed her gun into the woman's throat, and demanded her ID badge. The woman panicked and adhered to Seraph's demands immediately, passing the fearsome journalist her lanyard. Seraph said, 'I'm really sorry about this,' and she executed her now trademark head-butt again, leaving the poor young girl flopped against the wall as she ran back down the street.

Seraph tried to ensure she was presentable enough to enter the building without drawing attention to herself, smoothing her clothes and pulling her hair back into a ponytail as she neared her destination. She whipped the ID around her neck and got into character, adopting the persona of any other laboratory technician turning up for work. She followed the other people flocking into the building and tried to look as inconspicuous as possible as she queued up with the other employees to enter through the ID checkpoint in the lavish reception area, which rose up to the fifth floor above and showcased a giant waterfall streaming down, as well as many seating areas filled with luxurious settees and coffee machines on hand. She suddenly remembered she was carrying the weapons Ryken had stolen from the agents. *Calm down. Don't draw attention to yourself. You're not really a reporter, you're a bland office worker. A lab technician. Any ordinary person. They won't recognise you. Yeah right…* She tried to think quickly and logically. She needed to offload them. Putting her hands deep in her pockets, she tucked the two handguns inside her sleeves and pulled her hands back out. She saw a security guard staring at her, and as she smiled at him he seemed to carry on about his business, surveying everyone else. She saw her moment and appeared to turn to her right to stare at a screen on the wall, but as she did, she dropped one of the guns in a bag a woman in front of her was carrying. She turned back to face forward, and as the woman went forward through security and set off a number of alarms, Seraph spotted another opportunity amidst the ensuing chaos, dropping the other gun in a large plant pot nearby that contained a miniature palm tree. The poor woman went bright red, and was escorted off to a room by several security guards, as Seraph patiently waited her turn to go through security, still trying to appear as ordinary as possible. Seconds later, a different security guard waved Seraph through, and she moved along without any problem at all, hearing a positive beep after swiping the stolen card, and seeing the turnstile light switch to green. *Thank god.*

She didn't have any idea where she was going, but once she saw a sign for *Security Center*, she knew what needed to be done. She wondered what Ryken would be doing at that precise moment in time, and prayed he was okay. She hoped this would buy him some time at least.

She walked down a corridor and looked for the room she assumed would be there somewhere. Then she saw it, and looked through the glass window. There was only one security guard sat inside, and he was peering at the various images on the screens in his office. She tried the door but when she realised it was locked, she quickly moved to the side to stay out of view. She heard the handle and the door unlock, and the security guard peered around to see if anyone was there, but Seraph managed to remain concealed behind the door. As he moved back into the office and let the door shut behind him, Seraph caught the handle just before it locked, and she pulled the door open to let herself in, quickly shutting it behind her. The guard had no time to react as he eyed Seraph up and down. She was easily five inches taller than the middle-aged, balding man before her, and she knocked him out with one fell swoop, punching him right between the eyes. His body conveniently fell back in his chair, and she pushed him out of the way so that she could see the controls of the security system.

She went to the main computer, and found the control panel. She set the security level to low, turned off all the surveillance cameras and ran back out of the room, smashing the fire alarm on the wall outside as she did so. All the doors of the place unlocked to let everyone out. Entering the stairwell nearby, Seraph ran up the five floors to where she hoped Ryken would be.

Once she was on the fifth floor, she waited behind the stairwell door for all the staff that were floating about to get in the elevators and leave. When it finally seemed quiet, she emerged into the corridor and started walking from door to door, peering through each one as she went, trying to detect whether Ryken was inside one lab or another. She got to the end of one corridor when she decided to try the other one around the corner. She rushed round to start checking each of the offices back there, but an arm came out of nowhere to stop her in her tracks and quickly pulled her into one of the rooms.

The door shut and she desperately tried to escape her captor, but there was no moving out of his unyielding grasp. She heard his almost silent whisper in her ear, 'It's me. Stay absolutely still.'

He held his arms around her body, with his back up against the wall next to the door of the office they were in. She was immediately comforted by his presence and felt for his hand. Seconds later they heard noises out in the corridor, figures running about, shouting and peering through windows into offices. They heard weaponry slinging about, and heavy boots trudging. Ryken and Seraph both held their breaths as they prayed for the agents to leave, and after several minutes of silence, Seraph let her head fall right back against her would-be-captor's chest to look up into his face, and he bent his head down to kiss her forehead.

'Did you get what we came here for?' she asked hurriedly, turning to face him, still in his grasp.

Ryken shook his head in disappointment. 'I checked all three labs Seraph, and they've all been stripped. They are all totally empty, nothing's left. They've taken measures.'

Her nose was almost touching his and she saw no lie in his eye. They had gotten so comfortable with each other, that they stood so close without even blinking. 'Fuck Ryken, what the hell are we going to do?'

'Take a boat to a deserted island and never come back?'

'Ha ha, yeah, let's just waste all our efforts at the drop of a hat, after coming up against one little obstacle.'

'I have a horrible feeling our luck is about to run out okay. I say we cut our losses.'

'We can't. We've come this far. Remember what is at stake.'

'Our lives?' He was becoming slightly dejected, she could tell. She was exhausted and frustrated too, but something was driving her forward.

'There is something we are missing here Ryken, I can feel it in my gut. There is something we've overlooked, and I'm going to get to the bottom of it. I don't know what it is, but all this is just too weird.'

'Look, Seraph, can we just get out of here? Get somewhere safe and talk this through?'

'Okay.'

With that, Ryken checked the corridor and they ran for the stairwell, pounding down the stairs as quickly as they could. They got to the bottom and went out of a fire exit, slamming the door shut behind them as they left at the opposite side of the building she had come in through. They daren't go back to the bike, and when the building was no longer in sight, they started running and didn't look back.

CHAPTER 46

After pounding the pavements for what felt like miles, Ryken and Seraph were sure they were in Queens somewhere. They had traversed the ruined suburbs for so long, that everything looked the same. Every house was a filthy brown colour, every corner had a Convenience4U on it, and every takeaway stank of foul, greasy food. Their bodies had only the energy to run, not to think anymore, and they had no idea where they had ended up. They had twisted and turned down dozens and dozens of backstreets, not really knowing where they were going, only that they needed to avoid being seen. Seraph was developing a stitch, and she asked to stop behind a shabby food outlet. She held her hands on her knees, and tried to catch her breath, working out the stitch at the same time. Ryken tried to regain his strength too, but the pair of them were done for. It was starting to get dark, and they needed to rest somewhere.

He attempted humour. 'Two million and we can't even afford a bed for the night!'

'I know, right? This world is fucked. I can't even spend my money without someone knowing where I am or what I'm doing.' The strains of the day were starting to catch up with her, and inside she was beginning to despair. She needed some comfort and he knew without her even having to say. He took her in his arms, holding her head against his chest, stroking her hair. She didn't even have the energy to put her arms around him, limply falling against his body with hers.

'I wish I could take this all away Seraph, but I can't.'

Wearily she admitted, 'I know... What are we going to do Ryken? It feels like this is an impossible situation.'

They stood feeling as though there was nowhere to go, nobody who could help, no way of getting out of the situation without having to fight for their lives yet again. They were thirsty, hungry, tired and aching all over.

Ryken still suffered from the previous day's encounter with the agents, and he was running on empty. If it wasn't for Seraph, he could have happily crawled into a hole and died.

As he held Seraph, Ryken spotted something behind her. A man bounded out of his hydro-car, a Peugeot 9008, and left it running as he went into a Mexican takeaway just across the street.

'Quick, we're getting out of here.' Ryken pulled Seraph with him in the direction of the vehicle, and she soon cottoned on to his plan, with each of them slamming the doors shut as they got in the vehicle. It stank of body odour and cigars but as his and Seraph's escape route – it was priceless. Ryken sped off and heard the screams of the vehicle's owner behind them as they shot off into the darkness of the ensuing blackout. Seraph buckled herself in the passenger seat and let her head fall back against the headrest. She was exhausted, and she just needed to be away from all this.

Ryken relied on his instincts alone in a bid to drive east, and he kept going until he reached the Long Island Expressway. He kept to a steady 60mph to conserve power and avoid getting noticed. Seraph seemed to have fallen asleep in the passenger seat, but he continued on, hoping to find somewhere to stop for them to rest.

He had managed to drive quite far when he noticed the fuel gauge was starting to run low, so he pulled off the Freeway, without any thought of where he might go next. He hit Blue Point, which had been abandoned, and drove through, hoping to spot somewhere they could rest. The landscape was barren and unforgiving, and covered in darkness. There were loads of houses lining the beaches but they all looked ruined, battered by the rising waters. He didn't know whether any of them would provide decent shelter. The fuel level was running ever lower, however, and he would soon run out. He made a decision to pull into a white wooden beach house that looked totally abandoned.

He pulled up the gravel driveway, and the engine gave out as he reached the house. *I couldn't have timed that any better.* Seraph was still asleep, resting her head against the window, exhausted from the day's toil and their all-night lovemaking. He got out of the car and went to the passenger side, unbuckled her seatbelt and pulled her body out of the vehicle. She seemed to stir and tightened her arms around his neck, hiding her face in his shoulder. He reached a door of the property and walked into a kitchen to survey the scene. There were broken pots and pans thrown around, twigs, stones and bits of hay spread on the tiled floor and the smell of a house unlived in for decades. He saw a lounge off the kitchen and walked through, placing Seraph on a dusty couch covered in rubbish. He saw no better option at that moment, and needed to have a look around.

There were tins of food in the cupboards but they were well out of date, and the taps didn't produce any water. He gripped a banister to pull his weary body upstairs and found several bedrooms, but none of them looked as though they would be any good for sleeping in. He went back out to the vehicle, popping the trunk to see what might be hiding in there. He discovered bottles of beer, boxes of cigars, a tartan blanket and a bag full of dried snacks. He took them all inside, and saw that Seraph was sat up on the couch, wondering where he had got to.

'Where are we?'

'Somewhere on Long Island. The car died just as I pulled up the drive. Here, I found these in the boot.' He handed her a beer and a packet of chips. She slugged the drink after snapping the lid off, and broke open the bag of chips.

They didn't speak for several minutes while they munched the snacks and drank the liquid down. The bleakness of their situation was apparent. They couldn't travel, or go back to their apartments, and returning within even a yard of the city would be dangerous. It felt like they were alone without a single resource in the world.

They were both on their second bottles when she broke the silence. 'Ryken, there is something you're not telling me. I can feel it and see it in your eyes. Why weren't the samples there if Eve told us they would be?'

He knew this was coming, and yet he had hoped she wouldn't press him. 'They really weren't there, I searched that place high and low.' He was sat on a coffee table positioned right in front of the couch she occupied. He avoided her gaze, looking down at the floor. 'Eve may have believed they were there, but they have obviously been moved. Something has scared them into taking measures to move them elsewhere. You know it's not unheard of for them to just up and leave one lab for another, they do it all the time, at a moment's notice.'

She disbelieved him. She moved closer to him and lifted his chin with her index finger, looking him in the eye. 'Ryken, tell me. I trust you, please trust me.'

He twisted his lip as he fought back the urge to speak. He was fighting a desperate internal battle to tell her the truth, but he needed to protect her. He knew there were much larger things at stake. He kept looking her in the eye, but she realised he wouldn't reveal his thoughts.

'Fine, that's just fine,' she growled, before standing up to walk away from him, and opening a door to go outside.

She stood on the decking at the front of the house and looked out, gasping at the cold wind that rushed into her lungs. Even out there, the pollution of NYC still made it hard to see any stars in the sky, but Seraph used her imagination to envisage them. The wind rushed through her hair, and she breathed in the elements. The air was slightly fresher, but the familiar scent of the city still didn't seem too far away. Her heart hurt with a mixture of despair, new love and emptiness. Somehow, she couldn't believe

Eve would lead them into danger for nothing. She knew there was something she was missing about this whole fiasco, and yet, she was readying herself to cave in and admit defeat. The past week or so had almost crushed her spirit, sapped her strength and weakened her body to its very core. Earlier that day, she had been high with adrenalin and the way Ryken made her feel, and those feelings had given her immense strength. And yet, the reality was that they could never really be together unless this situation resolved itself properly. They needed that evidence. So many factors relied on getting that proof, and the enormity of its importance was hurting her brain so that she couldn't think straight. The one thing she had spent years trying to get, and the one thing she could never obtain.

Ryken came out and beckoned her back in with his hand on hers. 'It's cold, please come inside.' He led her back to the couch, and pulled her into his arms. 'If you trust me Seraph, then you will let me keep my silence for now. If you love me, you'll just stay here with me tonight, and we'll make our plans in the morning.'

She turned to look at him, with several emotions crossing her face, but she didn't have the energy to fight him. She fought back the sobs, breathing heavily as she said, 'I trust you with my life.'

He pulled her into his chest and held his arms around her tightly. She could hear his heart beating wildly, and his breathing was heavy. He spoke truthfully, trembling as he said, 'I would die for you, Seraphina.'

CHAPTER 47

It was around 7am the next morning and Seraph woke with a mouth that felt like sandpaper. She tried to suck some saliva forward to bring her tongue back to life, and suddenly she remembered where she was. She opened her eyes to survey the decaying house, and felt the blanket Ryken had tucked around her last night as she cried herself to sleep in his arms. Then a terrible feeling overwhelmed her. She shot up to look around, and couldn't see him anywhere. 'Ryken, Ryken, where are you?' But there was no response. She jumped off the couch, ran around the house, and couldn't find him anywhere. She looked outside and saw the car was still there. She ran out to see if he was loitering, shouting his name over and over again. He was nowhere to be seen. She was screaming his name, but there was no reply. She looked out at the grey waters, and spun around surveying the barren landscape. He had gone.

She fell to her knees, and screamed at the top of her lungs. Hot tears fell down her cheeks, and she pulled her hands into tight fists in fits of anger and despair. She had feared this would happen.

After gathering herself, she got up and went back inside, hoping he might have left her a note or something. But as she searched the place, she realised there was nothing. She didn't know when he might have left so couldn't figure out how far he would have gone. She went outside again, wracking her brain for options, and wondered whether she might find anything in the garage. She searched madly, but there was nothing. No vehicles, no fuel cans, nothing. There was only one thing she could do.

She powered up her Unicus and called Camille, who answered within seconds.

'Seraph?'

'I need help Camille, I'm stuck on Long Island, and Ryken's gone. He left me here and I've no idea how to get back, or where to go, or what to do. I'm just stranded, and I feel lost, Camille. Please help me.' She was rambling manically, and she took a deep breath as she could feel herself starting to panic.

'Seraph, my love, calm down, please, calm down. Are you on a secure line?'

'I don't know, I think so, I can't tell.'

'Listen very carefully, I'm going to call you back in a moment, but until then I want you to get back indoors and wait. Wait there, Seraph.'

'Okay,' and Seraph hung up, going back inside to wait.

Several minutes passed and she was starting to panic again when her Unicus sounded. 'Camille, Camille?'

'Yes, it's me. I'm sending someone to come and get you.'

'What about Ryken?'

'Seraph, just wait there. I'm sending someone for you. Send your co-ordinates to me at once, and we'll find you. Just hang in there, angel.'

'Okay, okay. I'll do that. But Camille, please find him for me. Please.'

'I'll do what I can, my love. Stay there, stay there my darling.' And with that, she hung up.

CHAPTER 48

Ryken had held a tearful Seraph in his arms until she fell asleep, and he had tucked a blanket around her body as she lay down on the dilapidated couch in the beach house. He had sat in an armchair, closing his eyes, willing sleep to come. However, no matter how hard he tried, he could not rest. He knew what lay ahead.

He seemed to go in and out of sleep for a little while, and at about 6am, he was shocked into life by the vibrating of a Unicus in his inside pocket. Seraph stirred a little, but didn't wake, so he looked at the screen and read the message: *The Plaza. One hour. Come alone.*

It was time. Ryken felt a sinking feeling of dread wash over him. He would have to yank every ounce of himself away from Seraph, and yet he knew it had to be done. Ultimately, there was no other choice. If he didn't do it, there would be no future for either of them.

He crept over to where she was sleeping and kissed her face ever so delicately so as not to wake her. He stroked her hair, and stared at her face, imprinting it on his memory. He would need her image to keep him going. He took a deep breath and soundlessly went out of the house. He hunted through a number of garages nearby to see if there was any spare fuel, but he eventually found something much better. A Ducati Tornado. It was unloved and would probably break down, but he had to give it a shot. He pushed it out of its hiding place, out of the driveway and then further down the road so that Seraph would not be woken by the sound of him starting it up. He caught sight of himself in a rear-view mirror and what stared back nearly scared the living daylights out of him. His face was black and blue, and his eyes were bloodshot, his face a pallid green and his mouth contorted with torment at leaving behind the woman he loved. The woman who had saved him. He almost didn't recognise himself.

Once out of earshot of Seraph, he started the machine. It took a few efforts but he eventually got it going and hopped on, heading back to New York with the engine spluttering along. As he rode the bike, thoughts of Seraph filled his head. Remembrances of their lovemaking, her bravery yesterday and her spirit. He nearly turned around and went back, but he didn't. He could have kicked himself, but instead he let the wind lash his eyes, tears streaming down his face as he rode on. He felt sick to the core; every inch of him knew that he may never see her again. Even the sky overhead seemed to mirror his sombre mood, with grey clouds tinged by brown dust and dreariness.

He took the Expressway, travelling back through the decaying neighbourhoods of Queens and Brooklyn, and across Manhattan Bridge with his fake U-Card. At that time of the morning, he didn't think anyone would be observant enough to recognise his face, and they weren't. He rode one-handed through the empty streets of Manhattan, which was yet to break into life, and he also knew that it would probably be the last time he would ever see the place. It had been home to him for the past eight years, and he never thought he would be leaving it. He had woken up every day feeling so grateful to live in the Big Apple that he couldn't wait to go out into the world and get on with the day. He loved the hustle and bustle, the crowding and the smells. He had always been a city boy at heart. That was pretty much the only kind of living he had ever known. However, he knew as he saw dozens of people asleep on the streets that there was a reason he needed to get this over with. He needed to help them see the truth for themselves, so that they could shake off their fears and rebuild their lives.

As he neared the Plaza, he manoeuvred the bike off the road and into the underground parking facility at speed, hoping he hadn't been followed. He got off the machine and headed for the doorway to the stairwell. He read the signs for *Reception* and climbed two flights of stairs to get there. He came up against a locked door, which had a combination entry system. He looked through the slit glass window and saw no signs of life in the hotel reception, but as he banged on the door to be let in, the shadow of a figure got closer to the door. It was Mara, and when she saw it was him, she unlocked the door.

'Ryken, come in, quickly.'

Ryken entered and closed the door behind him immediately. Once inside, he felt he had found sanctuary. The decadent surroundings were lost on him, though; he had so much whizzing around his mind. He needed to get this over with. She gestured for him to follow her, and they moved quickly. They went into an office behind the vast reception desk, and Mara left him there alone, saying, 'She'll be with you in just a moment. Help yourself to coffee.'

He sat at a desk with a mug in hand, rubbing his eyes, which were stinging from exhaustion. He suddenly heard, 'Hello Ryken.'

Behind him on the screen of the office vis-phone was a familiar face. 'We meet again, Camille?'

'Yes. Is Seraph safe?'

'She's in an abandoned house somewhere. She'll probably be calling you up soon to come get her.'

'It's a certainty. Look, we've got to act quickly Ryken. There's a drawer in the bottom of that filing cabinet next to you. It contains everything you need.' He looked down and was about to inspect its contents when she continued, 'But listen to me first. The guard at Officium's headquarters changes over at 8am. This is when they are most vulnerable, this is when you will attack. One of our undercovers learnt of a secret underground doorway on the south side of the building. There will be what looks like a utility worker's tent. Go inside and key *Orpheus* into the entrance gate system. This is our last chance to thwart them Ryken. We have to end this once and for all. You need to get to the director's office on the top floor. I'm going to send you his DNA fingerprint to your Unicus so that you can access his safe. You have the necessary software on your device, I imagine?'

He nodded.

She continued, 'Superb. We recently learnt he kept hard copies detailing all the research that was carried out on the 2023 virus, in case they needed to be able to deal with such a catastrophe ever again. Any digital information was destroyed decades ago, which is why we've never been able to hack the evidence. In the drawer, there's a page scanner. It's old but should work with the Wi-Fi on your Unicus. Scan the pages, and send them on to whoever you can think of. The data is more important than the vaccines Ryken. I know it will be tempting, but the data is all we need. We need to make sure these people don't get a second chance at wreaking havoc on this world again. In the drawer, you'll find explosives. Use them to destroy the labs and offices on the upper three floors. The best thing to do would be to rig them up outside the building so they won't be able to undo your work as easily. There's also a small device which we call the Imp in there, should you need a quick way back in or out.

'So many people have given so much for this Ryken, and they are all relying on you. I know you can see this through. Once the job is done, get yourself out of there as quickly as possible. Good luck.'

'Okay, I know what I have to do. Look after her Camille.'

'You know I will Ryken.'

She hung up and the screen went blank. Ryken went into the drawer and found a full set of body armour, timer devices, explosives, two PPKs and two AK-197s. There was also the slim, rectangular, A4-width scanner, and the high-tech Imp device. Nearly a decade ago, he thought he had done with combat, and now he was right back to square one. He stripped off his current clothing and pulled on the black cargo pants, black t-shirt and steel toe-cap boots. He strapped the bullet-proof vest around himself, as well as his protective legs and arm pads. He also pulled on a bullet-proof balaclava made of high-gauge metal fibres, and was ready to go, tucking the various weaponry and gadgets in his vest, the explosives in his trouser pockets and carrying the two AKs against the outsides of his thighs. Mara appeared at the door when he was ready and asked, 'Shall I show you out?'

'Yes, please.'

She walked with him, and he remarked, 'That was a pretty clever trick getting me in the cargo hold on the plane. Who knew what I'd find down there, eh?'

She winked slightly, eyeing him up. His militant appearance contrasted starkly with the decadent surroundings of the hotel. As she walked alongside him bolt upright, he noted that she must still practice her martial arts. Her limbs were taut and solid. She was beautiful and had an aura of infallibility about her. He recognised the women of RAO were strong leaders, complex and mysterious, but most of all dignified and full of integrity. He loved women, particularly this kind, and especially the most magnificent of all these fair creatures, Seraph, whom he hoped would one day become his wife and the mother of his children.

Mara began her pep talk, eyeing Ryken with unwavering eyes and a demeanour of absolute belief. 'All we needed was one person strong enough to take on this challenge, for this to work. It was fated that it would always be you, what with your combined combat and medical skills. I don't envy what it must have been like to have to divide your loyalties so determinedly to get where you did in their organisation Ryken, but you truly proved yourself to be incorruptible, unlike so many others we've tried to nurture over the years that have ended up entangling themselves too far. You and Seraph have sent them into a frenzy of fear. There is one other thing yet you have over them though, Ryken. You have love. Those automatons at the heart of Officium don't know why they kill, brutalize and maim other human begins. They have no thought for anything or anyone. They simply carry out orders and obey. You have a purpose much more worthy than theirs. Remember your ancestors, Seraph's parents, my father, my husband and many other people's loved ones. That is why you have to do what you must. They thought they could play God, and when it went disastrously wrong, they took whatever measures necessary to cover their tracks. Power in the wrong hands manipulated the course of human history forever.'

They reached a doorway at the back of the hotel, and Mara was about to let him out. 'Remember why you're doing this, Ryken. Most of the people in this world still don't understand why we are living like this, and they need to know.'

'Don't worry, I'm going to end this once and for all,' and he offered his hand for Mara to shake. She rigorously grabbed his with both of hers, and smiled warmly at the man standing before her.

'RAO prevailed because we were there from the beginning and knew what these people were capable of. They wouldn't have let you in unless they thought they could manipulate you. But you have her, just comfort yourself with that. She's a very lucky woman.'

'No, I'm the lucky one, fortunate to have found her when I did.' He looked out of the door, turned back to smile at Mara, and ran off.

*   *   *

Minutes later, Ryken had rounded the corner and was outside the tent. He checked there was nobody inside, and ducked in. It seemed deathly quiet in the area, and he wondered whether perhaps his and Seraph's antics yesterday had forced them to retreat inside. He keyed in the code and a manhole cover sprang open. He jumped in, and the door retracted back as soon as he was down. He was in a pitch-black tunnel, and after walking about thirty yards, he came to a set of climbing stairs and launched himself up. He found himself in a well-lit corridor with plastic floor tiles underneath his feet and cream painted walls.

He walked along precariously, waiting to see whether anyone had noticed his arrival. He strode on and came to an elevator. He pressed the button to go up, and just when he thought this all seemed a bit too easy, a woman noticed him in his full gear and screamed. She ran off down the corridor, shouting, 'Intruder, intruder!'

The elevator arrived and he stepped in. Pressing the button for the 20th floor, he heard the pounding steps of agents as the door shut. Seconds later he arrived and as the elevator doors opened, he took out his gun to damage the computer system in the lift. He walked out and took two pistols in his hands. He started firing off rounds, and screams from the staff rang out. He shouted, 'Everybody out, everybody get out now. I'm going to blow this place up!' He fired off some more rounds, shooting holes in the ceilings. He marched up and down the corridors between frightened members of office and laboratory staff running for their lives at the sight of the armour-clad menace rampaging about. Ryken went into an empty office amid the commotion and took out one of his AKs, pointed it at the window and held his finger on the trigger for three seconds. *This should do it*, he thought, and released his finger. A high-velocity blast made light work of the window, puncturing it instantly, and the recoil reminded Ryken of being shunted in a scrum during his rugby-playing days in the army. He replaced the gun, and took out his pads, strapping them to his knees and hands. He went out of the window and began setting up the first of the explosives outside, balancing perilously against the building on his knees. He attached the device to an iron frame and set it to detonate in thirty minutes' time. Quickly, he climbed to the top floor and set a detonator there too. He ascended to the roof and ran to the other side of the building, sliding along the edge and down to set two more detonators at that side too. Once they were ready, he moved back down to an office on the 19th floor, where he knew the deep-freeze units were kept. For personal reasons, he needed the phials, despite Camille's warnings. He took out the Imp – a slim, sophisticated rectangular device with a concentrated nuclear power cell. He clipped it around the metal join of a window and set it to pulse. He moved away quickly, up to the 20th floor, and heard the low rumble of what sounded like a seismic tremor. He reached down and kicked his leg against the pane; the glass shattering into dust as he did. He launched himself in as the material eroded. Just as he did so, an agent came upon him, trying to grapple him to the ground. Ryken shoved the man and whacked him around the head with his gun, before shooting him in the leg. Two more arrived and he shot them down too, before launching off towards the storage compartments. He madly searched for the ones he needed and found them, slipping them into a tiny refrigeration case, before bending down to tuck it into a small pocket at the bottom of his cargos. It was then he felt someone roughly tug his shoulders, pulling him back all of a sudden. He managed to swing his legs up in the air as he performed a semi-handstand, and grabbed the agent with his ankles, before twisting the neck of his attacker. He leapt back up and took out two pistols, one in each hand. One agent after another started leaping at him, and he had to shoot each one of them. He took a few shots himself, but he was impervious to their impact, he was in such a mode of concentration that he couldn't feel one single part of himself. He had to switch off to complete the task.

Ryken climbed over their bodies to get out of the laboratory and ran down a corridor, heading back in the direction of the elevator. This time he took the stairwell, smashing the door back into a wall as he raced back up to the top floor. As he took two steps at a time, another agent came his way, but he threw the man over his head as he raced on up. He got to the penthouse, the 23rd, and raced down another corridor toward the palatial director's office, which covered half the top floor. He turned the gold doorknobs to swing open the tall wooden doors into the office, before slamming them shut and lodging an AK between the handles to barricade himself in. He walked into the gigantic, air-conditioned room, observing the surroundings.

He breathed deeply and tried to slow down his heart, but he felt pure hatred as he walked further into the room. The art deco wood-panelling and ceiling crevices seemed so vile to him. He saw high shelves littered with stuffed animals and various antiquities, while in the lounge area he saw a globe liquor cabinet, tall brass lamps, numerous high-backed, worn-out leather chairs, matching pouffes and solid side-tables dotted about. The lighting was dim, and there wasn't a natural window in the place. Ryken shuddered with the feeling that this was a mausoleum of hell itself; a den of iniquity in which the director gathered his depraved minions about him. As he moved quickly between the items of well-used, old-fashioned furniture in the lounge, he reached the office area and began searching for what he wanted. The safe. He tried to put himself in the position of the director, trying to imagine where he might have hidden such a thing. He began frantically searching through oak cabinets and cupboards pushed up against walls at either end of the room, throwing them open and slamming them shut as he tried to discover where his destiny lay hidden. There was nothing. It wasn't going to be that simple. He walked toward the far end of the room to view the semicircular library that reached up to the top of the high ceiling. A very large, wide writing desk sat just in front of that. It was dark oak, with a green leather pad laid on top. A gold, art deco lamp shone a sliver of light amongst the darkness at that end of the room. *It wouldn't be here near the desk,* Ryken reasoned.

He turned about and was beginning to despair when he saw something. The sliding ladder was positioned at one end of the library, but Ryken saw the parquet floor was scratched at the other end more prominently. He looked up at the shelves, and nothing seemed out of the ordinary. There were simply rows and rows of burgundy, gold, navy-blue and racing-green-bound leather books, all of similar width and height. However, he noticed a lot of the books on that side had no lettering on the spines. He leapt toward the ladder to pull it to the other side, racing up after he had done so. He pulled a couple of the suspicious objects out and found they were merely cardboard boxes made to look like writing material. He pulled a load away, throwing them madly to the ground as he decided that this was it. This was where it would be.

Fuck. He could hear banging outside the door and realised he wouldn't have much more time. They would soon get in.

Once he had thrown away the dummies, he saw the safe. It was a large, grey metal panel on a high shelf with a sophisticated locking system that would only open up with the DNA of the director. Ryken took out his Unicus and loaded up the hack-software on it, before connecting to the safe via Wi-Fi. He found Camille's message with the DNA fingerprint and overrode the safe's security system to convince the lock he was the director. Within seconds, the safe clicked open. *Thanks Camille.* Ryken retrieved the numerous files from inside and slid back down the ladder.

As he threw the documents onto the desk, he suddenly felt as if a ghost had entered the room, and the banging outside the door subsided. He saw out of the corner of his eye a figure, which had appeared from behind a gold curtain hanging against a full-length fake window across the room.

'Captain Hardy, I've been looking forward to your arrival.' The gravelly voice, revealing a habit of after-dinner brandy and cigars, spoke in an accent seeming to belong to some Cambridge or Oxford-educated gentleman of substance. Ryken recognised him to be Crispin Childs, the head of Officium.

Ryken took out a pistol immediately and pointed it at the man. 'Don't move a muscle.'

The very elderly man stood with his hands held together in front of him. His white hair and tanned complexion contrasted starkly, while his cordial, patriarchal demeanour did nothing to assure Ryken of his humanity.

Ryken held the man's gaze and waited. He tried to calm his heartbeat, sure the man would be able to tell even from a few metres away how tense he was. He held the gun in the air, but his arm felt as if it were about to break in two. He was fighting the urge to simply shoot.

'Did you think it would be that easy? Did you really think we would let you in that easily?' The man tutted, and grinned mockingly. 'You must be out of your mind to think that we would allow you and that wench to simply undo years of progress just like that.'

Ryken held his arm out straighter all of a sudden, wiggling the gun in his opponent's direction, absolutely furious at the term he had just used. He remained silent, knowing any word would make him seem weak.

The old man continued, 'We knew as soon as you became an agent what you were up to. As if we would ever believe someone like you, the son of the great Nathaniel Hardy, could be acting for any purpose other than revenge.'

Ryken couldn't help himself, growling, 'I didn't delude myself that I was safe even for a second, I promise you.'

'No, but I bet she did. Told her about your little sideline, have you?' The man goaded Ryken with a menacing smile.

Ryken was battling an overwhelming desire to just shoot the monster down. However, some part of him wanted answers and resolution. He wanted to know how a man could have become so detestable, losing any semblance of remorse.

'She thinks that she can make you bend to her will. Well, now you will bend to mine.'

'Why are you doing this?' Ryken asked, moving in front of the desk and continuing to follow the director's movements with his gun as the old man went to sit in his huge black leather desk chair.

With his hands resting casually on the armrests, he began, 'Fate tasked me with bringing this world back to reality after the Ravage. People believed they could turn their backs on those who slaved away for their country for years, gave their lives, turned up for work every day on time and laboured for the benefit of their people, all the while getting pitiful rewards and little thanks.'

'I am not some imbecile you can brainwash, Childs. Get to the point before I blow you away.'

'When you offered yourself up as an agent, I allowed you to undergo the training, certain that you would come in handy one day, just as your father did. I've no doubt the dressmaker sent you to us, and I would thank her if she weren't dead. When we realised you and Miss Maddon were both heading for the airport, we put out the news about the storms on the networks to trap you both in the UK. She has been a terror for years, and we spotted a way to finally deal with her without getting our hands dirty. We knew it wouldn't be long before you got her in the sack. Unfortunately you had help, and then we had to lift the ban on the skies to let you loose again. However, we knew you would come home and we knew you would try to get hold of the vaccines.'

Ryken felt sick. He felt as if he could easily tear across the room and bash the living daylights out of the loathsome creature before him. He wanted to smash his body to pieces with the disgustingness of his spiel.

'I'm offering you a chance. If you leave the country today and take her with you, we will deposit five million ED in whatever account you wish.' The director got two U-Cards out of his pocket and placed them on the desk in front of him. 'You will take these, and you and she will go, and never return. Leave today and you need never fear for your lives again. We can have a jet ready and waiting to take you wherever you want to go within half an hour. We will deposit another five million ED in five years' time, and every five years after that. We will guarantee your safety, security and anonymity. As long as she never steps foot in this city again.'

Ryken's eyes wavered and the director knew he was tempted. He grinned and a set of pearly white dentures gleamed back.

In return, Ryken suddenly smiled menacingly at the elderly fellow and started laughing hysterically, before saying, 'You puerile fuck. You hoped you could simply tempt me just like that, with your treasures and your so-called security and anonymity? There is something you have no understanding of in this world, and it's called decency.'

'Just take the money and go Captain Hardy, before you pay with your life.'

'I'd rather die than see you continue to manipulate this world without impediment. I'd rather die than turn.'

'And if you die, what will happen to her? Think about that Hardy, think very hard, and very carefully.'

Ryken didn't respond. He knew doing so would reveal too much.

'We could have killed you when you were sleeping in that shed with her in Warwick. We tracked you from your chip.'

Ryken looked deeply troubled at the revelation but tried to shake it off again.

The director continued, 'Yes, we had one implanted in you. All this time, and you never knew… We've monitored your movements all this time. Why didn't we kill you then and there? Because she obviously hadn't yet fallen for your charms by that point. And because of the sensitive information she has and the danger of that being released. If New York society crumbled, so could our entire business empire, from the stock market downwards. It could take years to rebuild the damage. We knew she was probably the type to die rather than give up the information so easily. We knew you would be instrumental in freeing us of her once and for all. If you don't do this, we'll just have to deal with her ourselves, however we see fit. It would be much easier on everybody if you just take her and go.'

'I'll never accept your terms.'

The director stood up slowly and moved around the desk with his brittle legs looking as though they could buckle at any moment beneath his massive bulk. He moved toward Ryken to look him directly in the eye, and Ryken saw the look of devilry staring back at him, of absolute and unwavering faith in his own shameful beliefs, morals and codes.

'I thought you might need some extra convincing, which is why I came prepared.'

Ryken's pupils widened so that he had almost no retina left. He gritted his teeth at the director's proximity, and almost broke a tooth with the fury he felt. He could feel his face getting redder underneath the balaclava and he pulled the headwear off violently to avoid becoming even more agitated.

He threw it to the ground and stared at the director, spitting, 'Throw whatever you've got at me. We'll see where it gets you.'

The director smiled almost innocently, before retrieving a remote control from his pocket. The top of one of the oak cupboards across the room flipped over to reveal a holographic pad. Within seconds, a full-size image sprang up.

Ryken's heart thudded in his chest, and each beat felt like it was popping his skull with the sound reverberating around his ears. Blood seemed to shoot to his head all of a sudden, and he battled the fury within. His hand shook with the gun in it, and his arm fell by his side for the first time. He breathed heavily and almost collapsed with the feeling of light-headedness. He fell to his knees and hung his head.

There was a man blindfolded, bound and gagged in the image, seemingly alone in an empty room somewhere. Grey hair. Same hulking physique as him.

His father, Nathaniel.

With his head still bowed, Ryken muttered, 'Where is he?'

'In the basement. If you don't do as we say, he will be dealt with.'

'If I do carry out your demands, how do I know he won't still die?'

'You don't. But you will still have five million and that little temptress to keep you amused.'

Ryken kept his head facing the floor, and knew resistance was the key. 'Do your worst. Kill us both. I'm ready. I'll do whatever it takes to protect her. My death will ensure her safety, you know that. She'll keep going until she nails you.'

The director turned red and seemed to have lost some of his cool, struggling as he ranted on. 'You stupid, little boy. You think that this world is black and white, good and evil, rich and poor? You ignorant little fool. We never meant for the virus to escape, but it was such a force of nature, we saw that it was somehow meant to be. I have tried to protect millions of people from themselves. They all thought they could keep procreating without any consequences. This world is small Hardy, and it's going to keep getting technologically and geographically smaller and smaller. Soon, it will be so small, only the fittest and strongest will be able to survive, just as in 2023.'

Ryken lifted his head to stare into the distance, saying calmly, 'You're wrong. People are better than you think, you just haven't got the capacity to see that. This world can change of its own free will. There are those out there who can lead better than this, better than you. People can evolve and adapt to the new world on their own, without bastards like you trying to tell them how.'

'Delusion seems to be your tragic flaw, son.'

Ryken looked up to eye the murderous villain across the room from him, and he sneered, 'I will never give in. Just kill me now.'

'Just leave Hardy, take the girl and the money, and we will release your father. We can all just carry on as before, but you will be slightly richer for it.'

Ryken was knelt on the floor, trying to appear as if he wasn't working out a plan in his head. However, in actual fact, his brain was working on maximum output. He knew deep down what needed to be done. He was seeking a solution, a way of accomplishing all the things he needed to. He sought a path through the maze, and he turned to look at the director, whose tremulous breathing had given him away.

He revealed, 'Eve Maddon was the dressmaker. She was married to Tom Bradbury, but he didn't die in 2023. He took a new identity and became Stephan Dulwich.'

Ryken stood up having regained himself all of a sudden and moved toward the director purposefully. He pushed the man back so that he fell in his desk chair with a thud. He hovered above the frail old man and eyed him with a cold glare. He threatened him with a massive clenched fist held in front of him, reinforcing his own belief in himself.

'All this time, you've had a simple fucking dressmaker running rings around you, you absolute cretin. Look at *you* old man, thinking you can rule the world with your iron fist! You're a madman. You have absolutely no idea what people are capable of when they turn their minds to it. She sacrificed her whole life to protect him. She loved him that much, she became what she did. You sit there, and you listen to me, before I throttle the living daylights out of you. She isn't dead. She's alive, and she's coming for you. She will get you when you least expect it, and you'll finally pay. She won't stop until you're done for. She'll keep going until you finally get what you deserve. It doesn't matter how much money or technology you have, or what vile threats you make, you will never get her. And why? Because she has the love and loyalty of followers all over the world. People who believe unwaveringly in her. Look at you, what do you have? Those dogs you call your police force, who would realise if they weren't so pumped full of drugs, what you really are. I'm giving you a chance now, director, to leave and never return. Leave and hide, otherwise she will get you, I can guarantee you that. Even I don't know where she's waiting for you, but she will keep waiting, until the time is right to finally thwart you once and for all. She will bide her time until she can send the milliner to blast the brains out of your skull bit by bit.'

Ryken felt sure that the director was in defeat, and took several deep breaths to calm himself down after his speech. The elder man sat there absolutely shocked to the core, unable to move or make a response. Ryken coolly picked up the pile of documents off the table and began pulling the pages out on top of a sideboard nearby. The director watched him as if he had become disabled, his eyes bulging from the revelations, knowing there was no lie in Ryken's eyes. Ryken found evidence of research into the Indonesian flu strain; memos, emails, employee records and various other documents. He scanned the papers, one after another, and took out his Unicus to download the information, before tagging it on to a new message. Restricting the sender info, he sent it on to generic addresses including Americanpress, pressuk, worldpress and NewYorkChronicle. It would surely get picked up by one of them.

Ryken noticed the man's face had turned purple. He was going into cardiac arrest, breathing hoarsely and holding his hand to his chest while his other arm went limp. Ryken had no sympathy for the man. Frantically double checking he had done what he needed to do, he headed to the doors of the office, and prepared for the next onslaught. He breathed deeply and recovered, readying himself. He remembered her face, and what they had, and he knew what needed to be done for that to remain untarnished. He looked at his watch and saw he had three minutes to go before the roof was blown skyward. He needed to get out. He shot at the AK holding the door shut across the room, knocking it out of its resting place. Dozens of agents rushed in, tumbling over each other to get to him. He took his remaining

AK and aimed, shooting them out of his way. Two got to him without being shot, and he had to battle against them to get out, thumping them about as if they were rag dolls. He roared as he head-butted one, and kneecapped the other, but as Ryken escaped, he heard one say, 'We need backup.'

Ryken sprinted back to the stairwell, up to the roof, with pistols in hands. He shot another three agents waiting for him on the roof, ran to the edge and waited to see whether he would have more company. He had taken a few direct hits and knew his armour wouldn't hold out much longer. As he assessed his situation, he looked down at the ground and thought he saw a figure looking up at him, but he couldn't be sure. Then he saw her red hair. His heart stopped. *What is she doing here?* Gunfire rang out from the door across the way, and he turned back to face his opponents. He charged at them, and as he looked at his watch, he saw he had thirty seconds left. He thought fast and decided there was only one thing for it…

CHAPTER 49

Seraph had been sat there for more than an hour, going out of her mind with worry. She tried contacting Ryken several times, but all she got was his message service. She left dozens, pleading with him to get in touch with her, begging him to come back. She felt totally bereft without him by her side.

Watching from the kitchen window, she saw a hover-car pull up outside on the drive and leapt out of the house to see who it was. The driver got out and she saw it was Lucius.

'Seraph, come on, get in!' He seemed panicky and desperate to get back on the road, so she ran round to the passenger side and got in.

They were heading back to NYC within seconds, with Lucius speeding off as fast as he could make the vehicle go. Seraph turned to look at the youth, 'I thought you would be back in England by now.'

He turned sideways, saying, 'I thought so, too. But my mother said we needed to stick around for a while.'

'What for?'

'They don't keep me abreast of anything important, I just get told where to go and what to do.'

'Where's Ryken? Do you know that?'

'I don't know anything. I only know I've been told to come and get you, and take you to the Plaza.'

'Come on Lucius, are you holding out on me?' She spat as she spoke, viciously demanding information.

'I've no idea, honestly. I was just told to get you back to the city as soon as possible. There's a big shit storm going down at Genevieve Tower and we need to get somewhere safe before it gets worse.'

She eyed him, asking, 'What did you say?'

'There are police vans everywhere, surrounding the place, some intruder has threatened to blow it up or something.'

Seraph was straight on the Unicus and sent a mass message to all her contacts, asking, *What's going on at Genevieve?*

She searched for the latest news stories, and found one relaying what Lucius had just told her. Seraph knew it was whispered to be Officium's secret HQ, but she had never been able to find out for sure. The whole place was sealed shut with thick iron girders to prevent anyone but those who had special access getting in. She didn't know what the key was, but she would need to find out.

'Lucius, you're taking me there instead, and don't fight me over this.' She swung her ceramic weapon out from her pocket to load it, and he gulped, swallowing hard as he nodded in agreement.

A flood of messages appeared in her inbox and she read them one by one, but they all pretty much said the same: *There was a break-in, someone is trying to retrieve something.*

She sent out a message asking, *What is the access key?* However, the various people who responded didn't know.

Seraph suspected Ryken had known of another laboratory but had not revealed its existence, instead going it alone to protect her in the process. She looked across at Lucius, 'Have you got any weapons in here? Anything at all? We're going in and it's not going to be pretty.'

'In the boot, I've got a couple of stun guns and a kangaroo knife. But Mum will kill me if I let you take them. She gave express instructions to take you back to the Plaza.'

'The man I love is out there in danger Lucius. I will kill you if you don't let me take them.' Seraph was irritated by the obedient youngster.

They travelled all the way down the Expressway and could see the disused, unkempt Brooklyn Bridge up ahead. Lucius powered the vehicle across at top speed, reaching 150mph. Seraph realised he was going to jump the wall with this vehicle, using a well-used ramp to lift it into the air and bring them right over the structure that stood just after the end of the bridge's crudely sawn-off road. She held her breath as they flew through the air, squeezing her eyes shut and praying for a safe landing. As they hit the ground with a thud on the other side, she turned to look at the youngster, who seemed totally calm. 'Nice driving. Or is that flying even…'

'Thanks,' he grinned, feeling he had done his bit for the cause.

Lucius took the vehicle through the city streets, never travelling in a straight line for more than a few minutes, to ensure they couldn't be followed very easily. Seraph got ready in the passenger seat, preparing for whatever she might come up against. She reloaded all her weapons, shoving them into various pockets. She knew she would probably be spotted as soon as she went anywhere near the place, but she didn't care what happened to her anymore. Nearing their destination, Seraph asked Lucius to drop her a block away from Genevieve Tower. The vehicle stopped with a thud and she got out on Madison Avenue. He sped off into the distance, and she surveyed the scene around her. The streets were almost completely empty. Whenever anything like this happened, people went indoors and didn't dare come out for days. Just being on the street made you guilty at a time like this. She could hear the drum of action in the distance; police marching around, voices shouting into radios and helicopters heading in one direction. She stood trying to decide how she was going to handle this, and came to the conclusion there was nothing for it.

She ran on her feet as light as she could toward the corner of Fifth and E 57th. Her heart was thumping with thoughts of Ryken and where he might be right at that precise moment in time. She wished she could just transport herself to wherever he was. As she got close she could practically hear the voices of the officers, and stopped abruptly to peer round the corner. There were people everywhere. She eyed dozens of officers and agents, all crowded around waiting for their colleagues inside to let them know what was happening. There was no way she could take on all these people at once. She needed a plan, a way of getting in the backdoor or... something...

Her Unicus sounded loudly and she nearly dropped dead in that moment. She hoped nobody in the vicinity heard it, and she answered as quickly as possible. She whispered, 'Hello?' without even checking who it was. As she spoke, she checked around the corner to find out whether she was done for, but luckily in all the commotion, nobody seemed to have heard.

The voice on the other end of the line belonged to Camille. 'Seraph, get out of there, what are you doing? Get to the Plaza right now. You don't know what you're up against. You'd never get out.' Camille sounded different to her usual self, angry and desperate, unlike her normal calm and collected persona. Seraph brought the Unicus up to her eye level to peer at Camille, who looked uncharacteristically upset.

'Camille, where is he? Come on, there's something going on here. Where's Ryken?' Seraph betrayed her similar despair.

'He's inside Seraph, and he's not coming out without a fight.'

'Camille, I'm desperate, I think he's going to do something stupid. I need help.'

There was a deep intake of breath on the other end of the line, and Camille spoke, 'Seraph, this is bigger than you or I now.'

'I just can't stop myself going to him!' Seraph was wild with despair, trying desperately to think of a way of ending the nightmare. She kept pulling at her hair and swinging her fist about in mid-air.

Camille shouted, 'No, no! You can't Seraph, please, please, no! For Eve, please don't go looking for him. Please. No good will come of it. No. I'm coming over there myself, right this minute I'm boarding a jet, and you're not going to go anywhere but back to the Plaza. Promise me I will see you there.' A solitary tear of desperation ran down the Frenchwoman's face, so upset at the prospect of something happening to her friend.

Seraph wanted to scream, and she was slowly realising there was nothing she could do. She was defeated. She wanted to tear the whole building down with the anger, hurt and frustration she felt right in that instant. 'Okay Camille, I won't go. I promise. I'll see you there.'

'Thank you, thank you. Please go now, Seraph, go now.' Camille left the screen and Seraph started walking, intending to go around the block to the Plaza. However, as soon as she set off, she heard shouting among the agents, and running. She went back to peer at them and saw they were all heading inside, sprinting with everything they had; guns, full armour and batons at the ready. *Dumb pricks, all for one man. One man stronger than the lot of them put together.* With the square in front of the building empty, Seraph went to investigate, ignoring Camille's pleas. She dare not go inside for fear of what she might find, but she was so inquisitive, she wanted to know what was happening. She waited a couple of minutes, but it seemed like an absolute age as her heart pounded in her chest and she willed Ryken to come flying out of the sky toward her. Just as she had that thought, she heard gunfire above. She almost jumped out of her skin, rocking back on her heels as she fell to the ground and scrambled for cover behind a police car. She looked up to see what was going on and could see nothing. The gunfire continued, and she reckoned it was coming from the top of the building. Then she saw him. It was Ryken standing on the roof, looking down on her. He had full armour on, but she knew it was him. He held a pistol in each hand, old fashioned weapons for an old fashioned gent, but she couldn't make out his face very well from twenty-odd floors below. She wished she could, and she hoped he was smiling. There was more gunfire, and he turned around, tearing off back across the roof out of her sight. Several more rounds of gunfire rang out, and she heard a catastrophic, high-pitch noise she couldn't possibly have prepared herself for. Even shielded by the car, she felt the blast shunt her body and the screech of the explosion made her put her hands over her ears. There were several loud bangs and she fell flat to the ground. She could feel the heat emitting from the building, and she continued to protect her ears, hoping it hadn't really happened. She closed her eyes, but when she felt some chunks of rubble fall on her back, bouncing off her leather jacket, she looked up from where she was laid and saw the entire upper half of the building on fire.

She got up to survey the damage and another bang rang out as bits of the building started to collapse around itself. Suddenly, she realised. *Where is Ryken?* She started to run round to the other side of the building, shielding herself with one arm from tiny bits of falling rubble as she went, and holding her other hand against her mouth to prevent herself breathing in the smoke and dust. She could barely see where she was going, only able to make out the outline of the building from where she could see the fire. She ran around the back, and saw only remnants of destruction. There was no sign of him anywhere. She shouted, 'Ryken, Ryken, where are you!? Ryken, Ryken!'

Nobody responded to her cries, and as she moved further away from the building to get a better look at the top floor, another explosion rang out and the top three floors vanished beneath flames and dust. In that moment, her heart stopped. She forgot to breathe. Her lungs suddenly seemed to collapse in on themselves, and her legs gave way beneath her. She fell on the pavement, falling flat on her bottom. She could feel saliva running from her mouth, and snot dripping from her nose. She lost all control over her body, and she nearly died in that moment from grief and despair. Her head fell between her knees and she suddenly realised she needed to breathe. She took one deep intake of breath, and in the next, she screamed at the top of her lungs until her whole body hurt. Her shrieks echoed between the surrounding buildings, even over the whistles and bangs still going on in Genevieve Tower nearby. Her anguish was only compounded as the skies opened and down poured battering blobs of icy water. Her hair matted and her clothes sodden, all she hoped was that the storm would wash her away and obliterate all conscious feeling. Then she felt arms go around her. She looked back wildly to see if it was him, but it was Lucius. She tried to shake herself free of his grasp, refusing to leave the place until she knew what had happened to Ryken. He was persistent and grabbed her torso roughly, yanking her body off the ground and toward safety. As Lucius pulled her along the sidewalk around the corner to the Plaza, she couldn't cry, nor feel even one single part of her body. Inside, she was numb, empty and just as dead as Ryken.

CHAPTER 50

THE TRUTH – A SENSELESS TRAGEDY
April 13th, 2063
By Francesca Robinson, Editor, *NY Chronicle*

Yesterday an anonymous document was uploaded to various newswires around the world, containing files that seem to prove conclusively that a cover-up had taken place in 2023. These documents also appear to confirm Professor Mara Dulwich's theories, many of which have long been refuted by some amongst senior medical circles. What we now know for certain, however, is that a potent and mutating strain of avian influenza left only the strongest and fittest alive because of its ability to "read" its victims' medical histories and encourage the symptoms of former illnesses to re-exhibit themselves, on a much more extreme scale. Having never come into contact with humanity before, this was how it learnt to thrive, weakening its hosts by aggravating past ailments. It seems an inoculation couldn't be immediately created because of the lack of fertilised eggs available to cultivate a vaccine, following the cull of all domestic fowl during the spring of 2023. Despite this, the files suggest a vaccine is thought to have existed, but Officium never disclosed any information about it.

We've now learnt Officium was set up by Crispin Childs, a child genius who became a microbiologist at eighteen, before turning his attention to politics and taking on the mantel of UK PM in 2014. Childs was publicly vilified by the British Press only two years into his premiership after it emerged he had used his country's treasury to fund some particularly unsavoury habits. As early as 2016, he began recruiting a number of former politicians to join him in establishing a number of research laboratories in strategic locations around the globe. It was their belief that the future of the world's people rested primarily on tackling emerging flu viruses before they had chance to wreak havoc. Desperate to regain the popularity he had lost during his time in public service, Childs and the other figureheads of Officium hoped to be called on in times of future disaster. Ninety-two-year-old Childs has seemingly disappeared into thin air since yesterday's events.

It has also emerged that the rare but beautiful Indonesian Mocking Fowl was the carrier of the H8K1-Z strain of flu, and we now know it was a group of researchers recruited by Officium that transported the creature to the UK for testing. The corporation consequently spent decades trying to hide their part in the research of the virus, simultaneously using the ensuing chaos to further their interests. With such a swollen population, the world was vulnerable to viral attack, but it seems Officium never really intended the flu to escape so catastrophically. Sending people to the cities enabled them to set up a network of constant surveillance, making it easier to track possible threats to their administration.

We are also told that one of the earliest victims of the influenza was Stephan Dulwich, previously known as Tom Bradbury, a British zoologist from Yorkshire, England, who contracted the disease during his travels in New Guinea and changed his identity in 2023. His wife was the recently deceased bridal gown designer Eve Maddon, who kept up the pretence of spinsterdom to protect him and ultimately head up resistance group, RAO.

The truth would never have come to light without the efforts of virologist Doctor Ryken Hardy, who we believe may be responsible for sending out the anonymous message yesterday after breaking into Genevieve Tower, situated near a probable meeting place of RAO – the Plaza. Reliable sources suggest that Hardy had been working undercover as an agent. Tragically, Officium's headquarters were destroyed by a series of explosions yesterday while he was on the roof, and his fate remains uncertain. There is little left from the wreckage, and therefore Hardy is presumed dead.

The Global Health Organisation's part in the conspiracy has also been uncovered. It appears many of their members received bribes from covert slush funds deep at the heart of Officium, agreeing to become the mythmakers who convinced the world it would never be safe again. Their warnings against procreation were no doubt to prevent any further population explosions, which would have made it even more difficult for Officium to keep tabs on the planet's inhabitants.

In nations everywhere, people are rejoicing at the truth finally being revealed after decades of secrecy, fear and corruption. Citizens are daring to leave the cities with renewed hope, heading back into the countryside to make a fresh start, venturing out into a new world.

CHAPTER 51

Three months later...
Seraph was laid in bed in her apartment. She had been there ever since the day Ryken had died, and she had hardly moved a muscle. She refused to take off his blood-splattered shirt, and she hadn't changed the sheets he had slept in with her. The one thing she had spent her life trying to achieve was done, and yet the cost had been so high. She had lost the only thing she had ever really wanted. She'd had a fleeting glimpse of life with him, having only just discovered what real love could be, and then he was torn away from her. She was a wreck, hardly ever washing or eating, never answering calls or the door.

Camille had arrived at the Plaza the day of the explosion, and Seraph had cried into her arms for hours, sobbing and wailing in disbelief. Camille had wanted to take her back home with her, but Seraph wouldn't go. She wanted to be alone to deal with her pain, and she had holed herself up ever since, refusing to accept any help. She had no hope of ever getting herself back on track. She couldn't go back to the days of rampaging the streets of New York for stories, and yet she couldn't move on either without Ryken. He had freed her of her responsibilities, and yet, he wasn't there anymore to help her go on. She was hiding away, burying her feelings deep down, and trying to get over the anger she felt towards all the people outside who had a new lease of life because of him, while she had nothing left.

There were no more agents, no more people after her, and no more battles to be won. She slept for hours on end, feeling as though years and years of exhaustive work had finally caught up with her. She dreamt of the way he had made love to her, and she wailed at the thought that she couldn't even bury him. Sometimes she wished she had never even known the great love he had bestowed on her, because thinking of it only agonised her. She would never be able to love anyone else because of how much he

237

had loved her.

However, today was different. She woke with a ravenous hunger and went to the kitchen, feasting on some bread in the cupboard. She poured herself a glass of juice, and drank that down too. As she shuffled back to her bed, however, she suddenly felt nausea wash over her and she was unable to control it, rushing off to the bathroom to throw up everything she had just scoffed.

Wiping her mouth dry afterward, she felt the urge to eat again, and yet she told herself she shouldn't eat anything if she was sick. Heading back to her bed, she lay there with her head spinning, and could feel her stomach churning. The more she closed her eyes, the more she felt nauseous. She sat up to see if that made her feel better, but there was no change. She moved back into the apartment. Sitting on the couch, and looking out of her windows, she suddenly had a thought. But, she had just reckoned it had been because of her grief...

She hadn't had her period since Ryken had died, but she brushed it off. Throwing some clean clothes on, she caught sight of her ghoulish face in the mirror as she left the apartment, but she didn't care.

After going to the store, she came back with a one-use ultrasound kit. She had clumsily done the sums and if she were actually with child, she calculated that she must be at least thirteen weeks pregnant. She already knew the truth in her heart, but she daren't believe it.

She landed on the bed with her coat on still and lifted up her black sweater. She slapped a sticky gel-pad on her lower abdomen and attached two nodes to it, before plugging the wiring into her Unicus. Her device instantly found the relevant application and she heard a slight whirring as it downloaded information from the sophisticated scanning pad. She held her breath. The thirty-second wait seemed like an age, but when she finally got her result, shock flooded her entire body. The Unicus revealed: *Gestation is approximately three months. Preparing for video imaging. Do you want to record?*

Seraph stared at the device almost in disbelief before hastily realising she did, shouting, 'Yes!' She couldn't believe what was happening. But then she saw them. On the screen, two foetuses flickered into focus, and seconds after that, she heard their strong, rapid heartbeats. The cold, robotic voice of the application snapped her from her reverie. *Foetal scan completed. Twin elements detected. Expected due date January third, 2064.* She saw the two blobs laid in her womb and felt a connection to Ryken. They were his. She touched the screen and shook with nervousness as realisation swept over her and she thought about what that meant. She would be a mother. She took a few minutes to absorb the news, but when she finally had, she held her tummy and cried with joy. She was going to have his babies, twins even. She felt like she had got him back in a way, and yet she knew she would be facing it all alone. She cried with the various emotions running through her head, and knew that she had to be strong for her unborn children. She would love them just as she had loved him.

CHAPTER 52

Three months previously...
Mara had just gone back to the cockpit, and Seraph was in the toilet reeling from the revelation about Ryken. Meanwhile in the cargo hold, he was sitting feeling desperate, with a rouge slap mark across his face. He felt sick to his stomach, scared out of his mind of losing the one person he had ever loved. He realised it only hours after meeting her, and he knew that he would never stop loving her. He could only hope she would forgive him eventually.

He started to wonder whether his mind was playing tricks on him, but he heard rustling behind a pile of boxes, and felt sure there was someone else in there with him. 'Hello? Is there anyone there?' he asked.

Seconds later, an elderly lady was stood before him. She was elegant, uniquely dressed in some sort of African-inspired smock dress and distinctive pieces of jewellery. She had extraordinarily long, platinum grey hair running down her back, and piercing green eyes. He stood up to survey the woman, looking her directly in the eyes. He noticed the resemblance immediately, and ventured, 'Eve? Am I right?'

'You are right, young man. And you are, of course, Ryken.'

He scratched his head, wondering whether he should speak. He simply said, 'But you're dead? And you're here?' She sat down and motioned for him to sit next to her on a bench. He wondered whether he was going mad, having seen all these similar-looking women around him on this one jet. He surveyed her face and saw the same mouth and round cheekbones that Seraph also had. He could have easily been surveying what Seraph would look like in decades to come. The woman had obviously led a full life, and yet she didn't look withered or tired, she looked vibrant and healthy. 'And if you don't mind me saying, you don't look as if you're at death's door either.'

She was eyeing him up, getting the measure of him, and she finally deigned to speak again, 'I am dead, though Ryken, aren't I? At least in the eyes of the world, the world which believes whatever it is told.' She smiled, asking, 'Did you get my invitation by the way?'

He grinned, starting to piece together everything in his mind, and he knew this would prove to be a very scintillating conversation. 'She's devastated you're dead. There must be a reason for all this.'

Slightly defensive, Eve shifted and moved toward him to look him directly in the eye. 'Believe me, I wouldn't have done this to her unless it was absolutely necessary. I needed to be dead and I'm going to tell you why.'

'I really hope so, because right now she despises me.' He rubbed his red cheek, explaining, 'Your daughter just told her about me being an agent.'

'That was naughty of Mara wasn't it, but I needed to get you down here. And yes, I know about your employment my dear. I knew about your job even before you did. I gave you that role because I knew you wouldn't let me down. I've watched people like you for most of my life Doctor Hardy, and believe me, nothing shocks me more than to think of someone who worked for Officium coming within a mile of Seraph. But I had faith that a gentleman like you would do the right thing, and even though deception is sometimes a hard road to take, it can lead us to something better.'

He chastised himself again for lying to Seraph, not telling her the truth from the start, and Eve noticed the torment cross his face.

Bluntly, she asked, 'You love her, how could you not?' He turned to look at the old lady with a look that gave away his turmoil, and she assured him, 'Ryken, you've proved yourself enough already. Now you need to hear what I have to say. Listen, if you never do anything else ever again, listen to me now.'

She took his large hands within her own, holding them gently as she spoke. Her skin felt like tissue paper, but her hands were warm and comforting. He was mesmerised by her eyes, and felt so intimidated by her, he had to fight the urge to look away in embarrassment as she drew him into her gaze.

'Ryken, I died because I needed to get her over to England so that she would cease her investigations temporarily. No other reason would have brought her over so swiftly. I also needed to make my enemies think they had got rid of me. The news of the dressmaker's death has no doubt reached Crispin Childs, but he doesn't yet know why I am what I am. He has no idea that Tom Bradbury, that is to say Stephan Dulwich, was my husband. We trod very carefully over the years, and somehow managed to retain that secret.

'So, I needed to die for so many reasons, and yet I knew it would cause hurt. I foresaw it would turn a lot of people's worlds upside down. But I have been working for this cause for so long, waiting patiently for the right time, and this was it.

'Seraph's recent investigations in New York have unsettled Officium. She recently turned her attention to a debauched senator who we know is high up in Childs' group, possibly even his prospective successor. It is thought Childs is dying and he's desperate to secure his legacy. I received word that agents have been watching her every move. I got the overwhelming feeling that I could no longer protect her. I had been secretly feeding her information about the city's officials for years, and she never knew it was me. It was her protection, and I paid several brave men and women to gather this information for me, some of whom lost their lives in the process. However, I began to fear they would stoop to any level to finally get Seraph off their backs.

'Therefore, with all these factors in play, I decided it was finally time to take decisive action. I needed someone from the inside, and you proved the perfect choice after Camille pointed you in the right direction all those years ago. They know about your father Ryken, and they suspect you, but they hope you can still be corrupted and that is why you remain alive. They probably put out the story about the storms to ensure you and Seraph would come together, enabling them to keep an eye on you both with greater care. However, they didn't realise that I was also aiming for the same end, and that I could see what they couldn't. I could see that neither you nor she would be broken by them, and together, you will beat them. I foresee a test Ryken, a test of your mettle, and it is only you who can decide which way you go. But I have faith in you.

'Now, this is what you are going to do when you get back to New York. You will be dropped back at your respective apartments, and you will stay there Ryken. You will stay in your apartment and wait.'

He shook his head, pleading, 'I can't leave her, what if they stake her place?'

She pulled a small Unicus from one of the deep pockets in her dress and handed it to him. 'Take this. It's secure. I will contact you if I hear anything. If she needs you, I will let you know.'

He took the device and looked it over before hiding it in his inside pocket.

'She has a letter containing instructions, and that letter also has many other revelations that will not be easy for her. She doesn't know it yet, but she will need you. There are worse things ahead to face. We can never get complacent Ryken, never let yourself believe this is over, until it really is. You can't breathe a word of our conversation here to her, you understand? I know it will be hard, but it's for the greater good. You cannot risk her safety. You cannot tell her I'm still alive. In fact, I mean for you to never tell her. I won't make her grieve for me twice. Promise me.'

'I understand. It won't be easy though, you know she's like a dog with a bone when she knows something's not right.'

'I know her better than anyone, and believe me, you're going to have to do some expert lying.' She continued to hold his hands between her own, in a motherly way, squeezing them whenever she thought he needed comfort.

He looked at her, knowing there was more she had yet to say. He waited and asked, 'Tell me what I have to do, Eve.' He just wanted to get it over with.

She looked at the floor, trying to breathe away the dread that was creeping across her face. She knew he didn't need to see that. She looked up, with her eyes shining brightly, and said very matter-of-factly, 'You need to die, Ryken.'

He deliberated for a few moments, taking it all in and nodding, before she continued to explain. 'You need to wait until the time is right. I will let you know. Keep that Unicus with you at all times. They are gathering at their New York headquarters, which I'm sure you have knowledge of. You and Seraph will go to one of their old lab buildings, the one in Brooklyn, you know which I talk of?'

'Yes, but there won't be anything there, will there?'

'No, but we need to convince them that they have beaten you. Seraph doesn't need to know that this is a ruse. We need to throw her off the scent too. The security won't be that difficult to break, now that what we need is elsewhere. You won't find anything there, and then you will leave the city. This is their ultimate aim – to get you both out of their way. They will imagine that they have beaten us, but when they are least expecting it, we will strike at the very heart of their organisation. The milliner will contact you with instructions, and you must follow them to the letter. My forces will continue to strike fear into their arrogant, cold hearts until the time is right. I've no doubt those who are not entirely loyal in their group have already started disbanding, and the director's plight will finally have begun unravelling. He will be arrogant enough to believe that he still has a chance, but we know better.

'You will die after completing this task. You know there will still be survivors of Officium out for revenge, and we can't risk your relationship with Seraph compromising her.'

He recognised an affinity with the old lady; the way neither of them bent to the will of others or their weaknesses. Their ultimate self-belief was what made them what they were, remaining steadfast amongst the corruption. He absorbed everything she had said, and knew what had to be done. Deep down, he was secretly pleased he was going to be part of this. He could finally right a few wrongs. He knew it wouldn't be easy, but he trusted Eve, and he knew she was a force to be reckoned with. He guessed, 'You chose me because of my father, didn't you?'

She didn't seem shocked by his suggestion, maintaining her gaze. 'Yes, that, and so many other reasons.'

'I need you to tell me what you know.'

'People who suffer addiction will do anything to feed it, unless they are strong enough to battle against it. They will also do anything to hide it, and in your father's case, they bribed him to become an informant, otherwise they'd reveal his secret vice. Colleagues of his across Manchester who tried to investigate Officium were killed and his inner demons got the better of him.' Ryken seemed to breathe a sigh of relief at having his suspicions confirmed, before she continued, 'My own mother was an addict too, and after I finally realised I couldn't help her any longer, I never saw her again. She died in 2023 and I truly regretted not making peace with her. She never met Tom or Mara, but perhaps we might meet her again in better circumstances yet… maybe in a realm beyond this world.'

He understood completely.

He enquired, 'How did you manage to stay so strong, after everything?'

She appeared taken aback, slightly offended almost. She stood up, with some effort, and turned away from him. She hid her face from view, and she gathered herself to make a reply.

'I learnt long ago to survive on nothing Ryken, even before I married Tom, and that is what you will have to do too. To have had him in my life at all was a blessing I was thankful for every day. When he died, I had to become something more, something indestructible, in order to really become the dressmaker. Fate found me and moulded me to become seemingly infallible. But I had a lot of friends to help me along the way, and they got me through. You, however, will have to go it alone. You know what needs to be done, anyway, don't you?'

He nodded. Somehow his mind had become clear, and he knew what his place was. He knew the path that lay ahead of him. 'Where do you mean to go when this is all over?'

'Mara and I mean to stow ourselves away somewhere incredibly quiet and desolate, and live out the rest of our days in peace, away from all this. We can finally just be mother and daughter. Only you and Camille will know the truth Ryken. I have to detach myself completely otherwise I will never be free. This world will go on without me, and I will go on without the world. My last days need to be mine and mine alone. Someone like me cannot simply just come back from the dead. You can, however, to take care of her. My precious angel. She is strong, so very strong, but she needs you more than you realise. She reminds me of myself when I was young. Simply surviving, until one day a man turned my head and showed me what it could be like to really love someone, to really be with someone who knew what I was feeling without me even speaking, who finished off my sentences before I did, who made me complete and pushed me to be the best I could be. A soul mate, life partner and best friend. Even during the worst of times, love can spring up from nowhere and prove to be transformative, inspiring and live-giving.'

He could have cried, knowing what she had lost, and yet she had not succumbed to bitterness. He shook his head in disbelief and admitted, 'I've never heard anyone talk so honestly about love like that.'

'Ryken, love her as if every day is the last. She just needs time and for you to be there for her. Believe me, she'll not let you go easily once she's got you.'

He stood up to take the woman's hand in his own, and bent down to kiss the back of it generously. He said, 'It's been a pleasure meeting you.'

Her face tinged with blushes, even at her age she couldn't ignore the attractiveness of this man.

'Goodbye Ryken. Remember everything I've said. I'll be in touch. Now go, and wait.'

'I will. And Eve, thank you.' She bowed her head, and he returned to the cabin above.

EPILOGUE

Heavily pregnant, Seraph wandered through the streets of Paris, dressed in a long-sleeved, floor-length purple velvet dress, with a green suede belt under her bump. Her red hair was pulled up in a tight messy bun, with strands flowing over her face. She had that glow of impending motherhood; her body humming with maternal happiness. She felt alive like never before, and her veins ran with the potent, nutrient-rich blood that fed Ryken's babies inside her. Her hair and skin were awash with loveliness, and she had gained an extremely womanly physique that she had embraced to its fullest. She felt happier, stronger and more powerful than she ever could have foreseen. She had achieved the pinnacle of womanhood, and felt certain she was meant for no other role in life more than this one.

Wandering around the Place du Tertre in Montmartre, the sharp smell of the oils overpowered her nostrils as she stopped to view various paintings in the process of being created, receiving admiring glances from the artists. She snacked on grapes as she left the square behind to wind her way through the streets and head to the market. However, she remained unaware of an admirer stood in the distance observing her movements between the tall white townhouses. He was plucking up the courage to say hello to the woman he loved, and he could not believe she was pregnant. He couldn't stop smiling and could have stayed like that forever, following her as she drifted around silently while he soaked up her intense beauty.

She wandered around makeshift stalls set up at the base of the steps leading up to the regenerating Basilique du Sacré-Coeur, picking up a silk neckerchief from one, and two beautifully knitted shawls from another for her children. She smiled to herself as she passed random people, knowing secretly that her babies' father helped to set them free. She spotted other expectant mothers, who seemed to be numerous at that time, and they shared a knowing smile.

Just as she was about to purchase a piece of meat from a butcher's cart for her and Camille's dinner that night, she felt a presence behind her. A heavy hand touched her shoulder, and someone's breathing was right next to her ear. He spoke in a broad Mancunian accent, saying, 'You are the most beautiful mother-to-be I've ever laid eyes on.' Strong arms went around her, and she smelt his familiar scent – one of musky sandalwood.

Her heart skipped a beat and she wanted to pinch herself to make sure she wasn't dreaming. She tried to calm herself down for the sake of her babies, but she couldn't. Her whole body was in shock, trembling, willing it to be him.

She slowly turned around and standing before her was Ryken. She nearly fell over and put her hands to her mouth, sending her shopping to the ground, causing chaos as everyone around them scrambled to help pick up rolling oranges and various other items. Ryken said, 'Pardon, pardon, merci.' He took her bags in his hands, and motioned for her to join him on a wooden bench nearby. She fought desperately to control her emotions, but the tears were already falling and she was shaking like a leaf.

She asked, 'Ryken… is it really you?' He nodded in response and took her cheek in his hand, before she continued, 'Why did you let me believe…? Why has your voice changed?'

'There is so much to explain, but for now can I hold you?' She nodded, biting her lips to stop them trembling any more. He pulled her close to him, and she let the tears fall and fall. He nuzzled his nose in her hair and started kissing her all over her face. 'Oh god, I love you Seraphina, so much. You're my world.'

She pulled away to look at him, with such joyful tears rolling down her cheeks. He was supremely handsome, no longer the battered and bruised shadow of a man she had last seen him as. He was dressed in a long tan overcoat, with his customary jeans and boots and a cream polo neck. She stroked his hair, which had grown long around his ears, and ran her fingers all over his face, which was bearded. He had lost a lot of his heavy musculature but he looked stupendous. He smiled so broadly and looked as if he could have burst with emotion. He grabbed her fingers and kissed them, before moving over to kiss her passionately on the mouth. He pulled away to stroke her bump gently, proudly asking, 'When is he or she due?'

She smiled a cheeky grin, giggling as he asked, 'What…? What is it?'

'Children,' she said, 'Our twins are due any day now.'

He raised his hands to his face in disbelief, his eyes aglow with wonder and delight. He grabbed her again to kiss her, and she held him tight, making sure it was really him.

'I'm so sorry I put you through this, Seraph. But no man is more proud than me right now. I knew you would remain strong.'

She felt for his hand, bringing it up to where her heart was. 'It kept beating for you Ryken.'

He cried too, wiping a tear from his eyes. He breathed deeply, trying to regain his composure. 'Do you know what we're having? What sex?'

'No, I wanted it to be a surprise. They're not identical, so we could have one of each yet.' She smiled and giggled as she spoke, so happy to have him back, so delirious with joy.

He took a deep breath, trying to steady himself, rubbing his thumbs across her newly freckled cheeks. 'You really do look radiant. You really do. I just can't explain quite how stunning you are.'

She looked down and stroked her stomach, rolling her fingers over the bumps of baby limbs she could feel shifting under her skin. 'Don't try to flatter me, I feel like a house Ryken.'

He chuckled, 'Don't be stupid, you look immensely wonderful. I thought you were perfect before but…' He went to kiss her neck delicately, brushing fine bits of hair away from her skin. His touch sent shivers down her spine and shockwaves through her body, especially with the concoction of hormones already swilling about inside her. He whispered in her ear, 'If you want those babies out now, I know a way. I've missed you so much.' His breath made her hairs stand on end.

Her eyes danced as she shot him a mock-horrified look, before offering him a knowing glance. She didn't think to ask for an explanation about where he had been; she simply knew she was so grateful to have him back, so happy to have the father of her children by her side once more. They stood up together and walked off hand-in-hand, not noticing the faces of passers-by who thought they looked like the most handsome couple they had ever seen, and also the happiest.

And now these three remain: faith, hope and love.
But the greatest of these is love.

ABOUT THE AUTHOR

Sarah Michelle Lynch lives with her husband and daughter in the East Riding of Yorkshire, England. She read English at Hull University before working in journalism for several years. It was then a long period of maternity leave that offered her the time to write a novel. Beneath the Veil, the first book in the Ravage Trilogy, is succeeded by Beneath the Betrayal. The third part, Beneath the Exile, is a work in progress.

Made in the USA
Charleston, SC
09 February 2013